THE VISIONARY
MAYAN QUEEN

THE VISIONARY MAYAN QUEEN

YOHL IK'NAL OF PALENQUE

BORN 550 CE – ACCEDED 583 CE – DIED 604 CE

LEONIDE MARTIN

Mists of Palenque Series Book 1

Made for Success
P.O. Box 1775
Issaquah, WA 98027

The Visionary Mayan Queen: Yohl Ik'nal of Palenque

Designed by DeeDee Heathman

Library of Congress Cataloging-in-Publication data

Martin, Leonide
The Visionary Mayan Queen: Yohl Ik'nal of Palenque

      Mists of Palenque Book 1
         p. cm.
      ISBN: 978-1-61339-867-8 (pbk.)
      LCCN: 2016902393

To contact the publisher, please email service@MadeforSuccess.net or call +1 425 657 0300.

Made for Wonder is an imprint of Made for Success Publishing.

Printed in the United States of America

CONTENTS

List of Characters and Places

Yohl Ik'nal – Characters
(*historical person)

Royal Family of Lakam Ha

*Yohl Ik'nal** – first female ruler of Lakam Ha (Palenque) 583-604 CE

*Kan Bahlam I** – ruler of Lakam Ha 574-583 CE, father of Yohl Ik'nal

*Ahkal Mo' Nab II** – ruler of Lakam Ha 565-570 CE, older brother of Kan Bahlam

Xoc Akal – mother of Yohl Ik'nal

*Hun Pakal** – husband of Yohl Ik'nal

*Aj Ne Ohl Mat** – ruler of Lakam Ha 604-612 CE, son of Yohl Ik'nal and Hun Pakal

*Sak K'uk** – ruler of Lakam Ha 612-615 CE, daughter of Yohl Ik'nal and Hun Pakal

*Kan Mo' Hix** – son of Yaxun Zul, husband of Sak K'uk

*Janaab Pakal I** – son of Sak K'uk and Kan Mo' Hix, ruler of Lakam Ha 615-683 CE

*K'uk Bahlam I** – first ruler of Lakam Ha 432-435 CE (Bahlam lineage founder)

Main Courtiers/Warriors of Lakam Ha

Yax Kab – elder statesman, trusted advisor of Kan Bahlam

Mut Yokte – Nakom/War Chief of Kan Bahlam

Chakab – warrior, strong supporter of Kan Bahlam, later Nakom/War Chief

Tilkach – trusted court advisor to Yohl Ik'nal

Itzam Ik – trusted court advisor to Yohl Ik'nal

Buluc Max – Royal Steward to Yohl Ik'nal

Mas Batz – dwarf of Royal Court of Yohl Ik'nal

Nobles of the Opposition in Lakam Ha

Ek Chuuah – distant cousin of Yohl Ik'nal, moves to Usihwitz, plots against Lakam Ha

Yaxun Zul – wealthy noble, royal lineage, leader of opposition to Bahlam family

Chak'ok – warrior, member of opposition

Kab'ol – warrior, member of opposition, brother of Ek Chuuah

Uc Ayin – noble courtier to Yaxun Zul, stays neutral

Attendants/Tutors

Sak Nicte – best girl/woman friend to Yohl Ik'nal

Na'kin – girl/woman friend to Yohl Ik'nal

Tulix – girl/woman friend to Yohl Ik'nal

B'ay Kutz – Royal Tutor to children of Yohl Ik'nal

Priests/Priestesses

Lahun Uc – High Priestess, mentor of Yohl Ik'nal

Wak Batz – High Priest, chief ceremonial authority

Mat Ek' – Priestess of Ix Chel

Villagers

Nohpat – farmer in village near Lakam Ha

Halil – wife of Nohpat

Tz'un – daughter of Nohpat

Uxul – son of Nohpat, gifted stone carver

Characters from Other Cities

Zotz Choj* – Sahal/ruler of Popo' 560-578 CE

Chak B'olon Chaak* – Sahal/ruler of Popo' 578-595 CE

Hix Chapat* – son of Popo' ruler

Hohmay – daughter of Popo' ruler

Joy Bahlam* – Sahal/ruler of Usihwitz circa 586 CE

Zac Amal – Nephew of Usihwitz ruler

Cauac Ahk* – Sahal/ruler of Yokib 510-602 CE

Cities and Polities

Matawiil – mythohistoric origin lands at Six Sky Place
Toktan – ancestral city of K'uk Bahlam, founder of Lakam Ha dynasty
Petén – lowlands area in north Guatemala, densely populated with Maya sites

B'aakal Polity and Allies

B'aakal – "Kingdom of the Bone," polity governed by Lakam Ha (Palenque)
Lakam Ha – (Palenque) "Big Waters," major city of B'aakal polity, May Ku
Popo' – (Tonina) in B'aakal polity, linked to Lakam Ha by royal marriage
Yokib – (Piedras Negras) in B'aakal polity, later allied with Kan
Wa-Mut – (Wa-Bird, Santa Elena) in B'aakal polity
Sak Tz'i – (White Dog) in B'aakal polity, later allied with Kan
Anaay Te – (Anayte) in B'aakal polity
B'aak – (Tortuguero) in B'aakal polity
Mutul – (Tikal) great city of southern region, ally of Lakam Ha, enemy of Kan
Nab'nahotot – (Comalcalco) city on coast of Great North Sea (Gulf of Mexico)
Oxwitik – (Copan) southern city allied with Lakam Ha by marriage
Nahokan – (Quirigua) southern city, ally of Oxwitik

Ka'an Polity and Allies

Kan – refers to residence city of Kan (Snake) Dynasty, Lords of Ka'an Polity
Uxte'tun – (Kalakmul) early home city of Kan Dynasty, usurped by Zotz (Bat)
    Dynasty
Dzibanche – home city of Kan dynasty (circa 400-600 CE)
Ka'an – "Kingdom of the Snake," polity governed by Kan
Usihwitz – (Bonampak) in B'aakal polity, later enemy of Lakam Ha, allied with
    Kan
Pakab – (Pomona, Pia) in Ka'an polity, joined Usihwitz in raid on Lakam Ha
Pa'chan – (Yaxchilan) in Ka'an polity
Uxwitza – (Caracol) allied with Mutul, later with Kan
B'uuk – (Las Alacranes) city where Kan installed puppet ruler
Maxam/Saal – (Naranjo) southern city, initially offshoot of Mutul, then ally of
    Kan
Tan-nal – (Seibal) southern city, ally of Maxam
Imix-ha – (Dos Pilas) southern city, ally of Tan-nal and Kan
Kan Witz-nal – (Ucanal) southern city, ally of Kan and Tan-nal, former Mutul ally

Waka' – (El Peru) ally of Kan, enemy of Mutul

Places and Rivers

K'uk Lakam Witz – Fiery Water Mountain, sacred mountain of Lakam Ha
Nab'nah – Great North Sea (Gulf of Mexico)
K'ak-nab – Great East Sea (Gulf of Honduras, Caribbean Sea)
Wukhalal – lagoon of seven colors (Bacalar Lagoon)
K'umaxha – Sacred Monkey River (Usumacinta River), largest river in region, crosses plains north of Lakam Ha, empties into Gulf of Mexico
Michol – river on plains northwest of Lakam Ha, flows below city plateau
Chakamax – river flowing into K'umaxha, southeast of Lakam Ha
Tulixha – large river (Tulija River) flowing near B'aak
Chih Ha – subsidiary river (Chinal River) flows into Tulixha
B'ub'ulha – western river (Rio Grijalva) flowing into Gulf of Mexico near Nab'nahotot
Pokolha – southern river (Rio Motagua) by Nahokan, near Oxwitik

Small rivers flowing across Lakam Ha ridges
Kisiin – Diablo River
Bisik – Picota River
Tun Pitz – Piedras Bolas
Ixha – Motiepa River
Otolum – Otolum River
Sutzha – Murcielagos River
Balunte – Balunte River
Ach' – Ach' River

Maya Deities

Hunab K'u (Hun Ahb K'u) – Supreme Being, source of all, giver of movement and measure
Muwaan Mat (Duck Hawk, Cormorant) – Primordial Mother Goddess, mother of B'aakal Triad
Hun Ahau (One Lord) – First born of Triad, Celestial Realm

Mah Kinah Ahau (Underworld Sun Lord) – Second born of Triad, Underworld Realm, Jaguar Sun, Underworld Sun-Moon, Waterlily Jaguar

Unen K'awill (Infant Powerful One) – Third born of Triad, Earthly Realm, patron of royal bloodlines, lightning in forehead, snake-footed, called Manikin Scepter

Ahauob (Lords) of the First Sky:

B'olon Chan Yoch'ok'in (Sky That Enters the Sun) – 9 Sky Place

Waklahun Ch'ok'in (Emergent Young Sun) – 16 Sky Place

B'olon Tz'ak Ahau (Conjuring Lord) – 9 Sky Place

Ix Chel – Earth Mother Goddess, healer, midwife, weaver of life, fertility and abundance, commands snake energies, waters and fluids, Lady Rainbow

Hun Hunahpu – Maize God, First Father, resurrected by Hero Twins, ancestor of Mayas

Yum K'ax – Young Maize God, foliated god of growing corn (overlaps Hun Hunahpu)

Wuqub' Kaquix – Seven Macaw, false deity of polestar, defeated by Hero Twins

Hun Ahau – (Hunahpu), first Hero Twin

Yax Bahlam – (Xbalanque), second Hero Twin

Wakah Chan Te – Jeweled Sky Tree, connects the three dimensions (roots-Underworld, trunk-Middleworld, branches-Upperworld)

Xibalba – Underworld, realm of the Lords of Death

Xmucane – Grandmother, Heart of Earth, Goddess of Transformation

Bacabs – Lords of the Four Directions, Hold up the Sky

Titles

Ahau – Lord

Ixik – Lady

Ix – honorable way to address women

Ah – honorable way to address men

K'uhul Ahau – Divine/Holy Lord

K'uhul Ixik – Divine/Holy Lady

Ah K'in – Solar Priest

Ah K'inob – plural of Solar Priests

Ix K'in – Solar Priestess

Ix K'inob – plural of Solar Priestesses

Nakom – War Chief

Sahal – ruler of subsidiary city

Ah Kuch Kab – head of village (Kuchte'el)

Chilam – spokesperson, prophet

Batab – town governor, local leader from noble lineage

Kalomte – K'uhul Ahau ruling several cities, used often at Mutul and Oxwitik

May Ku – seat of the *may* cycle (260 tuns, 256 solar years), dominant city of region

Yahau – His Lord (high subordinate noble)

Yahau K'ak – His Lord of Fire (high ceremonial-military noble)

Ba-ch'ok – heir designate

Juntan – precious one, signifies relationship between mother and child as well as between deities and ahau, also translated "beloved of"

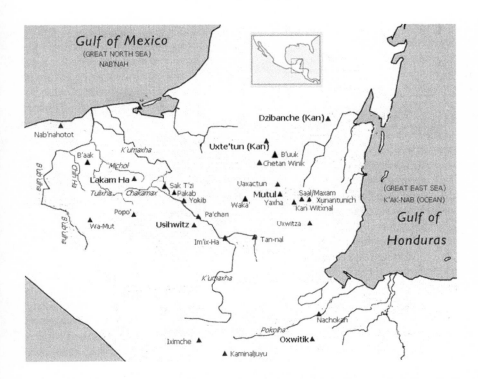

Central and Southern Maya Regions in Middle Classic Period (500-800 CE)

Names of cities, rivers and seas are the ones used in this book. Most are known Classic Period names; some have been created for the story. Many other cities existed but are omitted for simplicity.

Inset map shows location of Maya Regions in southern Mexico, Yucatan Peninsula and Central America.

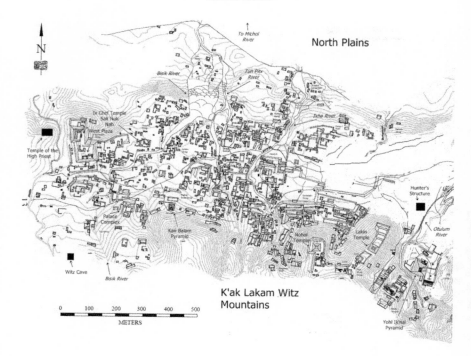

Lakam Ha (Palenque) Western and Central Areas
Older Sections of Settlement circa 500 – 600 CE

Dark boxes are fictional structures added for the story. Structures important to the story are labeled. This does not signify that these structures were actually used for purposes described in the story. The city extends further east, but these sections were built later.

Based upon maps from The Palenque Mapping Project, Edwin Barnhart, 1999. A FAMSI-sponsored project. Used with permission from Edwin Barnhart.

Lady Muwaan Mat was born. Eight years after her birth, she binds the deer hoof. Then on 4 Ahau 8 Kumk'u it ends, the era, 13 Baktuns. A year and a half after the hearth was measured at the edge of the sky, the First Hearth Place, Hun Ahau (God I) entered the sky. On 9 Ik 20 Mol he dedicates the 6 Sky Ahau place, the 8th House of the God. It is the name of the house of the north. Over 750 years afterwards, then he arrives at Matawiil. On 9 Ik 15 Keh he is born at Matawiil. It is the penance of Lady Muwaan Mat, she fasted, she let blood, 3 times a mother. Then over 800 years after she was born, she tied the white headband on herself, Lady Muwaan Mat. It is 9 Ik 0 Sak. She was the first ruler.

> Tablet of the Temple of the Cross, dedicated by Kan Bahlam II
> Period ending 9.13.0.0.0 (March 18, 692 CE)
> Based on translation by Gerardo Aldana, *The Apotheosis of Janaab' Pakal*
> University of Colorado Press, 2007

Here were the remains of a cultivated, polished, and peculiar people, who had passed through all the stages incident to the rise and fall of nations; reached their golden age, and perished, entirely unknown. . . We lived in the ruined palace of their kings; we went up to their desolate temples and fallen altars; and wherever we moved we saw the evidences of their taste, their skill in arts, their wealth and power. In the midst of desolation and ruin we looked back to the past, cleared away the gloomy forest, and fancied every building perfect, with its terraces and pyramids, its sculptured and painted ornaments, grand, lofty, and imposing . . . we called back into life the strange people . . . pictured them, in fanciful costumes and adorned with plumes of feathers, ascending the terraces of the palace and the steps leading to the temples; and often we imagined a scene of unique and gorgeous beauty and magnificence.

> Excerpt from John L. Stephens, *Incidents of Travel in Central America, Chiapas and Yucatan, Vol. II*
> Dover Publications, New York, 1969
> Originally published in 1841 after Stephens' visit to the Palenque ruins.

YOHL IK'NAL — I

BAKTUN 9 KATUN 6 TUN 2 (562 CE)

1

THE GIRL HURRIED along forested paths toward the waterfalls, her bare feet squishing in humus. A colorful shawl covered her head and she drew it closer around her shoulders against the morning chill. Mist draped the mountains and clung to the canopy of the tropical forest. Vaporous fingers reached into the trees forming ephemeral lianas. Branches heavy with moisture gathered mist into brief droplets before releasing them to the wet soil below. Wetness was upon the mountains, the forests, the uneven earth. All was wetness, silence, stillness. Only the mist moved stealthily among the trees and crept toward the city of stones.

She peered anxiously toward the east, as the dawn sun ignited the mist into a shimmered golden glow. Birdcalls broke the misty silence: twitters, soft hoots, squawks, shrill cries. A steamy halo heralded the sunrise. Downward she plunged, following a path twisting in tight turns over roots and rocky outcroppings. The steep descent brought her past waterfalls that roared into foaming pools, past stone structures grouped around open plazas, and into denser forests.

Soon she found the place, a short way off the path marked by a small cascade. Again she glanced skyward into the luminous mist. Pushing aside ferns and bushes that splattered her with droplets, she came to the small clearing with a cluster of rocks in the center. The natural outcropping reached to her shoulders, an irregular tumbled group with one remarkable feature. She had discovered it several moons ago, and kept it secret. This was her special place. She folded her shawl on a smooth rock and sat cross-legged, as was her people's custom. Eyes closed, she focused on the dawn chorus of birds greeting the day.

The girl waited for the sun's signal. With luck, the mist would thin enough for the sunrays to strike her face. She loved the sudden heat and light that launched hundreds of red sparks behind her eyelids. Body still, breath bated, mind alert she waited. Only the birds with their raucous celebration, the steady fall of droplets, and the distant roar of waterfalls broke the hovering silence.

The sun burst suddenly through the mist, stunning her face and igniting red sparks in her closed eyes. It was the moment. Heart pounding, she took one deep breath and focused her entire attention behind the eyelids. Her eyes flew open. The clear quartz prominence situated on top of the highest rock blazed with light, bursting into radiant sun-flames. Partially blinded by the brilliance, she shot her consciousness into the quartz and was projected along scintillating pathways into another world.

It was a world she had visited before, though not always at the same place. Even after practicing for at least four moons, she had not learned how to control her journeys. She did not seek help from her parents or teachers, being afraid they would force her to stop the journeys that were a source of such delight. Though she hinted to a few friends, none of the other children recognized it. Maybe no one knew. So she kept her secret, and visited the special place as often as she could.

Now she was in the cold windy place, located on a flattened hilltop with vast meadows of grass and gentle green hills. The hilltop grass was strange, long and thin reaching past her knees. Sparse rocks dotted the hillside, bordered by shrubby bushes dense with aromatic purple flowers. Winds always swept across this place, making the grass wave endlessly. Hardly a bird or animal ever appeared, although once a flock of black hawks crossed over silently. She wandered around the hilltop, looking closely at everything, feeling and smelling and touching. So strange, such a different and austere place, so unlike the ebullient jungles of her home.

The sky was vast. She had never seen such an expanse of cool sky, muted blue streaked by thin gray clouds. The sun was not strong. She wondered if someone had defeated the great Sun God and taken away most of his powerful light. How did people ever get warm here, she wondered. Were there people in this desolate place?

As if her thought manifested its own answer, she heard footsteps crunching a distant rocky path. A chill of fear arose and she rehearsed the procedure for returning home. She had learned by trials to focus intensely on her special place with the quartz, and envision the small clearing in the jungle. When this image was perfectly clear and filled her mind, she suddenly found herself back home. But she had never been afraid before.

The footsteps became louder. The girl crouched behind some bushes and waited. A thin wavering voice rose over the rim, making sounds that saddened the girl's heart. Was it a form of singing, a song of grief? None of the sounds were recognizable, no tones or rhythms familiar. She waited, prepared to leap or run or fight.

She was astonished by what stepped lightly onto the hilltop, singing the eerie song. It was a girl, close to her own age, but so totally different as to take her breath away. This girl's hair was the color of corn silk, pale golden and braided in two long ropes. Blue eyes, much bluer than the limpid sky, in a face so pale as to appear colorless. Clothing that covered her completely, a skirt almost reaching the ground, a heavy shawl around the shoulders, garments covering arms to the wrists. The colors were muted green, purple and tan in a squared design, and dark shoes enclosed the feet. As odd as the creature appeared, at least she did not seem dangerous and certainly was not very large.

The dark-skinned girl stood up and raised an arm in greeting. The other spun suddenly and gasped, eyes wide and mouth agape. Slowly she raised an arm to mirror the greeting. Moments passed as the two stared and appraised each other. Something passed between their minds, their consciousness met and mingled.

The girl from the jungle tried speaking.

"Greetings of Father Sun. I am Yohl Ik'nal, daughter of Lord Kan Bahlam of Lakam Ha. I come to visit your world from time to time."

The pale girl tilted her head quizzically but did not seem to understand. She spoke in an unintelligible language that had rhythms unlike any that Yohl Ik'nal had heard. Seeing that words would not suffice, the pale girl walked slowly forward and offered the dark-skinned girl a morsel from her pocket that appeared to be hard cake. Yohl Ik'nal accepted it and nibbled cautiously. It was sweet and grainy, not at all unpleasant. She nodded and smiled but had nothing to offer back.

The pale girl pointed to her chest and said: "My name Elie. Eh-l-ee."

"Eh-l-ee" repeated Yohl Ik'nal slowly, as the other nodded.

"Yohl Ik'nal. Yo-hl Eek-naal," she said, pointing to her chest.

They repeated each other's names several times, touched clothing and hair, eventually touched fingertips to faces. Brown eyes gazed into blue eyes, searching deep into the soul, finding kinship. Yohl Ik'nal wondered if communicating with mind images might work. She led Elie to a grassy place where they could sit, and pointed to her forehead while squeezing her eyes closed. Elie followed suit, and for some time the girls sat facing each other, eyes closed, concentrating intensely on each other.

Slowly images began forming in Yohl Ik'nal's mind, and she could sense that Elie was receiving her communications. After some time, neither knew how long because time was suspended in this strange world, a flow of mental communication ensued.

Elie was from a large city, much larger than Yohl Ik'nal could imagine, full of crowded streets and tightly packed houses, where people used long-legged animals to pull rolling boxes for traveling. Elie lived inside her house much of the time because it was often cold and cloudy and rainy. All her people covered their bodies with lots of clothing and wore hats. They burned black chunks in odd fire pits built into the walls of houses. It kept them warm in the chill northern climate. They cooked and ate food inside. Elie had a garden with colorful flowers, different but beautiful, and went there whenever the weather permitted. All this was wondrous to Yohl Ik'nal and not much to her liking as she mostly lived out of doors with little clothing. The animals amazed her and she longed to see the huge ones with horns as well as the graceful long-legged ones upon which Elie's people depended so much.

Elie inquired how Yohl Ik'nal came to this place, and the dark-skinned girl communicated her process. It was not dissimilar to Elie's way of arriving, for she sat in a quiet space focusing on a small flame until it carried her off. Elie called this going to the "fairie realm" and told of many other places she visited, full of tiny creatures with gossamer wings and mysterious forests with magical animals. This particular place, the windy hilltop, belonged to beings she called the Celts who practiced magic. Sometimes these beings met her here and told her secrets about the other worlds.

Yohl Ik'nal invited Elie to come to her home, the place of many waters, Lakam Ha in the jungles with bright sun and colorful creatures. Elie promised to visit some day, but like Yohl Ik'nal she could not control where her journeys took her. The girls looked with yearning at each other, now feeling a bond of shared adventure and wanting more. Suddenly Elie jerked her head, eyes darting back and forth.

"Mum is coming," she said in her strange language. "I must return, goodby and I hope we meet again soon." Closing her eyes and scrunching her forehead, Elie suddenly disappeared.

The wind whipped Yohl Ik'nal's black hair, and she was acutely aware of how cold she felt. Shivering in her light tunic, she stood and turned slowly, gazing at the alien landscape as if to imprint it indelibly in her memory. Only the rustling of windblown grass reached her ears. Stillness surrounded her. Closing her eyes, she envisioned her secret place with intense yearning for its warmth and light, and returned.

2

"Lady Xoc Akal, I am concerned about your daughter."

The High Priestess of Lakam Ha, Ix Lahun Uc, spoke gravely. As mentor of the noble girl from the ruling lineage, the priestess took her sacred charge seriously. She had free access to the ruling family's private quarters and arrived unannounced.

Xoc Akal released herself from the backstrap loom where she was weaving, a favorite art of noble women.

"Then you must speak of this to me," she replied, settling onto a floor mat and gesturing for the priestess to sit beside her.

Lahun Uc carefully folded her thin form into the cross-leg posture Mayas used for sitting, annoyed by creaks from protesting joints.

"Let us have cacao." Xoc Akal signaled attendants to bring the warm beverage laced with chile, certain that the priestess would appreciate its spicy, bitter jolt on the wet winter day.

Pale light slanted through narrow windows in white plaster walls. The rectangular chamber had one door covered by a heavy fabric drape. Chevron patterns in black and yellow against a white background rippled in the moist wind that blew from the patio. The drape hung from a pole suspended in round hollows on each side of the doorframe. A wooden lintel spanned the upper doorway, mortared into the plaster walls. Furnishings were sparse in typical Maya style; several colorful floor mats, a painted ceramic jug for water with gourd dipper, tidy piles of cotton thread waiting for the loom to form them. Plant, insect and mineral pigments produced the vibrant red, green, blue, and yellow colors. One luxury item graced the room, a small alabaster vase of creamy golden hue. It smooth sides, translucent even in dim light, curved gracefully to a small lip.

Xoc Akal's shawl lay nearby where she dropped it before entwining herself into the backstrap loom. The simple shift she wore had yellow borders at neck and hem, leaving arms bare. Her skin was moist, partially from effort but mostly from the humid air. She nodded as the attendant returned with steaming cacao in ceramic cups brightly adorned with dancing figures.

Lahun Uc inhaled deeply, savoring the biting and earthy aromas as chocolate mingled with chile. She sipped the astringent beverage, thankful for warmth in her gut.

"Now it comes upon six tuns (360-day "years") that I have taught Yohl Ik'nal," the priestess began. "She learns the occult arts rapidly—too rapidly. I fear her journeys will take her beyond her ability to control them. She goes so easily to other realms, other times and places. There is danger she will be trapped by denizens of these other dimensions, or she may become lost and unable to retrace the thread of connection to her form in the Middleworld."

"Has she found difficulty returning?"

"An occasion or two, she appeared unable to return when it was time. Not such that I was required to journey to her dimension for retrieval, although I almost began that process once. So far, she has been able to return when I called her with mental intensity."

The High Priestess looked sternly at Xoc Akal.

"Are you aware of journeys she takes without supervision?"

"No, Holy Priestess, I am not aware of such things."

Xoc Akal fretted that she was not adequately observant of her daughter. Yohl Ik'nal had been independent from early childhood, with a habit of leaving home for long periods. Her attendants complained that she slipped away when they were distracted. They made the rounds of friends' homes and nearby plazas, even searching along river banks and nearby forest trails, but the girl eluded them.

"She is known to disappear, not infrequently," Lahun Uc observed dryly. "It is my suspicion that she journeys alone, and this is dangerous."

The mother bowed her head, acquiescing.

"Journeys across time and space should be undertaken with supervision. It is especially difficult to time travel, for the spirit becomes disoriented through multiple veils and may lose the thread of consciousness linking it with the body. Your daughter could be lost in a past or future time; if spirit wanders too long the body will die."

Lahun Uc was stating the obvious, but she knew that Xoc Akal had little interest in Maya occult arts. Weaving, dancing, feasting and children, the usual noble women's pursuits, had occupied her attention.

"This must be controlled," Xoc Akal said, hands fluttering in dismay. "She respects you, Holy Priestess. Will you speak with her, set rules for her? As you say, she is in danger, both from wandering in the jungle and forays to other dimensions."

Asserting her high rank to regain face, she added firmly: "It is time she realizes her sacred obligation to the Bahlam family and our B'aakal polity."

"It is so," the priestess agreed. "Soon she will be of age for the transformation ceremony into adulthood. Should our ruler, Holy Lord Ahkal Mo' Nab continue with no issue, Yohl Ik'nal will be the only direct descendant in the family. This becomes of greatest concern, that she be capable of transiting portals to the Triad Gods and ancestors appropriately. She must learn to control her journeys . . . as well as her worldly explorations."

"You speak truth . . . though it pains the ruler that succession might not pass through his children. I will speak at once to Kan Bahlam. My husband recently mentioned the ritual to confirm Yohl Ik'nal as bearer of the royal lineage. He must obtain consent from Ahkal Mo' Nab, and this is delicate, as you appreciate."

"Yes, delicate but necessary for the Bahlam dynasty to continue."

"We deeply value your loyalty," said Xoc Akal.

Lahun Uc nodded. Long had she supported the royal family of Lakam Ha, and would continue while breath infused her body.

"This shall we decide," she stated with finality born of authority. "Once you speak with Kan Bahlam, and he obtains consent from his brother, will I begin concentrated training to prepare Yohl Ik'nal for the transformation and bearer of royal blood ceremonies. She must remain with me in the temple. Our priestesses will constrain her movements, and I will discipline her journeys. So shall we mold a potential heir to the throne."

Xoc Akal's eyebrows shot up, forming crescents on her slanted brow.

"Ruler? Never has a woman ruled B'aakal. Mother of rulers she might be, but ruler herself?"

"She is the last of the purest bloodlines to the founder. The Bahlam dynasty will end if some other high-ranked noble succeeds to the throne, even if married to Yohl Ik'nal."

"Think you this is possible? There will be much resistance from the men."

"Except for one man, her father Kan Bahlam. Your husband, My Lady, has both the prowess and the passion to seat his daughter on the throne."

YOHL IK'NAL — II

BAKTUN 9 KATUN 6 TUN 14 (568 CE)

1

THE STONES IN the firebox were ashen-gray, signaling readiness to receive the waters that would produce waves of steam. Already the sweat chamber, with its low ceiling and narrow entrance, radiated intense heat. Smooth stones formed a seating platform along the sidewalls, absorbing the heat, waiting, anticipating. Stooping to enter the *Pib Nah* (oven house), the attendant brushed sweat from her eyes as she gauged the stones' readiness. Giving a nod of satisfaction, she backed out and hurried down the long corridor leading to the quarters of the *ahauob* (nobles).

The corridor was flanked on one side by square pillars and the other by a thick-walled chamber. A low corbelled arch formed the ceiling, joining pillars and wall. The pillars opened onto a sunken courtyard with stairs ascending to corridors on all sides. Carved stone figures of stylized jaguars with pudgy faces and large teeth adorned the stairs. Bright sunshine heated the smooth white stucco of the courtyard, while the covered corridor retained morning coolness. When the attendant reached the ahauob quarters, she clasped her left shoulder with right hand and bowed to the priestess standing by the entrance.

The High Priestess Lahun Uc was dressed in a white cotton shift bordered with woven red and yellow bands, anchored above her breasts and falling just below the knees. A lizard headdress clasped her hair in a topknot, from which dangled braided strings ending in azure droplets of jade. Colorful cloth bands crossed in mid-forehead and sprouted a lotus blossom. Woven reed wrist-cuffs dangled shiny copper discs that clinked melodies as she moved.

Without speaking, the priestess pushed aside the cloth screen hanging across the doorway and entered the room. Inside the small chamber the young *ahau* (noble) waited, seated meditatively on the wall bench. Only a single T-shaped window allowed light to enter, and copal smoke undulating from several censers increased the chamber's obscurity. The young woman looked up as the priestess entered. Their dark eyes met knowingly, nothing more was needed. Both knew what must happen. Rising slowly, the young woman gathered her loose robe and on bare feet followed the priestess out of the chamber.

Yohl Ik'nal had been fasting and making oblations to the deities for three days. Taking only water and fruit juices, she repeated chants and incantations for hours on end. Hunger disappeared after the second day. Now her body felt transparent, so light it nearly floated. Dizziness resolved into infinite space, and she entered an unbounded reality where she might become lost in vastness.

Instructions from the High Priestess for this purification were explicit. She must search her conscience for any grievances she had committed against her people, family or the Gods. Any jealousies, any resentments, any accusations must be purged. Any false thoughts she held must be identified and rectified.

The effort required for this inner accounting kept her linked to her body, though she would prefer to float in timelessness. She summoned to mind, as precisely as possible, many hours of teachings and practices given to noble children. After that came rigorous training in the Temple of the High Priestess. Had she lived according to the highest principles? Had she regularly recited the names and kept the days of the Gods? Had she been duly obedient to authorities?

No. All these obligations had not been well met.

Memories of training in the High Priestess' temple burst through her mind like crashing cascades in Lakam Ha's tumultuous rivers. She had resisted the discipline, resented the confinement, yearned for her former freedom to wander jungle paths and travel to distant places. The shamanic techniques demanded by Lahun Uc were double-edged; they gave control over visioning and dimensional travel, and brought her in profound contact with Maya deities and ancestors. But they restricted spontaneity and imposed a culturally defined focus on her journeys.

Using the High Priestess' vision serpent technique, she imbibed mind-altering concoctions of plants or frog secretions. These drew her consciousness into spirals of incense that became the vision serpent, from whose mouth deities and ancestors emerged. She could then ask questions or receive instructions. Using the Wakah Chan Te—Jeweled Sky Tree technique, she learned to descend into deep underground caves, meet her power animal (*uay*), make requests and be guided to ascend the Three-Level Jeweled Tree from its roots in the Underworld, through the trunk in the Middleworld and along branches into the Upperworld. Toward the end of this training, she made journeys deeper into the dangerous Underworld, with close supervision.

The deep Underworld journeys frightened her. One time her uay took the form of a lizard and guided her through watery caves dripping calcareous spines from ceilings. On a slippery boulder, wraith-like figures danced around blue flames, their spindly limbs flapping as bloated bellies jiggled. Skeletal faces leered in toothy grimaces and bloodshot eyeballs popped out of open sockets. They signaled her with bony fingers to come closer. Chills ran up her spine, teeth chattered and body shivered in the cold gloom. Splashing through knee-high water she approached the mirage, nudged forward by the lizard. Suddenly the flames shot higher and twisted into a huge blue snake. It reared its fanged head and fastened red beaded eyes upon her. Tongue forking and vibrating it hissed commands that drew her like a magnet.

She resisted but could not hold back. Terror flooded her body and she twisted frantically, but the magnetic force pulled her up against and into the snake. She became the snake. Primal power surged through her. Pounding heart became the earth's drumbeat; surging blood became the sap of plants and flowing *itz* (life force) of creatures. Creation, death, transformation and rebirth were her essence. All moved by and through her as the serpent of the life cycle.

The lizard helped her return and the High Priestess interpreted this journey. It was a great gift from the creator goddess and sign of empowerment. She was designated as one who could work with primal life forces to benefit her people. Mayas of high rank, rulers and priesthood must navigate all three worlds, learning to handle Underworld powers, to fully manage the needs of their society.

But she was unable to return to the cold, windy place on the grassy hilltop. Maybe the only way to journey there was using the crystalline sunrays of her special place. She wondered about the pale girl Elie, and her strange world. Would they ever meet again?

On one occasion she found opportunity to slip away to her special place. It was during the family celebration for the birth of her brother, a time when she was released from temple confinement for a few days. In the hubbub of ceremonies and feasting, when her attendants were recovering from quaffing fermented fruit juices, she crept out before dawn. Stealthily she plied the path beside the cascades, her feet noiseless as a jaguar's paws on the dry humus, it being the season of bright sun and less rain. Settled on her stone, she waited until the rising sun ignited the quartz into flames, and projected her consciousness on the brilliant rays.

The season was also warmer on the windy hilltop. She welcomed the weak sun, inhaled fragrances of dry brush now tipped with seed pods, and peered across endless waves of grasses tawny with seeds.

Elie! she called in her mind. *Elie, come visit!*

Time seemed long in the waiting. Could Elie still receive her calls? Would Elie respond; was she able to return to the hilltop?

There seemed to be some difficulty. Yohl Ik'nal could sense Elie's consciousness though the girl's form had not appeared. Perhaps Elie no longer was capable of making the journey into another dimension.

Closing her eyes and focusing strongly, she mentally communicated to Elie: *Can I help you? Here, use my awareness as a thread to follow.*

She sensed a struggle, and then a bursting forth of Elie's awareness and suddenly the girl was beside her on the hilltop.

Elie was bigger and surprisingly tall. Her complexion remained moon-pale framed by corn silk hair. The sky blue eyes were startling in their clarity.

Eagerly the girls embraced, touching each other's faces and clothes. Yohl Ik'nal felt how happy Elie was to meet again, and sensed her fear that they might not have another visit. Standing apart, they appraised the changes several years brought. Elie was much taller, her people of larger stock.

Are things well with you? Yohl Ik'nal mentally asked.

I have difficulties. Not much freedom. My father plans marriage for me soon. To a man I do not like. My mother watches me closely. I cannot visit the fairie realm. Until you called me now, I was not sure I could travel here anymore. These ideas were transmitted by Elie and Yohl Ik'nal understood. She communicated back: *Our lives are similar. I have lost my freedom too. I am being trained by a strict priestess to become bearer of the royal blood. They will marry me to whoever best suits their needs. This may be the last time I can come here.*

Holding hands, the girls gazed longingly into each other's eyes. Both desired to escape their worlds and go somewhere together where they could have the lives they wanted. Elie sent a strong plea: *Don't forget me, Yohl. Somewhere, sometime we will know each other again.*

You will *come to my world. I can sense it.* Yohl Ik'nal surprised herself with the certainty of her knowing.

Elie smiled and her blue eyes sparkled. She asked to know more about Yohl Ik'nal's world. Through vivid mental imagery they shared about their families, cities and activities, each in wonderment over how exotic the other's world appeared. All too soon, the girls realized the moment of return had arrived. In parting, the poignancy of Elie's intention echoed in Yohl Ik'nal's memory: *My greatest wish is to be in your world. May Spirit make it so!*

Ocellated turkeys gobbled in the distance, pulling Yohl Ik'nal back into her self-examination. Untwining her legs, she stretched tight muscles. Attendants had placed a gourd of fruit juice inside the door flap and she drank with gratitude. Taking a deep breath to revive her brain, she resumed her examination of conscience.

Not only was she disobedient in her journeys, but also jealousy and resentment had marred her emotions. Resentment over how dramatically life would change when she was designated as bearer of the royal bloodline. Already gone was her freedom to journey and losing this source of adventure was frustrating. In addition, she was jealous of her friends and worried about how their friendships would change.

Her three closest friends were noble girls whose family compounds were nearby. They played, explored, danced, dreamed and laughed together as equals. They were close and shared intimately. But once she was designated, courtly protocol would require her friends to treat her with deference, to hold her at a distance.

Tears trickled down her cheeks with these thoughts.

It is not fair. They can have some choice about their lives, the men they marry and things they want to do. But I will have very little choice about anything. Her life would not be her own, but in service of her city and dynasty. Why could she not be resigned to her fate? Surely this failing displeased the Triad Deities.

An even worse offense, she reflected, was how she came to resent the birth of her little brother. At first she was delighted with a new baby, holding and singing to him. After the novelty wore off, she found herself jealous of her father's affection for his son. She had been the focus of his attention before, basking in his praise: "My precious Heart of North Wind Place (that was what her name meant), you blow sweetly into my arms, has there ever been so beautiful a girl?"

Her confinement in the temple and the new baby changed everything. Now she was not often home and lacked opportunity to attract his attention. Yohl Ik'nal adored her father, Kan Bahlam. She loved everything about him, his smell, his strength, the large fine hands and gleaming jade insets in his teeth. She thrilled at his rich baritone voice, doted on his stories told while she sat in his lap. Just the pure maleness of him was a delight. He seemed infinitely wise, masterful and kind. It broke her heart that he was so taken by his son, and she resented both his affection for her brother and being a girl.

Then the tragedy happened. Before a solar year had passed, her baby brother was dead, stung by a scorpion in his bed. Just remembering it now brought tears to her eyes. She was flooded with guilt. Had her evil thoughts summoned the scorpion, directed his venom into her brother? She had desperately entreated the Triad Deities for forgiveness, and now she again called for their absolution. She had meant no harm. She just wanted her father's love back. Her father's grief was intense, and her accusatory thoughts toward him dispersed in waves of compassion. She vowed to make it up to him, to replace in his heart the son he so loved.

Now that opportunity was upon her. As bearer of the royal bloodline she could perpetuate the Bahlam dynasty descending through her father, should his brother Ahkal Mo' Nab remain childless. She must perform the ritual perfectly, embody the sacred qualities of the B'aakal lineage, and convey to the nobles and people of Lakam Ha that she was worthy.

As the preparatory time drew to a close, Yohl Ik'nal still felt torn about the coming rituals. Both a great honor and immense responsibility were being conferred, but it came with a great price. Did she really want it? Was she capable? Did she have any choice?

"No, I do not have a choice," she chanted repeatedly. "My father wants this. It is very important to him; I must do it for him."

She had undergone the purification. She had performed proper oblations to the Gods, memorized how to speak their names, relate their history, and count their days correctly. But her emotions often overcame her reason, and her obedience was faulty. Her conscience was not entirely clear.

Doubt nagged the edges of awareness as she followed the High Priestess along the corridor. Was she truly ready for this all-important ritual? Could she carry it out?

Ceremonially they proceeded through the corridor toward the *Pib Nah*, first the priestess, and then Yohl Ik'nal followed by the attendant. With each step the priestess shook a rattle of monkey tree pods, making hollow clacking sounds ending in a decrescendo of dry murmurs. Yohl Ik'nal was in an altered state, nearly floating outside her body. Only the brushing of long dark hair against her shoulders and the sensation of cool stones below her feet anchored consciousness to her body.

At the narrow entrance of the square stone structure rising slightly above the women's heads, they paused. The priestess began a mournful chant, shaking the rattle and clinking the copper discs at her wrists. From beside the Pib Nah where an open culvert channeled the nearby creek, the attendant brought a jar full of water and entered the structure. The sound of boiling water and vapors of steam emanated from the entrance. The attendant quickly exited and drew the door curtain down. She carefully twisted and bound up Yohl Ik'nal's hair with white ribbon, until it perched like a twining serpent upon the crown of the Ahau's elongated skull. Finishing her chant, the priestess motioned for Yohl Ik'nal to enter the Pib Nah for the final purification.

Dropping her robe, the young ahau stepped into a dark cave of steamy heat. Settling carefully on the hot stone bench, her naked body received the purifying vapors.

The main plaza of Lakam Ha was lined with people, leaving the brilliant white center bare. Large buildings framed two sides, and the others were lined with residences of the ahauob, situated close to the Bisik River. The south building had wide stairs descending to the plaza. Ascending the stairs were two columns of Ah K'inob (priests) and Ix K'inob (priestesses), attired brightly in feathered capes and headdresses, adorned with jade and shells. Rows of censers poured out spirals of copal smoke. The buildings shone red-orange in the sun, their roof-combs painted white, yellow and blue. From the main plaza, complexes of stone buildings clustered on level areas of the narrow mountain ridge, while wood and thatch huts clung among trees on the slopes.

The city of Lakam Ha, Place of Big Water was situated on a plateau of K'uk Lakam Witz, "fiery water mountain" hovering over fertile plains that stretched north to the Great Waters. It was a city beloved of the B'aakal Triad Gods, for they had thought to place it on this Holy Mountain long ago, when the Bacabs, Lords of the Four Directions, raised the sky and parted it from the waters. In that ancient time the Land of the Mayas arose from the waters like the back of a huge turtle shell, for they had willed it.

The day was hot and clear. Smells of jungle humus mingled with pungent copal, incense made from dried tree resin. Flocks of squawking parrots flew overhead and the roars of howler monkeys reverberated in the distance. Clay flutes, drums of hollow logs and turtle shells, wooden sticks, pod and shell rattles created plaintive and rhythmic melodies. Dancers performed in the plaza, enacting the coming of age story that was the purpose of the ceremony. It was a rite of transformation, when someone moved into a different phase of life, never to return to the previous status. Life changes such as puberty, adulthood, and marriage required this rite. Transformation to adulthood took place when 18 tuns (17.75 solar years) were attained.

When the dance ended, drummers struck a stately cadence. All eyes shifted to the platform above the stairway. The crowd murmured greetings when two richly dressed ahauob appeared, well-known and respected nobles through whose veins flowed the sacred blood of the B'aakal Triad, Kan Bahlam the father and Xoc Akal the mother of Yohl Ik'nal. They raised arms in salute, using the open-palm hand sign of blessing as the villagers cheered then fell silent.

Like a flock of birds suddenly changing direction, the crowd shifted toward the west building. Standing on the stairway was a collection of nobility together with the most respected warriors and artisans of Lakam Ha. They gazed up toward the platform as long wooden trumpets blared from rooftops and musicians drummed a rapid rhythm, escalating to a crashing frenzy. In the sudden silence that followed, the ruler of Lakam Ha appeared, the *K'uhul B'aakal Ahau*, Holy B'aakal Lord Ahkal Mo' Nab II, elder brother of Kan Bahlam.

Standing between two ornate censers, wreathed by copal smoke, Ahkal Mo' Nab raised one arm to bestow blessings as he made the sowing gesture with his other hand. This hand sign replicated the motion of sowing corn seeds into the ground. It was the archetypal hand sign of Maya rulers, who were embodiments of the Maize God, First Father—Hun Hunahpu, the bringer of life, sustenance and abundance to his people. The crowd roared approval, reaffirming their sacred social contract. In return for the ruler's intercessions with Gods to bring beneficence, they gave their love and support and effort. Thus Maya society maintained harmony and balance with nature and spirit worlds.

Attention shifted again to the parents of Yohl Ik'nal. Speaking in clear tones that carried across the plaza, they told of their daughter's accomplishments. She excelled at sciences, understood the workings of nature and the stars, and knew the sacred calendars. She played lovely flute melodies, danced gracefully, spoke and used hand signs eloquently. She recited the Gods' names correctly, read glyphs and performed oblations. She gently tended children, guided her household properly, honored elders and ancestors. She kept a calm demeanor and brought peace with her presence. She was, in all ways, an exemplary daughter who now had reached adulthood.

At each pause in the recitation, musicians rattled and drummed as the crowd murmured approval. Excitement was building, for the moment approached when the young woman would appear.

The High Priest and Priestess, standing on the top stairs, stepped onto the platform beside Yohl Ik'nal's parents and rapped their beribboned staffs seven times against the stones. In unison they chanted: "*Uht-iy 4 Chuen 16 Uo, u-pib-nah ek-uan-iy, Ix Yohl Ik'nal.*"

"It happened, on this auspicious day, the sweatbath is set in place, for Ix Yohl Ik'nal. She has arrived at the age of adulthood, her parents have said so, she has prepared and been purified, all has been done according to what is prescribed. Ix Yohl Ik'nal is spiritually and physically clean, she is reborn into a new life. As an adult, *Halach Uinik*—real human, she is fully formed. She takes her place in Lakam Ha as a woman of the B'aakal dynasty, bearer of the sacred blood. She is now her own person.

"Come forward, Ix Yohl Ik'nal."

Intense silence settled upon the plaza. The crowd's anticipation was palpable. Softly in the distance birdcalls insinuated melodies into the silence. A shape began to coalesce, seen dimly through copal smoke. Each deliberate step gave the apparition more form, until the young woman was suddenly visible. The crowd drew a collective in-breath, exhaling with a sigh.

Yohl Ik'nal stood on the top step of the platform. Her heart thundered in her ears and pounded against her chest. Blinking through the smoke, she looked around the plaza at an immense sea of faces, all eyes trained on her. Sweat formed tiny beads on her trembling upper lip. Nothing could have prepared her for this moment. Many times she had watched her uncle, the ruler, stand before the people. Sometimes she was also standing among the royal family on the platform. But never before had the people directed their full attention to her.

The blast of energy from the crowd felt like a shock wave against her body. Every nerve vibrated, sending prickling sensations along her spine and electric tingles to fingers and toes. Waves of nausea threatened to make her retch, and only maximum determination kept her upright. Nostrils flaring, she inhaled deeply and willed her rebellious gut to stillness. Her eyes lost focus and the crowd became a blur, an odd comfort that allowed her to regain poise. She raised clammy palms toward the people in the blessing sign and hoped her hands were not shaking.

To the crowd below, her appearance was regal. Almost as tall as her father, her stately form was adorned sumptuously in a towering headdress of quetzal feathers, beads and shells held by richly embroidered fabric and a huipil (shift dress) of yellow with red and green borders. The waistband held a medallion of *K'in Ahau*—Sun Lord's face. Below the waist, a woven-mat skirt covered the huipil, connecting her with the Maize God and the generation of life. This mat also signified the *Popol Nah* (Council House) and her role as advisor and decision-maker. Maya leaders sat upon woven reed mats when they met in council. Brightly colored reed sandals covered her feet; wrist and ankle cuffs jangled metallic beads. A large jade pendant hung at mid-chest, carved in the face of K'uk Bahlam I, the first Halach Uinik—real human ancestor of her lineage.

Now was her time to speak to the people, her first formal speech as an adult of the sacred blood. She must demonstrate her knowledge and her memory. The ruling lineage carried this responsibility; they were the ones who remembered. They knew the history of their people far into ancient times, and even what came before that. Not everyone in the lineage had clear memory, however. The ability to remember in part determined who was selected as ruler. Not just remembering, but also communicating with ancestors and Gods. All her training had brought her to this point. Now she must speak.

Yohl Ik'nal drew in a deep breath. She hesitated a moment, tempted to glance at the High Priestess, her mentor. Would she be worthy of her training? Would the sacred blood run true and fire her memory? Uncertainty rippled through her heart and her eyelids flickered, but she kept her gaze directed toward the square. She sensed her father's strong presence and felt his encouragement.

Fastened to this moment in time, arms too heavy, her tongue felt huge, choking her, adhered to the roof of her mouth. Could she utter even one word, much less recite a complex poem?

Quickly, before panic closed her throat, she breathed out, lowered her arms and began to speak.

In a clear, pure voice that surprised her and carried across the plaza, Yohl Ik'nal recited the creation story of B'aakal, her people and land.

"It was before the Fourth Creation, in times long ago.
Ix Muwaan Mat was born.
Of her birth it is said, she entered the sky
on the Day of Lord (Ahau), Month of Conjuring (Tzek),
for she was to bring the new creation."

Everyone knew the Gods' first three creations had failed. The animals could only howl and screech and growl and twitter; the mud people dissolved when it rained; the stick people had no hearts and little minds. None could properly honor the Gods, name their names, keep their days and give suitable gifts. The great saga bound all B'aakal people together and none ever tired of listening. They swayed to her rhythmic cadence as she recited.

"Seven tuns after her birth came the new Creation,
when all counts of the long calendar returned to zero.
The Gods of the sky, of the earth, of the underworld
knew what they must do.
They did three stone-bindings in the sky:
The Jaguar Throne Stone at the 5 Sky House;
The Water Lily Throne Stone at the Heart of the Sky;
The Serpent Throne Stone at the 13 Sky Earth-Cave.
These three stones formed the First Hearth Place,
patterned the stars so homes on earth would have hearthstones.

"Then the Lords of the First Sky took their places:
9 Sky Yoch'ok'in, 16 Ch'ok'in, and 9 Tz'ak Ahau.
These were Lords of the Jeweled Tree
that reached from the Middleworld of earth,
into the Upperworld where the Gods lived.
These Lords required gifts, these bundles were their tribute,
they were adorned with precious jewels, with necklaces and ear spools.
Ix Muwaan Mat adorned them,
she did tribute in the way required.

35

"And also for the new Creation, the underworld Gods were put in order.
The Underworld Ruler K'in Bahlam—Sun Jaguar
received bundles from the six Lords of the Underworld.
They gave their gifts and all things were in order.
It was done. The Fourth Creation came to pass.
The hearthstones were seated, the Jeweled Tree was raised.
The Lords of the Sky and of the Underworld took their places.

"Eight tuns after her birth, Ix Muwaan Mat did
the Deer Hoof Binding ceremony to designate herself as heir.
She carried the burden of creating the lineage.
The time was not yet, it was still to come, her travail for the lineage.

"Two days after the Deer Hoof Binding ceremony,
First Father Hun Ahau entered the sky, sited the House of the North,
in the 6 Sky Ahau place, creating the origin-lands of Matawiil.

"Now was the time of Ix Muwaan Mat's travail.
It was time for the birth of the B'aakal lineage.
It happened, 750 tuns after House of the North was sited.
Hun Ahau the Son of First Father was born of the penance of
 Ix Muwaan Mat in the origin-lands of Matawiil.
He is the Lord of the Celestial Realm.

"Great was the travail of Ix Muwaan Mat,
for next was born in 4 days a second son,
Mah K'inah Ahau the Lord of the Underworld,
called K'in Bahlam, the Sun Jaguar, the underworld sun-full moon.
And soon thereafter, 14 days after the second son, was born the third son,
Ahau Unen K'awiil, Lord of the Earthly Realm,
and keeper of the royal blood.

"Thus were born at Matawiil, through the travail of Ix Muwaan Mat,
the three patron Gods of Lakam Ha, the B'aakal Triad.
Let the people of Lakam Ha always remember their Primal Mother,
for through her comes our life and our sustenance."

Yohl Ik'nal paused, her gaze sweeping around the plaza. All sense of personal self had evaporated; she embodied the cosmic storyteller reciting the age-old tale of origins. Despite the hot sun, the people stood in perfect stillness with rapt expressions. Sweat dripped from brows and trickled down backs, but went unnoticed. Copal incense infused her lilting tones to create a hypnotic state, enhanced by deep-seated memories that the ancient story evoked. With bated breath they waited for the ending.

"One final ceremony was required for creating the lineage of B'aakal.
There must be the sacred office of *ahaulel* (rulership).
There must be the first *k'uhul ahau* (ruling lord).
She, Ix Muwaan Mat the Primal Mother,
she first earned the right to tie on the White Headband of ruler.
It was done. 800 tuns after she was born,
Ix Muwaan Mat tied on the White Headband.

"Her three sons, the B'aakal Triad
thought to themselves, this place needs people
to know the Gods, to speak their names and keep their days.
These three decided to create the Halach Uinik—real people.
And then was created the first person, the modeling of the first mother-father,
with yellow and white corn for the flesh, for the bones and legs and arms.
This first person, *U K'ix Kan*, was simply made and modeled,
there was no mother and no father.
By sacrifice and their *uayob* (spirit companions) alone,
the B'aakal Triad created the first human.

"*U K'ix Kan*, mother-father of the B'aakal lineage,
tied on the White Headband 1300 tuns after
Ix Muwaan Mat became the first ruler.
Then came the time of duality, the mother-father divided
into female and male, so the Lords of B'aakal could live in the Middleworld.
This was done, the dividing, by nine maize drinks given by
Grandmother Xmucane, Heart of Earth, Goddess of Transformation.
More than 1200 tuns later,
K'uk Bahlam I was born, he of Toktan.

"It was accomplished, in the Fourth Creation,
the birth of a son from a man and a woman, Halach Uinik, real people,
the progenitors of the B'aakal lineage.
The son, the ruler, Holy B'aakal Lord, K'uk Bahlam I,
whose blood flows through all rulers of Lakam Ha.
And in this way the Triad Gods, the three sons of Ix Muwaan Mat,
created the B'aakal lineage, the founders of Lakam Ha."

It was accomplished. The prophetic words echoed in her mind. *She* had accomplished the entire recitation and done it correctly. As self-awareness returned her face flushed, whether from heat or pride she cared not.

Yohl Ik'nal heard the long sigh that escaped the collective throats of the crowd as they bowed, arms crossed over chests in the gesture of honoring. Once again the story was told, once again the Triad Gods of B'aakal found it fit to bring forth the great lineage that created and maintained Lakam Ha. That the story had been well told was acknowledged by the deeper than necessary bows of the High Priest and Priestess.

Drums initiated a soft cadence as the High Priest chanted, his reedy old voice wavering through the recitation of titles for the *K'uhul Ahau,* the Divine Ruler who was the Gods incarnate, Holy B'aakal Lord Ahkal Mo' Nab. A slender man with narrow features, Ahkal Mo' Nab advanced slowly toward the platform where Yohl Ik'nal stood. Two noble attendants followed him, each carrying with great reverence an ornately wrapped bundle. As the ruler ascended the stairs to stand before the young woman, she sank to one knee, arms crossed and head bowed. The drums ceased and the priest's chant ended.

After a pause, Ahkal Mo' Nab spoke: "Ix Yohl Ik'nal, daughter of Ah Kan Bahlam Ahau and Ix Xoc Akal Ahau, you who are now transformed into an adult, bearer of the sacred blood of Ah K'uk Bahlam Ahau our lineage founder, you who have recited correctly the names of the Gods, retold their history and kept clear account of their dates, you are now acknowledged as lineage bearer. In recognition of this, you will carry the god-symbols for all people to see. You will bear the symbols of rulership as have all the leaders of B'aakal, for this is your right and heritage."

He gestured for his attendants to unwrap their bundles, taking the symbols in his hands.

"Rise, Yohl Ik'nal," he intoned. "Receive the K'awiil scepter and the K'in Ahau shield."

She stood and looked directly into her uncle's eyes. The family resemblance was striking; they shared the same strong jaw line and almond eyes with straight brows, similar full lips and prominent noses, and both had elongated skulls sweeping from brow to crown. He offered the K'awiil scepter into her right hand, and placed the K'in Ahau shield on her left arm. Although both were heavy, she bore them without apparent effort.

The K'awiil scepter was made of carved obsidian as long as her forearm, portraying the Triad Deity Unen K'awiil who was patron god of the ruling lineage. A smoking knife protruded from a mirror on his forehead, and one leg became a serpent that represented his uay (animal spirit). K'awiil was the serpent-footed lightning god, who connected the sky and earth, Gods and humans, and whose vision was infinite. He gave power to the K'uhul Ahau, the god-ruler, for visioning and communicating with deities.

The K'in Ahau shield featured the face of the sun god with square eyes and swirling pupils, long nose and a forehead mirror, placed on a four-petaled flower that was the sun glyph. Maya rulers were the embodiment of Father Sun, K'in Ahau, for they maintained proper relations with solar forces and sunlight.

The Holy B'aakal Lord was the only person who normally could touch these accoutrements of office. It was a high honor for Yohl Ik'nal to carry them, and she trembled inside. It was not fear, but the magnitude of what she was about to do. Next she would walk the entire periphery of the plaza, carrying the K'awiil scepter and K'in Ahau shield, displaying these powerful symbols of rulership to the people of B'aakal. It would mark her forever as someone apart, different, not simply noble but of the sacred lineage descended from the Gods. Through her body and blood, future rulers might be born. It signified her role as priestess and visionary, as holder of the memories. The people would respect her at a distance, elders would consult with her, and nobles would come to her for spiritual guidance and dream interpretations. Her future was being set, and it would not be ordinary.

She had passed over a threshold. The ritual had indeed transformed her and she felt the difference. Strength and confidence soared through her, evaporating fears and doubts. She turned slowly, feeling jolts of lightning coursing up her arms from the symbols of rulership. Her body felt ablaze with power. Catching her father's eyes, she rejoiced in his obvious joy.

This is your gift. Her eyes held his like an embrace. *I have done this for you.*

The drums took up a brisk tempo, joined by lilting flutes and accented by mournful wails of long wooden horns. Yohl Ik'nal lifted her head high, making feathers of her headdress sway and bobble, and descended the platform stairs to the plaza floor. Her parents and the High Priest and Priestess followed. Eyes straight ahead, she walked the plaza at the crowd's edge, holding the symbols so they were clearly visible.

From the nobles' platform, two different pairs of eyes watched her closely with new feelings—one with admiration and the other with jealousy. Both were young men, not much older, and both were distant relatives. The eyes of Hun Pakal observed her as if he had never noticed her before, which in fact he hardly had. Busy with the physical training of young men involving mock combat, races, ball games, hunting and contests of strength, his path seldom crossed that of the palace women. He did know who she was and might even have exchanged a few words at social gatherings. But she certainly had not made much of an impression. Today all that changed. He was struck, taken by her graceful movements, strong presence, and radiant beauty. Why had he never noticed this before? Her irresistible mix of strength and gentleness captivated him.

The other young man's response was completely opposite. The eyes of Ek Chuuah narrowed as he observed the high ritual, a ritual he coveted for himself. His family also claimed sacred bloodlines, but not pure enough to give him rights as a lineage holder. From early childhood, however, he had yearned for power and position. He observed the Holy B'aakal Lord with intense respect and modeled himself after the ruler. He dreamed of assuming such revered leadership, receiving the people's adulation, holding counsel with nobles and priests as he dispensed wise advice and strong edicts.

Inside he burned for this power. And now he watched his distant cousin, a young woman of no particular distinction, undergoing the ritual of lineage bearer. That title he wanted fiercely for himself. Hot toxins of jealousy exploded through his body. He boiled with resentment. All his stifled rage erupted at Yohl Ik'nal and he hated her. She became the symbol of everything that stood between him and his ambition.

I will find a way. Powerful jaw muscles bulged as Ek Chuuah ground his teeth. His mind reasoned coldly despite erupting emotions. *Lineage succession is not indelibly set. Sacred blood courses through my veins, and it is hotter and stronger than hers. Our ruler Ahkal Mo' Nab has no children. At his age, if he has produced none, he is unlikely to have any. His brother's family, and especially Yohl Ik'nal, be cursed! There are ways to discredit them. Now is coming the time for another part of the lineage to take over. My part.*

2

Lakam Ha overlooked the broad plain across which the K'umaxha (Sacred Monkey River) coursed. The plain fanned north to the Nab'nah (Great North Sea) whose waters were grey. Several waterways led to this distant sea, but the K'umaxha was used most for travel. The setting sun was swallowed by the blue waters of another great sea though few had visited this distant place. In the east was K'ak-nab the fabled azure sea, color of precious jade, where traders obtained red spondylus shells and stingray spines for sacred ceremony. Lakam Ha was truly a place of many waters, its small rivers cascading from upper slopes through ravines and limestone boulders, pausing in quiet pools cloaked by lush greenery. The small rivers connected to large arteries leading to the seas that surrounded the turtle carapace holding up the lands of the Mayas.

From the narrow, irregular shelf of land on which the city perched, high escarpments ascended to steep mountains in the south. Many rivers cut through the mountains and offered transportation through the dense jungle. Farther south the mountains rose exuberantly to impressive peaks, home of highland rain forests perpetually bathed in cold mists. Here lived the prized quetzal bird whose feathers adorned regal headdresses. Reports by traders told of a narrow isthmus far to the south that could be traversed in less than a day's travel. Beyond that, another immense land arose with a river as wide as a lake and mountains reaching so high that they must put the traveler into the Upperworld.

The polity of B'aakal was under the oversight of Lakam Ha. Close relationships existed with nearby cities. To the north were ally cities of B'aak and Nab'nahotot. Within the polity along the Sacred Monkey River were the cities of Yokib and Pa'chan. Tucked into the hills was Usihwitz, an artistic center with accomplished muralists. Popo' sat on the banks of a tributary flowing south, isolated by nearly impassable jungles. Beyond these cities to the southeast began the territory of another polity, the powerful Mutul, among the oldest and greatest of Maya cities.

Toktan was a legendary city cloaked in mystery. It was the birthplace of Lord K'uk Bahlam, the first fully human ancestor of the ruling lineage. None could say exactly where Toktan was; perhaps it existed in another dimension.

Yohl Ik'nal was expected to learn about the geography and politics of cities in the B'aakal polity. Now that she was designated as bearer of royal blood, it was her responsibility to study governance. She would soon attend her first Council meeting, and sit upon the mats at the Popol Nah. Much to her delight, her father Kan Bahlam, a seasoned statesman, undertook her instruction.

"The basis of our social organization is cooperation." Kan Bahlam fully enjoyed the mentor role with his daughter. "There is hierarchy, yes, for each is born to a certain status with implied roles. The spirit comes into a body perfectly formed for that status. This shapes our destiny, ordained in all wisdom by the deities. Society also follows its destiny, following patterns given by the Gods to maintain harmony and order. As long as people keep these sacred laws, they attain personal satisfaction and we continue in peaceful coexistence with other cities."

He explained to her the *may cycle*, a venerable tradition given by the Gods. Mayas, the people of the *may*, were keepers of calendar knowledge that included the *may* cycles. These cycles shaped the political landscape of B'aakal polity, as they had formed the sociopolitical substructure of Maya society from long distant times. This way of organizing society was a brilliant gift of the Gods, who in their wisdom understood the limitations of humans, their tendencies toward selfishness and acquisition and lust for power. In the *may* cycles, authority, power and prestige were rotated among different Maya cities in a clearly defined and timed process.

The *may* cycle followed the numerology of 13 by 20. This was based on the Maya 360-day "year" called *tun*. One *may* cycle lasted 260 tuns (256 solar years), consisting of 13 *katuns* of 20 tuns each. It was divided into two parts of 130 tuns each (128 solar years). The city selected to be the seat of the *may* became the spiritual, ritual and political center of its region. Called the *May Ku*, this city built plazas and temples to hold regional ceremonies and was considered the crossroads, the navel of the world. Using creation symbolism, the city denoted a sacred ceiba tree (*yax che*), a sacred grove (*tzukub te*), and a sacred well (*ch'en*).

Yohl Ik'nal had studied Maya calendars and knew the most important ones: *Tzolk'in* of the sacred numbers 1-13 that interwove all the others; *Haab* the 360-day calendar of 18 months having 20 days and one short 5-day month (*uayeb*) to follow the annual course of the sun; and calendars tracking the movements of Venus, Mars, the Pleiades, and the moon. Many calendars shaped the lives of Maya people, guiding every aspect of daily, seasonal, cyclic and ritual activities. So intricate and complex were these calendars, whose number approached 60, that special calendar priests—*Ah K'inob*—had emerged to interpret them.

"What is very important," Kan Bahlam said, "is that the *May Ku* city controls political and economic functions. It decides tribute requirements, manages land apportionment, makes appointments to public office, and sets schedules for ritualized 'flower wars' and ball games to demonstrate prowess of leaders and warriors."

"Have we had a flower war?" asked Yohl Ik'nal.

"Not in my lifetime, so far," her father replied. "We have not needed one. Now listen closely to this. The *may* cycle consists of 13 katuns. Each katun is ritually seated in a different city in the region, determined by the May Ku city. Thus every 20 solar years another city is honored and recognized, holds subsidiary rituals and selects its katun priests and katun spokesman/prophet (*Chilam*). This katun city makes local political and economic decisions independently. Do you see the beauty of this strategy?"

Yohl Ik'nal thought for a moment.

"The katun city feels important. It exercises local power and this satisfies the ahauob. Leaders of the city have much to occupy their attention."

"Yes, very well said. The most significant strategic result is ensuring cooperation with the May Ku city. There is little motivation to oppose or rebel against the political hub of the region. Each city knows it will get its turn as katun city. How wise the deities are who constructed such a system."

When the *may* cycle approached midpoint, a council of leaders and priests took place to select the next May Ku city. The current seat and the forthcoming one shared ritual and ceremonial functions during the second half of the cycle. The current seat gradually decreased its building programs and rituals, until at the end of the cycle the major ceremonial areas, roads, and idols were ritually destroyed and the city was "abandoned." Not everyone left the city; most commoners and many nobles stayed. Often the ruling dynasty and their retinue left to found another city. New ruling families emerged to launch the city's next phase. The new May Ku seat began its building program in preparation for increased duties.

"The *may* cycle was modeled on cosmic cycles," Kan Bahlam concluded. "It reflects a sacred pattern, beloved of the Gods, and prevents disruption of the social order. Power and prestige are shared predictably, according to the calendar, and the chaos of political upheavals is avoided."

Thus the Maya people kept the laws of the Gods, counted their days and honored their names in an orderly pattern, exactly as did the celestial bodies of the cosmos.

"When did Lakam Ha become May Ku?" asked Yohl Ik'nal.

"We were chosen as seat of the *may* at the beginning of Baktun 9 (436 CE). At the half-way point the May Council met and again selected Lakam Ha for the forthcoming *may* seat. Though not usual, it is acceptable for the same city to serve as May Ku for two consecutive cycles. That decision was made at the turning of Katun 13 (564 CE)."

Yohl Ik'nal calculated dates. This May Council had taken place four years before she underwent the transformation ritual into adulthood and was designated bearer of the sacred blood.

3

"Now comes something important."

The messenger's sonorous words echoed off the plaster walls of the Popol Nah, the Council House of Lakam Ha.

Ahkal Mo' Nab, Holy Lord of B'aakal, moved his regal head slightly and eyed the messenger. His slender body straightened but remained relaxed in the customary posture, one leg tucked under the other that dangled from the low stone throne covered with a jaguar pelt. He motioned gracefully with one hand, signing for the messenger to continue.

Yohl Ik'nal was all attention. Eyes wide, she surveyed the rectangular room, walls lined with benches slightly lower than the ruler's throne. The benches were covered with woven mats, cushioning the stony hardness. It was her first time in the Popol Nah, and she sat proudly beside her parents as an adult of the sacred blood.

Kan Bahlam studied the messenger with experienced eyes. This messenger was a well-respected noble, a seasoned runner and traveler who had visited many cities. He had relayed numerous important messages before, and was not prone to exaggerate. Clearly the messenger was excited, his black eyes sparkling and his body taut.

Kan Bahlam could read men. More than once this keen insight had steered his brother Ahkal Mo' Nab away from hasty or inopportune decisions. He was concerned about his brother, noting traces of fatigue around eyes and mouth of the thin face. It seemed the ruler had lost yet more weight, and his skin appeared sallow, despite his wardrobe attendant's efforts to mask these. Few appreciated how the ruler disguised his sickness, but Kan Bahlam knew well the cost of these efforts.

His mind wandered for an instant to the dank swamps of their adolescent quest. The two royal boys, born only one year apart, entered the transformation rites at the same time, companions facing the challenge of surviving in dangerous terrain while pursuing their jaguar prey. Young men of royal blood who were potential heirs must hunt and kill a jaguar, bringing back the pelt to signify their victory over fear and their mastery of the most powerful jungle beast. Only then could the jaguar become their *uay* to guide and counsel them in matters of power and the Underworld. They would earn the right to sit upon the jaguar-skin draped over the ruler's throne.

Both succeeded in their quest, but Ahkal Mo' Nab brought something else home beside a jaguar pelt. A few weeks later he was seized by a ferocious fever, sweating and shaking with bone-rattling chills, struggling with a fierce opponent who brought him to the edge of death. Priestly ministrations and rich offerings by his father ameliorated the Death Lords and the boy survived, but was severely weakened. His body was never again strong although his mind recovered its sharpness. Now in middle age, he was weakening steadily as the minion of the swamp was hard at work again

Kan Bahlam had long believed that this sickness, this life-sucking swamp fever that robbed his brother of so much strength was at the root of his childlessness. Though married to a robust woman, Ahkal Mo' Nab had failed to produce offspring in their 20 years together. Given his declining health, it was doubtful an heir would be brought forth. Thus the lineage succession would fall to Kan Bahlam and his family—to be precise, his only living child, his daughter Yohl Ik'nal. This troubled him; male succession was preferred although Maya custom did not dictate patrilineal descent.

The messenger's resounding voice pulled Kan Bahlam back to the present.

"There is discontent among the ahauob of Usihwitz and Yokib. It is said, they speak of it, that the May Council decided unjustly. Why should it be, they ask, that Lakam Ha becomes the May Ku again? Is it not enough; is it not just that Lakam Ha now luxuriates in the honors, the tributes, the construction of many new buildings? This is what is just, they say: 'it is enough for Lakam Ha to prosper for 260 tuns enjoying the katun celebrations and the dispensation of katun privileges. Some other city should be the next May Ku. Let us share this bounty, why keep it there?' So they speak, so they argue, in Usihwitz and Yokib."

Indignant murmuring filled the Popol Nah. Various nobles gestured and signed each other their surprise and concern. All waited for Ahkal Mo' Nab to speak.

"So they spoke ill." The ruler emphasized each word. "The May Council was fairly constructed and represented all the cities in the B'aakal polity. On the Council sat priests and ahauob of every city, Usihwitz and Yokib included. Why do they complain?"

"So say they, that the men of their city were weak," answered the messenger. "They who now complain were not at the Council and are angry they did not

45

have a say. It is a long time, beyond their generation, until the next *may* seating and they covet the prize now."

The ruler gestured for others in the Council House to speak, turning from long habit toward his brother.

"More is to be seen here, the roots go deep," Kan Bahlam said. "Sahal, speak of what you learned in other places you visited." He nodded at the messenger.

"My travels also took me to Popo'. This city in our polity, far from the river, we think about as a slow-moving place isolated by the vast jungle. But in fact there is much foment in Popo', much movement, much involvement that is surprising. When I was there, several ahauob had recently returned from Kan, in the Polity of Ka'an, the Snake."

Murmurs of surprise rippled through the Council House. Kan was the name of the ruling dynasty of a distant polity called Ka'an. Their primary city was Dzibanche, but frequently the dynastic name was used instead. Many days of travel were needed to cover the terrain from Popo' to Kan.

"They spoke little to me of their business with Kan," the messenger continued. "Of their purpose, they described trade but I saw few foreign goods in Popo' markets. One evening I sat late with an old merchant, praising his fine flint and obsidian, even buying a knife to loosen his tongue. Then he spoke of strange things, things he heard from the ahauob who visited Kan. Things so strange, I hesitate to speak of them."

Kan Bahlam exchanged a quick glance with Ahkal Mo' Nab. It was not lost on the other nobles present. The tension in the Popol Nah rose palpably.

"It is of importance that you speak these strange things," the ruler urged. "Let it be noted in the Popol Nah that you are simply repeating what you heard from the merchant of Popo'. Here we do not hold you accountable for the truth of what you heard, that you now repeat."

The messenger nodded gravely, eyes downcast. His reputation was important; he did not want it sullied by inaccurate information. Breathing deeply, he raised his eyes and glanced around the Council House, as if holding each ahau to the ruler's guarantee.

"Uitah Chan, the Kan ruler is an ambitious man. His building program is impressive since Dzibanche became May Ku of Ka'an polity. His ceremonies are the richest and most elaborate, his feasts the most delicious and generous. Sahals and priests are becoming fat and wealthy. Dzibanche is expanding its sources of tribute, bringing other cities under its provenance. There was fear in the old merchant's voice, fear he learned from the ahauob who visited Kan. So it was I asked the old man, why are the nobles afraid? Had I not listened and sat with him a very long time, very late into the night, I do not believe he would have answered. But he did answer, saying the ahauob spoke of changes in warfare methods by Kan. He did not understand well, not being a warrior, but spoke of more blood, more death in the warfare of Kan."

Silence gripped the Council House. Each ahau struggled to grasp the significance of this change. For generations, from ancient times, a protocol governed encounters between warriors of different cities. This "flower war" took place in the spring when flowers appeared. The ritualized combat permitted young men to test their courage and strength without killing. The *may* cycle was god-given to bring harmony to governance; the flower wars brought contained competition that served all parties well.

In the flower wars, the warriors of two cities met in a designated field in-between their homes at an agreed time in the spring. Adversaries of equal rank engaged in combat, which was a test of strength and skill with non-lethal weapons. There were matches of spear throwing, wrestling, racing and club wielding against poles. The most dangerous combat was with flint or obsidian knives, the objective being to draw first blood from shallow cuts. Occasionally an overly aggressive warrior caused more serious wounds, with death sometimes resulting. But killing was proscribed; overcoming the opponent and capturing him was the goal.

When one combatant was declared winner, he grasped his opponent by the topknot of hair that warriors wore, and cut off most of the long tail. This signified defeat, and the loser had to work in the victor's city until his hair re-grew. It usually took nearly a year. The loser then chose to remain in the victor's city or return to his home city. Often the man found a woman to marry or a new work opportunity, and remained. Many new alliances and fresh bloodlines were developed through this system.

This system of mock battle worked well for generations. But now Kan appeared to be increasing the lethality of warfare.

"This is information that troubles me greatly," said Ahkal Mo' Nab. "How is this related to the discontent of Usihwitz and Yokib?"

"Holy B'aakal Lord, I do not know," demurred the messenger.

Ahkal Mo' Nab invited the other ahauob to speak, which many did at length. In the Council House, each noble could express his or her view and offer suggestions. Kan Bahlam kept silent, however, his thoughts swirling rapidly. Deviation from the flower war protocol was not without precedent; he remembered incidents in southern regions involving Mutul and Uxwitza. Campaigns to overthrow dynasties or seat puppet rulers had occurred before, but never so close to home. He would speak later to his brother about his thoughts, in private.

A slight movement beside him drew his attention to his daughter. A surge of regret arose that her first Council House session involved a puzzling and serious problem. Catching her glance, he was surprised by the deep comprehension he beheld in her eyes. Tight lines in his face relaxed as he felt a wave of relief. On a deep, intuitive level he apprehended that she had the mettle for rulership.

He determined to take her with him when he met privately with the ruler.

4

Sunlight blazed fire into her eyes. Bursts of brilliance burned through her closed eyelids with blinding intensity. Heat seared her face. The sun was too hot, too close.

"K'in Ahau, your light is blinding me," Yohl Ik'nal cried.

Glowing streamers of molten fire reached from the sun's surface toward the earth, swirling and twisting like ferocious serpents. Their strong magnetic field drew her toward them, closer to the blasting furnace of burning light. She struggled against the magnetic pull, but could not resist its power.

The sun was immense, its intense heat melting her.

"K'in Ahau, release me, I am burning," she pleaded. "I beg you, let me go!"

But the Sun Lord was relentless and continued to draw her into his cauldron of gaseous flames. As her body fell into the sun, she did not incinerate but was suddenly catapulted along a magnetic arc into deep space. Floating, soaring in vastness she saw stars flickering in the darkening indigo of space. A white band arched across the sky, milky and translucent. She recognized the Celestial Caiman (Milky Way) who swam through the night sky, his devouring mouth seeking souls after death as his tail tipped the horizon plunging him downward, like an immense canoe carrying his cargo to the Underworld.

She was drawn through the dark rift of the Caiman's underbelly, and propelled past Tzab Kan, the seven stars (Pleiades) called rattles of the rattlesnake tail, ancient origin of the celestial Maya ancestors. The magnetic currents suspended her near the Heart of the Sky, the Creative Source that brought into being her people's part of this vast universe, the home of Hun Ahb K'u the Supreme Creator Deity.

Fascinated, she watched as the spiral galaxy slowly turned, its widespread arcs circling around the mysterious dark center in majestic rhythms, forming a cyclic pattern. Groups of stars moved gracefully in space following trajectories within the arcing arms of the spiral. Some stars had planet systems and undulated in their cycles, like the movements of snakes through water. All was spirals, circles and ovals, cycles upon cycles, comings and goings in a grand cosmic dance.

Suddenly she plummeted downward along an arc of the great spiral until she hovered in space above a brilliant star with eight planets circling around it. The star looked familiar, could it be her sun K'in Ahau, the solar lord? She recognized the cloud-shrouded blue planet as her home, the earth called *Kab'* or *Lum* in her language. Her heart leapt at its beauty, so watery and full of life. Awe, gratitude and love filled her.

Then she saw the great calendar wheels her people had created to follow the cycles of the sun, K'in Ahau. As the sun traveled the arc of the great spiral, making its own undulating cycle with its planets, an unimaginably long cycle appeared— the complete traverse of the arc around the Heart of the Sky. The time span was beyond her comprehension. Another calendar wheel appeared near K'in Ahau, smaller and following a much shorter time cycle, though still immensely long by standards of a human lifetime. As the sun followed the elliptic course of this cycle, it moved closer at one end and farther away at the other from the Heart of the Sky.

Abruptly the wheels and cycling stars froze. Eerie sensations prickled along her spine, raising her alertness. Something significant was happening. She focused intently and tried to make sense of the frozen pattern. There was something significant about the location of K'in Ahau and its planets on the elliptic cycle. They were near the farthest end away from the Heart of the Sky. Then the cosmologic images began shimmering and dissolving.

A gust of chilling air blast against her skin and she woke shivering.

Yohl Ik'nal drew blankets around her shoulders, sitting up on her pallet and drawing her knees close against her chest. It took some moments for the chills to end. The dream remained vivid and she reviewed its details, committing them to memory. This was a significant dream, she was certain. Tomorrow she would discuss it with her mentor, the High Priestess Lahun Uc.

Early that morning Yohl Ik'nal traced the familiar route to the temple of the High Priestess. The temple was a short walk across two plazas and up a long stairway from her family compound. Scarcely a moon cycle had elapsed since her training there had ended, with its enforced residence. Ruefully she realized that she missed the predictable temple routine and the discipline of study.

The High Priestess was finishing a lesson with acolytes when Yohl Ik'nal arrived. The young woman waited impatiently in the reception chamber, fingering the woven sitting mats and looking distractedly at wall glyphs. Finally, Lahun Uc entered the chamber and sat upon her elevated bench.

"Greetings, Yohl Ik'nal, to what do I owe this unexpected visit?"

"Salutations, Holy Priestess, and please forgive this interruption. It is a matter of importance or I would have requested an audience. Last night came a dream that left me both confused and full of wonderment. Perhaps you can assist me to understand its meaning."

Lahun Uc nodded, signaling her to continue. Dreams often brought significant messages or portended critical events, and the Maya respected these communications from deeper dimensions of consciousness.

"K'in Ahau drew me into his body as the dream began, and I feared I would burn up. Instead, he sent me far into the distant reaches of the sky and I saw many incredible stars beyond the Great Sky Caiman and the Tzab Kan. It seemed I was taken to the very center of our star system, the Heart of the Sky, then shown immense cycles of our sun, K'in Ahau and his planets."

Yohl Ik'nal described her dream in detail. The High Priestess knit her thin brows in concentration, eyes burning into the depths of the young woman's soul. When the recounting finished, the priestess pressed her eyes closed and seemed in meditation. Then she spoke in a husky voice that startled her visitor.

"This is indeed an extraordinary dream. It is of utmost importance. Truly, I am astounded by what K'in Ahau has shown you. What you have seen is knowledge reserved for only the most advanced calendar priests, those who have passed through many initiations to prove their comprehension and spiritual worthiness. Never have I known one who is uninitiated to have this revealed to them. Ah, but it was the action of K'in Ahau, the Lord Sun, and we must take it as his initiation of you."

"But, Holy Priestess, what did I see? What does it mean?"

"This I cannot speak of," Lahun Uc said. "It is secret knowledge, the arcane calendar arts that only the High Priest has authority to reveal. We must see our chief calendar priest, the Foremost Ah K'in, Wak Batz."

Lahun Uc sent one of her priestesses ahead to request audience with Wak Batz. She and Yohl Ik'nal followed more sedately, crossing several plazas then climbing long stairways to the temple of the High Priest. This secluded temple was situated on the northwest rim of the plateau, on a craggy out-cropping ascending the mountainside. It commanded a breath-taking view of the plains and river below, stretching to distant horizons that shimmered in the morning heat.

The women were shown into a small chamber bordering the High Priest's quarters. Scarcely had they settled onto mats when the bent form of Wak Batz appeared. He seemed immeasurably old to Yohl Ik'nal. Small and wizened, his body contorted into folds and angles while thin limbs remained remarkably straight. Sunken cheeks and eyes made his nose even more enormous and his teeth protrude in a permanent grimace. Today he wore no adornments of office, leaving his lop-sided chest bare with ribs clearly defined. Had he attained twice 52 tuns, the revered age of 104 tuns that made him almost immortal? Each of his numerous wrinkles carried her people's history and wisdom.

After the formal greetings, the High Priest inquired into their mission and listened to the re-telling of Yohl Ik'nal's dream. He too sat with eyes closed in meditation as she finished. After a time of silence, the High Priestess spoke.

"You see why I brought her to you at once. It is beyond my purview to explain the meanings of these revelations by K'in Ahau."

"Ah, yes, so it is, so it is," he murmured, still inwardly focused.

At last he came to his decision. When his eyes opened, they held a luminescent glow that lit his entire wizened face. A shimmering aura surrounded his head that both the young woman and High Priestess could see.

"It happened, in your dream, that our Sun Lord-K'in Ahau revealed to you the most secret, most sacred and esoteric of our many calendars." His usually thin, reedy voice took on resonant tones. "It is the calendar we call *Tzek'eb*, and it traces the Great Solar Year in the journey of the Tzab Kan (Pleiades) stars as they move closer and farther from the Heart of the Sky. You see, our own Sun Lord is one of the Tzab Kan; our Father Sun has seven brothers and together we all form a single cosmic family. As in any family, we will have better times and worse times. We have our seasons of light and of darkness. All of this occurs in a very long time span, so very long that few can comprehend it. This Great Solar Year is the cycle of the rise and fall of consciousness and civilization upon our beloved planet, *Kab'*."

"Is this calendar known to my father?" Yohl Ik'nal could not resist asking.

Maya rulers and leading nobles all studied the calendars and were expected to possess sound understanding of their cycles and significance.

"Even your illustrious and erudite father has not attained this knowledge," Wak Batz answered. "Nor his brother, the ruler. Often it is better that those who must bear the burdens of our people's needs, must make the sacrifices and intervene with deities, keep their vision focused on cosmologies that are closer to home. The full realization of *Tzek'eb* and its implications could discourage their efforts. You will see."

He exchanged glances with Lahun Uc. Sighing deeply, he continued.

"It seems K'in Ahau decrees that you are to understand this Great Solar Year, the Tzek'eb. Why this is so, is not yet clear to me. The Sun Lord must have some plan for you, perhaps it will be revealed in due time. Even as K'in Ahau travels across the sky of Kab' and we note the seasons, so K'in Ahau has his own seasons in his cosmic cycles. The longest cycle is his own birth, growth and death. But that is beyond all comprehension, except in the infinite possibilities of the Long Count Calendar. Of that cycle I do not now speak.

"The cycle you saw is the Great Solar Year of K'in Ahau. It is his movement around a twin star in our area of the Celestial Caiman, one of his brothers in the Tzab Kan. This long cycle takes 26,000 tuns (25,650 years) and brings our sun and planets closer to the Heart of the Sky, then farther away. It was known in very ancient times, and we inherited this knowledge. It is tracked by the changing zodiac signs on the eastern horizon at spring equinox. These changing signs mark our movements from one age, or Sun, into the next. We have been in Bahlam, sign of the jaguar, moving toward Coz, sign of the parrot. When 5200 tuns (5125 years) are completed, there comes another Creation, another Sun. Now we are in the Fourth Sun of the Great Solar Year, in the declining cycle. When the next, the Fifth Sun begins, we again start the ascent from the farthest point moving toward the nearest point.

"Your dream confirms this. You saw our sun and planets on their cycle, near the farthest point. Hmmm, yes. For this I am grateful. It coincides with my calculations."

Wak Batz fell silent, lost in contemplation. Yohl Ik'nal waited until her patience could endure no more.

"Holy Priest, I am confused," she said. "Your calculations and my dream place our sun at its lowest point in the cycle, but if this means a declining age, why does it appear that our people are increasing in knowledge and ability, that our society is developing?"

"Ah, your mind is sharp to pose such a question." Wak Batz nearly chuckled. His glowing eyes caught and held hers. "You are destined for greatness, that I can see."

Lahun Uc studied her student with new interest.

"Now comes your answer, my young inquirer. Yes, the Maya people seem ascendant; our cities are growing and accomplishments increasing. Yet we are in the autumnal fluorescence of our civilization. There were greater ones who came before, in the legendary lands of Atlantiha, in the great sea of the east. Their knowledge and powers far exceeded ours, but few retain memory of those times. Atlantiha was a great civilization even before Matawiil, the land of our ancestors Muwaan Mat, Hun Ahau—First Father and the Triad Deities. Our ancestors of Matawiil were descendants of the exalted leaders of Atlantiha, whose land was destroyed in the great inundation. It was the beginning of the descent, the loss of high knowledge. Slowly this golden age deteriorated, although groups of people held onto the knowledge for thousands of years.

"What we have now, in the Maya people of our time, is a late flourish of this advanced civilization in Tamuachan, as we call our Maya lands that rose from the turtle's back after the flood. In other lands, far across the great eastern sea, societies have fallen into darkness and barbarism. This is the time for the Maya to be great; after greatness follows darkness."

Tears sprang to Yohl Ik'nal's eyes and she looked pleadingly at Lahun Uc.

"Why must this be so? What is the purpose of it all?" Her voice choked.

"It is the Cosmic Law, the nature of cycles. The Creator of All has ordained these cycles in its infinite wisdom." Wak Batz softened his habitual grimace into what resembled a smile. "The cycle is not at its end, Yohl Ik'nal. There is much yet to come. You have an important role in what is coming."

Wak Batz turned to Lahun Uc.

"This is most irregular, but I will instruct Yohl Ik'nal in the esoteric calendar arts. As she was recently under your tutelage, it is fitting that you arrange this as a continuation of her studies. I will come to the priestess' temple, as not to arouse curiosity. The nature of these studies we must keep in strict confidence. Not even her parents shall know what she studies."

"So it shall be," the High Priestess agreed.

"Yohl Ik'nal, you must take a vow of secrecy about your dream and the calendar meanings we have discussed," the High Priest said gravely. "Do not mention it to your father, mother or anyone at all. The High Priestess and I will be your only confidants. Understand the seriousness of this. Such knowledge would be destructive for those not initiated. Give us your vow."

Trembling at the magnitude of holding this knowledge, she pressed her lips tightly to avoid sobbing as tears continued to gather, sending a trickle down her cheeks. The hardest thing was not being able to talk to her father. She felt disoriented, off balance that he was not privy to such information. Her world was even more deeply shaken than by being designated bearer of the royal blood.

The stares of the priest and priestess caught her in a vise. There was no escape.

"My vow . . . it is given . . ."

Her voice caught as a sob escaped.

"We are witness to your sacred vow. Soon we will meet again," said Wak Batz.

Lengthening shadows reached across the courtyard and a cool breeze swept through columns into the veranda. The family of Kan Bahlam sat on mats as their afternoon meal was served. Food was prepared and consumed outside, since the stone walls absorbed and radiated heat. The well-ventilated pole-and-thatch kitchen serving the Bahlam residence was located just outside the courtyard, keeping its activities away from the more enclosed living quarters. Its earthen floor and open-lattice walls allowed heat and smoke from burning charcoal to escape. Servants did all the cooking and serving, bringing ceramic bowls of stews, platters of fruit and drinks of juices in beautifully decorated cups. Small gourds were used as scoops, or thick maize cakes dipped into savory dishes.

While her parents chatted about daily events, Yohl Ik'nal brooded about her encounter with the High Priest and Priestess. Her head was whirling and her mind felt fuzzy. Why did she have to know this? Resistance swelled and pushed against the knowledge that her people were destined for inevitable decline, that they were in the final fluorescence before their world unraveled. Hopelessness flooded her. What help could she possibly offer? Yet the High Priest said that she would have an important part in what was to come. It did not seem possible to help much feeling so desperate, so alone.

Looking at her handsome father, her heart wrenched. He did not know. He went through his days assuming their world would continue. Torn between the aching need to tell him and seek comfort in his wisdom, and the desire to protect him, she could barely stifle her sobs. When food arrived, the pungent spices almost gagged her. She picked at the fruit platter and drowned maize cakes in her stew bowl, hoping her parents would not notice. But her mother did.

"Are you unwell? You have hardly touched your meal."

"This day has been long, I am tired." She hoped her mother would not ask about her day.

"What did you today? You were away most of the time."

"I made a visit to Lahun Uc. I find that I miss being at the temple." Desperately she hoped to avoid more probing.

"Of what did you speak?" Now her father had joined the inquisition. It was time to use whatever skills she had at dissembling, something she was certain her new status would require. Gathering up her determination, she tried to keep her voice normal.

"We spoke of calendars and the cosmologic structures, these I studied most recently with the Priestess. She wishes to instruct me more, as the lessons were not completed before my ceremony. Should it be acceptable to you, I will continue to meet with her."

It was certainly close to the truth. Her father seemed pleased and her mother had returned to eating, losing interest as soon as calendars were mentioned.

"Indeed, this you should do," he said. "One can never learn enough about the calendars, they are so complex and numerous. It does demand great concentration which can be tiring." He smiled and the jade insets in his teeth gleamed.

"Eat, it will restore your strength," her mother mumbled with mouth full.

The food was no more appetizing than before, and she knew another bite would make her nauseous. Smiling weakly, she signaled an attendant to remove her dishes.

"The food does not sit well upon my stomach. It is no fault of the cook, simply that I am not feeling well. With your permission, I shall retire to my chamber and rest."

Her mother signaled permission while her father appeared perplexed. She quickly escaped before he could grill her further. Once safely ensconced in her chamber, she flopped on her sleeping mat and allowed tears to flow. She cried quietly to avoid alerting her attendant. Pure despair washed over her as a black pall descended. Grasping her knees and rocking back and forth, she wallowed in a pit of darkness, unable to think.

Time passed and the sky turned ebony. Stars sparkled in their distant celestial dances, taunting her through the small window. Emptied by her catharsis, eyes dry, she gazed into the imperturbable Upperworld and found a spring of determination burbling upward inside her.

She was not helpless. She could seek answers for herself. She could use the shamanic skills that Lahun Uc had taught her.

She sat upright on the woven mat, cross-legged and very still. Intention took shape to get information about her dream and how it related to her life. The uncanny sequence could not be accidental. First she was designated bearer of royal blood, next she attended her first Popol Nah and learned of foreboding events, and then her dream revealed immense human and planetary patterns that shaped Maya destiny.

Using shamanic practices, she joined her mind with the Jeweled Tree, the ceiba whose roots penetrated down into the Underworld, whose mighty trunk rose through the Middleworld of earth, and whose lofty branches soared into the

Upperworld in the sky. She saw herself seated at the base of the tree, merging into its sturdy trunk covered with thick thorns, becoming fluid as its sap so that her spirit could rise. Upward and upward she went through the arteries of the tree, into the branches that became smaller, through the capillaries of the tiniest twigs, until her spirit evaporated out of the cloud-touching tips into the sky above.

Floating in the domain of Gods and ancestors, she shaped her questions. Inter-polity conflict and the nature of warfare had not crossed her mind before; now she needed to understand. The messenger in the Popol Nah revealed serious disturbances of social order. First was the discontent within B'aakal cities over the May Council's decision to make Lakam Ha the May Ku for a second cycle. What forces of change propelled this questioning of long established, god-given protocols that maintained the balance of power? Second was the escalation of warfare by Kan, violating the venerated flower war tradition that managed ambition and aggression in men. Surely the Gods had shown great wisdom in providing this model; by what right and for what purpose would a city overturn it?

The cosmic calendar appeared with cycles of rising and falling stars that formed the eras or "Suns" of Maya timekeeping. As things began, so they ended. As cycles completed, other cycles started. Cycles embedded in cycles, from the vastest to the tiniest. Again she saw the Tzek'eb cycle of K'in Ahau and its planets, moving closer and farther away from the Heart of the Sky. As it moved farther away, the exalted consciousness of the highest age began to wane, slowly at first then more rapidly until times of darkness, of constricted consciousness and all the atrocities this brought, reigned during the farthest point.

As Maya civilization deteriorated in the descending cycle, the social structures given by the Gods to maintain harmony began to crumble. Human ambitions and greed began to outbalance the divine wisdom of cooperation and sharing. This phenomenon was underlying the changes reported by the messenger. It was the harbinger of darkness.

Sadness tugged at her heart, quickly replaced by calm acceptance born of the visionary state. Such was the way of the cosmos and the divine forces that shaped and ordered it. The cycle of existence simply was. To dance as a star was her people's fate, until the ultimate dissolution into cosmic dust.

She felt her awareness being drawn back toward earth and knew her vision would soon end. A final question formed quickly; what was her role, what was she to do?

Times of strife and conflict, betrayal and plotting formed a matrix followed by a burst of brilliant light which transformed Lakam Ha into a large city with magnificent structures, level upon level climbing the steep mountainside, architecture she could not have imagined. A ruler yet to come, of creative genius and incomparable leadership, would shape this new city and leave an unrivaled legacy of Maya civilization. His mission was to preserve Maya knowledge, their wisdom and esoteric practices, their unique relationship with time and the cosmos as reflected on earth.

This great ruler would come from an issue of her body, from her blood and loins and the holy B'aakal lineage of which she was the keeper.

5

Ahkal Mo' Nab II, K'uhul Ahau of Lakam Ha, Holy B'aakal Lord, mediator with the Gods and bringer of abundance as the embodied Maize God, was not feeling well. During the night his thin body was shaken with fever, his bed pallet drenched with sweat. This morning he was weak, drained of the vigor that his 45-year-old body should rightfully have. He was steadily becoming weaker. Each attack depleted his reserve and lowered his life force. Shuddering, he sensed the relentless approach of the Death Lords of Xibalba. Not imminent, not yet at his threshold, but not so far away.

He sighed, thinking of his strong and still youthful wife who was denied children by his infirmity. Greater than this personal emptiness, however, was the lack of dynastic succession through a son. Now he accepted the inevitable, that the lineage would continue through his brother Kan Bahlam.

The ruler's ruminations were interrupted by attendants bringing him a bowl of nourishing liquid made of ground maize, peppers and venison broth. The Shaman-Priest had carefully instructed them about the ruler's needs after fever attacks, and also sworn them to silence about these episodes. They bathed their K'uhul Ahau once the fever broke with tepid waters infused with medicinal herbs, and wrapped him in dry cloaks of soft cotton. They encouraged him to drink plentiful clear water conveyed into his quarters by Lakam Ha's extensive aqueduct system that also supplied chambers for bathing, eliminating and steam baths.

To satisfy his attendants, who would report the meal to the Shaman-Priest, the ruler tried to eat but his appetite was small. He gestured for them to leave the bowl with him, signaling that he be dressed in casual garb for his brother's visit this morning. To his surprise, two visitors appeared shortly at the door of his day chamber: Kan Bahlam and his daughter, Yohl Ik'nal.

"*Ma'alo k'in*, greetings of the day," said Ahkal Mo' Nab, concealing his surprise.

"*Ma'alo k'in*," father and daughter said in unison, bowing while grasping the left shoulder with the right hand, gesture of respect and honor.

The day chamber was larger than most. Its outer door opened onto an interior plaza while the inner door gave access to the sleeping chamber. Two tall rectangular windows faced the plaza where small trees and shrubs in ceramic pots added color. The ruler sat on a raised platform covered by woven mats and his guests settled cross-legged onto mats on the floor. The mats were richly woven in bright colors and intricate designs, made of dense cotton that provided cushioning. A similar woven drape covered the inner door, hanging from a wooden pole wedged into small holes on either side to give the sleeping chamber privacy.

"Here beside me is my daughter," began Kan Bahlam. "That of which we speak today also pertains to her. It is time that she enters into these things, these considerations. May the Holy B'aakal Lord be in agreement with this understanding."

Ahkal Mo' Nab nodded gravely, his right hand signing acceptance.

"It is fitting that she is here. This understanding we share."

Yohl Ik'nal kept her eyes discretely downcast, hands folded in lap. When her father told her about this meeting with the ruler, she knew why. But there was much more she needed to learn, and her mind was alert and focused.

"The meaning of the messenger is clear," Kan Bahlam continued. "This discontent of Usihwitz and Yokib is not solely of their doing. It is fed by the ambitions of Uitah Chan, ruler of Kan. He plots and schemes for expansion and his gluttonous eyes are turning toward the land of B'aakal. To support his objectives, he sows covetousness into the minds of young nobles with little to do. He puts ideas into their minds, that they could be victorious warriors and gain greater things than are possible in flower wars. That they might even become rulers, displacing the traditional lineages of their cities. When such foment occurs the social order becomes unstable. Then shifts in power can occur, rulers made vassals, lineages unseated and overlords set in place to control the city's resources. Uitah Chan is putting this strategy into motion."

Silence followed as Ahkal Mo' Nab closed his eyes. Without these bright beacons of intelligence, his face appeared wan and drawn, skin tinged faintly yellow. Yohl Ik'nal absorbed the implications of the ruler's appearance, for she knew some things about illness and healing. Her heart felt heavy.

"It was done, this undermining of rightful order, in the time of Tuun K'ab Hix of Kan and our father Kan Joy Chitam," the ruler said in measured tones, as if forming words was an effort. "The Kan ahauob seated 12 year-old Aj Wosal of

Maxam after his father's untimely death and left a Kan overlord for many tuns, gaining much tribute. Often have I wondered about that death, although it was claimed to be natural."

"And shortly before that, Kan interfered in the affairs of Pa'chan," Kan Bahlam added, "though to the credit of Pa'chan the encounter left a Kan captive in their city. That which happened more recently between Kan and Mutul is of greater concern."

"With that I fully agree. The snakes of Kan have reached far southward, insinuating into the domain of the great and ancient Mutul, our friend and trade partner. Is it only six tuns since this shameful event? When Uitah Chan installed a puppet ruler at B'uuk, I became suspicious of his intentions. Next was a wily move, to stir the fires of discontent in Uxwitza that smoldered for years in resentment of Mutul's dominance, a position fairly won through flower wars and the decision of the May Council."

"Much have those events troubled me," said Kan Bahlam. "Still we are lacking definite information. It is puzzling that we had no contact with Mutul since its 'chopping down' ten tuns ago. We do know that Kan became the patron of Uxwitza and encouraged their dishonorable behavior in this event."

"It is said by the Calendar Priests, that the 'chopping down' of Mutul was as expected, part of the ritual termination of monuments and structures that must occur when the may cycle is completed," Ahkal Mo' Nab reminded his brother. "And Mutul was completing its second may cycle at that time."

"That is true, but Uxwitza seized upon the time of Mutul's ritual termination to enter the city and wreak havoc," countered Kan Bahlam. "Now follows what I have concluded about this event. The warriors of Uxwitza, accompanied by a contingent from Kan, took advantage of the turmoil in Mutul as its grand structures were being sealed and its monuments chipped. Remember that many fires blazed, symbolically 'burning' the stone monuments while mourners cried and did ceremonies and scattered ash everywhere. There must have been intense chaos; Mutul had been supreme for 520 tuns and her people could not imagine life in the declining may cycle. Perhaps even the ahauob and priests resisted. Into this disarray came the foreigners, who undertook destruction in earnest, fought in the plazas and desecrated some of Mutul's sacred shrines. It is also possible that ahauob of Mutul who opposed the ritual termination, who refused to accept Mutul's retirement from power, joined the foreigners. Possibly these ahauob were cultivated by Kan in the days before the may cycle end."

After a pause, Ahkal Mo' Nab asked: "Is it your thinking that the death of Wak Kan K'awill, ruler of Mutul, was accomplished by Uxwitza and Kan?"

"Of this I cannot speak with certainty. The Holy Mutul Lord died very soon after the ritual termination, and he received full royal burial with honor by his people. This I have heard from reliable sources. And, the rulership continued in the Jaguar Paw lineage as expected. But he was not an old man, so we can doubt a natural death. It is possible that dissident ahauob of Mutul were involved. This still remains unknown."

"Such a ferocious attack on Mutul violated the divine laws of the may cycle. People were killed and the city's sacred shrines desecrated. This is against what is righteous and ordained in the cosmic order."

"And Mutul must still suffer now, her city and people in disarray. Probably this is what shut down communications. Indeed, we are in troubled times for the snake-eyes of Kan are directed toward B'aakal."

Yohl Ik'nal listened attentively to this recounting of events of which she had no knowledge. Much had occurred in the Maya world outside her concerns. It was clear that the innocence of childhood and the sheltered status of women had ceased to be her refuges. Even as she had envisioned, the time of conflict and deterioration of Maya civilization was upon them, and now it became her concern.

The brothers' conversation paused, and Kan Bahlam looked at his daughter.

"You must learn of these things." The gruffness of his voice concealed emotion. "And of more. All is not well in Lakam Ha."

Turning toward the ruler, he asked: "May I speak frankly?"

Ahkal Mo' Nab nodded, his eyes measuring Yohl Ik'nal.

"There is talk that our lineage lacks the proper line of descent, that our ruler has no sons and is unlikely to produce any. Some whisper that a fresh branch is needed, sprouts from another family of the sacred blood. Some young men are gathering, grouping around the leader of this talk."

"Who is that man speaking such?" shot Ahkal Mo' Nab.

"Ek Chuuah."

"That puppy! His sacred blood is thin. Men listen to this foolishness?"

"So it seems."

"We will bring this to a halt. Soon we will do the deer hoof binding ceremony to name you as my heir," the ruler said decisively.

Kan Bahlam lowered his head slightly in acquiescence. It was inevitable, and he was prepared for it—and for the consequences affecting his daughter.

"Our people need some distraction, some activities to bring their idle minds back to order," the ruler continued. "Usihwitz and Yokib need a few lessons about respecting their May Ku city and keeping away from the temptations of Kan. We will schedule a flower war with them in the next season of flowering. And we will send some observant merchants to Kan for trading, to learn more of Uitah Chan's plans."

The brothers discussed details of these events, selecting ahauob to take charge and organize different aspects. As their discussion finished, the ruler looked toward Yohl Ik'nal and asked: "What make you of these happenings, Yohl Ik'nal?"

"Much have I learned today," she replied. "And much I do not know about the workings of power among men and cities. What I see you plan today, in your wisdom and experience, appears good. That difficulties will continue I do not doubt, but the Triad Gods will guide you."

"And of the succession? You know what is to follow."

She hesitated, recalling her vision. It was the ruler's right to know.

"Much am I troubled by these recent events. I made vision quest by means of the Jeweled Tree to the Upperworld to seek understanding. It was shown to me that our lineage will continue intact, but not without difficulties." She spoke in a clear, strong voice that commanded the men's attention.

"One will come, a ruler who will bring Lakam Ha to great creative heights and leave a legacy the world will admire for untold times. We will face adversity but the B'aakal lineage will continue. Details were not revealed, but the vision showed that I will indeed be the bearer of royal blood to continue the Bahlam dynasty."

"An auspicious communication from the Upperworld," said Ahkal Mo' Nab. "It appears you are becoming skilled as a seer. May your vision hold true."

Yohl Ik'nal bowed her head as her father regarded her with pleasure. The powers of a seer would command respect and inspire awe. Both were necessary for successful leadership.

What she did not speak, however, was prohibited by her vow of secrecy. She did not reveal that after this apex of greatness a vast shadow would fall upon Lakam Ha, the Maya people and the entire world.

6

Mists steamed from stucco as the late afternoon sun warmed the plazas, damp from the midday rain. Wispy spirals wove among treetops and draped lofty roofcombs crowning temples high on the hills. In a large courtyard, smoke from cooking fires joined with mists and steaming stewpots to create a succulent haze. Laughter and murmuring voices made sun-glossed droplets quiver upon soft waves of sound. Random flute notes and drum thumps darted as musicians tuned.

The household of Kan Bahlam and Xoc Akal was preparing a feast in honor of their daughter's transformation to adulthood. Cooks stirred large clay pots simmering with stews of venison and wild turkey mixed with beans, squash, tomatoes and sweet potatoes and liberally seasoned with salt, peppers, coriander and oregano. Women bent over flattened grinding stones, rolling corn kernels with tubular stones into fine flour. This maize was mixed with water to form dough for flat cakes. Leafy green chaya leaves or mashed beans were added before cooking them on hot stones over open hearths. The maize dough was also made into drinks by adding milk and water, usually served hot. Another flavorful drink was made with toasted corn kernels that were ground finely with chile peppers and cacao.

Ceramic bowls with geometric patterns and fanciful figures were filled with fruit cut into wedges and served fresh, including guava, papaya, nance, sapodilla, mamey, pitahaya, ciricote, wild grapes, plums, and avocado. The tropical forests provided an abundance of fruit and the Maya cultivated their favorites in terraced gardens. Nuts from cashew trees and cocoyol palms were boiled for snacking, or dried and ground into flour that served as a substitute for maize.

Starchy yucca root and other vegetables were boiled and seasoned with annatto, an orange colored spice that gave piquant flavor and golden color to sauces. For added taste, chile, black pepper and tomato were mixed into these annatto sauces.

Fermented drinks were much enjoyed at special ceremonies. Most common was balche, made by fermenting bark of the *balche* tree in water and honey. This produced a strong-flavored and potent alcoholic beverage, used to excess in certain religious rites. From toasted maize they made *picul-aqahla* having lower alcohol concentration; it's very name means "a drink in abundance" and it was the mainstay of banquets. Other alcoholic drinks were made from fermented brews of broad beans and squash seeds.

In honor of this great occasion, a special dish was baked in an oven dug into the earth, called *pib*. Fire was started in the bottom of the pit, and when coals became red-hot, stone slabs were placed over them. A wild peccary was tonight's choice for the pib, prepared for roasting and wrapped in many layers of banana leaves, seasoned with maize gruel and spices. Over the wrapped packet they filled the earth oven with leaves, branches and stones. Pib or pibil was a favorite dish among the Maya, tender and succulent after the meat was roasted in the covered oven for several hours.

Xoc Akal passed among the cooks, attendants and musicians to ensure that all was proceeding well. She glanced west checking the sun's progress, smiling inwardly as the horizon assumed the green layer typical of early tropical evenings. Soon the westward glow would fade from green to indigo as Father Sun settled into the watery Underworld and the starry Lords of the Night took their places in the sky. Tonight the moon was at first quarter and would hang in mid-heavens, with Venus off her lower tip. This lovely configuration held symbolic importance, one of the reasons why this time was chosen for the transformation ritual of Yohl Ik'nal. The waxing moon signified the maiden's ripening into an adult woman. Venus was the wandering star of destiny, whose deity Lahun Chan could be fierce. When Venus rose as Morningstar or Eveningstar, it could bring malign influences unless properly propitiated. But when Venus was "captured" by the tip of the moon, it became a cooperative force for unfolding one's life purpose.

Tomorrow night Yohl Ik'nal would climb to the mouth of the Cave of the Xaman near the summit of K'uk Lakam Witz, the sacred mountain upon which Lakam Ha was situated. There she would do vigil as the Moon and Venus came into view, make offerings, pray and meditate upon her destiny and purpose. But tonight they would celebrate.

At dusk the torches were lighted around the courtyard, and guests began to gather. Ahauob of the highest classes, nobles, merchants and warriors came in festive dress to partake the largesse of the ruler's brother. Men wore hip and loincloths of white and black, embroidered in designs of red, yellow, blue and green. Loincloths hung below the knee, slightly longer in front with tassels or fringes at the bottoms. The men were adorned with necklaces and pectoral collars of jade, obsidian and colored stones in brown and blue tints. Many wore diadems of stones or metallic beads, or small headdresses of feathers and beads. Those of the noblest lineages had elongated skulls, a genetic trait sometimes copied by others using head compression boards during infancy. Wrist cuffs and heavy bracelets were common. Most men wore woven and embroidered sandals though some went barefoot. Men wore their hair long, pulled into a topknot and either twisted around the crown, or dangling down the back.

Women wore huipils, shift dresses secured above the breasts. Huipils varied in length, often hanging below the knees, though some were waist length with an underskirt. At times they had woven waistbands. These colorful garbs used all the Maya palate in dazzling embroidered designs. Women were adorned with jewelry equally heavy and large as the men's, and both sexes wore large ear sporls, weighted for balance. These heavy sporls elongated the earlobes. Most women braided and twisted their long hair into fanciful creations, weaving in feathers, beads and ceramic figures. Headdresses worn for social occasions were smaller than those for public rituals.

Numerous mats were spread around the courtyard, and guests gradually settled onto them sitting in small groups. The host family and higher nobles gravitated to the long veranda fronting the palace, opening onto the courtyard through a series of columns. As they settled onto mats the musicians struck up a lively tune, rhythmic drums and wooden clackers underlying cheerful wooden flute and ceramic whistle melodies. The music ended with a wooden trumpet fanfare as Kan Bahlam rose to his feet.

"Greetings of the evening, and welcome to our celebration." His deep baritone voice resonated off stone and plaster. "You have all witnessed the transformation ceremony of our daughter, Yohl Ik'nal, a ceremony that found favor in the eyes of the Triad Gods and the people alike. As the ceremony happened according to the calendar, now also happens the celebration. All is in order, as given and ordained by the Gods. This night we will feast, we will drink, we will dance to show gratitude, to give recognition of the abundance and protection that is drawn to us by our Holy B'aakal Lord, Ahkal Mo' Nab, K'uhul Ahau of Lakam Ha."

The musicians played another fanfare, more elaborate and drawn out, as torches appeared through the main palace doorway. A contingent of priests emerged and in their midst walked Ahkal Mo' Nab followed by his wife. Waves of throaty cheers greeted his entrance. In the wavering torchlight, the slender ruler seemed larger and more vigorous than Kan Bahlam knew was the case. They had discussed whether the ruler should attend the ceremony, since he was weakened by nightly bouts of fever. But, not attending would communicate a message neither man wanted. They agreed the ruler's presence would be brief, but was necessary.

Ahkal Mo' Nab made the rounds, walking among seated guests who by protocol remained still as the ruler spoke to some, touched hands with others, smiled at all. His wife graciously gestured and chatted with women. Music played softly during this social ritual, and when the royal pair took their places on the mat with Kan Bahlam's family, the serving of the meal began.

Attendants moved quickly through the crowd, bearing large gourds full of steaming stews, reed platters heaped with maize cakes and ceramic bowls full of cut fruit. Diners sipped stew from the gourds or used chunks of maize cakes to scoop mouthfuls. Fruit was eaten with fingers, seeds carefully discarded into smaller bowls. Decorated ceramic cups of picul-aqahla were distributed to both men and women. Balche would be served later to those, primarily men, who wanted stronger spirits.

Murmurs of anticipation announced the first servings of roasted peccary from the pib, which were ceremoniously carried through the crowd to the royal families. Moist and aromatic with herbs, tender chunks were served in gourd bowls, scooped onto maize cakes or eaten with fingers. Much finger-licking and smacking in appreciation followed initial tastes of this treat. As soon as bowls or cups were empty, alert servers replaced them with brimming new ones. The meal was exceptional, and the guests immersed themselves in complete enjoyment. Laughter and muted conversation filled the courtyard with merriment.

Yohl Ik'nal shared a mat adjacent to her parents with her three closest girlfriends. Two had preceded her with their transformation to adulthood ceremonies, although none as elaborate as hers. They laughed together and talked of shared experiences, much as they always had, although Yohl Ik'nal perceived that the girls accorded her a subtle deference, and sent appraising glances under lowered lids. She felt the difference and a small current of sadness drifted across her heart. She teetered on the cusp of whom and what she would become, but a demarcation was ritually anchored when she was acknowledged as lineage bearer. Her fate diverged from that of her friends.

The girls had eaten lightly and were badgering Na'kin about her romantic interests. The oldest of the group, Na'kin was being courted by a popular young man and her family looked upon him with favor.

"Were these said, his vows of devotion?" asked the youngest girl Tulix, now about one tun from her own ceremony.

"What of it, were it so?" countered Na'kin coyly.

"So it was? Have you not just said so?"

"Said I so? Where are your ears? They must be filled with moon water."

"Not so much moon water as yours with moon-ing sighs," Tulix archly retorted.

All the girls laughed as Na'kin blushed. She feigned reluctance as she allowed the others to draw a few little intimacies out. Clearly she was receptive to the attentions of her young admirer.

During a lull in conversation, Sak Nicte who was closest to Yohl Ik'nal studied her friend with a mock-serious scowl.

"Then comes this thought, I do think it, that we ask such questions of Yohl Ik'nal," she pronounced weightily.

Startled expressions greeted her comment, not the least from the subject herself.

"Of what speak you?" blurted Tulix first. All eyes bore upon Yohl Ik'nal, who shook her head in confusion and furrowed her brows.

"I know not of what you speak," she said firmly.

"Perhaps she should know!" "Now you must tell!" the other two exclaimed.

With a sly smile, Sak Nicte related: "A certain young man has been asking many questions about the daughter of Kan Bahlam, since her transformation ceremony. This certain man has spoken in glowing words of her beauty, her majesty, her noble spirit. He was seen watching her from across the plaza with eyes full of admiration. His friends are making jokes of how smitten he is. Of such things, I have heard much."

"Who is it? Who—who? You must tell!"

Yohl Ik'nal looked quizzical. She certainly had not noticed any young man taking an interest in her. But then, she was immersed in her ceremony and the political considerations she now had.

"Do you want to know?" Sak Nicte asked Yohl Ik'nal.

"It appears I must," she answered ruefully.

After a suspense-building pause, Sak Nicte replied: "Here come the words, then. The name of the one who seeks information about Yohl Ik'nal, who speaks in such admiration of her, who sighs to see her pass. Now it comes, now it passes my lips."

All the girls' stared mesmerized at Sak Nicte's lips, which moved silently then pouted and parted in a huge grin.

"Speak! We do not hear you! What did you say?"

Laughing, Sak Nicte shook her head and pointed to her lips. Again the girls focused breathlessly. In a forced whisper, just enough to be heard above the crowd, she said: "The name . . . his name . . . Hun Pakal."

Tulix gasped, Na'kin sighed, and Yohl Ik'nal looked even more quizzical.

"Hun Pakal! What a handsome man!" from Tulix.

"Hun Pakal! He is good friends with my sweetheart," said Na'kin.

"Hun Pakal, son of the scribe who is my father's distant cousin?" asked Yohl Ik'nal.

"The very one." Sak Nicte crossed her arms triumphantly.

In the ensuing silence, each girl examined Yohl Ik'nal's face and found nothing there with any emotional charge.

"She is innocent of this information," observed Na'kin as Tulix nodded confirmation.

But Sak Nicte would not be discouraged. Leaning forward, she drew the girls' heads together and whispered: "He is here tonight. Watch, observe, you will see."

Music began as the meal remnants were cleared away and the mats moved to the edges of the courtyard. The time had come for dancing, which the Maya greatly enjoyed. Two lines were forming, men on one side and women the other, facing in pairs. Drums, rattles and wood clackers beat a stately rhythm as flutes and whistles warbled intertwining melodies. Bodies straight, the dancers used a toe-heel step while moving arms in small arcs, palms outward and almost touching the partner's. In perfect unison the pairs stepped in place and made matching arcs with closely aligned palms, creating circles in the air between them. After several minutes, each dancer spun around and moved one partner to the right. New dancers joined those without partners, or the end man danced down the line to join the woman at the other end. Soon the courtyard was full as feathers bobbled, jewelry clanked, loincloths flared and torchlight glinted off stone and metal.

The four girls soon joined the dancing, Na'kin pairing with her sweetheart and the others waiting for an open man in the line. Yohl Ik'nal danced gracefully, glad for distraction from their conversation, while a bit apprehensive that her unknown admirer might suddenly appear—if she could remember what he looked like.

She did remember. With a jolt, she realized the young man across from her was Hun Pakal. Yes, she did recall those features, though matured from the boy she occasionally saw at gatherings. She had to admit that Tulix was right, he was handsome. Half a head taller than she, his body was muscular and lithe, moving with contained power in the stately dance rhythm. He had the noble's elongated skull, prominent nose and large sensuous lips with dark almond eyes looking intensely into hers. Did she see something special in those eyes?

They spun around and moved to the next partner. Hun Pakal glanced over his shoulder and she felt a quick shiver as their eyes met in an unspoken promise. She was surprised that her heart was beating more rapidly than the exercise demanded.

More vigorous dances for men followed, allowing a display of stomping footwork, spinning and leaping. Then women demonstrated their grace and knowledge with delicate and intricate steps accompanied by symbolic hand signs telling stories or conveying feelings. After a long women's dance sequence in which Yohl Ik'nal drew an admiring chorus at her virtuosity, she sought refreshing water at the adjoining cistern plaza. A wall separated the cistern plaza from the courtyard, and through the open doorway torchlight created a flickering rectangle.

She sat on the low rim of the cistern, dipping a gourd tied to a long pole into the clear water. Underground streams cut veins through the limestone ridge supporting Lakam Ha, and many openings were made to access these for household use. She sipped the wet coolness and splashed a little on face and neck. Relaxing in the semi-darkness, she did not notice the figure enter the plaza.

Suddenly she straightened, alert to another presence. Turning to look, at first she did not recognize the man standing near. His face was in shadow as torchlight framed his body. But already she knew the contours of that body.

"Hun Pakal?" she said tentatively.

"Ix Yohl Ik'nal," he replied softly.

They watched each other in silence for long moments. She motioned to the rim beside her, and as he sat she offered water from the gourd. He drank thirstily, and nodded thanks. The space between them was charged with energy.

"Much do I enjoy, and much appreciate this excellent gathering to honor your transformation to adulthood," he said a little stiffly.

"My heart is glad that you find pleasure here," she replied.

"More pleasure than you can imagine," he blurted, hand touching his lips as if to recall the words.

"My father is a generous man, and my mother an excellent hostess." She spoke quickly to cover the embarrassment. "Was this not a truly fine feast?"

"Most truly fine," he assented, regaining some poise.

"And most entertaining dancing," she continued. "You danced well."

"And you also."

She glanced away, uncertain where to go with the conversation.

"All is well with your family?" she asked. "I am regretful that I have not visited with them for some time."

"All is well with my parents. You recall my sister died several tuns ago? We are recovered and know her spirit dwells in the stars with the ancestors."

"Yes, I recall. Her death was in childbirth? I am certain her spirit is a shining star now. Brave deaths of laboring women and honorable warriors receive the blessing of Ix Chel, our Mother Earth Goddess, Lady Rainbow. By the goddess' promise, their spirits avoid Xibalba and go to the stars."

"Salutations to Ix Chel." Both made the salutation hand sign.

"You have no other brothers or sisters; am I correct?" Yohl Ik'nal strained to remember what she could of his family.

"That is correct. Now we both are only children."

They laughed, more to ease the tension than for any real reason.

"Often have I wished for a brother or sister," she said wistfully, remembering her infant brother's death.

"Have you been lonely?"

She glanced quickly into his eyes, dark and deep with kindness. She nodded, wondering that he would so quickly realize this.

"It must be so," he said thoughtfully. "Due to your family position, and especially now that you are recognized as lineage bearer. But you have women friends, tonight I watched as you laughed together . . . Ummm, and I have seen you with them."

Now she laughed in earnest.

"You were watching us?"

"Many eyes were directed toward the veranda where the ruler sat with your family, and you were just beside them." He sounded a bit defensive, but quickly changed his tone. "Yes, Yohl Ik'nal, I was watching *you* and I have been watching you. I am thinking much about you."

"Oh." She lowered her eyes and felt a flush on her cheeks.

"This I ask, that I may continue to watch and think about you."

His voice had a vibrant timbre she had never heard before. It set off resonances deep within her being, sending another shiver through her chest. He moved a little closer on the cistern rim, not touching her, but she felt heat radiating from his body, burning her skin.

"Oh." She could only murmur again, aghast at her loss of words.

Silence hung heavy between them. She kept her gaze averted, eyes downward. Why was she so confused and befuddled? This was entirely unlike her usual way of being. Her downcast eyes watched his hand, brown and strong, that rested on his thigh. Another flight of shivers was set off as she noticed the rippling muscles of that thigh. As if in slow motion, his hand began moving and she watched in utter fascination, mesmerized as the hand slowly lifted toward her face. Gently, like the brush of a swallow's wing, his hand cupped her chin and he lifted her face until their eyes met. Long and hungrily he gazed at her, sending the full impact of the bright flame in his eyes.

"This I ask," he whispered, "that I may continue."

From somewhere deep inside, from an unknown and untapped source of exquisite sensations came the reply. Not her mind, but her heart spoke in a language both new and unfathomably ancient.

"Yes, you may continue, Hun Pakal," she whispered.

The god-bundles were almost ready. Two round pieces of white cotton fabric lay open on the stone altar, ready to receive the offerings. Yohl Ik'nal had deeply contemplated these offerings, meditating upon the Moon and Venus, seeking to intuit what their deities would most desire. Already the bundle for Venus held a piece of choice peccary roast from the feast, wrapped in banana leaf and tied with red and yellow embroidery. A fine obsidian blade, jade jewelry and shiny metallic beads surrounded the peccary. For the Moon, there were maize cakes in which dried berries and fruit were mixed, made by her own hand while chanting Ix Chel's many names. A fine mica mirror was added to reflect the Full Moon's brilliance, accompanied by blue stone beads and a thorny oyster shell from the distant sea, precious for its red hues that invoked both sunrise and renewed life.

She sat back on her heels contemplating the bundles. Something else was needed, very special and personal, something of herself. Rising quickly, she found her most elaborate headdress, worn for her transformation rite. With a tiny knife she cut off a splendid quetzal feather, long and intensely blue with a shimmering iridescent oval at the tip. Lahun Chan, the demanding and often ruthless deity of Venus would certainly be pleased with this offering. Carefully bending the feather in a circle around the other offerings, she tied the Venus god-bundle securely with colorful braided threads.

What else for the Moon? Tonight *X'yum Uc* was in her waxing crescent, the maiden phase but soon moving toward fullness. How could she attune to these energies through gifts of her own being? Her quest tonight was to explore her destiny, to anticipate what might be required in fulfilling new responsibilities of lineage bearer. One who bears the lineage . . . certainly that meant having children of royal blood who might become leaders, even rulers, of Lakam Ha. Blood and childbearing, all concerns of Ix Chel, goddess of fertility, pregnancy, childbirth, healing, abundance, weaving and watery things. Ix Chel, Moon goddess, Earth Mother goddess, Lady Rainbow, special to women in all phases of life.

In a flash of memory, it came to her. What was more significant to Earth Mother and the Moon in her maiden phase than the first menstrual blood of young women? In her puberty transformation ceremony, she ritually saved her first menstrual blood. Small pieces of bark paper were used to catch drops of this blood, considered highly potent for magical and ritual purposes. She located the ceramic bowl into which she had placed the blood-spotted papers, hidden behind mats in a corner, not thought of in years. Taking out six pieces, one for each year since menarche, she reverently placed them in the Moon's god-bundle. Tying it with more braided threads, she hummed a song to Ix Chel and knew it was complete.

As dusk fell, the High Priestess Lahun Uc came to conduct Yohl Ik'nal to the Cave of the Shaman. Two male attendants carried torches, long-handled flint axes for path clearing, and large knives in their belts for protection against night predators.

"It is time, are you prepared?" asked Lahun Uc.

"All is prepared, Holy Priestess," Yohl Ik'nal answered, clasping left shoulder in a bow of respect.

"Now we go."

The High Priestess gave hand signs; one attendant picked up Yohl Ik'nal's bag containing things she would need during her vigil, and the other led the procession toward the towering mountain behind the palace. The High Priestess clanked metal discs and chanted, as Yohl Ik'nal grasped her god-bundles and held them close against her breasts. The path was wide and smooth for some distance from the palace, but soon curved upward ascending the steep hillside, becoming narrow and rocky. Trees and brush obscured vision most of the way, but from time to time an opening in the foliage gave views of the city below. Dozens of buildings dotted the level plateau, their roofcombs catching sunset's final glow. Lower structures settled into gloom. Flickering lights from cooking fires in numerous courtyards twinkled like fallen stars far below. Vast plains faded into muted blue-green haze where the plateau fell off beyond the farthest buildings.

Now the climb was steeper, commanding concentration in the semi-darkness. The four climbers were breathing hard, but pushed on steadily. Rocks clinked as they turned underfoot, and the air moistened as mists crept around the heights. Higher and higher they climbed, the trail taking them to the far side of the mountain where ridge after ridge undulated into the distance, covered with jungle foliage. The High Priestess stopped chanting to catch her breath for climbing. The lead attendant paused occasionally to whack away lianas and brush obstructing the path.

As night deepened, sounds of the jungle emerged. Insects chirped, whirred and clicked rhythmically, frogs croaked and night birds gave eerie calls. In the distance, the prolonged roars of howler monkeys echoed back and forth. Throaty snorts and cracking brush announced the rapid departure of peccaries and deer as the human intruders interrupted their forage. Although the attendants kept ears attuned for the soft, short grunts of jaguars, they heard none.

The trail broke through the jungle into a clearing that the torchlight quickly illuminated, revealing the mouth of a cave. Two huge boulders were placed on either side, carved with many hieroglyphics. A round stone altar sat between the boulders and the cave entrance, a gaping crevasse high enough to admit a standing man. The attendants took positions in front of the boulders, the High Priestess and her charge stood in front of the altar.

The priestess intoned greetings: "Guardians of this cave, ancient ones who serve the Witz God, we salute you and we greet you. It is I, Lahun Uc, High Priestess of Lakam Ha who call to you. Here with me is a young woman, Yohl Ik'nal of the ruling lineage, who has come to do vigil and seek guidance from the spirit world. You who are keepers of the Cave of the Shaman, we ask that you appear and give permission for this vigil."

After a lengthy silence, they heard footsteps from inside the cave. An old shaman slowly emerged, bent form draped in a dark cloak. He fixed deep-sunken eyes on the two women, speaking in a quavering voice: "It is known that the young one comes. Permission is given that she abides for her vigil at the cave entrance. Not to enter the cave, that is not permitted. Alone she must be. You may light fire in the clearing. Return for her at dawn."

Nodding repeatedly, head bobbing as if beyond his control, the old shaman turned and shuffled back into the dark mouth of the cave, disappearing from sight. The attendants gathered branches and soon a modest fire blazed in the well-used fire-pit. They stacked additional branches nearby. Fire was the best method to keep predators away and all Maya learned this early.

"We leave you now," said Lahun Uc. She touched fingertips with Yohl Ik'nal and gazed intently into the young woman's eyes. "You are ready. Whatever else is needed, you must discover for yourself."

"You have mentored my heart and spirit well. Receive now my gratitude once again."

The women exchanged faint smiles, and then Lahun Uc turned and with the attendants disappeared down the jungle path.

Yohl Ik'nal removed a thick mat from the bag, placing it between the altar and cave entrance. There was a blanket to ward off the night chill, a gourd of water, sprigs of aromatic herbs, a ceramic whistle, an embroidered altar cloth and her incense burner with a supply of copal. Laying the god-bundles on the mat, she chanted the purification song while brushing the altar with the herbs. Blowing the whistle, she circled the altar nine times to seal ritual space from invasion by the Bolon Tiku, the fearful Nine Lords of the Night. She arranged the cloth in the altar's center, whispering prayers and making hand signs for blessing and empowerment.

Taking the incense burner, she approached the fire and glanced around the edges of the clearing to make certain that no creatures hovered there, neither night animals nor meddling spirits. Nothing alerted her perceptions, physical or intuitive. She used two sticks to move glowing coals into the censer bowl, returned it to the altar and dropped pieces of copal onto the coals. At once pungent smoke arose, carrying the acrid and sweet odors of copal tree resin to her nose. She sniffed appreciatively, enjoying the tickling sensation and evocative smells.

Kneeling on the mat with arms outstretched, she began the chant sequence that brought her consciousness into ritual space.

"*Dzu bulul h'yum k'in, dzu tip'il x'yum uc*
Already the Master Sun has set, and the Mistress Moon has risen
Pepenobe cu lembaloob ichil u lol caan
The butterflies shine amid the heavenly flowers
C'suku'unob ka' c'kiikob a'ek'ob
Our brothers and sisters the stars
A'k'abe, Hun Ahb K'u, a' k'ab cuk'alala
The night, Hun Ahb K'u, is your hand that closes
Tichile cu yuchil tu lacal
And within it everything happens
Hebix u topol nek'e, hebix u hok'ol yalche y tip'il lol
As the seed buds, as the flower emerges and blossoms
Beyo hebix u zihil le uinick
In this way is born the human being
Bel u yuchul tu lacal tu k'ab Hun Ahb K'u
Thus it is that everything happens by the hands of Hun Ahb K'u

Ti tech in dzama in uinclil yetel in vol.
To you I surrender my body and my spirit."

Yohl Ik'nal meditated, allowing the waves of thought to drift away. She sensed her consciousness expanding in larger and larger spheres, beyond the clearing, above the mountains, into the dark night and twinkling stars. She waited until her inner vision could perceive the crescent moon rising above the tree-lined horizon, dangling Venus from the lower tip.

Opening her eyes, she looked over her left shoulder and there was the moon, hovering just above the trees and startlingly large. Shifting to view the moon squarely, she sat cross-legged and watched the crescent slowly climb. Venus shone brightly at the lower tip, assuming a blue tone intermittently.

"X'yum Uc, Mistress Moon," she whispered, "I greet and salute you. Yum Venus, Master Lahun Chan, receive my homage. Tonight this one, daughter of Ahau Kan Bahlam and lineage bearer of the Holy B'aakal Lords, sits to do vigil with you upon the Sacred Mountain, K'uk Lakam Witz. Here I offer what I have brought, god-bundles with gifts for you each. Accept these offerings of precious things, things of my heart and hands and body. Now they are yours, now I am placing them upon the altar, may they find your favor."

She rose and took the two god-bundles to the altar, placing one on either side of the incense burner. She added more copal and fanned the smoke over the bundles with graceful hand signs for purifying and giving. Standing, she lifted her hands toward the Moon and Venus, palms open and facing the heavenly bodies. She drew down their energies through her palms, and then crossed both arms over her chest in a deep bow of respect and honor. Sitting cross-legged she meditated again and focused on the Moon and Venus until she sensed that they had accepted her offerings.

"Tonight in this vigil, this one has a request of each of you," she said. "This one would know something of her destiny, what she is called to do in this life in the Middle World. You, Beings of the Upperworld, can see so much more from your view high above. You have power to set the paths of those creatures that walk the Earth. When we call upon you, you can send your influence between dimensions. We are, in truth, all connected through the Yax Che, the Sacred Ceiba-Jeweled Tree that reaches through all dimensions. This I have learned; this I do believe. X'yum Uc, Mistress Moon, Yum Lahun Chan, Master Venus, hear my request and respond."

For a while Yohl Ik'nal sat with eyes closed, aware and open, receptive. She waited patiently, keeping the mind still and thoughtless. Night sounds of jungle insects and crackling fire barely penetrated her consciousness. Time was void, meaningless in this expanded state.

Images began to build in her inner vision. Sounds of strife, conflict, chaotic movements within Lakam Ha. Women wailing, children crying, men screaming as torches filled the plazas that were splattered with blood. Warriors from elsewhere were chipping and defacing glyphs as Lakam Ha's men fought back. Gradually these images faded and she saw herself in council, but she was leading the discussions in the Popol Nah. Her face was older, jaw set strongly and hair showing gray strands. She sensed that Lakam Ha was restored but still troubled. This, she knew, came from Venus.

In her expanded state, she received this information dispassionately. Any surge of emotion would break the connection with the Upperworld beings. Calmly she waited, shifting focus to the Moon. New images formed, those of family life. She saw herself with two children, a boy and girl. The boy, older than his sister, had a weaker aura that seemed fragmented. The girl's aura shone brightly, golden and strong, her presence commanding. The deity K'awill, patron of the B'aakal lineage, hovered near the girl. Then she saw Lakam Ha, dramatically changed. The city was much larger, with pyramids and palaces of breath-taking grandeur, radiating grace and harmony. Numerous people went about daily activities in peace and prosperity. Visitors with strange countenances wearing exotic clothes mingled with the townspeople. The Great One to come who sprang from her lineage blood appeared next to her daughter, now a much older woman. All was well, all was magnificent, the Gods smiled upon Lakam Ha. Then the images, sent by the Moon, began to fade.

As the vision was ending, a tiny part of her consciousness formed the question that was all-important to her, and projected it toward K'awill.

But wait, tell me, who is the father of my children?

Clouds swirled across her inner vision. She focused intently, trying to hold back any hopes about who this might be. Her consciousness settled toward acceptance and openness. A face was forming in the clouds, unclear at first but resolving into newly familiar features. The eyes, the lips and shape of the body she seemed to recognize. Hun Pakal. Surely it was him. Or was it? The ephemeral features blurred and distorted. Her eyes scrunched and forehead wrinkled to make the image sharper. It was Hun Pakal . . . it must be him.

Gratitude flowed from her heart with intensity that surprised her.

She became aware of breath and body. Consciousness was shifting, drawing inward from its vast expansion, condensing into the physical. Discomfort in her back and knees made her realize the vision had ended. She stretched out her legs and moved her shoulders, changing position. Opening her eyes and glancing around, she noted that the sky was still completely dark and full of stars. The Moon and Venus hovered on the opposite horizon; many hours had passed. Only a few coals remained in the fire, giving little light to the opening in front of the cave.

Before moving, she thanked the Moon and Venus for their visions and bid them farewell. Standing stiffly, she went to gather additional branches for the fire. As she squatted to pick up branches, a rustling movement nearby made her freeze. Breath bated, she listened and looked into the darkness beyond the woodpile. At first she saw nothing, but her vision adjusted enough to detect light reflected off a pair of eyes no more than two arms-lengths away. Large, tawny eyes at a height denoting a sizeable animal. A faint grunt was all she needed to know she was facing a jaguar.

Hair rose on her neck and arms as her heart pounded. She remained crouched, not moving, staring into the jaguar's eyes. Forcing herself to breathe slowly and deeply, she countered feelings of fear with respect for the powerful animal, a symbol of mastery.

"Greetings, Noble One," she murmured soothingly. "Welcome to this night of vigil. Have you done vigil also? Have you watched me for long? Come in peace, come in love, come in friendship. You are the uay of rulers, keeper of the greatest power, and it is fitting that you are here this night. For this night I have learned about my destiny; that rulership will pass through me and into my children and their children. I bid you bring strength and courage and determination to me as my path unfolds."

The jaguar remained still, unblinking. Yohl Ik'nal waited until she felt completely calm and at peace. Then she took several branches, moving slowly, and backed toward the firepit. The jaguar's eyes followed her every movement, but it remained in place. Soon the branches burst into flames, casting light to the periphery and she saw a fine, large female jaguar with two sleeping cubs. Settling onto the mat, she kept eye contact until the jaguar blinked and looked away. A short time later, the jaguar yawned and firelight glinted off her fangs. She nuzzled her cubs, waking them and leading them back into the jungle.

YOHL IK'NAL — III

BAKTUN 9 KATUN 6 TUN 18 — BAKTUN 9 KATUN 7 TUN 0 (572 CE—573 CE)

1

THE CITY OF Lakam Ha was buzzing with activity. Households packed bags of clothing and bedding, cooking implements, food supplies, and decorative gear. When a large bag was full, both men and women used tumplines across their brows to carry burdens that rested on their backs. The Maya had no pack animals; deer and tapir could not be domesticated for such purposes. Musicians and dancers arranged their instruments in similar bags, merchants their goods, and warriors their weapons and cloth armor. Older children walked and toddlers were carried on women's hips in a cloth sling. Nearly the entire populace was preparing for a journey, one that would keep them many days away from their homes. They were going to the *lol pisba'h*, the flower war.

The household of Kan Bahlam made preparations more elaborate than most. The ahauob would make the journey in a *ch'akte*, a palanquin with wood platforms on horizontal poles carried on the shoulders of four strong men. Palanquins were adorned according to rank and wealth; the finer had vertical poles supporting cloth sides and roof decorated with embroidered designs, fringes, ribbons, bells or chimes. The palanquin of Kan Bahlam was the largest and finest of all, and bore a standard in front with the glyph of the B'aakal polity—for now he was ruler of Lakam Ha.

Two years previously, his brother the former ruler Ahkal Mo' Nab died. The ruler's deteriorating health caused postponement of the flower war they had planned. Then an elaborate burial and a year of mourning were required before Kan Bahlam could formally accede on 9.6.18.5.12 (December 3, 572 CE). These events commanded his attention and absorbed the people of Lakam Ha, and put on hold the personal lives of the new ruler's family.

Now, as the K'altun approached, it was a fortuitous time to schedule the flower war. The K'altun or stone binding ceremony was performed at the end of the katun that consisted of 20 tuns (19.71 solar years). According to Maya calendars, these 20-tun periods each had certain qualities that could bode ill or well, and that repeated cyclically. When the ruler conducted a suitable ceremony for the K'altun, and offered the proper god-bundles, favorable qualities could be augmented and unfavorable ones mitigated. More than seven moon cycles would elapse before the katun end in the winter season. Now it was spring, the season of flowers.

Kan Bahlam considered the timing of the flower war carefully. By his thinking, having this long-anticipated event preceding the K'altun ceremony would amplify the energies, especially as he fully expected Lakam Ha's warriors to be victorious. During the previous tun, he sent messengers to Yokib, Popo' and Usihwitz announcing that the Holy B'aakal Lord was calling the lol pisba'h—flower war. Using stately Maya protocols, the messengers "invited" these cities to participate, but actually it was a royal summons that was rarely, if ever, ignored. As expected, these cities were now sending their warriors and most of their people to the plains below Lakam Ha.

Stretching between the mountain plateau of Lakam Ha and the K'umaxha River were broad plains with little brush. It made a perfect site for large encampments, had nearby water from tributaries, and provided grassy space for the competitions. Already streams of people were converging upon the plains, selecting areas for temporary shelters and setting up places for cooking. When all had arrived, there would be more than 5,000 people at the flower war.

In the third palanquin serving Kan Bahlam's family, Yohl Ik'nal braced herself for the bouncing rhythm of the bearers' footsteps. She drew back side flaps to better see the surroundings during this daylong journey. Leaving the palace and passing through the city, the procession began a steep descent following the course cut downhill by the Bisik River running northward. City workers had long ago created a wide path alongside the river. The path surface was even and covered with finely crushed *sahcab*, white calcareous sand found beneath limestone caps.

Sahcab was used to bind building stones, and for the sakbe, the "white way" forming raised roads through the jungle. On the path it bonded into a firm layer making walking easier. Each year after the heavy rains, more sahcab was applied and flattened with rolling logs. The path had many switchbacks to compensate for the steep hillside, and descent was slow. Lovely cascades, pools and waterfalls draped by lush foliage and lianas graced the view and soothed the ear.

When glimpses of the plains appeared between trees, Yohl Ik'nal could see wisps of smoke from hearth fires far in the distance, and a stream of travelers from her city wending their way over gentle rises. Lulled by the steady motion of the palanquin, she drifted into daydreaming. Images of her father's splendid accession ceremonies were followed by memories of the previous ruler's difficult final days. She remembered his urgent need to caution Kan Bahlam about containing dissident forces within Lakam Ha, and consolidating support for succession passing through his brother's family. Which meant her, she thought with a tinge of apprehension. She knew her father was building this support among priests and nobles. He was also training her in k'uhul ahau skills needed by the ruling lord of a polity.

Drowsing in the warm sun and soothed by steady movements when the bearers reached the level plains, these weighty concerns slipped away. Her reverie moved to more intimate considerations, as the image of the anticipated father of her children appeared. She had seen little of Hun Pakal in the past few years, primarily in ceremonial circumstances. Though it saddened her, this situation was completely normal within the requirements of her royal status, and she accepted it without question. Her personal desires must be subjugated to her duty to the ruling succession, the needs of the people, and ultimately the Triad Gods.

But now a fresh opportunity presented itself in the flower war. The ahauob of Lakam Ha would be living in close proximity making interactions easier, more casual. Instead of palace walls, she would dwell in a tent-like structure with four poles supporting a canopy and hanging fabric walls with a door flap. Her mother and female attendants would share the tent, which was richly adorned with woven designs and feather fringes. Her father stayed in a separate tent, even more elaborate and containing an adjoining "throne room" with open sides, where he would receive homage from visiting nobles.

Soft rain began falling just after Kan Bahlam's tents were set up, as rulers and leaders from the assembled cities gathered in his portable throne room. Rituals of greeting and honoring were followed by review of flower war rules and establishment of the sequence of contests. Priests from each city would officiate at the contests to assure impartial judging of winners and application of penalties. It was understood that competitors would be matched by status, and that losers were bound to work for the winner's city during the months it took their hair, topknot cut at the moment of victory, to re-grow. In some cases, tribute would be accepted in place of work time, if the man served his city in a crucial capacity and could not be spared. For group competitions not involving one-on-one contests, awards would be given to those who excelled. The priests jointly would make such decisions.

The night rain was sparse, dawn heralded by golden shafts of sunlight breaking through rapidly clearing clouds. The day promised to be warm and bright, the grass fresh and damp until trampled down underfoot. Yohl Ik'nal woke early, intent upon being present from the start. She ate lightly of their morning meal of maize porridge, papayas and melons. Sounds of people moving, laughing and talking filtered into her tent and she impatiently urged her mother to dress.

When the royal women were properly attired, hair prepared and simple headdresses attached, they walked through the tent city to the place of honor prepared for the K'uhul Ahau's family, giving a central view of the field. The women settled to seated positions on reed mats covered by soft woven fabrics. As the mats were large, Yohl Ik'nal signaled her friend Sak Nicte to join her.

"Now comes something special," exuded Yohl Ik'nal after her friend's formalized greeting to the ruling family. "Much have I anticipated this flower war, the first in my lifetime. See how many contestants are gathering!"

"Indeed it is so," Sak Nicte replied. "This day will hold group competitions, yes?"

"So it is planned. Competitions for running, spear throwing, blowing darts, and swinging clubs. The next two days will offer one-on-one contests."

"So many handsome young men!" Sak Nicte spread her hands toward the milling group. She smiled mischievously. "It may happen that among so many are two for us."

Yohl Ik'nal laughed as she scanned the group, seeking a familiar shape.

"Should that be so," she retorted, "we shall shortly be confined to home with babies at breast, as are our friends Na'kin and Tulix, and miss such exciting events."

Xoc Akal turned toward her daughter, unable to resist the young women's conversation.

"It is best not to set your heart on a particular man, for the arc of necessity and the wind of fate may not hover there. The greatest satisfaction comes from embracing the destiny given by the Triad Gods of B'aakal. Such has been my life and I am content."

Xoc Akal knew her husband was planning a match for their daughter. Recently this topic was the focus of a discussion in which several advisors joined the royal pair. The man chosen must serve critical purposes; he must bring a loyal following by kinship and fellowship that would support succession through Yohl Ik'nal, he must be a respected warrior-leader, and he must be of appropriate blood-lines. Part of the flower war's purpose was to watch the competitors, to see which young men stood out in prowess and charisma. While preference was for men of B'aakal well-linked to the founding lineage, it was not out of the question that a younger son of another city's ruling lineage might be the most opportune match.

Watching her daughter's face carefully, Xoc Akal searched for a fleeting expression that might hint of feelings. But the young woman maintained a placid countenance, even as their eyes met. *She has been well trained*, thought the mother. For she suspected, actually intuited for there was no evidence, that her daughter had a suitor.

"Well spoken, my mother. As always, your words are the expression of pure wisdom. Long shall they be my model and guide."

Yohl Ik'nal turned her gaze toward the field and continued light chatter with Sak Nicte as the crowd gathered around the sides of the open area. Though she had revealed nothing, her heart was pounding and her thoughts swirling. Had her vision been inaccurate? Surely she had followed the rituals precisely and purified her body and mind to receive the vision clearly. But now doubt crept in. Perhaps the yearning of her heart had shaped the appearance of a destiny that she desired, instead of the one ordained by the Gods.

The sound of conches interrupted her musings. These large seashells blared like mournful horns, honoring the Lords of the Four Directions as priests waved smoking copal and chanted incantations. Her father Kan Bahlam led the procession of rulers, highest-ranking nobles and priests from all the gathered cities. Solemnly they marched around the field then stood at attention. From the center he spoke the welcoming and officially opened the flower war.

First came the races. Men who served as messengers, whose work was running long distances between cities, excelled in the foot races. There were races of speed, then of endurance as runners circled the field many times. Yohl Ik'nal appreciated their graceful limbs and agility and was pleased to see Lakam Ha's runners win several races. But she knew that Hun Pakal would not be racing, that was not his skill. Perhaps he would throw spears or use the dart pipe.

Targets were set up at one end of the field for dart blowing. Wooden birds covered with cloth to which feathers were sewn served as targets, placed on branches of tall trees cut for the contests and shorn of leaves. The dart pipe was a special skill cultivated by the Maya, used primarily for hunting. In the story of the Popol Vuh, one of the Hero Twins, Yax Bahlam (Xbalanque) crouched at the base of a ceiba tree and blew a dart to knock off the proud usurper Wuqub' Kaquix (Seven Macaw). This arrogant macaw had proclaimed himself the Center of Creation as the north star of the polar region, while in truth it was the underbelly of the Celestial Caiman—the Dark Rift of the Milky Way—that that led to this center. In unseating the false center, Yax Bahlam set the stage for creation of proper humans. The macaw lost his teeth from the dart and was sentenced to having a wrinkled featherless face.

Straining to see as she might, Yohl Ik'nal could not detect Hun Pakal's form among the contestants. Finally, she relaxed into enjoying the display of marksmanship. In the final rounds, effigies of the red macaw were set atop tree branches. Contestants crouched at the tree base in the stance of Yax Bahlam, depicted in many works of ceramic and codex art. Each time a dart hit home on the bird's head, the crowd cheered enthusiastically.

As the bright sun reached mid-sky, food and drink were brought around. Both observers and contestants moved about, mingling and attending to personal needs. Canopies were set up to shield the rulers and ahauob from the sun. Yohl Ik'nal and Sak Nicte strolled among tents of their city, followed dutifully by attendants. Walking around, the two greeted many from Lakam Ha and some strangers but not the object of Yohl Ik'nal's interest. By mischievous glances, Sak Nicte revealed her awareness that her friend's perusals were not as casual as they appeared.

When the contests re-convened it was for spear throwing. Yohl Ik'nal riveted her attention and soon was rewarded by the appearance of that body, so familiar yet so unknown, of Hun Pakal. Dressed only in a loincloth and neck collar, his strong muscles rippled as he dashed forward several steps, spear balanced in right hand. Ending in a leap, he heaved the spear in a long arc. The large flint point glistened in the sunlight with feathers fluttering from the shaft. She was close enough to hear the swooshing sound and solid "thunk" as the point embedded in the ground near the final marker. It was an excellent throw, farther than any spears yet hefted. Did she only imagine that he cast a glance in her direction as he retrieved the spear?

Quickly she lowered her eyes and turned to make conversation with Sak Nicte, hoping her mother had not detected any particular interest in this spear thrower. But her friend picked up subtle cues, raising an eyebrow as she remarked that this was the best throw so far.

There were several rounds with eliminations, and in the final throws again Hun Pakal exceeded all others. He was awarded the grand prize, with lesser prizes for all finalists, a good number from Lakam Ha. A group of young men gathered around Hun Pakal, cheering and lifting spears. They stomped in a spontaneous victory dance that brought them in front of Kan Bahlam's mat. The ruler stood and touched each on the shoulder, praising their abilities.

Suddenly Hun Pakal was standing before Yohl Ik'nal. He knelt and offered her a feather from his spear, smiling into her eyes. She reached to accept the feather, breathlessly silent as Sak Nicte congratulated him. Other men came to bow in honor of the royal women and he disappeared into their midst.

Yohl Ik'nal hardly noticed the final event, club swinging. Burly men excelled in handling the heavy bulk of wooden clubs, some embedded with flint spikes. Wooden effigies of warriors were planted like posts into the ground, and the clubbers attempted to decapitate them or knock them over. The observers called encouragement or hooted at failures, and again Lakam Ha's men prevailed.

After the contest, the royal women walked back to their tent. Yohl Ik'nal lingered behind, giving her mother time to be out of hearing range. Sak Nicte walked beside her, as their tents were close.

"Show me the feather again," she entreated.

Yohl Ik'nal took it from a fold in her skirt. It was an eagle feather, brown with a white tip, long and strong.

"He is a fine warrior, an asset to our city," she said, trying to hold a neutral tone.

"So he is, and well-loved by his companions. He will be a good match for someone well-placed," Sak Nicte remarked, sounding casual herself.

"Yes, that is so." Wistfulness crept into her voice, despite her intentions.

Sak Nicte grasped her friend's arm, turning to meet her eyes.

"It is there, that special fire burning in his eyes. I saw it when he gave you the feather."

Yohl Ik'nal looked deeply into the young woman's eyes, as if seeking a sign.

"It is not impossible, is it?"

"It is not impossible. He was impressive today."

Kan Bahlam, the High Priest Wak Batz, and three trusted ahauob sat drinking hot maize mixed with cacao and spiced with chile pepper. It was the favored drink of Maya nobles, sharpening the mind and stimulating the imagination. Flames from torches cast mutating forms across the nearest side of the throne room, while the far sides retreated into gloom of a starless night. Attendants stood at each side assuring that no listening ears were near. The leaders of Lakam Ha were strategizing.

"Zotz Choj, Sahal of Popo' is chagrined by today's victories," spoke Yax Kab, an elder with much experience in the intrigues among cities. *Sahal* was the title for rulers of subsidiary cities in a polity. "If we continue to prevail, there will be no force for rebellion in this city."

"Likewise with Usihwitz, whose contestants made a poor showing," added Mut Yokte. A powerful warrior with scars testifying to near escapes from jaguar claws and opponents' knives, he was cousin to Kan Bahlam and a loyal supporter. He served in capacity of *Nakom,* "war chief" or military leader for Lakam Ha.

"Yet there remain two days, the most important, those of one-on-one combat," High Priest Wak Batz reminded them.

"We of Lakam Ha are prepared," retorted Chakab, youngest of the group. He raised a heavily muscled arm making the hand sign for victory. "Today our men excelled and fanned the fire for further victories. Passions are running high to win."

"Of this I am confident," Kan Bahlam said. "When I have defeated the ruler of Yokib, this agitation for change will be smothered. The snaking arm of Kan will retreat into its lair. But let us speak of things within our own city. How fares the seditious plotting of Ek Chuuah and his cadre?"

The young man, dismissed as a puppy four years previously by the deceased ruler, made headway during transition times in Lakam Ha. Surreptitiously at first then more openly, he gathered a group of dissidents who fed upon dissatisfaction with Lakam Ha's leadership. They complained that not enough tribute was exacted from polity cities, that ceremonies were not splendid enough, that the building program was not as grand as a May Ku city deserved.

"Today Ek Chuuah did well in spear throwing, not far behind Hun Pakal," observed Mut Yokte. "His cadre also won several prizes with club swinging. They swell with pride."

"They murmur that the flower war is long overdue, while capitalizing on it to advance their position," added Yax Kab.

"Now comes the worst of their corruptions," observed Wak Batz. "They whisper that the ruler's daughter Yohl Ik'nal is unfit to keep the succession, an untried woman and not yet married. It is time, Holy Lord, that you select a husband for your daughter. She must be seen doing more public ceremonies, and making decisions in the Popol Nah. I know you have been training her, is she now ready to take more leadership?"

Kan Bahlam replied thoughtfully, for he was indeed considering these very things.

"To the last, she is ready. She will take significant part in the K'altun ceremony and our people will see that she carries the sacred blood well, and knows how to give proper rituals and offerings. We must set up a program for her to shine forth in the Council House. Of this we will speak further, and involve the High Priestess. To the first, her marriage, I am in accord. This flower war will reveal the right alliance for her, the man who will bring the greatest following and earn the highest respect of our people through his achievements."

"If this choice was based on today, Hun Pakal would rank high," offered Chakab, with a touch of regret since he found the ruler's daughter most attractive. But he was already married and thus not eligible.

"The prowess of this young man has not escaped my notice," Kan Bahlam assured his advisor. "What of his following? He seems well-liked by many."

"Indeed that is so. His family is large, and he gains affection readily among peers. He inspired a sizeable group of men to train rigorously for the flower war, and gave expert instruction in tactical skills of one-on-one combat both unarmed and with knives. Without doubt he will comport himself well in these contests. Several times he consulted with me to learn from my experience," Mut Yokte noted. "In this he is prudent, as he has little direct experience in combat, for he is young."

"Young but wise," Wak Batz observed dryly. Nice strategy to befriend one of the ruler's closest advisors, should one have designs on the heir. "As your distant relative, he has the sacred blood of the K'uhul Ahau lineage from both sides of his family. His blood-lines are suitable."

"We will see what emerges in the next two days. Should an ahau of another city prove most victorious, we might see a preferable alliance," remarked the ruler.

"Or should Ek Chuuah prevail, might an alliance with him not preempt his opposition?" suggested Yax Kab.

"It is said often that you are a great strategist, Yax Kab," said Kan Bahlam tersely. "But I am loath to invite the scorpion into my nest. He is not a man to trust, nor is he worthy of my daughter."

Silence fell upon the four men after the ruler's strong statement. The older men remembered the death of Kan Bahlam's son from a scorpion sting. The ruler's mouth had a grim set, revealing his own sad recollections.

They drained the last of the cacao mixture from tall ceramic cups having exquisite scenes of dancers and anthropomorphic beings performing rituals, painstaking in every detail.

Kan Bahlam shifted position and stood up, indicating that the session was ending. The other men bowed low, clasping right hand to left shoulder, and turned to leave. A subtle hand gesture toward Mut Yokte ordered him to remain. Once alone, the two sat again as the ruler spoke softly, so even the attendants could not hear.

"Mut Yokte, you once had friendship with the Nakom of Usihwitz. Have those ties persisted?"

"This I believe is so, although we have not met for many tuns. What we shared together, those dangers, are never forgotten."

"That I can well appreciate. Now comes a request that may be difficult. This I ask of you because we have long been close, and my trust is total. My purpose is to remove the sting of the scorpion, that perpetrator of sedition, from Lakam Ha. Speak to the Nakom of Usihwitz and request that he set his most ferocious and skilled warrior against Ek Chuuah on the final day of the flower war, the contest with knives. This warrior must seek to wound Ek Chuuah significantly, such that he requires time to recover. There will be anger toward Usihwitz but the warrior will claim it was accidental. Ek Chuuah will then be required to reside and recover in Usihwitz and perhaps he will find life there more hospitable. Assure the Nakom that Usihwitz will benefit, that their ruler Joy Bahlam will remain in my favor and their tribute will decrease."

Kan Bahlam watched his Nakom closely, finding neither surprise nor disapproval in the warrior's expression. Such strategies were not novel to those seasoned in Maya politics. Mut Yokte nodded, seeing immediately the advantages of removing the dissident ringleader. In the time needed for recovery and service to the victor's city, the cadre of dissidents would be broken apart with tactics of co-optation or threat. And there was a real possibility that Ek Chuuah would never return.

"It is accomplished," Mut Yokte responded in a low voice.

The second day of the flower war dawned bright and hot. Contestants oiled their skin for wrestling, even though the oil would trap sweat on the steamy battlefield. Their faces and chests were painted in geometric designs of black, red and white. Muscled limbs and bodies glistened, powerful physiques were revealed by tight loincloths. Hair was pulled atop their crowns and tied into a topknot with long trailing tails, some braided and others loose.

Lesser nobles and warriors of all four cities were the morning contestants; in the afternoon the elite ahauob would compete. Each contestant sought an opponent from another city, and these two would struggle one-on-one until a man was subdued, kept pinned to the ground and unable to continue fighting. When victory was clear, a referee would approach and cut off the loser's hair just beyond his topknot. This signified a commitment to serve the winner's city until the loser's hair reached its former length, usually more than a solar year.

The victorious man rested for a short while, then re-engaged with another warrior who had not yet fought or who was ready for another fight. The strongest men might conquer three or four opponents, although those more experienced knew the risk of fighting when tired. This error often led to defeat and servitude for one who would otherwise be much lauded at home.

At the sound of conches, men streamed onto the field and quickly found suitable opponents. The field became a mass of swinging arms and twisting legs, straining pectorals and pounding feet accompanied by a cacophony of grunts, groans and snorts. Numerous referees wearing bright red and yellow headdress plumes circulated among the wrestlers, slicing off ponytails of the defeated. Cheers and hoots from the crowd punctuated the contests as favored warriors either lost or won.

After some time observing the swarming, sweating contestants, Yohl Ik'nal and Sak Nicte decided a visit to the market was in order. Merchants never failed to take advantage of such large gatherings, setting up makeshift markets near the encampment. It was a nice opportunity to see goods from other cities and perhaps obtain an unusual fabric or piece of jewelry, new spices or implements. The noble maidens' attendants brought woven bags to carry their mistresses' treasures, and smaller bags full of cacao beans to use for purchase. Cacao beans were accepted everywhere for barter, along with jade and semi-precious stones.

The market consisted of six rows of merchants who spread mats on the ground to display their wares. Some had raised canopies against the sun and rain, sitting in welcome shade as the day was hot. When Yohl Ik'nal and Sak Nicte found interesting items, they knelt on mat edges to finger wares and speak with merchants. First to catch their eyes were jewelry and gems. Several merchants featured jade in a profusion of colors; pale green with creamy streaks, verdant jungle shades, brooding near-black darkness, bright yellow-greens, and occasionally the rare blue jade. Many pieces were carved into pectorals, pendants, necklaces, earplugs, wrist and arm bracelets, tiaras and hair clasps. Jade also was fashioned into vases, containers, plates, cups and figurines.

Sak Nicte selected a fine necklace of pale green and nearly white beads, while Yohl Ik'nal chose a tiara with blue-tinged jade and pink marble beads alternating in double strands. An intricately carved teardrop jade hung over the forehead nearly to her nose bridge. Its swirled pattern represented the spiral star cluster from whose center the Maya originated.

They walked past merchants offering obsidian, chert and flint mined in mountainous regions to the south and north. Traders brought these stones long distances, using rivers and navigating along the coastlines in long canoes carved from a single huge tree. Sunlight gleamed off smooth surfaces and caught the brilliance of metals such as copper and silver that decorated handles of finer knives and spears. Gold was rare in the Maya regions, although traders from the far north mined it in abundance and occasionally brought worked gold to southern markets.

Pottery and ceramics from participating cities were abundant, in a style prevalent along the low sierras. Color combinations of red, black and orange were used over a cream primary slip. Linear designs dominated although a few figures could be found. This polychrome technique was applied most typically to wide everted-rim tripod plates. Cylindrical vases were rarely painted. Deeper vessels with convex bases and both tilted and flat rims were orange slipped and incised.

The relative simplicity of local pottery contrasted sharply with imported ware from farther south in the lowlands and coastal regions. These colorful polychrome ceramics depicted Maya deities, anthropomorphic figures, animals, plants and people engaged in symbolic activities or partaking in daily life. Glyphs along borders or near the figures described events or recited prayers or poems. Plant pigments of white, black, red, yellow, blue and green were used. There were flat plates for maize cakes, deep bowls for stews, and cups of different sizes as well as large containers for storage of grains and liquids.

Browsing at a fabric merchant's mat, Yohl Ik'nal drew in a sharp breath when she uncovered an unusual piece of material. Buried under a pile of typical woven cottons was the most exquisite cloth she had ever seen. Made of thin transparent material that felt silky to the touch, it was pure sky blue with occasional large orange rounds in which geometric symbols appeared in bright golden-yellow. One border was trimmed with smaller rounds of the same colors on a white background. The fabric slipped sensuously through her fingers, cool as spring water rippling over pebbles.

"Sak Nicte, look at this!" she exclaimed. "Never have I seen such fine fabric."

Her friend kneeled and handled the seductive material.

"Oooh, so lovely, so delicate," crooned Sak Nicte. Glancing at the merchant, she asked: "Where is this from?"

Bowing from his seated position, the small man with a narrow face and pinched forehead spoke in a dictinct highland accent.

"Honored Ladies," he replied, "this very fine material is most rare, most unusual. It is made in the Mountains of the Sky Gods far, far to the south, in a land always wrapped in mists. The tree that gives its flowers to this fabric lives only in this high place, and not many such trees are to be found. Yes, it is very rare and very dear. It is of the highest quality, and there is a small piece here. You are most astute to notice this wondrous material."

The women exchanged glances; they knew the price for the fabric was high. But nowhere had they encountered such material. From the merchant's foreign appearance and dress, they knew he was from far away.

"It is so, this fabric is unusual and wondrous," Yohl Ik'nal acknowledge to the merchant. To her friend she added, "But I do not know to what purpose I could put such cloth, see how it is transparent. Even with double thickness, you can see through it."

"There is one proper and special use for it," murmured Sak Nicte. Moving to whisper in her friend's ear, she said, "Would this not be perfect for your wedding night? To greet your husband in the chamber of your marriage pallet? Ah, such a dress would surely fire his passion!"

Yohl Ik'nal blushed and lowered her eyes, but smiled. Quickly her imagination pictured how she would appear to Hun Pakal in the flowing and revealing silky robes that could be sewn from this exquisite fabric. Her pulse quickened as her own passion stirred.

"This blue color is also special," continued the merchant. "The clay mineral for the dye was taken with great ceremony from the heart of the Mountains of the Sky Gods; many offerings were given in honor and gratitude. Then it was heated in a consecrated bowl during a special ceremony using the purest white copal from the mountain ceiba tree. Precious indeed is this white copal, dear to the Gods of earth and water. Chaak dispensed his watery blessings into the bowl to dissolve the blue powder; precious to our Father of Waters is this clear blue color. It is a sacred fabric," the merchant whispered reverently, making the Chaak hand sign.

Yohl Ik'nal knew she must have it, regardless of price. She tried to haggle with the merchant, whose initial request was astonishing, but he would not reduce it by much. Finally, she parted company with nearly all her cacao beans, but her heart sang as she walked away with the rare fabric tucked carefully into the attendant's bag.

Passing by the remaining merchants on their way out, the women admired multi-sized shells from eastern and western coasts. Tiny white clams and snails were used in personal adornment and jewelry, larger conches made instruments blown during rituals, and pearly insides of oysters were inlaid in ceramics or jewelry. The bright red thorny oyster called spondylus was much favored for ceremonies and burials. Scraping the white lining from the shell revealed its orange-red under layer, the sacred color of the east, of rebirth and renewal. Bundles of stingray spines were tied with thongs, the sharp pointed spines valued for sewing, ceramic work and bloodletting ceremonies.

There were mirrors made of pyrite plates, feathers of birds such as the ocellated turkey and eagle, and pigments for dyes including indigo, annatto and red cinnabar used for burials. A few choice foods were offered, including salt brought from salt flats along the coast of the eastern sea, dried peppercorns and chiles, gum from the zapote tree for chewing, tobacco, honey and beeswax.

Although much in the market was of good quality, merchants usually kept their finest goods for private trade with elites. The ahauob were concerned about status reinforcing goods and would pay premium barter for fine polychrome ceramics, eccentric lithics, highest quality carved jade, resplendent quetzal feathers, obsidian for scepters and bloodletting and magnificent spearheads for their ritual warfare.

The sun was high overhead when the two noble women left the market, now crowded with shoppers during the midday break. The sound of voices questioning, remarking and bartering rose in a steady murmur. Parting company fondly, the two friends returned to their tents for a meal and rest. But Yohl Ik'nal was too excited to doze. This afternoon Hun Pakal would compete, and the new fabric kept stirring her romantic imagination.

Clouds gathered on the western horizon as the contests resumed. Towering thunderheads rose above flat gray bottoms, promising rain later. Rumbles of distant thunder rolled across the plains. Elite ahauob surged onto the contest field, wearing little but embroidered loincloths and paint. Their skins glistened with oil for hand-to-hand contests of strength and agility. As if pre-planned, contestants from different cities faced off, although to observers it was difficult to distinguish them.

But not for Kan Bahlam. The Lakam Ha ruler recognized his men instantly, knew each by name and disposition, and knew family and friendship links. His eye sought Hun Pakal and cadre, but instead saw Ek Chuuah with his followers on the closest side of the field, in front of the royal family's mats.

They have deliberately positioned themselves in front of me, the ruler mused. He was displeased with Ek Chuuah's smirk, no doubt intended to throw insult, though not obviously at the royal family. Body language spoke eloquently as the warrior strutted in defiance and supreme self-assurance. His men fanned around him, some mimicking their leader's stance.

Once engaged in conflict their focus shifted to opponents, arms and legs entwining and twisting, chests heaving and shoulders bulging. No direct blows were allowed, so finding the correct grasp to down an opponent became paramount. They could trip each other or pin arms behind the body, and use neck clasps that choked and cut off breath. Ek Chuuah was strong and cunning, and quickly downed his opponent. The referee cut off the man's ponytail signifying defeat, and the man retreated to the sidelines. Immediately Ek Chuuah engaged another opponent and displayed prowess by bringing that man down in a short time. Other warriors in Ek Chuuah's contingent were similarly successful, only a few losing the struggle.

Kan Bahlam simmered and clenched his jaw. This demonstration of strength, with its undercurrent of defiance, was insolent. It was indeed well that tomorrow this vexing scorpion would be taken out of action.

On the mat next to her father, Yohl Ik'nal strained to see across the field without rising. She anxiously sought sight of Hun Pakal without alerting her mother. Too many contestants writhed and groaned close-by, flailing arms and legs blocked her view. Absently she noted the performance of Ek Chuuah and his men, wishing they were on the other side of the field. Although aware of his trouble-making, this was far from her consideration at the moment. When she saw one of Ek Chuuah's followers defeated, his ponytail cut and his sagging form reluctantly retreating to the sidelines, it dawned on her that Hun Pakal might suffer the same fate.

She drew a sharp in-breath and shifted position, trying to see more clearly. A surge of combatants pushed through Ek Chuuah's group and thinned the space. Near mid-field she saw Hun Pakal struggling with a larger opponent. Fear gripped her as the man threw Hun Pakal to the ground, but the agile warrior from Lakam Ha immediately sprang up and slipped a leg between the opponent's knees, causing him to fall. Hun Pakal pounced upon the fallen man and pinned his arms behind his back; fight as he would the trapped man could not rise. This soon brought the referee to cut the man's ponytail in defeat.

Yohl Ik'nal sighed in relief, earning a sharp glance from her mother. Turning her eyes to the side, Yohl Ik'nal stretched and yawned.

"The contests are long," she remarked.

"Our men perform well," her mother replied.

"Yes, but surely they will not fight much more. Many have already battled three opponents, that is sufficient."

She fervently hoped Hun Pakal had fought three and would stop now. Looking toward where he was last seen, she saw others struggling. Her eyes swept the periphery of the field, but could not detect him. She looked down at her hands, fingers tensely intertwined, and waited.

"Ah, Hun Pakal seeks another opponent," her mother observed.

Yohl Ik'nal looked up and he was there, right in front, so close she could almost touch him. Mesmerized, she watched the struggle that seemed interminably long. Sweat dripped from both men, and the sound of heavy breathing and bodies colliding assaulted her ears. Slowly Hun Pakal wrestled his opponent down, though the man resisted mightily, and finally the victory was attained.

Hun Pakal was obviously exhausted, but he raised his head smartly and smiled directly at Yohl Ik'nal. Her gaze was lost in his for an eternal moment, and she did not try to hide it. He was victorious; he was not a captive going to another city. That was all she cared about.

Xoc Akal observed the silent interaction, and it confirmed her suspicions. She allowed hope to well for her daughter's happiness, for Hun Pakal was consolidating his position with his victories. To the relief of both women, Hun Pakal left the contest field.

That evening Xoc Akal went to the tent of her husband. The promised thundershowers had arrived at dusk with dramatic swords of lightning fanning across metallic skies and deafening booms of thunder heralding an intense but brief downpour. Now light rain fell and the ground released fresh earthy fragrances. As they sipped hot cacao and chile, the royal couple conversed privately.

"It is happening as you hope, the flower war?" asked Xoc Akal.

"It is well, our men bring many victories and our strength is rightly displayed," replied Kan Bahlam.

"This flower war is wise, my husband, you have led the people properly. Think you the dissension among polity cities will end?"

"End perhaps not, but decrease it will. Should our victories continue tomorrow, few will care to challenge Lakam Ha." After a thoughtful moment, the ruler added, "What Ka'an polity is capable of, I am not certain. Many generations of Ka'an leaders have meddled in affairs of other polities. Their on-going rivalries with Mutul are a good example. I fear more is brewing with them. There may be troubled times ahead."

Xoc Akal nodded, placing her hand on his arm.

"Only so much can one man do," she murmured. "Ultimately the patterns of stars determine our destiny, and the whims of the Gods shape how it plays out in our lives. You are doing what you can to mediate their influences in the Middleworld."

"It is so, you speak wisely."

They drank frothy, spicy cacao in silence for a while.

"Have you settled on a husband for Yohl Ik'nal?" asked Xoc Akal.

"This event will bring him forth," her husband answered. "This I will announce at the closing ceremony."

"Who do you consider the most likely candidates?"

"Several men of Lakam Ha have performed very well. Of these Hun Pakal stands out, and his bloodlines are excellent. The younger son of the Yokib ruler has deported himself admirably. An alliance with Popo' would be prudent, but I have not seen a man of high enough lineage who stands out in the contests. Among our people, a cousin of Mut Yokte fought impressively today."

"Hun Pakal has a large following, and his men had many victories," offered Xoc Akal.

"So it is. Tomorrow we shall see if their prowess holds true."

"Tomorrow will be dangerous for armed battle as rain makes the field slippery." Xoc Akal glanced at her husband with furrowed brow. "Must you fight tomorrow? You are not so young now; it would not be dishonorable to decline."

"This, to fight in the flower war, I must do," said Kan Bahlam firmly. "All must see that the ruler of B'aakal is still strong, an opponent to be respected. But I will only fight once, with the Yokib ruler Cauac Ahk who is near my age. Do not worry."

Xoc Akal sighed.

"Worry is the part of women when their men battle. Even when we know it is a ritual battle without serious wounding. Mistakes happen, or warriors become overly aggressive. Men have died in flower wars."

Kan Bahlam wondered if his wife suspected his plan for Ek Chuuah, but chose not to speak of that. Keeping silence even with intimates was the wisest course in such controversial leadership decisions.

"It is true, that I also will be relieved when tomorrow's contests are over," he admitted. "Lakam Ha has not lost many men to service in other cities, but enough will be going. I should much regret losing such good men as Hun Pakal, though I doubt he will be anything but victorious. He seems to have high motivation to out-perform everyone in these contests. Think you he has ideas about our daughter?"

They caught each other's eyes and smiled. Rulers seldom missed subtle cues about their peoples' intentions; this was key to their ability to lead.

"Think you not?" she teased.

"Think I so," he chuckled. "Hun Pakal may indeed be my choice."

"That would please Yohl Ik'nal."

"Ah." Kan Bahlam realized he had not been aware of his daughter's feelings toward the young man. It pleased him to think that her heart's desire might be fulfilled as he accomplished what was needed for the dynasty. Everything depended on what happened tomorrow.

Misty tendrils undulated from the combat field as morning sun warmed the wet earth. Shallow puddles settled in depressions packed down by hours of stomping feet. Small clusters of grass hung weakly making a futile attempt to recover, while much of the field was bare ground. Although it was early, many observers were already placing mats in choice positions to obtain better views of the final day's contests. This was the most exciting and dangerous day, the day of one-on-one combat armed with flint knives as long as a man's forearm.

Fewer warriors participated in armed combat, this being reserved for the higher elite levels. Full regalia were customary, resplendent in design and color, rich in symbolism. Quilted cotton vests with colorful patterns protected the trunk, at times augmented by similar cotton jackets that hung to the knees. Pants or skirts covered the thighs, also quilted and patterned. Among the K'umaxha River polities, flexible shields made of thick woven mats were folded around the left forearm, used to block knife slashes. Some warriors preferred round wooden shields covered with deerskin, painted with lineage emblems or war deities and decorated with feathers. Sturdy sandals were bound with leather thongs about the ankles.

Headdresses were elaborate and significant. Most were shaped as stylized heads of the warrior's uay, his spirit animal. Among rulers the jaguar was frequent, and shields bore depictions of the jaguar sun god, deity of war and the Underworld. Headdresses sporting various bird effigies were common, including hawks, eagles, cormorants, macaws, and parrots. Serpent headdresses were used by snake lineages, less often seen among the cities of B'aakal although some families bore the Kan name. The serpent, Kan was the uay of the ruling family of Ka'an polity.

Conches announced the arrival of contestants at the field. Multiple conches sounding together created discordant harmonics, fitting for the edginess settling over observers. Next came assorted drums in rapid cadence as warriors grouped on the field according to their city. Each group was led by the city's ruling ahau or sahal.

Kan Bahlam, K'uhul B'aakal Ahau appeared on the field wearing the jaguar headdress that represented his primary lineage. A small K'awiil perched above the jaguar's head, representing the patron god of rulers. A huge stream of feathers fanned back in a graceful arc, a shimmering iridescent rainbow of ocellated turkey and quetzal tail feathers. In front a smaller feather arc dangled above the forehead. Around the neck was a splendid collar of jade mingled with red, blue and golden beads. Cuffs of leather extended from wrists to elbow, borders adorned with copper and silver discs.

He wore cotton armor quilted with golden and blue threads, and a flared waist-collar of leather and metal discs. His wooden shield bore the face of the jaguar god of the underworld, a sun with closed eyes surrounded by white flower petals. Brilliant blue quetzal feathers alternated with those of the red macaw at four points around the shield.

The bobbing and swaying feather headdresses created a festive appearance. Sunlight glinted off metal and beads as the last wisps of mist disappeared. Conspicuously placed around the field periphery were teams of healers, priestesses and priests of Ix Chel, goddess of health and healing. They carried soft cloths for bandaging wounds, salves and powders of soothing herbs, unguents to stop bleeding, and brew for relieving pain. Wounding was expected; the victor in each contest was the warrior who drew first significant blood. Tiny nicks frequently occurred, but to win the cut must be large enough to produce a flow of blood. Most commonly these cuts occurred on the neck, upper arms, thighs and lower legs. By long established protocol, the face was never a target in these ritual battles.

The contests between the four city rulers took place first, in the center of the field. The ruler of Lakam Ha was set against Yokib, Popo' against Usihwitz. It was agreed among these rulers that the defeated man need not serve in the victor's city but would substitute another ahauob, or the service might be waived completely. This contest was primarily for prestige and to demonstrate prowess, and everyone took it most seriously.

Kan Bahlam of Lakam Ha and Cauac Ahk of Yokib were both middle-aged men, although muscular and vigorous. They cautiously circled, feinted and parried seeking advantage, as both were seasoned warriors. Quick strikes were deftly deflected by knife blade or shield. Rapid twists or leaps allowed them to escape slashes aimed at the lower legs. Cauac Ahk drew first blood with a prick on Kan Bahlam's guard hand, but this was too small to count. The other pair of rulers followed similar maneuvers, at times slipping on wet ground.

The royal women of Lakam Ha clasped each other's hands tightly, sitting close together on their mat. Sak Nicte kept an arm around Yohl Ik'nal for support. Xoc Akal moaned softly when her husband's hand was nicked, but kept her gaze steadfastly upon the contestants and held her head high. Yohl Ik'nal felt confident that her father would prevail; it was Hun Pakal she worried about.

Soon her intuition proved correct. In a cunning feint toward Cauac Ahk's legs, Kan Bahlam unexpectedly swooped his knife upward as his opponent spun away and sliced deeply enough into the upper arm to cause a gush of blood. The cut was skillfully done, cutting just through the full skin thickness while not severing muscle. Cauac Ahk dropped his knife and knelt. Waiting a long moment so all could observe the victory, Kan Bahlam touched his opponent's shoulder and spoke clearly that no service was required. The defeated ruler rose, and both men saluted then left the field.

The Popo' and Usihwitz rulers were younger men, and fought longer. Both had several small pricks before the Usihwitz ruler Joy Bahlam placed a significant cut on Popo' ruler Zotz Choj's thigh. As the wounded ruler knelt, his opponent demanded a substitute ahauob for service and the elected man came to kneel beside his defeated ruler, subjecting his ponytail to the knife. It was a bitter moment for the Popo' ruler, and he seethed with anger at his opponent's victory strutting. Even the soothing ministrations of the Ix Chel priestess binding his wound did not calm his ire. Soon the analgesic brew she urged him to drink brought welcome drowsiness.

The field filled with finely attired ahauob, grasping sharp obsidian or flint knives and seeking suitable opponents. The array might have resembled a dance, with a sea of bobbing feathers and glinting metals had not the ground become splattered with blood. The shouts and cries of combatants mixed with groans of pain, screeching blades and thudding feet. Action was fast and the Ix Chel healers stayed busy.

Again Yohl Ik'nal strained to see Hun Pakal, no longer trying to hide her concern. Sak Nicte stayed close, murmuring reassurances in between exclamations about deftly executed moves by various of their warriors. She was enjoying the contests, not being attached to any combatant and feeling assured that no serious injuries would occur.

"See how clever he is!" Sak Nicte remarked.

Yohl Ik'nal had no idea which warrior her friend meant. Her attention riveted upon Hun Pakal fighting mid-way across the field. His opponent looked too large and strong, but soon she realized he was not as clever as the man her friend admired. Hun Pakal confused the larger man with rapid slashes that were clumsily deflected with an arm shield. With the opponent on the defensive, Hun Pakal moved in close and placed a good cut just above the neck collar, drawing enough blood for victory. This win secured, he moved toward the field's edge seeking another combatant. Soon he was re-engaged in fight strategies with a smaller and quicker warrior.

"Why must he fight more?" whispered Yohl Ik'nal.

"The better to win you," her friend whispered back.

"It is so frightening."

"You must be brave, for overcoming fear will often be your lot," Sak Nicte said not unkindly. "Remember your destiny. Much more there will be that you must withstand."

In later years Yohl Ik'nal would recall her friend's prophetic words.

With dry eyes and drier mouth, Yohl Ik'nal steeled herself and kept watch as her beloved won another victory, and engaged yet again. In the third struggle, he suffered a small cut on the upper arm and her heart dropped sickeningly. The referees did not consider it enough although a trickle of blood crept down his arm. When she felt almost unable to bear more suspense, Hun Pakal made a decisive cut on his opponent's lower leg that gushed blood profusely. After the victory hair-cutting, the man limped quickly to the waiting priestesses and Hun Pakal strode proudly to the royal family's mats.

He bowed low, right hand clasping left shoulder, to Kan Bahlam. The ruler nodded acknowledgement and smiled, for he was growing in conviction that this young man should become his son-in-law. No other had performed as well or as consistently in the flower war. He gestured to the side of his mat.

"Stay beside me, Hun Pakal," the ruler said. "Bring him drink and tend his wounds," he directed his attendants.

Hun Pakal glanced toward Yohl Ik'nal sitting on the adjacent mat. Their eyes met briefly but long enough that he caught the glisten in hers, whether from tears or excitement he could not tell. He sat obediently at the back of the ruler's mat and relaxed into the attendants' ministrations.

Kan Bahlam had one more important thing to observe, the fate of Ek Chuuah. So far the young man had fought well and subjugated two opponents. He was strong and wily; it was regretful that his ambitions made him an opponent and not an ally. After a drink on the sidelines, Ek Chuuah returned to the field for his third opponent. Immediately a burly man from Usihwitz presented the challenge to fight, multiple scars marking him as experienced in battle. How fitting that Mut Yokte would set this up as the third contest, when Ek Chuuah was tired and the likelihood of defeat the greatest.

It was a well-balanced fight, however, despite the veteran's experience. Ek Chuuah was quick and made surprise moves that almost brought the decisive cut, but his opponent recognized every strategy and avoided injury at the last moment. Perhaps the veteran was fresher or had incredible stamina, but his energy held as Ek Chuuah began to flag. The young man moved awkwardly to avoid a slash, his right foot coming down on a slippery area sending him off balance. As he struggled to recover footing he momentarily dropped his guard, and the veteran moved in targeting the slipping leg. He made a vicious slash behind the right knee, obsidian blade cutting deeply and partially severing one of Ek Chuuah's hamstrings.

Ek Chuuah screamed as his leg gave out and he collapsed onto the muddy ground. Blood gushed profusely as the referee declared victory and the veteran cut off the ponytail with a flourish. Two priests noted the serious injury and quickly carried Ek Chuuah to the sidelines, applying pressure to stop blood flow. They discussed the injury with the referee who shook his head disapprovingly.

Usihwitz observers nearby gasped, while Ek Chuuah's cadre gathered around, murmuring angrily. Several observers from Lakam Ha hooted and signaled an infraction of rules. The veteran insisted the deep cut was accidental, expressing regret for the injury. After some heated argument among referees, they decided in favor of an unfortunate accident, and service to Usihwitz was required of the loser.

Kan Bahlam smiled to himself, observing these happenings from his mat at a distance. Some of Ek Chuuah's men came over and pleaded with their ruler to intervene. Kan Bahlam explained patiently that he must support the priestly referees in their decisions, and indeed it appeared to him an accident, albeit unfortunate. Such things sometimes happened in the heat of struggle, as everyone knew.

In the end, there was nothing but to accept it as an accident.

Kan Bahlam was pleased. Yohl Ik'nal was grateful that Hun Pakal escaped from such an accident. Xoc Akal read her husband too well, regretted that such tactics were necessary, but would never speak of this. He did what he must.

The sun had passed zenith and started its afternoon decline when the last combatants finished. Clouds were gathering again in the west, and a cooling breeze swept across the plains. Conches called to the four directions as priests circled the combat field carrying incense burners with smoking copal. They used these sacred copal fumes to cleanse and purify the area, to remove all anger, aggression and suffering so that the land might be restored to harmony. The Maya lived in balance with nature, honoring the ways of their Earth Mother, always restoring what they had disturbed.

The final ceremony was conducted by Kan Bahlam, assisted by his wife and daughter. Each recited salutations to the four Chaks, Bolon and Pahautuns that kept the energies of the directions. Honorific phrases were offered to K'in Ahau, Lord Sun and Hun Ahb K'u, Creator of Movement and Measure, all forms and beings upon the earth. When these rituals were complete, Kan Bahlam spread his arms and made hand signs for an important announcement.

Murmurs from the crowd dissipated quickly into silence.

"People of B'aakal, we have seen these magnificent contests, we have appreciated the skill and prowess of our warriors in this flower war." Kan Bahlam spoke in his commanding voice that carried easily to all edges of the gathering.

"Much am I pleased by the warriors of our cities, and much have I found happiness in the presence of so many friends and citizens of our polity. In this we re-affirm our associations and solidify our cooperation. It is in keeping with the ways of the Gods that humans live in harmony and order, as we do in Holy B'aakal."

These political statements were pointed reminders that the cities present owed allegiance to Lakam Ha, as the May Ku seat and as the dominant city of the polity. That this allegiance meant tribute in both materials and labor was understood; and for this tribute the Holy B'aakal Lord, K'uhul Ahau Kan Bahlam, would keep relations in good stead with the Gods and assure peace and abundance. Such was the social-political-spiritual contract of the Maya.

"Now comes something very important, very dear to my heart," he continued. "This has been weighing upon my thoughts, the marriage for my daughter and heir, Ix Yohl Ik'nal. In anticipation of this flower war, it became clear that the man suitable to become her husband would appear. That man with great prowess, courage and strength, that man who excelled in his victories and won admiration of many followers, he would be the match for my daughter. That man of the sacred and noble blood, of ruling lineages beloved of the Gods. That man has come forth to me."

Yohl Ik'nal was frozen; stunned as she stood just behind to her father's left. Her eyes widened and her breath stopped as she struggled to maintain a calm façade. But the pounding of her heart made her neck-collar quiver, sending sparkles of sunlight across her chin. She forced herself to breathe regularly but could not unclench her fists.

"That man, who has come forth through his victories in this flower war, is Hun Pakal of Lakam Ha."

The crowd roared, especially Hun Pakal's contingent. Yohl Ik'nal felt faint with relief, but instinctively drew herself up to her full height and lifted her chin firmly.

"Hun Pakal comes from a noble family of Lakam Ha, from both mother and father's sides there is sacred B'aakal blood whose descent is traced to the Triad Gods." Kan Bahlam continued reciting Hun Pakal's pedigree and qualifications, signing the young man to approach. Hun Pakal bowed with arms crossed on his chest, the gesture of highest honoring. Kan Bahlam placed his hands upon the young man's shoulders in the greeting of kinsmen. Their eyes met in mutual acknowledgement. Then Hun Pakal approached Xoc Akal, who gave the kinsfolk greeting. Last he stood before Yohl Ik'nal as she placed trembling hands upon his shoulders, hoping only he would see the glistening tears of joy in her eyes.

2

Lakam Ha was in a festive mood. The city's warriors had excelled during the flower war and the daughter of their K'uhul Ahau Kan Bahlam, Holy Lord of B'aakal, was soon to be married. The ruler's choice for her husband, Hun Pakal, was a popular one with most of the nobles and common people. Hun Pakal was well-connected among elite circles, had a large following of young men eager to support his goals, and was greatly admired by commoners for his congenial nature and recent victories. Indeed, he had brought honor and recognition to Lakam Ha and reinforced its right to continue as the May Ku center of political and ritual power in B'aakal.

Preparations were underway for a grand ceremony with a lavish feast, to be enjoyed by all in the central plaza. The farmers did not grumble that they must provide huge amounts of corn, squash, peppers, and fruits for the feast. Nor did their women complain about the hours of food preparation and cooking, or the labor they would give in serving the feast. They relished the opportunity to prepare special honey-maize cakes, filled with chopped cashew nuts and dried berries that traditionally were offered at weddings. The priests anticipated brewing great quantities of balche; they enjoyed partaking of the intoxicating beverage as much as the townspeople. Musicians practiced new melodies and created sweet songs to celebrate love and fecundity.

Xoc Akal, the bride's mother, supervised the most skilled weavers in making the wedding dress. Although she was a competent weaver, on this occasion she preferred the oversight role, freeing her imagination for design. She selected a dark blue fabric of soft cotton, on which white starburst patterns would be embroidered. White patterned borders with star glyphs added dramatic accent. The bride's headdress was a work of art, with indigo and white feathers, woven lotus flowers of pale rose and yellow, and the beaded tiara from the market at the flower war. Its pale blue jade and rosy pink beads complemented the dress perfectly.

Several days before the wedding, Yohl Ik'nal sat in consultation with the priestess of Ix Chel, Mat Ek'. An imposing middle-age woman with silver streaks offsetting coal-black hair, Mat Ek' was the primary teacher of the goddesses' healing arts in B'aakal. Her herbal knowledge was legend in the region; people traveled long distances even beyond the polity's borders to obtain treatment. The focus of her meeting with the ruler's daughter was conception—or better, the prevention of it. The Maya possessed extensive knowledge about reproductive physiology, including herbal remedies for menstruation, conception, pregnancy and childbirth. There were herbs to both prevent and to enhance conception.

Maya elites planned conception to assure particular characteristics for the child. This was done through understanding how stellar configurations affected life on earth, how one's qualities, consciousness and destiny were shaped by patterns of stars, planets and constellations. Maya astrology interacted with celestial realms, using potent rituals to invoke cosmic influences and direct them to people or places. This was the domain of the calendar priests and priestesses.

The birth date of Maya rulers was of utmost importance. The celestial forces it invoked would have beneficent or malefic consequences for the entire people. Maya ruling families usually had few children, often spaced several years apart. This was a deliberate strategy, for rulers often led long lives and wanted to both assure the succession and avoid contentious factions. It was not unusual to wait five to ten solar years before having the first child.

Since birth date is determined by time of conception, the planning of conception was all important. The Maya knew pregnancy usually lasted 260 days, a sacred number that was one basis for the Tzolk'in 13x20 = 260-day calendar. To plan conception accurately, they had to identify the time of ovulation. This was accomplished by detailed knowledge of menstrual cycles and physical signs of ovulation that included changes in the quality and quantity of cervical mucus. Methods of divination and herbs to induce ovulation were additional tactics, if necessary.

It was this information that Mat Ek' taught Yohl Ik'nal. At present, Yohl Ik'nal must follow instructions to prevent conception. For this, the priestess used *Ix Ki Bix*, the female Cow's Hoof vine that grew in the wet forests, looping around tree trunks. Under its dark bark, the thorny vine was mahogany-red. Many plants used for women's conditions had reddish tints, the colors of womb membranes and menstrual blood. A handful of chopped vine was boiled in three cups of water until a dark red color appeared. Taken for three days before the woman's menstruation, it would prevent conception for five cycles. Then another treatment could be used to continue the contraceptive effect.

When conception was desired, the woman ceased taking Ix Ki Bix for one solar year so fertility would be restored. However, to carefully regulate conception according to the dates determined by the calendar priests, a short term contraceptive was used made of cedar bark tea. Taken three days before menstruation, the effect lasted only one cycle. During the cycle when conception was desired, no tea would be taken at the preceding menses.

For Yohl Ik'nal and Hun Pakal, the optimal time to have a child was still several years away. Even before the marriage, calendar priests began their complex calculations, based upon birth constellations of the couple and desired star patterns. Determinations to assure the sex of the child were based partly on stellar configurations, combined with specific coital positions. To guarantee dynastic succession without dissent, Kan Bahlam had commanded the calendar priests to plan that the first child be a son.

"Here is much information, Lady Yohl Ik'nal," said Mat Ek' as she finished her teachings. "Is this clear to you, need I explain more?"

"It is most clear, you have taught well," replied Yohl Ik'nal. She hesitated, not sure how to frame her question.

"Will the drink of Ix Ki Bix, that I will take tomorrow in anticipation of my moon flow, have any undesirable effects?"

"This drink may at first cause the digestion to be unsettled," Mat Ek' replied. "But that should go away after the first use. Your digestion should be normal before the marriage takes place and undisturbed when next you take the drink."

"Does it affect the reproductive system in any adverse way?"

"No, your moon flow will be the same amount and quality. Nothing will be noticeably changed."

"The, ummm . . . response to . . ." Yohl Ik'nal blushed and hesitated, but Mat Ek' perceived quickly the gist of her question and smiled.

"This drink will not affect your passion or enjoyment of your husband," the priestess replied. "Many times have I given this to our women, and none has told me of such problems."

Yohl Ik'nal nodded, feeling the blush fading. Mat Ek' would be her advisor and healer over the coming years, at her side during childbirth, her consultant for concerns about the health of her family. Many confidences would pass between these women. Their eyes met in acknowledgement of this special relationship.

After Mat Ek' left, Yohl Ik'nal fingered the maroon-colored woody twigs, sensing the potency of their earth medicine. She was grateful that Lakam Ha had such expert healers to guide people's lives according to the great cosmic plan. Putting the herb away in a covered quartz jar, she reflected how her life was changing. Soon her time would be taken by the duties of a wife and the political and social requirements of the ruler's daughter. That such requirements were increasing she had no doubt. The time to establish her leadership was at hand, and she greatly desired to meet the challenge well.

A childhood memory had returned to her in recent days, not thought of in several years. She felt her special place calling her. Was the clearing with its quartz-crowned rock cluster by the waterfalls still hidden, undiscovered? Or had it been removed for building, the quartz used by gem-workers, the stones chiseled into blocks. A deep yearning stirred to re-visit this place of early visioning, of adventurous journeys to other realms. After her marriage there would be no opportunity to disappear for such adventures.

She waited until nearly dusk, and then stealthily slipped through less-used palace passages. Once outside, she drew a shawl close around her head and shoulders to avoid recognition. Wearing the plainest clothing she possessed, the ruler's daughter managed to pass through the central plaza without notice. Few people were about, as most were gathered around evening cooking fires in family compounds, sharing meals and friendship. The path down the eastern cascades was wide and often trod, with buildings clustered at intervals. It bore little resemblance to the narrow forest path of her childhood. She passed a large housing compound of noble families near a wide pool. The amount of new building surprised her. She feared that the clearing no longer existed.

Staying at the path's edge under trailing lianas, she remained in deepening shadow. Although she could hear voices from the plaza, no one noticed her. Soon the path narrowed and descended steeply. It appeared little used and the jungle closed in. The murmur of a small waterfall drew her onward. She hoped it was the cascade marking the opening for the path to the clearing. Standing beside the cascade, she could not detect any opening in the dense forest foliage. Disoriented, she strove to recall which direction led to the clearing. It must be opposite the cascade. Approaching the foliage, she made several test pushes into leafy walls to no avail.

Closing her eyes, she concentrated upon finding the path. Only intuition would lead her to the clearing. She pictured the natural outcropping of boulders, the flat stones on which she sat, and the clear quartz that burst into brilliant flames when struck by morning sun. As if drawn by a magnetic force she moved into the jungle, pushing aside branches and lianas. Although some thorns caught her shawl and scratched her arms, she kept her direction and soon found the foliage less dense. Remnants of a path led into the clearing.

It was as she remembered. The irregular mounded stones loomed less tall but still bore the quartz, although small bushes found footholds in the surrounding flat stones. She located the place where she used to sit and wait for sunrise. Now it was dusk, the sky taking on a greenish glow in the waning light. She had never tried to make the journey at night, but always used brilliant morning sunrays to propel her consciousness across dimensions. Why not simply imagine this? Surely the inner vision would accomplish the same results, especially as she was now trained in visioning.

Sitting cross-legged, eyes closed, she slowed her breath and focused inward. When body and mind were still, she summoned the image of herself as a young girl sitting in this place, waiting for the sunrise to ignite red sparks behind closed lids. When this image was strong, she imagined opening her eyes to the blazing sunrays shooting through the quartz. With strong intention, she projected her consciousness into the quartz. Instantly she felt herself propelled along flaming pathways into that other world.

She was in the cold windy place, the hilltop surrounded by vast meadows of grass. It was the deserted place where she met the strange girl of corn silk hair and blue eyes. Drawing her shawl tight against the cold, she walked to the edge of the hilltop, smelling the pungent brush now devoid of purple flowers. The grass was brown, the sky clouded and gray. It seemed the season of dormancy was approaching, plants falling into their period of sleep. No bird sounds came to her ear, no animal calls or smells, only the sighing wind as it rippled across the grassy plains.

She called to the girl, Elie. Mentally she sent a summons, a request for Elie's presence. For some time, all was stillness and her vision empty. Then a scene formed that was impossible to interpret. A golden-haired woman stood beside the rail of a large wooden boat, so huge that it was incredible. It was like a modest mountain, its deck more than the height of three men above the water. Tall straight-limbed trees with billowing white cloth for leaves stood in a row along its center. Clusters of ropes were attached to them. Whole tents could be made from one piece of this fabric, so great was its size. Many men scurried around tending to the fabric and ropes. Two better-dressed men of commanding stature were observing the work. The men seemed hard and intent.

The golden-haired woman leaned against side rails and looked out across a vast expanse of water. No land could be seen along the horizon in any direction.

This must be the great northern sea, thought Yohl Ik'nal. She was astonished that the sea could be so immense. *The woman must be Elie, grown up as I am.* There was a resemblance in eyes and mouth that made it likely, where was she going? But it was not possible to enter the woman's thoughts or contact her consciousness. The expression on the woman's face was one of eagerness and curiosity.

She is going on an adventure, perhaps she is coming to visit my land, as she promised.

The thought of home snapped her back to the rocky clearing. She sat for a few moments, reflecting upon her journey and grateful for the vision. What it might mean for people from such a far away, vastly different culture to come to the lands of the Maya, she could not fathom. She knew Elie had a good heart and would do no harm, but the men seemed ominous. Their thin lips and small sharp noses, ruthless eyes and wind-dried ruddy skin left a menacing impression. Flitting on the edges of her mind was the realization that this journey of her friend and the stern men was in a distant future.

Bass blares from eight long trumpets resonated throughout Lakam Ha, their summons echoing through courtyards and alleys. Standing on the top platform of the city's tallest pyramid, the trumpeters projected four blasts in each of the four directions. The mid-morning sun burned through thin mists hovering around mountaintops, dispelling the last tendrils. In the sun's annual journey across the sky, it was now halfway between its farthest north and farthest south positions. This was the time of balance, when day and night were equal in length. The calendar priests marked equinox by sighting first rays of the rising sun at the central marker of the sun pyramid. At the solstices, the first rays hit either the north or south marker when the sun reached the extremities of its annual travels.

It was the time of fall equinox, leading to renewing winter rains. While an important time in itself, the day was doubly important for it marked the wedding of the daughter of Kan Bahlam, K'uhul B'aakal Ahau. The ceremony was performed in the central plaza so all people of Lakam Ha could partake in this holy ritual. The marriage ceremony reenacted union between the B'aakal royal family and the lineage founders, the deities of Matawiil. Proper rituals anchored spiritual into physical and sealed the union of lineage holders. As above with patron Gods and goddesses, so below with humans of royal blood. This was necessary and kept the realms of humans, nature and deities in alignment.

After the ceremony, commoners and nobles alike would indulge in a great feast with much dancing and drinking that would continue through the night.

In the center of the plaza a thick rope marked off an area in the shape of a square representing the cosmos. For the Maya, the cosmos was quadripartite, having four parts with multiple expressions that repeated from the infinite to the smallest of things. The earth was formed to reflect the quadripartite cosmos, having four cardinal directions. Each direction had its Pahautun who held up the firmament; and each had its Bacab, Lord of Winds and its Chaak, Lord of Waters. The relationships among them formed an equal-sided cross, a symbol of highest reverence.

The cardinal points began with the east where the sun rises, Lak'in, Chak Zib Chaak, the red color of new light; then crossed to the west where the sun sets, Chik'in, Ek Zib Chaak, the black color of the watery underworld; then to the north, Xaman, Sak Zib Chaak, the white color of cold winds and polar stars; and last to the south, Nohol, Kan Zib Chaak, the yellow color of warmth, growth and emergence.

Flowers the color of the directions along with representative elements were placed at each cardinal point. The elements were fire for the east, water for the west, earth soil for the north, and wind symbols for the south. Colored cloth mats for each direction filled in the four quadrants of the rope square. In the center was a carved stone image of the Wakah Chan Te, the Jeweled Tree with its nine roots for the Underworld, thick trunk for the Middleworld, and thirteen branches for the Upperworld. This sacred tree connected the dimensions of Maya existence; all were necessary for the roots must nourish the trunk and branches, the trunk must convey sap with life force energies up and down, and the branches with leaves must draw in the sun's light and spiritual sustenance from the cosmos for life on earth.

Musicians began playing flutes, drums and whistles as people gathered at plaza edges. The ahauob stood on stairways around the plaza while chanting priests and priestesses surrounded the rope square. At each cardinal point, priests blew large conches with red-tinged shells whose blaring voice was echoed by higher tones of the priestesses' small white conches. The conch chorus announced the marriage ceremony.

From the south palace, the ruler's family descended broad stairs toward the rope square. They made a splendid troupe with bobbing feather headdresses, shining metallic and gemstone jewelry, and richly colored clothes of the finest fabrics and weaving. Simultaneously, another entourage emerged from the east side of the plaza. This was the family of Hun Pakal, also extravagantly attired in their finery. The groups came to the edge of the rope square, to cheers and whistles of the gathered people.

The High Priest Ah K'in Wak Batz and the High Priestess Ix K'in Lahun Uc entered the square and stood on either side of the sacred tree of life. Silence fell upon the crowd as the marriage pair emerged from their surrounding families and entered the rope square, she from the south and he from east.

The sun at zenith caught opalescent shells of Yohl Ik'nal's headdress. Silvery metallic discs glimmered in her huipil, spirals inside white starbursts. Sparkling like the stars, these flashes of brilliance contrasted with dark blue fabric draping her lissome shape. Hun Pakal radiated golden tones from metallic beading on his short skirt, as his magnificent neck collar shimmered in multi-colored jades from warm tan to bright forest green. Feathers of red, yellow, black and white hung in overlapping layers from the neck collar. His headdress was the stylized corn plant with long drooping feather leaves behind and cobs dangling in front. A tuft of hair arched over his forehead, representing corn silk.

The marriage pair was dressed to symbolize core concepts in Maya cosmology. The styles and colors of her attire conjured the Cosmic Mother, Ix Muwaan Mat, the creatrix and ancestor of B'aakal, through the deep blue of infinite skies filled with silvery stars and spiral galaxies. He embodied the young maize god, Yum K'ax, whose golden corn silks, yellow kernels and green foliage represented the power to sustain growth and life, bringing abundance to the people.

The couple stood beside the Wakah Chan Te, as the High Priest and Priestess chanted invocations to call down the presence of these deities and merge them with the humans readied by costume, and also by days of fasting, prayer and visioning, to be pure and fit vessels. Waves of copal smoke poured from censers and filled the air with woody pungency. Simply breathing these sacred fumes was enough to put most Mayas into an altered state of consciousness. Indeed, the entire plaza seemed to quiver in anticipation, breathless in this suspended moment, entering a shimmering dimension on the edge of different realities.

The contingent of priests and priestesses took up a soft, rhythmic chant as the couple went to each cardinal direction, beginning in the east, to perform element rituals. Together they lifted an incense cup with glowing coals and placed twigs inside; immediately a small fire burst forth and they murmured a prayer to the Lords of the East as they moved the cup in form of a Maya cross; from east to west, north to south, and then in a circle counter-clockwise and another circle clockwise. This completed, they proceeded across the square to the west, taking a cup of water, praying to the Lords of the West, and performing the ritual cross-clock movements. Next to the north, lifting a cup of soil and doing ritual for the Lords of the North, and last to the south, lifting a cup with smoking copal for the air and doing ritual for the Lords of the South.

Returning to the center, the couple gave symbolic gifts to each other. Drawing from ancient roots of Maya agricultural traditions, Hun Pakal gave her a cob of corn and several cacao pods as the raw materials for making food and drink. After accepting these, Yohl Ik'nal offered him a prepared maize cake and cup of cacao as the food fashioned from his raw materials. Both nibbled of the maize cake and sipped the cup of cacao, sweetened with honey to signify the pleasures of married life. Once he had eaten of food prepared by her hand, the marriage bond was made between them. Among commoners, marriages were sealed by this simple gesture without accompanying ceremony. A man would go to the palapa house of a woman, where she would feed him, and they were considered married.

The High Priestess spoke the phrases to seal their marriage.

"Hun Pakal, you have eaten of food prepared by the hand of Yohl Ik'nal," she intoned. "By this act, your marriage is accomplished. Now I will bind your hands that all may see that your lives are bound together in everything that happens. You are the provider and the seed; she is the preparer, the bearer and the nurturer. Together may you bring forth progeny, abundance and happiness with the grace of the Gods."

Taking a strand of red agate beads, she wrapped his right and her left wrists together, lifting their arms so the crowd could see. Approving roars issued from thousands of throats. The High Priestess then led the couple around the square with arms lifted, displaying the bound wrists to continued waves of approval.

The couple returned to the center, and the High Priest approached with a large cloak of purest white trimmed in a geometric border of red and black. He swung the cloak out in a dramatic flair, and then settled it around the couple's shoulders until they were completely enclosed.

"May the sacred energies of love and honoring life surround you and enclose you in their protection," intoned the High Priest. He seemed straighter, voice steadier than usual. "As this cloak is a barrier to the wind and cold, may you always protect your marriage from the dulling forces of daily living, from the negative forces of bitterness and resentment, from the harmful gossip of evil-sayers. Keep your hearts open to the truth in each other. Listen well and speak with care. Remember your highest loyalty is to each other, even as you are loyal to B'aakal and our Triad Gods. Here we invoke the deities' protection of your spirits so that love grows within you as one."

The High Priest and Priestess joined voices for a series of chants, with a chorus in response by the priesthood around the square. The names of all the Maya deities were intoned with a call for protection and guidance throughout the couple's life together and continuing to their progeny.

With this ritual the wedding was completed. The cloak and wrist cords were removed, and the couple walked slowly toward the royal family group, up the broad stairs and into the palace while wooden and turtle carapace drums beat a stately cadence. The sun had dropped midway through its afternoon descent, long shadows reaching across the city on the plateau. People returned to their homes and chores, while the priests and priestesses ceremoniously removed the marriage ritual accoutrements and de-sanctified the plaza. Soon thereafter the work crew readied the area for feasting.

Although the ahauob would feast and drink in the palace courtyard with the ruler and his family, and the commoners would over-indulge in rich food and drink that they only accessed on such special occasions, the marriage couple was by custom allowed to be alone this evening. They were still in sacred space, and remained so through their first night together as their marriage was consummated. The following day they would participate in another round of feasting and celebration.

But this night they were alone together. A light meal was brought to their chambers and left by discreet servants. The heavy curtains closing doorways were pulled tight. As dusk settled the couple, ritually undressed of their marriage costumes and bathed for purification, were reunited in their secluded chambers.

Hun Pakal was already there when Yohl Ik'nal entered. She wore the fabric from the market at the flower war, sewn by her own hand into a loose-fitting dress with long sleeves. The transparent material of pale blue, with large orange rounds decorated in yellow geometric symbols, draped gracefully around her form. It rippled and flowed with each movement, even with her breath. The silkiness caressed her skin with sensuousness that was cooling and exciting at the same time, making her skin feel tingly. She was aware of her erect nipples as the fabric slipped like water around every contour and revealed what lay beneath. Still in a state of ritual consciousness, she felt amazing calmness deep inside while her heartbeat raced.

Leaping to his feet, Hun Pakal drew in a sharp breath of admiration.

"Aaah, my precious one, you are so beautiful!"

She bowed her head, causing her long unbound hair to slip around her shoulders. She reached both hands toward him; he quickly moved to cradle her hands in his. He was dressed simply in white loincloth and short cape with embroidered border.

He slipped his arms around her and drew her close, fingering the fabric.

"Incredible, what fine material," he murmured. "Fine as it must be for one so perfect, so lovely."

They touched noses and he nuzzled the hollow of her neck. As the contours of their bodies melded, powerful passions coursed through both and food was entirely ignored.

In the melodic but clipped tones of the Mayan language, he breathed endearments into her ear.

"Ti hebix u hok'ol yalche y tipil lol," he murmured.

"You are as the flower that emerges and blossoms."

"Chamuibtasbon kolonton," she whispered back.

"You perfume my heart."

"Xk'uxub kolonton." His voice was husky with desire.

"My heart aches for you."

"Ti tech in dzama in wuinclil yetel in vol." Her heart pounded against his.

"To you I surrender my body and spirit."

And Yohl Ik'nal did surrender herself—heart, body and spirit—into Hun Pakal's impassioned embrace for a night of ecstasy beyond her imagining.

3

The great calendar of the Maya, the Long Count of the Baktuns that stretched into the past beyond the formation of stars and galaxies, and projected into the future beyond the death of planets and suns, had reached a significant point for the Maya of B'aakal. In this Long Count, set at 13 Baktuns followed by a string of four zeros when the present creation began, an important milestone had arrived. Now in the Fourth Sun, the era in which Halach Uinik—real people had come into being, the katun count rolled over from Katun 6 to Katun 7. The other three values—tuns, uinals and kins—were reset to zero. On this day in mid-winter, with pounding rains and boiling rivers, as Lakam Ha sat drenched upon its mountain ridge, the Long Count rolled over into the new Katun.

Baktun 9, Katun 7, Tun 0, Uinal 0, Kin 0, on the date 7 Ahau 3 Kank' in. (December 3, 573 CE)

It was time for Kan Bahlam, K'uhul B'aakal Ahau, to do the K'altun or stone binding ceremony to mark the end of the 20th katun. In Maya sacred numerology, katuns with the count of 5, 13 and 20 from the previous 20th katun required special ceremonies. This 20-count katun with its K'altun ceremony was of utmost importance; by properly enacting it the ruler maintained his polity's relationship with the Gods and kept the portal of communication open. In the ceremony, god-bundles would be given as offerings to the Triad Deities; these gifts must be intuitively selected to be pleasing and to satisfy the Gods' desires. For the first time, Yohl Ik'nal would play a key role in the rites.

The K'altun ceremony was not a public ritual. It was conducted in the most sacred shrine of Lakam Ha, a secluded underground sanctuary constructed below the floor of a modest temple to Ix Chel, located within a residential complex not far from the palace. The underground rectangular structure was accessed through subterranean passageways that connected to a small private ceremonial room inside the ruler's chambers. Concealed by a panel carved in low relief that was pivoted aside, the doorway opened to steep, narrow stairs descending into the passageway. Near the entrances at each end of the tunnel were stucco sculptures of the Celestial Caiman, *Tz'ihb'al Paat Ayin*, the primordial monster whose immense body could be seen crossing the night sky as the Milky Way.

Called the *Sak Nuk Nah* or White Skin House, the walls of the underground structure were painted white with rows of flowers and jeweled medallions of blue and orange. Along the ceiling was a band of geometric designs in the same colors linked by small circles. An altar throne with fish motifs sat in the center of the floor, signifying the watery underworld and bearing the symbols of the B'aakal Triad Gods. The floor and altar throne were painted the same pure white as the walls, creating the ambiance of endless cloud-borne dimensions.

The passageways of the Sak Nuk Nah connected the Underworld and Middleworld. Here the watery realm of death and the cloud-filled realm of spirit were united. After death, the spirits of ahaulel, Maya rulers, entered into the Celestial Caiman's body and the new ruler sat upon a throne carved with this crocodile motif. The link between deceased and living ahaulel, and their ability to access ancestral guidance, was portrayed in this symbolism.

Only the highest ranks of elite ahauob could enter the Sak Nuk Nah. A certain level of spiritual initiation and occult knowledge was necessary. The group gathering for the K'altun ceremony was therefore small and select. Although the other ahauob were not present, they kept vigil and maintained ritual consciousness during this auspicious day. The common people also offered simple prayers of support and kept silence as much as possible. Their future was at stake; the K'altun ceremony in the Sak Nuk Nah would set the destiny of the coming 20 years, determining whether the katun ahead would be one of peace or strife, prosperity or hardship.

How well the K'uhul B'aakal Ahau and his daughter accomplished the rituals was key to their people's future.

The high initiate ahauob, priests and priestesses gathered in the Sak Nuk Nah, including rulers and high priesthood of several B'aakal subsidiary cities. Within the small structure this group of fifty people found places to sit upon reed mats, waiting in silence. All had completed purification rituals and donned simple ceremonial clothing, primarily white garments with blue, black, or green trim. Drafts of cool air flowed into the room through the tunnels, chilling the stone walls and floor already cool from the winter earth. Torches mounted on wall brackets cast flickering light into the darkness of the underground structure.

The distant sound of rattles signaled the approach of Kan Bahlam and Yohl Ik'nal. As the royal pair approached through the passageway from their chambers, the smell of copal incense drifted into the room. Soon they entered, making a circle around the altar throne once in each direction, and then the ruler sat upon the throne with his daughter standing at his right side. Kan Bahlam wore a short skirt with mat designs and a headdress displaying symbols of K'awiil, patron god of rulers, and Yum K'ax, the Maize God. Yohl Ik'nal was attired as Ix Azal Uoh, a form of Ix Chel as mother earth goddess who wove the fabric forming the lives of her creatures. Attendants waited in the doorways until summoned, carrying small bundles wrapped in white cloth, ceremonial headdresses and bloodletting implements.

On momentous occasions such as K'altun endings, the ultimate sacrificial offering of royal blood was required. Blood was the most concentrated source of *itz*, sacred life-force energy. As the Gods gave life to humans, so humans offered back the blood that coursed through veins carrying that life force, the sustenance of their existence in the physical world. Droplets of blood were collected on bark paper in ceramic cups and burned to release their essence as smoke that coiled and morphed into Vision Serpents. These metaphysical entities opened the channels of inter-dimensional communication; from their gaping jaws would emerge divine or ancestral beings who delivered messages to the vision-seeker.

The messages sought during this ceremony focused on the coming katun, the next 20 years for the people of B'aakal. The nature of the messages, their beneficent or malefic intent, depended upon how the Gods received the gifts prepared for them.

First came the offering of god-bundles. Following lengthy chanting, during which Yohl Ik'nal fanned incense smoke upon all gathered, the ruler summoned attendants to bring forth the bundles. There were three bundles that Yohl Ik'nal had prepared for the Lords of the First Sky. Kan Bahlam had prepared three headdresses for the B'aakal Triad.

An attendant knelt, presenting three bundles on a silver tray as Yohl Ik'nal prepared to speak the critical invocation to the Gods. Tense anticipation filled the room.

"Lords of the First Sky," she prayed, "Lords of the Jeweled Tree born of earth and celestial vault, the shining tree of precious gems reaching from the Middleworld of people to the Upperworld of spirits, it is I your earthly daughter, Yohl Ik'nal, who offers to you each your *ak'tu'* gift-thing. These gift-things have I created with my own hands and work and effort, breathing upon them love and devotion and gratitude. You are the Jewels of the First Sky; you radiate brilliance and beauty beyond compare. You are perfect, yet you may have enjoyment of such beauties of the earth realm. Beauty to beauty goes; precious resplendence finds its matching radiance. These are my offerings."

She lifted the first god-bundle, holding it upward then moving it in the symbolic gesture of the Maya cross. Slowly she unwrapped the bundle to reveal a necklace of deep red coral beads interspersed with spirals carved from spondylus shell, rose-hued with hints of opalescence. These treasures had been obtained with great effort and considerable risk from off-shore reefs in the great eastern sea, where vigorous waves threatened to dash divers against sharp ridges and big-toothed fish called *xoc* or shark awaited distracted swimmers. A set of large earspools of red coral, carved with the sun glyph, complemented the necklace to perfection.

"To you, 6 Chan Yoch'ok'in, I offer this gift-thing. May it bring you pleasure."

The gathered elite immediately appreciated the perfection of this gift. The god's name meant "sky you possess/enter the sun" whose center was red fire.

Setting the bundle on the edge of the altar throne, she lifted the next god-bundle and performed the same gestures. Upon opening, the gold necklace and earspools inside this bundle caught the dancing torch flames and burst into blazing rays, dazzling the eyes with brilliance. This golden metal came from the central mountains, where it was mined with immense effort by vassals of Teotihuacan, most powerful city of this northern region whose influence penetrated the Maya lands. Gold was much valued there, and the cost to obtain such a collection was substantial. The large necklace with 16 rows of beads gradually increasing in size, and flower shaped earspools were unusual and impressive.

"To you, 16 Ch'ok'in, I offer this gift-thing. May it bring you pleasure."

Golden light was a fine representation of the meaning of this god's name, "emergent young sun." It invoked the first shafts of golden brightness slipping over the horizon at sunrise. Its costliness was in keeping with the crucial role of the sun in Maya life.

This bundle placed upon the altar throne, she lifted the final one, performed gestures as before and opened it. Here were necklace and earspools of jade, smoky veined and mysterious, so dark as to be nearly black. Yet the veins in the jade provoked a curious fascination, thin networks of pearly gray contrasting with hidden forest depths, a mesmerizing pattern. Acquiring such a large and fine collection with exact coloration and patterning must have cost dearly.

"To you, 9 Tz'ak Ahau, I offer this gift-thing. May it bring you pleasure."

This god's name meant "conjuring lord" and indeed the gift was deeply shamanic, with its shape-shifting qualities plumbing the depths of mystery. The assembled ahauob breathed an inner sigh of relief and appreciation as she placed the final bundle on the altar. The novice ceremonialist had divined to perfection the qualities for gift-things that merged with the essences of the Gods.

Kan Bahlam rose and bowed to his daughter, arms across chest in the gesture of supreme honoring. His eyes twinkled as they met hers, for he was well pleased. She bowed in return and sat, as he began the offerings to the B'aakal Triad.

By long tradition, these Gods received hats or headdresses as their gift-things. The art was in creating imaginative and symbolic headdresses that included all the important elements for each god. Kan Bahlam had reflected long upon this, acquired the finest materials and directed artisans personally in selecting styles and colors. After chanting the obligatory ritual prayers, in exactly the tone and cadence as had generations of rulers before him, he signaled for attendants to bring forth the gifts. Each headdress was held in turn by Kan Bahlam while circling the altar three times, showing details to everyone in the group.

The first born of the B'aakal Triad Gods, Hun Ahau was given the sacrificial bowl hat created from exquisite ceramic bowl pieces painted by the most talented Lakam Ha artists. Attached were implements used for bloodletting such as the perforator bone from a stingray spine, obsidian needles, tendrils of bark paper and clear red beads in dangling rows suggesting a stream of blood droplets. Red macaw feathers continued the theme of spurting blood and ahau face glyphs framed the head border.

The second born, Mah Kinah Ahau was given the white paper hat. It was the custom of B'aakal rulers to tie on a white headband when they assumed rulership. The underworld sun-jaguar, whose celestial body was the full moon, acted as the uay of this god. With white paper streamers and arching white feathery plumes, jaguar skin bands around the base and ahau face glyphs, the headdress incorporated these themes and added blue quetzal feathers for the watery qualities of the underworld.

The third born, Unen K'awill was given the fire sky-god hat with red as the prominent color. This serpent-footed deity depicted as an infant represented the royal bloodline of B'aakal. With infant glyphs around the headband, shining mirrors of pyrite representing the lightning force of K'awill, serpents coiling and twining atop and flaming red macaw feathers mixed with black-tipped white egret feathers, the headdress brought the qualities of the god into full expression.

After presenting each headdress to the group, Kan Bahlam placed it on the altar throne and performed hand signs that invoked the deities to merge with the hat. His powerful form commanded attention from unseen forces as well as human. All eyes were riveted upon the ruler and everyone sensed the uncanny chill of other-worldly presences. Many people there, Yohl Ik'nal included, experienced a tingling sensation up the spine and felt gooseflesh form on arms. No one doubted that the B'aakal Triad Gods had entered the chamber to claim their headdresses.

Drummers beat a solemn cadence as Kan Bahlam and Yohl Ik'nal prepared for bloodletting. The ruler sat on the altar throne flanked by the Triad God headdresses. Attendants brought needle-sharp stingray spines and bark paper inside a ceramic bowl that they placed on a mat between his feet. The blood offering of male rulers was traditionally from the penis, symbol of generative powers bringing fertility to all creatures and abundant growth to crops, especially maize. Attendants kept a censer of hot coals ready to light sticks which would set the blood-soaked paper on fire.

Yohl Ik'nal sat on a mat and placed the three god-bundles around her. For royal women, blood offerings were from the tongue or earlobes. Attendants brought spiny needles and ceramic bowl with bark paper, placing them before her. This was a moment she both anticipated and dreaded; it was her first sacrificial bloodletting. Psychologically prepared by fasting, purification and prayer, she had also imbibed a brew of pain-numbing herbs along with a mild hallucinogen. These brews were prepared from secret formulas by the High Priest and Priestess; few among the commoners knew they were used for the bloodletting rituals.

Even so, there would be pain. Her father warned her of this, and taught techniques to use for separating her awareness from the pain. It was required that this act be one of self-sacrifice, carried out by the sacrificer. Only by such volition, such strong acts of willingness and commitment, would the Gods be pleased and the offering be pure. But it was hard not to recoil against trauma inflicted upon such vulnerable organs. She worried that she might not be able to withstand the pain without flinching. How important it was to show no reaction she knew well; all those observing would be alert to the slightest hesitation or shudder.

Kan Bahlam went first, grasping penis in one hand the spiny needle in the other. Gazing into the distance, he projected all his concentration into the starry realm of the Gods and began breathing in deep and measured rhythm. Deliberately he withdrew awareness from the body. When he felt deep inner calm, a stillness that was at once emptiness and infinite expansion, he raised his hand and quickly plunged the needle several times into the penile shaft. No expression marred his restful features; no twitch shook his straight body. Blood flowed in small rivulets onto the bark paper, staining their whiteness with crimson splashes.

Yohl Ik'nal did not watch her father but kept her eyes closed, building inner concentration. Using the same breath technique, she projected her awareness into the realm of the First Sky Lords. The Jeweled Tree captured her attention with its sparkling gems and propelled her along its trunk and branches into the sky realms. But a small part of her awareness resisted, hung back thinking of the sacrificial act. Quivers of fear trembled around her heart. She breathed more deeply, commanding her attention to focus. This inner struggle continued, she knew not how long for she floated in timelessness.

This must be done, echoed the recesses of her mind. This must be done correctly.

From a well of determination she had not known before, there surged a current of incredible strength. Sudden calmness descended and her consciousness exploded into infinity; she was the entire cosmos.

Now! commanded the inner guide.

She stuck out her tongue, grasped the tip between pieces of bark paper and quickly stabbed the spiny needle upward from the bottom. This needle had a thin thread attached embedded with thorns to sustain blood flow. Through a power beyond her personal self, she did not flinch or alter her calm expression.

When the needle penetrated through the tongue, she grasped its tip and slowly pulled it upward until the entire length of thorny thread passed. In some recess of a disconnected brain, pain registered. But the pain seemed small and distant, inconsequential. Her consciousness floated in exquisite realms of starry gems and exalted beings radiating love and peace.

Attendants collected blood as it dripped from her tongue, ruby droplets that trickled onto and slowly saturated the bark papers. They lit the papers and shortly a thin column of smoke curled upward. Kan Bahlam's papers were already emitting smoke. The two vision-seekers focused upon their smoke columns that undulated and danced in the torchlight, morphing into serpents whose elaborate jaws gaped wide. From within these jaws would emerge messengers bringing predictions for the coming katun.

K'in Ahau, the second born of the B'aakal Triad, the Watery Sun Jaguar who traversed through the underworld at night, appeared in the jaws of Kan Bahlam's vision serpent. Part of the message dealt with a time of strength and prosperity for Lakam Ha and stability in the B'aakal polity. The other part dealt with death and dynastic succession and was meant for Kan Bahlam alone. In his expanded state he accepted foreknowledge of his own death easily, although later when his human emotions were restored he would feel grief. The exact moment was not revealed, but he was given to understand he must lose no time consolidating his daughter's position for dynastic inheritance. He realized that the hoof-binding ceremony to formally denote her as successor must be done soon. So would it be.

Unen K'awill, third born of the Triad, appeared in the jaws of Yohl Ik'nal's vision serpent. The infant deity of royal blood, protector of succession, brought her the personal message of two children to be born of her union with Hun Pakal. The first, a boy, would succeed to rulership but there would be serious problems. The second, a girl, would also become ruler during troubled times but would use extraordinary tactics to handle these difficulties. Her success would lead to a golden age when Lakam Ha reached the apex of power, prestige and creativity. In the coming katun, the polity would prosper although the seeds of strife and disruption were being sown. At the center of this disruptive nucleus she could see the form of a scorpion, scudding around snapping its claws and thrashing its tail to put stings of poison in the hearts of men.

Thus the katun messages for B'aakal were mixed; there would be peace and prosperity for 20 years while change approached and danger loomed on the distant horizon.

YOHL IK'NAL—IV

BAKTUN 9 KATUN 7 TUN 11 — BAKTUN 9 KATUN 7 TUN 13 (584 CE—586 CE)

1

NOHPAT SQUATTED AT the edge of his cornfield. His weathered brow furrowed more deeply than usual, for he was worried about the corn. Scooping a handful of soil, he lifted it to his nose, rubbing it gently to release earthy aromas. The soil smelled clean with no trace of mustiness. Its texture between his fingers felt normal, rich with nutrients left after flooding by the Michol River crossing the plain below Lakam Ha.

Perplexed, he shook his head and allowed the soil to trickle from his fingers and return to the field. This was a young field, only in its second season of cultivation. Most fields could be worked for five or six annual seasons, and then allowed to lie fallow for an equal time to replenish soil fertility. He had cut channels for irrigation, drawing life-sustaining water from the river. He had planted companion crops with the corn in the usual manner, those plants that corn liked, that created a system of mutual support and nutrition.

In-between randomly spaced corn stalks, squash vines spread their flat leaves and sported bright yellow flowers, some setting small fruits. Several varieties of beans climbed up the stalks, along with vines of the spiny green chayote squash. The entire chayote plant was edible; the oval fruit and its leaves were steamed and the white tuber dug up and eaten in the dry season. Leggy tomato plants spread and twined among their cohorts, and several types of chiles formed on small bushes. Other herbs and wild greens found footholds, their leaves giving the Maya pungent seasonings including oregano, coriander, annatto, and epazote.

To Nohpat's experienced eye, none of the plants seemed as vigorous as last year, although it was the corn that most concerned him. At this point in the growing season, two moons past the heavy rains, the corn ears should be half grown and beginning to show tassels. But those in his field were small, the husks beginning to wither and no tassels peeped from their tips. Even the long leaves of the corn stalk seemed listless, drooping and turning brown at the edges. It was not due to lack of water, he assured himself. Had he not re-cut the channels, providing a dependable water flow? Had he not searched for beetles and fungi that might damage the corn plants?

Rising with a sigh, Nohpat turned from his cornfield and started back along the path leading to his family hut. He glanced at the sun nearing mid-morning, and quickened his pace. When the sun was directly overhead, he and his family would receive an unusual and most auspicious visit. It was both an honor and yet a shame, for it acknowledged the plight of his cornfield. The Ah Kuch Kab, leader of his *kuchte'el* (village) had been sufficiently concerned to request the highest assistance, the intervention of the K'uhul B'aakal Ahau of Lakam Ha.

The villagers living in the low hills and plains at the base of Lakam Ha were organized in four groups of 20 families that formed a kuchte'el. As families grew and young adults started their own families, they often moved to another kuchte'el or began a new one. The Maya did not allow marriage between people having the same surname. They limited each kuchte'el to 20 families so that all would know each other well. Kuchte'el governance was by age-gradated councils each having two representatives from every family. There were councils for children between 7-14 years, youth between 14-28 years, adults between 28-52 years, and elders between 52-104 years. Boys and girls younger than age 7 belonged to the whole community and everyone was responsible for their care and education. Between ages 7-14 both parents had direct responsibility; mothers taught girls and fathers taught boys about their roles. At puberty, rites of transformation were enacted. Girls at age 13 received sexual education by lunar priestesses; boys at age 14 were taught this by solar priests.

Young men usually followed the trade of their fathers, though not invariably. Villages required farmers, builders, hunters, artisans, traders, healers, priests, h'men and shamans. Young women learned from their mothers the skills of preparing food, cooking, weaving, maintaining household animals such as turkeys and dogs, caring for minor illness and tending children. Either sex could become musicians, storytellers and dancers who brought joyful sound and movement to family events and community ceremonies.

The age-specific councils presented the needs of their groups to the community, and reviewed problems within their age group. Usually having to face peers, provide explanations for behaviors, and receive the judgments of the council was enough to correct difficulties. If it was not, another council was formed of representatives from all age groups, because the whole community needed to find solutions together. All were responsible for the joys, pains and problems of their village. Problems that could not be solved on that level required extreme intervention, which might be a High Kuchte'el council of representatives from several villages. At times it might necessitate the illumined wisdom of the High Priest or High Priestess of the ruling city, or even the divine intervention of the Holy Lord, the ruler who was the deity's earthly form, the mediator between the Gods and the people.

Elders were held in high regard by the villagers. At the age of 52, the completion of one full cycle of the Tunben K'ak, the 52-year calendar in which the Tzolk'in and Haab returned to their initial inter-acting positions, a person was considered an elder. Both men and women at this age had the obligation to understand the basic uses of sacred calendars, and recognize how life and village cycles related to the ecosystem of minerals, waters, plants and animals as part of the cosmic order. They could lead village ceremonies and provide wise counsel. Elder men often became Ah K'in, solar priests while elder women became Ix Uc, lunar priestesses.

When elders lived to 104 years, they attained a place of special spiritual significance. At age 104, the completion of two 52-year cycles, they were living symbols of Maya sacred numerology that was conjugated in their bodies. They had completed the entire cycle of life, their time as a human was symbolically finished and they were regarded as almost spirits. It was customary for young people to visit them, to watch their faces and touch their hands. Each wrinkle represented many years lived, and by touching them the young people could touch time and remember cycles of sun and moon. In this way, they pondered the cycles of time.

Nohpat reviewed the council meeting when his cornfield was discussed. No one could think of a reason why his corn plants should be sick. His family had been successful farmers for generations. They followed cultivation practices known as ideal for their soil and climate, rotated crops, left fields fallow, channeled water. They never failed to offer gifts to the Maize God, to Chaak for good water and rain, to Bacabs of the four directions, and nature spirits. Even the village priests and shamans could not see how a deity might have been offended. After much deliberation, the Ah Kuch Kab suggested that a higher level of difficulty was involved. Perhaps the Triad Gods, the patrons of Lakam Ha polity were in some manner displeased. This idea came because of the central role that corn played in Maya cosmology, because it had significance that reached into the very creation myths of the Maya people.

The Maya are people of corn. When the Fourth Creation came to pass, when real people were made and modeled successfully after three prior failures, it was done using corn meal and water to mold their bodies. In the First Creation, the creator Gods Gucumatz—Sovereign Plumed Serpent and Thunderbolt Hurakan—Heart of Heaven decided to make beings that would honor the Gods, call their names correctly and name the days properly. First they made birds and animals, but these could not utter the proper sounds, all they made were howls and screeches. After attempts to teach them failed, their "flesh was brought low" by the creator Gods, who relegated these creatures to be eaten as food.

In the Second Creation, beings were fashioned out of earth and mud. This was unsuccessful, as their bodies were misshapen and crumbled when wet, and their speech was senseless. They were incapable of the worship required by the creator Gods, and so they were destroyed as useless in a great inundation.

In the Third Creation, beings were made of wood. These manikins were more resilient and did not dissolve when wet, but there was nothing in their hearts and nothing in their minds. Although they could speak, their speech was equally useless because they had no memory of their mason and builder, no gratitude for being created. They treated their animals and implements badly, so were destroyed by a flood and also attacked by their animals, plants, utensils, and houses that had been abused. The few survivors were banished to live in treetops and became monkeys.

It was only in the Fourth Creation that the creator Gods were successful. This came to pass by asking help from Grandmother Xmucane—Heart of Earth and Grandfather Xipiyak—Heart of Sky. A sequence of events was set in place pitting the Gods' creations against the Death Lords of the Underworld. The first set of twins, Hun Hunahpu and Wuk Hunahpu, were summoned to play the ball game against the Death Lords, but lost. A second set of twins was born from the severed head of Hun Hunahpu that spit into the hand of Blood Moon, daughter of a Death Lord. Rescued from her father's vengeance, Blood Moon was succored by Grandmother Xmucane, and gave birth to Hun Ahau (Hunahpu) and Yax

Bahlam (Xbalanque). Finding their father's ball game equipment, they played and disturbed the Death Lords who summoned them to games below. But these twins were clever shape-shifters, out-smarted the Death Lords, won the right to life and resurrected their father as Yum K'ax, the Maize God, who brought forth people made from corn. These were Halach Uinik, real people, who could count the days and call the Gods' names properly. Thus came into being the ancestors of the Maya people.

Because corn was the essence of the people's bodies and the vessel of their spirits, the K'uhul B'aakal Ahau was coming to Nohpat's hut so the problem in his cornfield could be resolved.

The palanquin of the K'uhul B'aakal Ahau completed the steep descent beside the Bisik River cascades. Quickening their pace along the well-traveled path through gently rolling foothills, the palanquin bearers adjusted shoulder poles to assure their passengers a level ride. As the terrain became flatter, they passed through groves of cacao and vanilla bean trees, much valued by the ahauob of Lakam Ha. Lush orchards of cultivated avocado, mamey, papaya, ciricote plums, custard apple, nance and guava spread across the broad plains toward the Michol River.

Inside the splendid palanquin, Mat Ek' glanced at the B'aakal ruler who sat straight and alert, observing the groves and orchards carefully. A shadow of concern hovered in the Priestess of Ix Chel's eyes, caught by a quick turn of the ruler's head.

"Be not concerned, Mat Ek' for all is well," the ruler said with a smile.

"Of this my heart is glad, Holy Lady," the healer replied. "Ix Chel grant that all may continue, and you attain full completion of your pregnancy."

Yohl Ik'nal had acceded as K'uhul B'aakal Ahau 291 days after the death of her father Kan Bahlam, who "entered the road" on Baktun 9, Katun 7, Tun 9, Uinal 5, Kin 5 (February 3, 583 CE). The timing of her accession was deliberately planned on the Tzolk'in—Haab calendar combination that would be most auspicious, 9 Lamat, 1 Lahun. Nine was the number of completion and doorway to the next realm, the number of supreme foundation. Lamat was the day of the Venus star, of fertility, successful cultivation, good fortune and deep intuitive penetration. One was the number of unity, beginnings, creative spark. Lahun was the uinal (18-day month) of expertise, skill and remembering.

That day was recorded by glyphs carved on panels in temples of Lakam Ha.

Baktun 9, Katun 7, Tun 10, Uinal 3, Kin 8 on the date 9 Lamat, 1 Lahun (December 23, 583 CE). This recorded when the first woman ruler of B'aakal tied on the white headband and was ceremoniously seated upon the double-headed jaguar throne. Kan Bahlam had prepared his ahauob and commoners well, had cultivated broad-based support among powerful families and kept the priesthood aligned. Yohl Ik'nal had continued to impress the elites with her powerful ritual enactments and uncanny intuition. She was considered a true seer, a visionary who communicated with the deities. There was no doubt that the B'aakal Triad breathed their presences into her form and passed their intentions through her acts.

As grand as her accession was, it was shadowed by an event that happened nearly five solar years before. The priests and priestesses, and the few elites who knew the real circumstances had agreed to conceal them from others. But, as such events among ruling families are known by servants and workers, rumors leaked out. The esoteric calendric significance was understood by only a few, but the gist of the event was not hard to grasp. Yohl Ik'nal's first son was born on an inauspicious date.

Following the calculations of Ah K'inob, the solar priests and the advice of Mat Ek', Priestess of Ix Chel and acclaimed healer, the date for conception was carefully determined. The most auspicious date for birth of the next ruler had been determined, taking into account the needs and circumstances of B'aakal in the coming katuns. Yohl Ik'nal and Hun Pakal followed all prescriptions with impeccable precision to conceive the child. They ensured it would be a boy through certain positions and techniques during coitus, enacted on the date that would result in birth 260 days later.

The conception was successful and all rejoiced as Yohl Ik'nal's pregnancy progressed. She was healthy and vibrant, ate carefully as the Ix Chel priestesses advised, and kept ritual practices daily for calmness. As the pregnancy neared term, Yohl Ik'nal began to have disturbing dreams of turmoil and conflict. She had been advised against undertaking vision rituals while pregnant, to safeguard against opening herself to malicious entities. Although she discussed her dreams with Mat Ek' and the new High Priestess Usin Ch'ob, she could not retrieve sufficient details for accurate interpretation.

Hun Pakal tried to reassure his wife, but her uneasiness persisted. Recollections of an earlier vision quest at the cave of K'ak Lakam Witz drifted through her awareness. On the mountain she had received messages about her children; there would be two and the dynasty would continue through her bloodline, but what of the firstborn? She strained to remember. Faintly the memory returned. The boy was weak and the girl strong with the lineage deity K'awiil beside her. If truly the child she bore was a boy, there was reason for her uneasiness.

Labor began several days before the planned date. The sun was low on the horizon when Yohl Ik'nal summoned her birth attendants. Mat Ek' was already in the birth quarters, having kept continuous vigil beside her charge for the past two moons. The calendar priests were informed and started new calculations. Days began at sunrise and ended just before dawn for the Maya. As labor intensified, the priests produced a new date chart. Should the child be born during the night, the date would still be auspicious. But after dawn, a day of bad auguries began.

Despite the best efforts of Mat Ek' and her Ix Chel healers to encourage labor to progress rapidly, Yohl Ik'nal struggled throughout the night as the child would not descend into the birth canal. Mat Ek' determined that its shoulder was stuck in the pelvic girdle, and attempted to reposition the head properly by abdominal massage. Drenched with sweat and exhausted, Yohl Ik'nal strained with intense contractions hardly giving her moments in between to rest. Reluctantly Mat Ek' administered a drink of milky sap from wild poppies with an opium-like effect, although she knew this relaxation would slow labor. If Yohl Ik'nal did not relax enough between contractions for the child to be turned, her life was in danger.

Dawn broke with dark clouds skittering across the sky, threatening rain. Yohl Ik'nal dozed fitfully, waking to moan through yet another contraction. The High Priestess Usin Ch'ob had joined the birth attendants during the night, chanting in earnest to bring the child forth before dawn. Now changing tactics, she joined with Mat Ek' to invoke the compassion of Ix Chel as Lady Rainbow, patron of harmony between earth and cosmos, to finish the birth despite the undesirable date. Mat Ek' oiled her hands with boiled palm kernel oil, blew a spray of orchid water across Yohl Ik'nal's swollen belly, determined that the relaxing drink was at maximum effect, and pushed one hand through the birth canal between contractions to deftly lift the child's shoulder up. With the other hand on the laboring woman's belly, she repositioned the child so the head settled into correct position.

The boy was born a short time later. He was small but perfectly formed and appeared healthy, crying loudly. The bruise on his left shoulder would resolve in a few days. As Yohl Ik'nal rested and the child was swaddled, plans were set afoot to conceal the actual date of his birth. The Tzolk'in day was 11 Kimi, the number of chaos and imbalance joined with the day of death, finishing, disappearing. The

Haab was 2 Pax, the number of duality-polarity that combined with energies of knocking off course or deviating.

Not an admirable combination of traits for a future ruler. The calendar priests and Kan Bahlam agreed to report that the birth took place in the hour before dawn. All involved were oath-bound to pronounce the prior day as the birth date of Aj Neh Ohl Mat, firstborn son of Yohl Ik'nal and Hun Pakal.

Aj Neh Ohl Mat was now in his fourth solar year, a boy of pleasing countenance and form but shy and fearful. He still ran to hide behind the skirts of his mother or nursemaid when anything new entered his world. Yohl Ik'nal worried that he would not do well when separated from the palace women. Boys began male socialization and study with solar priests when they reached their seventh solar year. As the heir apparent of the royal family, he would face special pressures for bravery and self-assurance, two traits that seemed sadly lacking in his infantile character.

Now she was pregnant with a girl, carefully planned and conceived according to guidance she received from the Triad Gods through visions. The solar priests argued for another boy, as men were wont to do, but she was not swayed by their reasoning. Her relationship with the B'aakal patron deities had deepened through frequent ritual communications, and she took her guidance directly from the Cosmic Realm of the Upperworld. So strong was her surety of this guidance, so evident the deities' presence in her aura that the priests refrained from challenging her decisions. Hun Pakal had an uncanny resonance with his wife and unconditionally supported her.

This girl child was special. Yohl Ik'nal knew that her unborn daughter would be the keeper of the succession, as her visions at K'ak Lakam Witz had revealed so long ago. How and why this must be so, and what would happen with her son, she did not understand. But neither did she question the will of the Deities. It would be so, as it was ordained.

The baby kicked vigorously, summoning her mother back to the present. Yohl Ik'nal patted her belly that showed the distinct contours of pregnancy entering the final trimester. Several more kicks greeted her touch, and Mat Ek' noticed the movements. The women's eyes met in mutual accord that this pregnancy must go well.

"See, she is strong and healthy," Yohl Ik'nal observed.

"We must keep her that way. Was this trip to the village truly necessary?" Mat Ek' wrinkled her brow disapprovingly.

"This is without doubt necessary. Blight upon the corn fields would be disastrous for my people. It is something I cannot turn away from, for such a request is not made except when the village priests and shamans have tried all in their power. Something is happening with this farmer Nohpat that is outside their realm of experience. They are appealing to the highest power, even to the Triad Gods through me. It is my sacred duty as K'uhul B'aakal Ahau to resolve this difficulty."

The conviction in Yohl Ik'nal's voice and her calm certainty silenced Mat Ek'. Glancing surreptitiously, the healer marveled at the mantle of divinity that hovered around the ruler when she spoke of such sacred obligations.

The palanquin bearers turned from the main path and soon the thatched roofs of many huts came into view. The ruler's entourage of three palanquins and about 20 people on foot came to a halt in the village square as the Ah Kuch Kab stood stiffly alert, flanked by his kuchte'el headmen and shamans. The entire village gathered around the edges of the square, their excited murmuring fading as the palanquins were lowered. Yohl Ik'nal's palanquin rested next to the raised platform in the center of the square, the only plaster structure in the village. It was used for the most important announcements and ceremonies, and had been decorated with flowers and incense burners in honor of the royal visit.

The ruler had ordered minimal ceremony, but some was required in due course. The small group of palace musicians began a solemn drum cadence while the shrill bone whistle commanded attention. Court nobles in modest attire, by the ruler's orders, surrounded her palanquin and opened its drapes, assisting the ruler to step out onto the low platform. She moved gracefully, for her pregnancy although obvious was not heavy, and she proceeded to the center of the platform. There she was joined by the High Priest and High Priestess who occupied the other palanquins.

The Ah Kuch Kab and important villagers paid homage to the B'aakal ruler by bowing deeply, clasping left shoulder with right hand in the Maya salute. A short ceremonial welcome speech was given, then the problem with Nohpat's cornfields described and the village leaders' attempts to resolve it enumerated. Although all this was well known to everyone, protocol required a formal public pronouncement to set the parameters of this important occasion.

Yohl Ik'nal listened graciously, nodding to acknowledge each fact. When the villagers had finished, and all eyes were riveted upon her, she said simply: "Bring forth the farmer Nohpat, that he may lead me to his hut and his ailing cornfields."

The crowd of villagers responded simultaneously with a surprised in-breath. From among the crowd Nohpat emerged, head bowed as the Ah Kuch Kab introduced him to his Holy Lady, K'uhul Ixik. He scarcely glanced upward, avoiding her gaze as though it might cause him to burst into flames, and gestured hesitantly in the direction of his hut and fields.

"Lead the way, Nohpat. We will follow you there," she said gently.

Though she would prefer to walk, Yohl Ik'nal knew that both her pregnancy and her status required she ride in the palanquin. The three palanquins, 20 court nobles and most of the villagers slowly followed Nohpat along a narrow path bordered by trees and fields. The distance was not far, and soon his family compound came into view; the thatched living hut made of thin branches with clay fill inbetween, the cooking hut of the same branches with open areas between so heat and smoke could escape, and a smaller clay and wood structure for domestic animals. A couple of small dogs and koatimundis roamed in the open area surrounding the compound. Turkeys gobbled inside their pen. The sun was high in the sky and heat waves shimmered.

Yohl Ik'nal observed the cornfields close to the compound, noting the stunted ears and lethargic leaves. Even the complementary plants seemed to lack vigor. It was as though some vital energy was lacking, and the plants languished. Closing her eyes, she sensed into the plants' interiors, feeling the fluids moving through cell membranes, the leaves capturing sunlight and converting it into energy, the roots twisting through soil taking up water and nutrients. All these systems were working, but not very effectively. The plants seemed to lack motivation, to be low in life force. She did not detect a toxic substance, or an opportunistic organism, or an evil force sent to harm the plants. What was wrong, why were they not flourishing?

Immediately an answer flashed into her mind. She realized that the plants were unhappy.

Acknowledging this communication, she probed further into the plants' essences for why they were unhappy. She reached an understanding, from profound unity with the plants, that their care-taking family was unhappy, and this feeling permeated the plants that depended upon the family. It was a deep-seated and problematic unhappiness, not readily solved, and persistent for some time to have such severe effects.

Mentally thanking the plants, Yohl Ik'nal redirected her attention to the people around her as she descended from the palanquin in front of Nohpat's living hut. Two women and a young man emerged from the hut and stood wide-eyed before the noble entourage. The village leader explained these were Nohpat's wife, daughter and son. His son helped him in the fields, and his wife and daughter maintained the household. It was a typical farming family, from a long tradition of successful farmers.

The daughter was soon to be married; by custom the son-in-law would live with Nohpat's family for a year and work the fields. After that, they would move and add their hut to the son-in-law's family compound.

The son of Nohpat was young, strong and capable of carrying on the farming traditions. He was not yet seeking a wife.

Yohl Ik'nal focused her intuitive senses upon each family member, seeking a source of unhappiness. It came to her immediately and strongly. She sensed hopeless discontent in the son, heart-rending sorrow in the mother, confused irritation in the daughter, and simmering anger in the father, Nohpat. An unhappy family indeed. A family that did not understand the source of the problems, felt unable to cope with the issues, and saw no solutions. The son appeared to be the key in this conflicted family.

Yohl Ik'nal asked the names of the family members, and was told that Halil was the wife, Tz'un the daughter, and Uxul the son. She began in friendly conversation with Halil, asking about her tasks and how she spent the day. The worried-looking woman began hesitantly but soon warmed to the subject, basking in the Holy Lady's interest. After a while, the ruler asked Tz'un about her upcoming marriage and her hopes for a family of her own. The young woman was eagerly anticipating the creation of her own family; she seemed relieved to talk about a pleasant future. When the ruler addressed Uxul, the atmosphere had relaxed somewhat. He began by describing his work in the fields, but without enthusiasm. Yohl Ik'nal asked if he enjoyed doing any other activities. A spark lit his eyes, but he hesitated and glanced toward his mother. She nodded almost imperceptibly.

"To carve wood and stones, this is something I enjoy," the young man said.

"Carving is a fine skill and a talent not possessed by many. Have you carved for very long?"

"For as long as I can remember, Holy Lady."

"He began almost before he could walk," his mother added. "His fingers knew how to use the flint knife sooner than he could speak many words."

From the side, Nohpat grumbled, "He wastes many hours making useless decorations. Better he should make traps or spearheads for hunting."

Tension immediately surged in the family and the spark in Uxul's eyes dimmed. Halil's face took on an expression of profound sadness. Tz'un looked off into the distance as if she wished she were far away.

"Have you here some of your carvings?" asked Yohl Ik'nal.

"Yes, Holy Lady," Uxul answered, avoiding his father's sullen gaze.

"Then bring them forth. I would see your work."

Uxul disappeared behind the hut and soon returned with several pieces of carved wood and a few small stone figures. He carefully laid them before his ruler. One of the court nobles lifted the pieces for Yohl Ik'nal to examine. She turned the carvings between her hands and traced the graceful curves with her fingers. Here was the work of an untrained master, exquisite in proportion and detail. Jaguars, quetzal birds, turtles, bats, peccary, snakes, crocodiles, hawks nearly leaped from wood squares with intricate borders of vines and flowers. Faces of men and women in profile graced squares bordered by geometric patterns. Figures of Gods and Goddesses in full regalia and classic postures enlivened smooth rock. The young man had obviously visited frescoes and tablets in Lakam Ha, and made drawings from which to produce such exact reproductions. Perhaps he had also seen codices, though how he managed that was a mystery.

"Uxul, you have been called by the Gods to be a carver," Yohl Ik'nal said in measured voice that carried across the compound. "Rarely have I seen such perfection even among carvers long trained in major centers. This is indeed a rare and special gift. Your work in this life must be that of carving the glyphs and painting the frescoes of Lakam Ha. Is such a work in your heart?"

The young man was dumbfounded. His most secret yearning, his impossible dream had just been clearly stated by the B'aakal K'uhul Ahau, the earthly presence of the B'aakal Triad Gods, as though it was simply evident. He stared in dismay, unable to respond and acutely aware of his father's disapproval.

The tension in the air was palpable, a suspended screeching silence.

"You may answer without fear, Uxul. Is it in your heart and your dreams to be a carver in Lakam Ha?"

He swallowed, trying to moisten his throat. Words would not form on his lips, so he simply nodded. His eyes were wild with hope long suppressed but clouded by bewilderment.

"You shall return with me to Lakam Ha, and begin training with the master carvers in the palace. You will learn to read and carve the glyphs that immortalize the events of our city in the sacred calendars of the cosmos. The Gods will be pleased by the fine works you will create to honor them."

Yohl Ik'nal looked around at the gathered crowd that was too awed to make a sound. Such a thing had never happened in their village.

"Halil, woman of this home, do you release your son to become a royal carver?"

Shock and amazement marked Halil's face, and tears of relief streamed down her cheeks. For years she had understood her son's artist soul, and watched his skill blossom, but felt helpless to support his talent. She knew his spirit was dying and she could do nothing to change the situation. Now all had changed, in an instant, like the sudden thunderbolt of a goddess. Despite the consequences for herself, she responded quickly.

"Yes, Holy Lady, it is my joy to release my son for your carving works," Halil said.

Yohl Ik'nal turned to Nohpat who appeared struck by lightning. He was stiff with shock, disbelieving what he had just observed.

"Nohpat, man of this home, do you release your son to become a royal carver?"

His body shook and his mouth worked as he sought a response.

"He is my only son," Nohpat sputtered. "I am not a young man; I need his help in the fields. What am I to do if he is not here to help?"

"For a year you will have your son-in-law," Yohl Ik'nal responded. "After that, the Ah Kuch Kab of the village will provide a young man, perhaps the second or third son of another farmer, who will be glad to work good fields for himself and his family."

She turned to the village leader, her eyes commanding his reply.

"Yes, Holy Lady, this man of course we can find, there are many farming families with sons in our village," he replied breathlessly.

"People of the village, hear this. Family of Nohpat, hear this."

Yohl Ik'nal seemed to become taller and more powerful, her aura sparkled in the noon sun and some would swear later they saw Unen K'awiil, the serpent-footed deity of royal lineage, hovering above her shoulders.

"The corn of Nohpat is sick because the plants are unhappy, they cannot thrive. The plants are unhappy because the family of Nohpat is unhappy, they are not thriving. Uxul has been called by the Gods from an early age to be an artist, a carver of wood and stone. He yearned for this and learned to carve without formal instruction. His works are masterful. But he could not fully express this calling, this god-given talent, because of family duty and tradition. This is killing his spirit, making him sick and making the family sick. His mother Halil knows this, has known this for years, but felt helpless to do anything. His father Nohpat knows his son is unhappy, but does not understand his son's soul and calling. Nothing in Nohpat's life could help him understand this; it is not a failing or a fault. The sister Tz'un also suffers from the family conflicts and hopes to escape by marriage. This is not good for a family. The family has become very unhappy, and their crops have suffered because plants are sensitive, they can feel the emotions of their caretakers. The cornfields of Nohpat will only recover and thrive when the family restores its happiness and harmony."

She turned again to Nohpat and willed his eyes to meet hers. Unable to resist, he looked upward into dark pools of mystery beyond his comprehension.

"Nohpat, you are asked to make a great sacrifice for the good of your family and the health of your cornfields. You are asked to release your son to a calling that takes him away from you. His work in your fields will be replaced, but it is not the same as having your own son follow in your steps. This I understand. You will see him but not as often. His life will change and he will be different, he will experience things you do not understand. It is a great sacrifice, and I call upon you as your K'uhul Ixik to make it bravely."

Moments passed while Nohpat was allowed to let the significance of what was transpiring sink in. Yohl Ik'nal kept his gaze locked with hers, using psychic forces to bring his mind into acceptance. It was a critical moment.

Ultimately the farmer had no choice but to comply. His sacred ruler, incarnation of the Gods, commanded his agreement. But in truth he was swept up in powerful forces that made all this seem the natural progression of things, as extraordinary as it might be.

"Yes, Holy Lady, I release my son to your service." Nohpat spoke more distinctly than anyone expected.

2

The baby gurgled, pursing pink lips to blow cascades of bubbles over the strong brown hands tenuously supporting its head. Gnawing a tiny fist, it belched and then began hiccupping. The baby's father drew his brows together in an expression of grave concern.

"Is he sick? What is he doing?"

"He has hiccups; it is common in new babies. Lift him over your shoulder and pat his back."

The father awkwardly raised the baby and flopped him against a burly shoulder. This added loud wails to the hiccups.

"Why is he crying? Did I hurt him?"

"No, but you must move him more gently," laughed his wife.

"Here, you take him. I fear hurting him, he is so small."

She crossed the chamber and received the squirming, wailing bundle offered eagerly by her husband. A few moments of cooing and backstroking returned the baby to gurgling and fist chewing.

"Perhaps he is hungry, you should feed him," her husband suggested hopefully.

"Ummm . . . There are people I must meet, aaaah, to discuss matters with."

"Of that I have no doubt." She smiled to think of this brave warrior afraid of his own infant son. Best to let him escape his discomfort with an excuse. "It is perhaps time for feeding; do send in my attendant on your way out."

The relief flooding his face was comical. He bent and nuzzled her cheek, patted the baby's dark fuzzy head and quickly departed.

Ek Chuuah strode purposefully out his household compound, heading nowhere in particular. Instead of taking the wide plaster walkway toward the central plaza of Usihwitz, he turned onto a smaller path covered with crushed limestone that led to the river. Today he wanted to think, or more accurately, to scheme; something his mind was naturally inclined to do. Walking the path along the river provided more solitude.

Life in Usihwitz had treated him well. The warriors were first to befriend him, having admired his prowess during the flower war. Soon the Nakom—War Chief was consulting him about tactics and advice for trainings. The Ix Chel priestesses attended his wound and helped it heal without infection. The family who housed him considered it an honor and appeared somewhat in awe due to his reputation and bloodlines. As an elite ahau, he was asked to join the Popol Nah and sit in council with the city's leaders. There he drew upon experience with the larger, more complex political structure at Lakam Ha and impressed Usihwitz's ruler Joy Bahlam.

Glancing back over his shoulder, he noted the few tall temples of Usihwitz that rose above the forest canopy. It was true that this adopted city was smaller and less grand than his home. Continuing skirmishes with its domineering neighbor city Pa'chan, situated in a loop of the K'umaxha River, had weakened the Usihwitz dynasty. Pa'chan had put in place puppet rulers on occasion, most likely the underlying reason why Usihwitz sought alliance with Lakam Ha. As the circles of influence and alliance took shape, Pa'chan was drawn into the polity of

Ka'an while Usihwitz gravitated toward the polity of B'aakal. The Kan leaders, however, appeared to have designs upon Usihwitz to judge from recent visits by trading delegations. Joy Bahlam remained firmly neutral to overtures, keeping his commitment to B'aakal.

But that was something Ek Chuuah meant to change. The birth of his son, his first child, set off a storm of scheming about his future in Usihwitz. His lovely wife was the eldest daughter of ruler Joy Bahlam, and winning her hand was a fine accomplishment. This pleased him greatly. It showed how high his status had become in the city of his banishment. When the year of service was complete after his hair grew out from the flower war, his decision was unequivocal. He chose to remain in Usihwitz. Rage against Lakam Ha ruler Kan Bahlam made returning to his home impossible.

For he was certain that his wounding at the flower war was not an accident. There was something in the clever way that his opponent conveniently missed his target and slashed deeply to create a serious wound. The process seemed choreographed, even to Kan Bahlam's refusal to challenge the referee's call. An unfortunate accident, indeed. With an advantageous outcome that allowed Kan Bahlam to exile an opponent. Fury exploded at the injustice, at the blatant violation of sacred rules given by the Gods for conduct of these mock warfare games.

An uneven pocket in the path twisted his right leg and he winced in pain. The cut that almost severed his right hamstrings was well healed but still remained painful when stressed. Probably he would always walk with a slight limp. He seethed while rubbing the scar; it would prevent him from ever fighting as effectively as before. He often saw the Usihwitz warrior who wounded him, evidently in collusion with Kan Bahlam, but was wise enough never to confront the older man. Soon enough the old warrior would join the spirits, and the order of power would change in Usihwitz.

That thought brought Ek Chuuah back to his current scheming. Joy Bahlam was in declining health and had designated his only son as successor. The young man lacked charisma and leadership, his following was tenuous, and Usihwitz had a history of dynastic changes. It was the perfect set-up for bringing a new bloodline into rulership—his own. Married to the ruler's eldest daughter who had given him a son, well respected among warriors, accepted into a leadership role in the Council, more experienced in politics than most, he was the perfect choice as the next ruler.

To consolidate his position, he would spearhead a raid on Lakam Ha. Once Joy Bahlam joined the ancestors, convincing his weak-minded son would be an easy task. From conversations with Kan visitors, including a few warriors, he knew that support could be gleaned from the distant polity. The Kan ruler in Dzibanche had ambitions for expansion, and Lakam Ha was in his sights.

The path reached the river, also called Usihwitz because it passed close to the city. It was a tributary of the mighty K'umaxha River, major transportation artery giving access to the Chakamax River running just south of Lakam Ha. He stood on the bank, watching the current form swirls around posts placed for tying canoes. Around the next curve was the main docking area for the city, with a wide plaster walkway leading to the plaza. The rushing water masked men's voices in the distance. Breathing deeply of moist and pungent air, he concluded that his plan would work. The rivers were the access, and the foils. It might take a few years, but he could almost taste the sweetness of victory, and the satisfaction of revenge.

3

Sak K'uk sat at the edge of a small pool formed by an aqueduct that diverted flow from the Bisik River into the royal residences. Near the courtyard edge, a narrow rivulet broke off and burbled gently over its shallow rocky bottom. The courtyard off the children's chambers bordered the pool and the child frequently splashed in its cool waters. The dark haired girl, just over two solar years in age, was busily weaving twigs and leaves into fanciful shapes. Once satisfied with her creations, she set them in a semicircle between her and the building. Standing, she drew her tiny body as tall as possible and tilted up her chin, gesturing imperially and babbling rapidly at the twig figures. A mixture of simple Maya words and nonsense syllables, her speech continued for several minutes. From time to time she rose on her toes, gesturing forcefully to make a point.

Her speech finished with several loud exclamations, as she shook her finger at the twig figures. Dropping to her knees, she swept the figures into the pool and watched as the current carried them slowly into the stream.

"What are you doing, Sak K'uk?" Her mother, Yohl Ik'nal, had been watching from a shaded area of the courtyard.

"Bad men," the girl replied, pointing at the disappearing twig figures. "Not do, very bad, they go."

She gestured again toward the figures in a dismissing command, tossed her head and shot a winning smile at her mother as she pirouetted prettily over the courtyard.

Yohl Ik'nal clapped her hands in appreciation of the girl's dance and laughed. Her daughter never failed to amaze her. The girl's birth had been as easy as her older brother's was difficult, and their characters could not be more different. Sak K'uk was confident, assertive and self-assured beyond anything reasonable for such a small child. She seemed fearless, would explore any crevice and climb any branch, and frequently wandered off alone if not carefully watched. Her attendants and nursemaid were already cowed by her commanding manner and seldom crossed her desires. It made discipline nearly impossible. The mother learned early that coaxing worked better than ordering and had several creative techniques to lure the girl into cooperation.

Already her brother, although six years her senior, was intimidated by her strong personality and did her bidding. Yohl Ik'nal worried that her son Aj Ne Ohl Mat might never develop the character of a leader, and his little sister was not helping. That she was a born leader left little doubt.

The sound of footsteps approaching the courtyard interrupted Yohl Ik'nal's musings. She smiled as her husband Hun Pakal entered with two companions, trusted advisors from the royal court. She was expecting them, anticipating their report of a recent surveillance trip around the B'aakal polity. Gesturing that the men be seated on nearby mats, she called for Sak K'uk's nursemaid.

The girl tumbled into her mother's lap as the nursemaid approached. The determination of the little body to stay put was communicated immediately to Yohl Ik'nal. She sighed and waved the nursemaid to remain nearby, but did not try to dislodge the girl. It would only be asking for a scene; one she did not want exposed before the men. Stroking the girl's hair, she bent her head close to her daughter's ear.

"You may stay if you remain quiet," she whispered. "I must speak of important things with your father and our friends. Will you be good?"

"Yes, mother," Sak K'uk whispered back with a colluding smile.

"It is good to have you back, and to be with you all again," Yohl Ik'nal said warmly to the men. She reached to touch Hun Pakal's hand and their eyes met in fond acknowledgement. His fingers entwined briefly with hers, and then he became businesslike.

"This we have seen, the general mood of the cities of B'aakal, is one of calmness and content," reported Tilkach. The middle-aged noble was among her most trusted court advisors, a man whose large hatchet nose and severe mouth belied his good-humored character.

"It is thus, the year's crops have been bountiful, festivals were provided for the people by their Sahals and Ah Kuch Kabs, and calendar ceremonies performed as ordained by village Ah K'inob," added Itzam Ik, a young pleasant-featured man whose acumen in building trust among village leaders made him an indispensable asset. He was included in the inner circle of court advisors.

"When people's bellies are full, their work close to home, and their homage to the Triad deities enacted correctly by those entrusted to assure continued good fortune, then comes a time of satisfaction. The people and the city ahauob are less inclined to follow those who agitate for something different," commented Hun Pakal.

Yohl Ik'nal nodded in acknowledgement, and then posed a query.

"In regard to the city of Usihwitz and of Ek Chuuah, what have you found?" she asked.

Fourteen solar years had passed since the flower war in which Ek Chuuah had been injured and required to give service to his victor's city, Usihwitz. Although he could have returned to Lakam Ha after his hair re-grew, the embittered warrior had stayed. There was little doubt that he held deep grudges against the family of Kan Bahlam, and would seek to avenge this dishonor in some way.

"Ek Chuuah has insinuated himself into favor with Joy Bahlam, ruler of Usihwitz," Tilkach responded. "After recovering from his wound, he befriended the young warriors and taught them new strategies, for he is a clever combatant. He believes his wounding in the flower war was deliberate, and thus his anger simmers. Gaining respect as a tireless worker and fearless warrior, after a few years he was so favored by the ruler that his marriage to a royal daughter was approved. Now he has a son and his position among the leadership in the Popol Nah is assured."

"Joy Bahlam was my father's good friend," mused Yohl Ik'nal. "Strange are the ways of rulers to become fickle. Surely he must not trust Ek Chuuah, knowing the basis for his service and understanding the dark motives propelling this warrior. To give him such favor seems ill-advised."

"Holy Lady, the esteemed ruler Joy Bahlam is an old man. His hand upon the city is no longer strong. To protect his heir, to keep the rulership in his succession, he needs every alliance among the ahauob he can cultivate. There continues an undercurrent of dissidence among younger ahauob, slyly fed by the devious plans of Ek Chuuah. Although none said it openly, I suspect continued contact with Kan," observed Itzam Ik.

"We will not see Ek Chuuah back here in peace," observed Hun Pakal darkly.

"Were observed by you any hints, any signs of plotting against Lakam Ha?" asked Yohl Ik'nal.

"Much did I speak with merchants, warriors, courtiers and carvers but gained no specific information about such plotting," added Itzam Ik. "There was a trading group in the past two years from Kan, but none knew of a continuing relationship or of excursions from Usihwitz to the Ka'an polity. It seems that the Great Snake of Ka'an is busily occupied with its campaigns to the south. When Uneh Chan became Kan ruler, that was seven years ago, he directed incursions beyond Mutul. Much is our sadness that the polity of the Jaguar lineage is so humbled and dispossessed. These incursions were carried to Uxwitza, where Uneh Chan assumed a supervising position in ceremonies done by Yujaw Te'Kinich, ruler of Uxwitza. It is spoken of much in Usihwitz, this bragging by the Kan dynasty of its exploits in the south."

"Spoken of with admiration, especially among the circle headed by Ek Chuuah," observed Tilkach.

"But nothing is said of more solid actions," Hun Pakal added.

"Then will we wait and watch events at Usihwitz," said Yohl Ik'nal. "Now I would know of our other cities, of Popo' and Yokib, of Sak Tz'i and the smaller villages around them."

The men described at length details of their observations in these cities of B'aakal. In Popo' the rulership had passed seven years ago from Zotz Choj to his son Chak B'olon Chaak. This transition went smoothly and the young ruler appeared well favored by his people. Shortly after his accession, an upsurge in artistic expression and new water works occurred. In Yokib, the venerable ruler Cauac Ahk continued his long, stable reign with widespread support. He had weathered foreign influences early in his tenure, absorbing into local expression both the agents and cultural icons of the distant superpower Teotihuacan whose influence was felt throughout the Maya lands. Succession was in place with his heir formally acknowledged. Even in the small city of Sak Tz'i, the tenor of contentment and abundance pervaded.

Yohl Ik'nal stroked Sak K'uk's hair as she listened intently, noting nuances in the scouts' voices that might indicate something needing further attention. The girl nestled comfortably and kept silent, her intelligent eyes appearing to shine with understanding as she nodded now and then. Hun Pakal smiled inwardly at his precocious daughter, and wondered what her little mind comprehended. Perhaps he would find it surprising.

Attendants brought refreshing fruit juices while the ruler and her closest advisors discussed the types and amounts of tribute expected in this period of prolific crops. After both the first and second harvests, ahauob and prosperous villagers would bring offerings to the Lakam Ha court consisting of fruits, vegetables and nuts, pottery and fabrics, jewelry and body adornments. Farmers brought a portion of their dried maize. It was this tribute that sustained the royal court and nourished the workers who carried out the building projects that communicated in grand scale the greatness of the ruling dynasty and its May Ku city.

As the courtiers rose to take their leave, Sak K'uk catapulted herself into her surprised father's arms. The strategy session came to an inglorious end as father and daughter tumbled on the ground, laughing hysterically.

Later that day, as the sun dropped toward the horizon and ignited the underbellies of streaky clouds with golden shafts, Yohl Ik'nal and Hun Pakal strolled along the western plaza edge overlooking the vast plains below. From this huge, nearly empty plaza close to the royal residence complex, the mountainside dropped precipitously into craggy foothills where stunted trees struggled for a foothold. The Bisik River plunged rapidly down, breaking into cascades far below. The river and steep hillsides kept this far western part of Lakam Ha isolated from numerous complexes nearby, perched on terraces between three rivers; the Bisik, Tun Pitz, and Ixha.

Sunrays deepened and trees cast long shadows across smooth plaster plazas. The temple situated halfway between the Bisik and Tun Pitz rivers blazed into color. Later called Templo Olvidado by archeologists, it rose above a base of four platforms spanned by a wide staircase. The north-facing front had three doors of equal size, with square stone roof and tall roofcomb. The red-orange paint gleamed in the setting sunlight.

Turning her back to the plains, Yohl Ik'nal gazed at the glowing temple. It was recently built as her father Kan Bahlam's funerary monument. To her eyes, it was not finished.

"It is time to build," she murmured without shifting her gaze.

Hun Pakal turned to face the temple.

"What is it that you think to build?"

"My father's temple requires adornment and monuments. There must be frescoes on the roof and carved panels beside the doors. The roofcomb must bear figures, shapes to remind all who look that Kan Bahlam was the bodily form of the Triad Deities, and is now an ancestor who brings wisdom and guidance to his people."

Hun Pakal nodded. The art of carving stone into fine shapes and glyphs was advancing under the ruler's patronage of outstanding carvers, not the least being young Uxul whom she had brought from his village. The large terrace upon which the temple sat seemed to call for other structures to complement and extend its grandeur. His eyes swept farther east and north across the long ridge upon which Lakam Ha was based. Beyond the Ixha River there was little construction. Ridge upon sub-ridge undulated in an ocean of green.

"Much land remains upon which Lakam Ha can expand," he observed.

"So it is, the city will expand to cover the entire range of ridges." In the waning light a vision swept before her gaze; a magnificent city in red-orange and white with countless temples on mountain summits, a unique palace on an immense plaza, ceremonial and residential complexes draping the hilly terrain and cascading down the far eastern slope.

Glancing at her transfixed expression, Hun Pakal almost imagined what she saw.

"May the Gods will it," he said.

"They do."

4

The royal court of B'aakal gathered in an administrative complex across the Bisik River from the royal residences. A raised pathway spanned the narrow part of the river not far from where it emerged from the mountain as a burbling spring. Water management with aqueducts, squared bridges, walled pools, drains and conduits traveling under buildings were important features of Lakam Ha. These water features channeled the rivers through residential complexes for easy water access. A technique of gradually narrowing the stone conduits created water pressure. In some places the conduits had vertical channels forcing water to surge upward as fountains, or flow into vats serving as water reservoirs for elite homes. Household water structures also provided for waste removal, the equivalent of small stone toilets.

The royal court building, the K'uhul Ahau Nah (House of the Holy Lord), was a long low structure with five doors. The central door was largest, giving visual access from the plaza into the throne room. Interior doors on either side of the throne room opened to smaller antechambers with exterior doors. The final two exterior doors opened into lateral waiting rooms with no interior doors. Here stone benches lined the walls where visitors waited to progress to the antechambers.

No furniture occupied the antechambers; visitors would stand, squat or sit on floor mats waiting to approach the ruler. The throne was a wide platform elevated to waist level; the double-headed jaguar throne with pedestal legs ending in paws and a Witz monster mask on the front panel. Luxurious woven blankets and a jaguar pelt covered reed mats. Glyphs painted on the wall behind the throne declared the pre-eminence of the B'aakal Triad Deities. A pedestal beside the throne held an open-brimmed wicker basket with chevron and beehive designs; it served to receive offerings. At the opposite edge of the throne was the scribe's square table made of firm, tightly woven wicker. When the scribe sat with crossed legs, the table was at knee level for ease of writing.

The Court throne room was quite different than the Popol Nah, where the ruler sat in council with ahauob and city leaders. The Popol Nah throne was smaller and less ornate, flanked by wall benches slightly below throne level. The K'uhul Ahau Nah throne was not only more impressive but it stood alone in the room. As visitors approached the ruler seated on this throne, they sat or knelt on floor mats, scooting forward to take their turn making offerings and speaking with the ruler. The architecture and spatial arrangement of the rooms powerfully conveyed the ruler-subject, higher-lower dynamics. Visitors became supplicants, acknowledging the divine elevation of the ruler and their dependent status upon his or her intercession with deities and natural forces.

The K'uhul Ahau Nah was the place of formalities, of courtly discourse. The refined art of the courtier in bodily attire and habitus, in ritualized behaviors and conventions of speech, and in the all-important procedures of giving tribute created an ambiance in the court that was particular to Maya high culture.

The main plaza of Lakam Ha buzzed with activity on mornings when the royal court was in session. Ahauob, city leaders and prominent commoners such as merchants and traders congregated in the plaza. As they waited, the hum of conversation mingled with flutes, drums and rattles of musicians. Servants stood beside their masters, holding baskets full of tribute. Many noble women were present, attired in richly woven huipils and fantastic feather headdresses.

On this clear, sunny morning an air of excitement mingled with steam evaporating as the stoned warmed. The sahals of Popo', Yokib, Usihwitz and Sak Tz'i were present, bringing their first harvest tribute, along with the Ah Kuch Kabs of numerous smaller villages. The taking of tribute was a public ceremony, and commoners of Lakam Ha crowded around the plaza edges, waiting an opportunity to glimpse their K'uhul Ahau seated on the throne. They gloried in this social affirmation.

The stately cadence of royal drummers announced the ruler's procession. Silence fell upon the crowd as standard-bearers entered the plaza, followed by the royal guard in full warrior regalia. Scribes and artists were next, then the priests and priestesses. A long sigh escaped hundreds of lips as the ruler appeared, regal in her magnificent costume. Her impossibly tall headdress of woven bands, feathers and ceramic effigies was removed after she took the throne, replaced by a simpler though still ornate headdress of rulership. Behind her came members of the royal family and household.

Among this group was Mas Batz, a dwarf no taller than waist level, with thick stubby arms and legs, a lugubrious rolling gait and massive head that seemed neck less. His features were a parody of Maya ideals, with round bulging eyes, wide pug nose and puckered lips over a receding chin. To compound these oddities, he had a small hunchback on the right side. It was the custom of Maya rulers to keep dwarfs in their courts, or unusual attendants such as eunuchs, foreigners and criminals. These often were from lower classes, recruited to courtly service to enhance the power and authority of the ruler in several ways. Because of the contrast between deformed people and noble elegance, their presence marked the court as liminal space that transcends and detaches from ordinary society. This symbolized the ruler's duality as both the center of society yet outside of it, representing both societal union and distant divine Otherworlds. Dwarfs were believed to freely access the Underworld and mediate death transitions. They were often assigned to lay out corpses and burial goods, going through tomb doors too small for normal-sized people. Maya art depicted dwarfs accompanying the maize god; the dwarf personified the stunted second ear common to maize plants while the god expressed the full ripened ear.

Such confidants, who posed no threat to the ruler's power and succession, were permitted a level of honesty not possible with potentially competing nobles. These court attendants could express views not colored by future family ambitions, fear of property loss or status dispossession. Such exotic and unsettling attendants wrapped a veil of mystery around royal court activities, adding to its liminal quality as a zone between realities.

Thus the court, with its contrast between esthetics of high culture and deformed, marginal attendants, was exotic and foreign to the rest of society.

Yohl Ik'nal sat cross-legged on the wide throne with the scribe to her left. As he set up his bark-paper book, brushes and pots with paint, her attendants changed the headdresses and placed cushions at her back. Behind the scribe stood the royal guard, arms crossed on their chests. Jars with fruit juices were set beside the throne. A serving woman crouched beside them, holding exquisitely painted ceramic cups. Members of the royal retinue found places in the adjoining room to the left, sitting on mats or standing for better views. Mas Batz the dwarf sat conspicuously in front of the throne, glaring at any who approached.

The Ah Pop K'am Nah, Keeper of the Reception House Mat, took his position at the right interior door to allow visitors entrance into the throne room in order of importance. Buluc Max was an imposing figure, broad-shouldered and muscular with a barrel chest. In his pivotal role of dispensing privilege through the sequence of access to the ruler, his stern face and piercing eyes commanded obedience. Most striking was his voice, deep and sonorous, resonating through the open court building and across the plaza. As a royal steward he collected tribute and managed positioning of ahauob according to the ruler's wishes.

High-ranking ahauob, sahals and city leaders crammed into the antechamber. They jockeyed for position to catch the steward's eye and receive the honor of being among the first group admitted. With a subtle finger flick, Yohl Ik'nal signaled the steward to admit the first chosen. In his sonorous voice he called forth by name the sahals of Popo', Yokib, Usihwitz and Sak Tz'i, along with the ruler's closest courtiers and the most prominent merchants and village headmen. In all, ten men entered the throne room, sitting in two parallel lines according to order called. Each carried symbolic tribute, cradled in their laps until ready for offering. Later attendants would carry the complete tribute, consisting of multiple large bundles and baskets, to the tribute hall for tallying.

Again the Ah Pop K'am Nah's deep voice carried through the antechambers and into the plaza below now filled with lesser nobles and commoners craning necks for a better view of the throne room.

"The K'uhul Ahau of B'aakal would first speak. Listen well, oh people of B'aakal, to the words of your ruler. Now all hear the K'uhul Ahau!"

Yohl Ik'nal turned her body slightly to face the plaza, lengthening spine and extending neck to full seated height. Red, yellow and blue feathers swayed from her headdress; copper and jade jewelry caught and reflected sunlight. Her voice was clear and melodic, carrying easily across the plaza.

"It is time to build.
It is time to create.
To expand the beauty of Lakam Ha.
Beneath the Lords of the Night Sky,
before the Lords of the Waters.
Measuring, squaring in the sacred shapes,
modeling, forming in the sacred proportions.
The fourfold siding, fourfold cornering, measuring, staking,
halving the cord, stretching the cord in the sky, on the earth,
the four sides, four corners, as it is said, by the Maker, Modeler,
mother and Father of life, of humankind.
Giver of Breath, Giver of Heart, who gave birth to the Triad Deities,
to those begotten and born of the light,
ancestors of B'aakal, begetters of the k'uhul ahauob,
Knowers of everything in the sky-earth, river-sea.
Thus do they speak:
It is time to build, time to create,
temple mountains reaching the sky,
temple caves plunging into the underworld,
vast plazas shining in the Light of Ahau K'in, Lord Sun.
Places to speak their names, count their days, praise their work and design.
So it is said, so it is done."

The way one spoke was as important as the words one said. The words themselves were infused with *itz*, life force energy, the essence of divinity, the sacred current that permeated—that was—all things. To honor this sacred life force, words were arranged in a way that was beautiful, that graced the ears of listeners, mortal and divine. The cadences and rhythms of these orations created a poetic language unique to Classic Maya courtly expression.

Yohl Ik'nal had spoken well, and murmurs of approval rippled through the plaza. The commoners were delighted; more glorious temples and buildings, more spectacles to initiate them, more feasts and drinking to celebrate their completion. The ahauob and sahals and merchants and traders made quick calculations of how much could they profit weighed against how much they would be required to contribute in labor and building materials. For a large group of laborers living in modest thatched huts clustered between the Tun Pitz and Ixha rivers, it meant increased hard work mitigated by substantial food and gifts. Builders, water-workers and carvers fairly leapt with joy over the untold opportunities to express their crafts.

Mas Batz stood, bowed deeply clasping one shoulder, and danced a jig in place while hand signing his approval. The faintest trace of a smile curled the ruler's lips as her eyes slid toward the dwarf, without moving her head the least. In the fleeting moment of their eye contact, his communicated "good decision." Both knew, though it had not been spoken between them, that this building program was the perfect scenario for a powerful katun end ceremony when the current 20-year cycle completed on Baktun 9, Katun 8, Tun 0, Uinal 0, Kin 0 (593 CE). Seven solar years remained to accomplish the ambitious planning and construction that she envisioned.

Settling into protocol position for receiving offerings, Yohl Ik'nal twisted her body to the right side and placed her right elbow on right hip, hand extended with palm upward.

The first ahauob in line was Cauac Ahk, Sahal of Yokib. Now an elderly man, he stood straight and moved with agility. His wrinkled skin and sunken features could not detract from the vital energy that still permeated his form. Here was a ruler very much in charge, who had outlived his two older children. His youngest son would succeed as a middle-aged man, unless the ruler lived amazingly longer and the rulership passed to a grandson.

When Buluc Max signaled to begin the tribute offering, Cauac Ahk scooted forward nimbly and extended a large reed basket filled with yellow and white pom. This was his symbolic offering of copal resin, highly valued for incense. It demonstrated the value of his tribute, which he would report as soon as the ruler asked for it.

"Honored Lord of Yokib, we are graced by your visit," Yohl Ik'nal said solemnly. "What tribute have you brought for the K'uhul Ahau, for the Sacred City of Lakam Ha?"

"Holy Lady, the city of Yokib offers ten measures of dried corn, 8 measures dried beans, 6 bolts of cotton cloth, 20 baskets of tubers, squash, and nuts. We provide in addition 3 baskets dried fruit, 3 baskets palm nuts, 3 baskets tobacco, 3 baskets of gourd cups and 3 baskets cacao pods. Fine jewelry from the hands of leading Yokib artisans is wrapped in soft white cloth to adorn the royal family and ahauob. May these gifts receive approval of the Triad Deities and please you, Holy Lady."

"Thus is the Holy Lady pleased, Honored Lord of Yokib. In the person of the Triad Deities, she who is their earthly personification receives and approves these offerings." The ruler replied using court protocol. The scribe behind her carefully recorded each offering, type and amount.

Following the formal tribute dialogue, after the symbolic offering was placed in the basket, came opportunity for additional interaction. This highly public and closely observed process was meant for displays of power and status. Rulers could bestow favor or disapproval, embarrass or intimidate, put the visitor on the spot, or simply establish a congenial contact. The visitor likewise had a moment of public exposure with the highest authority of the polity, and could use it to advantage, whether for cooperation or subterfuge.

"Immense is our pleasure to have your presence in the Royal Court of Lakam Ha, Sahal Cauac Ahk," Yohl Ik'nal said warmly. "My heart is glad to see you well and healthy, Gods grant you many more such years. How fares it with your son and grandchildren? Did they accompany you to Lakam Ha?"

"So it is, Holy Lady, that my family now enjoys the grand hospitality of the Royal Court of Lakam Ha. For the youngest ones it is like a visit to the Upperworld, climbing the high mountain to arrive at a city in the sky, peaks wrapped in clouds and waters cascading over boulders, casting mists across the paths. They are enthralled, as indeed are we all to be in the Sacred Presence of the K'uhul Ahau of B'aakal." Hearing Cauac Ahk's strong voice, one would never imagine his advanced age.

"Tell me of happenings in your city," the ruler continued. "Is not a new ceremonial complex being built? It is apparent your first harvest was abundant, I trust the second will also be good."

"Indeed it is as you say. Waters flow to irrigate fields, rich soil is deposited as the rivers recede and our farmers follow time-honored techniques to preserve fertility. Of the new ceremonial center, work progresses well and we expect completion in another two years. Heard the Holy Lady of the new ceramic process our artisans now use? It produces a marvelous glaze of melon shade and holds paintings securely."

Congenial exchange continued as Cauac Ahk related other details of life in Yokib. The two rulers reminisced about previous occasions together, expressing respect for Kan Bahlam, Yohl Ik'nal's father now a Sacred Ancestor in the Upperworld. Neither ruler appeared to be pursuing an agenda, so courtiers relaxed and enjoyed the display of congeniality. Such demonstrations reinforced the social order and reassured the people that the ruling ahauob were satisfying the deities. Thus was fulfilled the social-spiritual contract between Maya rulers and their people.

In ending their interchange, Yohl Ik'nal extended a special sign of favor to Cauac Ahk by inviting his family to a private dinner with the royal family. Murmurs of approval welled from the crowd as the aged sahal gracefully accepted. Upon a hand sign from the K'uhul Ahau, the steward Buluc Max offered his arm to the Yokib ruler and assisted him to rise. This gesture would occur with every visitor as part of court protocol, but the elderly man was especially appreciative. The steward guided the Yokib Sahal to the stairs leading down from the throne room, where attendants and family waited.

Buluc Max signaled the next sahal in line to begin tribute.

Chak B'olon Chaak, young sahal of Popo' scooted forward and extended a large clay vase filled with cacao pods. This was his symbolic offering of precious cacao, representing the value of his tribute. He waited for the ruler to begin.

"Honored Lord of Popo', we are graced by your visit," Yohl Ik'nal intoned. "What tribute have you brought for the K'uhul Ahau, for the Sacred City of Lakam Ha?"

Her eyes carefully surveyed the smooth youthful face. His forehead sloped steeply upward from large nose in the straight profile so admired by Maya elite. On his elongated skull perched an elaborate headdress. Strong jaw and chin offset wide sculpted lips. Almond eyes above high cheekbones conveyed calm confidence although he was several years younger than she. Liking what she saw, the ruler's eyes alone conveyed approval.

"Holy Lady, the city of Popo' offers ten measures of dried corn, 5 measures dried beans and chiles each, 3 bundles of woven rugs, 3 bundles of cured skins, 20 baskets of tubers, fruits, squash, root vegetables and nuts. In the offering are 5 baskets of gourds, 2 baskets rare black copal, 2 baskets of conch shells and 3 baskets cacao pods. We offer a bundle of long blue quetzal and multicolored feathers, and a bundle of obsidian. From our deep forests come five jugs full of *kik*, gummy sap of the rubber tree, ready for mixing with morning glory juice to make adhesives and rubber products. From our skilled artisans are 2 baskets of fine ceramics and jade jewelry. May these gifts receive approval of the Triad Deities and please you, Holy Lady."

"Thus is the Holy Lady pleased, Honored Lord of Popo'. In the person of the Triad Deities, she who is their earthly personification receives and approves these offerings." The scribe behind Yohl Ik'nal nodded approvingly as he recorded these offerings.

The young sahal looked expectantly at Yohl Ik'nal, a hint of eagerness in his expression despite his resolve to remain unruffled. His tribute had been generous.

"Of the Sahal of Popo' it is said, he rules the city justly and wisely," Yohl Ik'nal continued, her hand gesture signifying respect. "Numerous are the voices that speak thusly, that praise the governance of the city of Popo' by the young ruler. Lands for agriculture and orchards are well managed; these lands produce abundantly and are prudently farmed for future productivity. New water works benefit the crops and city water supply. Artisans of the city practice their trades successfully and prosper, the people are satisfied, and the Gods are satisfied. It is in this way that the ruling ahauob fulfill their divine destiny; enact their rightful obligation, sacred and ancient, as emissaries of the Gods on earth."

A slight flush colored Chak B'olon Chaak's cheeks as he clasped his shoulder and bowed to the K'uhul Ahau.

"With gratitude do I hear your kind words, Holy Lady," he replied.

"You do honor to your father, holy ancestor Zotz Choj, a good friend of my father. This is pleasing to the ancestors in the Upperworld; it is fulfillment of the dynasty. B'aakal is pleased to have the Sahal Chak B'olon Chaak in charge of his city."

"It is thus to serve Sacred B'aakal that is my goal and my destiny." The sincerity of his voice left little doubt that he spoke truly.

Yohl Ik'nal was pleased with this young sahal. She decided to continue her plan of dispensing favor.

"It is known that you have twin children, a vigorous son and a lovely daughter. They are near the age of my son, Aj Ne Ohl Mat. Now comes something important. The K'uhul Ahau would have your children join our royal household at Lakam Ha. They are both of age for apprenticeship into their royal roles; we would have them study these skills with our leaders and teachers here. No finer training may be found in B'aakal. This is our desire and pleasure."

A nearly inaudible gasp arose as eyebrows raised and eyes shifted. This was a huge signal of regal favor, simultaneously linking the families of Popo' and Lakam Ha into a close alliance. Few missed the implications that a future royal marriage might result.

Chak B'olon Chaak swallowed quickly, his eyes widening in surprise. This unexpected summons of his children to the Lakam Ha court was a mixed blessing. While a royal marriage was a great honor, he would essentially be held captive to the K'uhul Ahau's objectives as long as his children were in her power. Her perspectives would shape their young characters. Loyalties would be built to the B'aakal dynasty of Kan Bahlam that had lifelong implications. However, the close alliance would benefit his city and his dynasty. A wave of pride swept over the young sahal, erasing his concerns.

"We of Popo' are greatly honored, Holy Lady," he declared. "To serve the desires and pleasures of the B'aakal K'uhul Ahau is our greatest accomplishment. As the wind is to the trees, as the stream is to the rocks, so shall the will of our Sacred Ruler, the Triad Deities incarnate, sweep over us in life-sustaining largesse. Ever to the Triad Deities do I bow."

Crossing both arms over his chest, Chak B'olon Chaak bowed to Yohl Ik'nal in the gesture of highest honor. She smiled at his well-phrased courtly language evoking the Triad Deities.

"More of this later shall we speak," she said, giving hand signs to her steward to arrange a later meeting. Buluc Max tipped his head in acknowledgement, sending her a significant glance. The steward offered his arm to the Popo' ruler as the young man arose and guided him to the stairs as voices below swelled in a symphony of approval.

Buluc Max signaled for the next tribute, from Usihwitz.

The representative from Usihwitz approached the throne. Short, powerfully built and darker skinned than most elite Mayas, his eyes were slightly crossed giving a shifty look to an already closed face. Zac Amal, nephew of ailing ruler Joy Bahlam, was impossible to read. The middle-aged man placed his symbolic tribute, a bundle of obsidian and jade, into the basket.

Yohl Ik'nal recited the court tribute protocol: "Honored Representative of the Lord of Usihwitz, we are graced by your visit. What tribute have you brought for the K'uhul Ahau, for the Sacred City of Lakam Ha?"

"Holy Lady, the city of Usihwitz offers eight measures of dried corn, 2 baskets of woven cotton, 3 measures dried beans, and 2 baskets cacao pods." Zac Amal droned an enumeration of tribute items, all noticeably less than tribute offered by preceding sahals. Except for two beautifully painted ceramic bowls, there was no special offering for the ruler. Blandly, he concluded with the formulaic response, "May these gifts receive approval of the Triad Deities and please you, Holy Lady."

The slight given by diminished tribute did not escape anyone's notice. The court waited with bated breath in the charged silence.

In the instant before her formal response, Yohl Ik'nal had to make a decision. She could put him on the spot by demanding more tribute, or disparage the agricultural skills of Usihwitz farmers for their poor harvest in a season of abundance. Or, most insulting of all, she could insinuate that the ruler had faulty relationships with the deities resulting in a poor harvest, which was a serious failing in a Maya ruler's central obligation.

She chose none of these responses. Instead, she continued as if the Usihwitz tribute was not out of the ordinary—except for omitting her words of approval.

"Thus does the Holy Lady accept your tribute, Honored Representative of the Lord of Usihwitz. In the person of the Triad Deities, she who is their earthly personification receives these offerings." Her voice was as neutral as his.

The scribe tilted his head and blinked as if to remove a speck from his eye. After this slight delay, he recorded the offerings. Courtiers who saw the scribe recognized this disparaging sign. They also noted the ruler's subtle disapproval. Zac Amal also did not miss these messages.

"How fares the health of the Sahal of Usihwitz, the Honored Lord Joy Bahlam?" Yohl Ik'nal asked, sincere concern in her voice. "Much is it my regret that he is unable to grace the Court of Lakam Ha with his noble presence. My revered father, now our Sacred Ancestor Kan Bahlam, held your ruler in greatest regard. Although many years have passed since last I saw Joy Bahlam, well do I remember his prowess at the great flower war of the past katun." She was setting the stage.

"It is thus, greatly to my sadness, that my Lord's health does not fare well." Zac Amal's voice stayed smooth as glassy water. Heavy lids half-veiled his crossed eyes, making them even more impenetrable. "Great is his sorrow that he cannot be here to attend the Court of Lakam Ha for the first tribute. He charged me to say unto you, his Honored K'uhul Ahau, 'The light of the Holy Lady's presence shines not upon me, and for this I am diminished'."

"Thus also shall I be diminished, should we not meet again in the Middleworld. It is charged to you, Zac Amal, to repeat these words to Lord Joy Bahlam. With no disrespect to the Learned Ah Kins of Usihwitz, I will send back with you my most skilled healer priest. May the Gods deign that he be successful in aiding your sahal."

Zac Amal clasped his shoulder and bowed in acknowledgement.

"So shall all of our city be grateful," he said, "should this healer priest of Lakam Ha bring relief to our beloved Lord. In their stead, and for Lord Joy Bahlam, do I offer our gratitude."

She asked a few questions about members of Joy Bahlam's family, while Zac Amal answered with courtly politeness. Behind half-veiled eyes he waited to see her trajectory, though he could well imagine where it might be headed. With her next remarks, it became clear.

"There resides in your city, I do believe, a distant kinsman of mine. He has chosen to stay in Usihwitz since his service after the flower war. Know you of his situation? He is called Ek Chuuah and is a warrior of great power."

Although she scrutinized Zac Amal's face and posture, he gave no hint of reaction and answered in the same neutral tones as before.

"Well-known in Usihwitz is Ek Chuuah," he said smoothly. "He is indeed, as the Holy Lady says, a powerful warrior. His choice to pursue life in our city is to our benefit, for he has contributed many skills and taught these to others. Surely the Holy Lady knows of his marriage to the ruler's daughter, and of their child. A fine family, dedicated to serving our Honored Lord and city."

"It is our happiness that our kinsman has contributed well to Usihwitz," Yohl Ik'nal continued. "Yet we regret he has not returned to visit his friends and relations in Lakam Ha. Perhaps he has undertaken travels to distant realms that prevent such a visit? Or may it be councils with foreigners that occupy his time. It seems he has learned unusual techniques of battle, new strategies and tactics. Such things might also benefit Lakam Ha, should he visit and teach us."

"Of this will I speak to him, be it the Holy Lady's desire. Surely Ek Chuuah is eager to visit his friends and relations in Lakam Ha. His sense of duty may be strained, however, between his city of birth and his city of residence. With our ruler's declining health, he has assumed many responsibilities that make it difficult to leave at present."

Zac Amal waited after giving little in his response, to see if the K'uhul Ahau would command Ek Chuuah to return or press on about his actions. Yohl Ik'nal noted that he avoided the topic of foreign contact, and realized he would reveal nothing of significance. She decided this display of her awareness about the Scorpion's activities was sufficient. The power structure at Usihwitz would be alerted that the B'aakal ruler kept abreast of events.

"Speak to Ek Chuuah of our interest in a visit," she resumed after delaying just long enough to evoke anxiety among those watching, and especially in Zac Amal, she hoped. "We do understand his responsibilities to an ailing sahal, and respect his commitment. Convey the regards of the B'aakal K'uhul Ahau who is also his kinswoman. For this do we give you thanks, Zac Amal."

The royal steward recognized that this dialogue was finished. He offered his arm to help Zac Amal rise, a bit more coldly than before, and guided the representative to the stairs as the crowd watched silently.

Mas Batz broke the tension by stomping his stubby legs and gesturing dramatically while calling for refreshments. Attendants quickly poured and distributed cups of liquid from the jars near the throne. This special drink was made of fresh corn milk mixed with fermented guava juice, produced only at the beginning of harvest before corn was dried into maize. Lightly sweet with a touch of alcohol, it was refreshing and stimulating. Murmurs of approval passed among waiting courtiers as they quaffed their cups.

The court session continued with the ruler accepting tribute from the Sahal of Sak Tz'i, nobles and merchants of Lakam Ha and headmen of several villages. After these came prominent ahauob and merchants of other cities. Most of the day was taken in this process, with occasional breaks for eating, drinking and relieving nature's call in the secluded toilets among the plaza aqueducts. A steady stream of attendants carried heavy tribute baskets and bundles to the palace storerooms, where each was tallied by scribes. This tribute would feed the Lakam Ha royal court, and provide lavish ceremonial feasts for the people at rituals prescribed by the Maya calendars. Such was the proper due of the May Ku, the "navel of the world," the city that served as seat of the 260-tun *may* cycle.

YOHL IK'NAL—V

Baktun 9 Katun 8 Tun 0 — Baktun 9 Katun 8 Tun 11 (593 CE—604 CE)

1

YOHL IK'NAL OVERSAW the building program at Lakam Ha with driven intensity. Seven solar years was not an abundance of time for what she meant to accomplish. The ruler met daily with architects and builders, and visited stonemasons in the process of setting huge square limestone blocks so precisely carved that their junction would not admit the thinnest obsidian blade. In the workshops of stone carvers, her ubiquitous presence kept workers focused and alert as they rendered complex Maya hieroglyphs and lavishly attired figures in bas-relief on panels. Of varying sizes, these carved panels would decorate outer walls and columns, line interior chambers with richly significant reproductions of Lakam Ha rulers and deities, and grace roofcombs with large figures that could be seen from a distance. Locally available limestone, dense and fine-grained, was the finest in all the Maya regions. It allowed carvers to fashion crisply cut edges and buttery smooth surfaces giving unsurpassed elegance to the art of Lakam Ha.

Uxul, the village stone carver, had the prestigious assignment of creating glyphs for Kan Bahlam's commemorative temple that housed his crypt. Uxul's art was featured prominently on the four outward-facing panels that flanked the temple's three anterior doors. These magnificent stucco glyphs were carved in deep relief so their details would be preserved through baktuns of rain and weather. Faces of the Lords of Time, swirls and geometric symbols fused in complex designs with animal and zoomorphic faces to tell the history of B'aakal rulers and their embodiment of the deities.

The temple's rectangular roof featured a procession of the B'aakal lineage from founder K'uk Bahlam I, ending with the seventh ruler, Kan Bahlam I. The Lakam Ha rulers' portraits were carved on the lower front roof, facing the plaza. They wore full regalia, every detail of function and decoration carrying important symbolic meanings. Above these larger than life size figures arose the narrow roof comb. In its center were three huge figures of the Triad Deities conferring their powers to the rulers.

It was an awe-inspiring sight from the residential areas a distance below the high plaza on which Kan Bahlam's temple stood. Taking advantage of the natural hill for elevation, the temple soared above four long rectangular plazas accessed by stairs spanning the entire plaza length. Simply ascending these tiers of stairs gave the feeling of meeting the sky, the domain of ancestors and Gods. Once standing upon the temple plaza, worshippers ascended another four tiers of stairs that narrowed at each level, until they reached the middle door of the temple structure.

Inside the temple's narrow room, murals depicted the major milestones of Kan Bahlam's rule in brightly painted glyphs and figures. A round central altar stone, embellished with carved glyphs reciting prayers of offering and salutation, held lovely ceramic incense burners that emitted the woody, enchanting odor of copal. Ah K'inob, the Solar Priests constantly attended this inner sanctum, performing rituals and receiving offerings.

Yohl Ik'nal was well pleased with her father's memorial temple. Several other structures were built on the temple plaza, including stucco and thatched roof houses for the priests and visitors making pilgrimage.

To house all the workers needed for the building program, she had additional living quarters constructed on the hillside between the Tun Pitz and Ixha Rivers. A series of eight terraces were created, climbing sequentially uphill to make flat surfaces for seventy-eight structures and fifteen small courtyards. Called the Xinil Pa' Group, its southern section contained the highest density of structures; small homes arranged around private courtyards. This provided families with their own areas, while concentrating buildings for efficient use of limited space. Water management features included drainage systems and altering the course of the Ixha River to maximize building area.

Part of her building program included expanding the aqueduct serving the main plaza (later called the Picota Group) with its Royal Court building and Popol Nah. This sophisticated example of water management was built of tightly fitted stones that fed water from multiple springs through a network of channels. Pressure systems forced water up into residences and fountains, and included wastewater drainage from bathing and toileting areas. At the aqueduct's exit, the flow rejoined the Bisik River, whose course was altered to turn sharply east, not following the flow dictated by natural gravity. The river passed through two other residential areas, then toppled downward in wide shallow cascades to join the Tun Pitz River flowing north towards the floodplains below.

The Nauyaka Group, situated adjacent to the western-most complex that contained the royal palace and large homes of the most prominent ahauob, received special attention. This residential area was built on flat land, bounded on the south by the Bisik River and on the north by a steep hillside. In this prestigious area were homes of elite nobles, priests and priestesses, and the wealthiest merchants and artisans. Most of the residential groups were connected by elevated platforms that provided easy walking well above the water pooling at ground level during storms.

Yohl Ik'nal added several new residential groups in this area, dispensing favor on additional elite by inviting them to live in closer proximity to the ruler. Of course, they were required to make extra contributions to construction for this privilege. When building was completed, the Nauyaka Group had seventy-four structures and seventeen courtyards.

But adding housing for elite and wealthy citizens was not Yohl Ik'nal's true motive in expanding the Nauyaka Group. This relatively isolated complex, with a panoramic view of the northern plains far below, hid the most sacred shrine of Lakam Ha; the Sak Nuk Nah—White Skin House—the underground structure dedicated to the Triad Deities. Above the Sak Nuk Nah at ground level was a modest structure with a uniquely triangular form. Ostensibly a temple to the young moon goddess, the nubile form of Ix Chel, it was tended by her priestesses who performed moon rituals in the adjacent plaza. The priestesses lived in the two attached rectangular buildings, performing divinations and healings.

Only the leading ahauob of the city, who had been initiated into the Triad Deity rituals, knew of this underground shrine. Part of their initiation was a pledge to keep the shrine's location secret. Other nobles and prominent commoners knew such a special shrine existed and that its location was secret. The occult mysteries surrounding the Sak Nuk Nah enhanced its significance and imbued the rituals held there with exceptional power. It was rumored that the ruler and heirs actually became Gods, taking on the form of one of the Triad during K'altun and other critical ceremonies.

Access to the Sak Nuk Nah was through underground tunnels carved many years before by workers now departed to other dimensions. An obscure storage structure beside the Ix Chel temple was the entrance for ahauob and priests/priestesses. They entered through a concealed door from a chamber inside the healing temple. Ahauob frequently visited the Ix Chel priestesses, so their comings and goings did not arouse any curiosity. Only those initiated were ever taken to this chamber.

The ruler's entrance was a longer tunnel leading from the royal palace to the Sak Nuk Nah. An impressive work of engineering, this secret passageway was a testimony to the skill of Maya architects. The tunnel entrance in the palace was hidden behind a carved panel of Ix Chel as moon goddess that could be pivoted aside by pressing a certain glyph. The panel was located in a little-used private ceremonial room that opened only to the ruler's sleeping chambers.

As the circle of initiates enlarged, Yohl Ik'nal wanted close-by residences for these privileged elite. And, the additional residential structures served to further disguise the area.

East of the Ixha River there were few buildings on the ridges. Nearest the river were workshops and residences of minor artisans and merchants, with terraces for home gardens. Beyond these spread pole, clay and thatched roof dwellings of commoners, surrounding shared plazas and gardens. A few large stone structures had been constructed by prior generations of rulers, notably a temple to the East perched high on the eastern slope of the tallest mount overlooking a flat meadow bordered by the Otolum River. This temple caught sunrise before any other in Lakam Ha, and was used for rituals of Lak'in, of sun initiation and beginnings of endeavors. Another temple dedicated to the South was built on a rise with southern exposure just beyond the Ixha River. Here ceremonies honored Nohol, or "big door" of the south through which flowed heat, power and abundance for growth and prosperity.

Nearby was an area of particular interest to Yohl Ik'nal. A small structure built there during her great-grandfather's time had been used for visioning rituals. It was situated on a modest hillock of bedrock east of the Nohol Temple, in dense forests not yet cleared for building. The small hillock nestled between steep hills as the Otolum River wrapped around its western edge. This location, with its feel of being cradled in the arms of the Great Earth Mother, was her choice for her funerary monument.

It was customary for Maya rulers to plan and begin building their funerary monuments, which were often completed by their successor. Rites of transition for the ruler from the Middleworld to the Underworld were of utmost importance. Properly enacted with rituals and burial objects, transition rites assured a successful navigation through underworld challenges. Death Lords must be overcome and outwitted in order for the rulers to ascend to the Upperworld where they established their presence as stars. The prototypes for this transition were the "Hero Twins" Hun Ahau and Yax Bahlam whose saga is poetically told in the Popol Vuh.

Yohl Ik'nal envisioned her burial temple as a solitary pyramid, embracing the bedrock hillock and rising substantially above to reach toward the sky. She was unique, the first woman ruler of Lakam Ha, and her monument must stand alone. It would remind the people of both her singularity and her oneness with the Great Mother, the primal goddess Muwaan Mat from whose womb all life springs. Her father Kan Bahlam's funerary pyramid also stood alone, signifying his innovative reign that successfully turned the inheritance pattern toward the female side of the B'aakal lineage. The several preceding rulers had traditional burial patterns. Their monuments were a line of adjoining temples at the southeast corner of the complex by the Bisik River. These six pyramids were built into the hillside overlooking the main plaza, foreshadowing the line of temples built later by Lakam Ha's most creative ruler.

The momentous occasion of the katun end arrived and was recorded.

Baktun 9, Katun 8, Tun 0, Uinal 0, Kin 0, on the date 5 Ahau 3 Chan (August 22, 593 CE) was a date that marked nearly seven solar years of the building program initiated by Yohl Ik'nal. Ceremonies were held on the highest plaza at the newly completed Temple of Kan Bahlam. The ruler enacted her first katun-end rituals with pomp and precision, in the high style expected of the Bahlam lineage rulers. She presented appropriate bundles to each of the Triad Deities and strongly embodied their presence.

In her vision following bloodletting, from the jaws of the vision serpent coiling in copal smoke emerged Mah Kinah Ahau, the second born of the B'aakal Triad, the Watery Sun Jaguar who traversed through the underworld at night. He conveyed a disturbing message that she recited in trance state to the elite initiates gathered in the underground Sak Nuk Nah.

"Katun 5 Ahau begins,
harsh is its face, its tidings.
Severe is its toll upon the ruler.
Then begins vexation by enemies,
then happens suffering in Lakam Ha.
Disrupted is the balance, the stability.
There is affliction borne by the offspring.
Then comes the blurring of the face of the Gods.
The red rattlesnake raises its head to bite.
The red stinging ant rises up to bite.
He who lies in wait is among you, it is his katun.
He is seen in the plazas on his mat,
the three-day mat person.
The rattle of the katun is shaken,
there is treachery of the katun at Lakam Ha.
Amid the affliction of the katun, the treachery,
Those greedy for dominion are turned aside.
The Mother of the Gods wears the Plumeria flower,
there is an end to the misery of Lakam Ha."

2

As the fall equinox drew near, there were days of bright sunshine that defied the tall billowing clouds hinting at rain. Early morning mists burned off quickly, and forests steamed under the strong sun. Many residents of Lakam Ha sought refuge in the cool, dim chambers of their thick-walled homes as insects buzzed and bit relentlessly. Even the birds and monkeys hid in leafy depths, strangely silent until refreshing evening breezes brought revival.

Not so the royal family. Led by Hun Pakal and Yohl Ik'nal, a small entourage toiled over hilly paths and across burbling rivers now at their lowest, heading southeast from the palace. Sak K'uk, ever eager for adventure, bounced energetically a few steps ahead of her father who led the way. She took short detours to examine an interesting bug or flower, humming to herself and tardy to respond when called back. Walking beside Yohl Ik'nal was her childhood friend Sak Nicte, now her chief female assistant at court. Close behind were several household attendants carrying baskets of food and drink, woven mats for sitting and canopies for creating shade.

Next to Hun Pakal was Hix Chapat, son of Chak B'olon Chaak the ruler of Popo' and ward of the Lakam Ha royal family for the past eight years. He and his twin sister Hohmay lived in the palace, participated in court protocol and training, and were schooled by the royal tutor B'ay Kutz. At fifteen solar years, Hix Chapat was muscular and athletic, participating enthusiastically in games and hunting, bearing himself proudly as the royal heir of Popo'. Hun Pakal was fond of the boy and made a point of cultivating him, teaching skills in competition and battle. Truthfully, he had more rapport with his ward than with his own son, Aj Ne Ohl Mat. Half listening as Hix Chapat described the trophies of his last hunt, Hun Pakal glanced back seeking his son's whereabouts.

Not surprising, he sighted Aj Ne Ohl Mat walking beside B'ay Kutz, engrossed in the pompous scholar's long-winded discourse on some learned subject. B'ay Kutz meant "fat turkey" in Mayan, and indeed the chubby little tutor seemed turkey-like as his pink wattles jiggled and round eyes blinked when he made particularly salient points. Aj Ne was a perfect foil to the fat turkey, his own lanky limbs and pointed face perched on a long slender neck making him appear decidedly stork-like.

"No athlete, this one!" Hun Pakal could not suppress his disappointment. Sighing, he turned back to the more satisfying, although self-aggrandizing monologue of Hix Chapat.

But Aj Ne Ohl Mat was not as engrossed in his tutor's ruminations as he appeared. Nodding often and muttering appropriately, his eyes darted frequently ahead to the young woman following his mother. Her lissome form moved gracefully, arms and shoulders bare in the hot sun. Dark ringlets danced beneath her headband as she walked with a hip-swaying motion, her shapely legs outlined through the thin summer skirt. He was smitten with Hohmay, the twin sister of Hix Chapat. Surges of yearning such as he had never imagined in his 15 years pulsated through him. Her demure demeanor during their studies and social time together had never suggested romantic interest, until recently when sultry glances beneath half-closed eyelids set his heart palpitating.

Or was he mistaken? Anguish flooded the boy and he tried to re-focus on his tutor's monotonous voice, to no avail. What had he heard, half-listening to his parents' conversation giving hints that she might be selected as his wife? Why had he not paid better attention? Overcome by insecurity and doubt, he dropped into wells of inner darkness and heard no more of B'ay Kutz's teachings.

Yohl Ik'nal had indeed been cultivating Hohmay as the future bride of her son. She wanted to solidify the alliance with Popo' and guarantee its longevity, especially since her katun predictions foresaw serious troubles ahead for Lakam Ha. Following her recovery from the trance and bloodletting in the prior year, she studied the notes made by the royal scribe. While she did not completely understand all the symbolism, the message of vexation, suffering and affliction was clear. This seemed especially focused on the ruler and offspring, which troubled her greatly. Treachery was certainly in the offing, but from whom and in what form she did not yet foresee. The ambitions of Ka'an were likely involved, given the imagery of rattlesnake bites, for they were the dynasty of the snake. She puzzled about the "three-day mat occupant" that implied someone taking over Lakam Ha's governance temporarily. Thankfully, the predictions ended on a positive note with the Great Mother Goddess fending off those seeking domination, and then restoring harmony.

She must undertake another vision to gain more clarity.

Meanwhile, she pushed to complete her building program and ensure alliances with other cities. This excursion today was related to the building program, an idea of the royal tutor B'ay Kutz. He thought the young royals would benefit from first-hand exposure to the out-lying parts of Lakam Ha development, and possibly be inspired to contemplate what their future contributions might be. After all, they were nearing adulthood and before much longer would be assuming leadership roles.

Ruefully, Yohl Ik'nal admitted that her physical vigor was less than a few years ago. Her joints were already aching and her breath shorter than she liked. Glancing ahead at Hun Pakal, her heart swelled at his continued vigor as he strode easily beside the young Popo' heir.

He will outlive me, she reflected with uncanny certainty.

The failing health of Popo' ruler Chak B'olon Chaak was also sobering. He was younger than she, and reports of his prospects were not good. Soon young Hix Chapat would return home to prepare for taking over rulership. She felt assured that his training and experiences in the court of Lakam Ha would provide a sound foundation for this critically important transition.

The royal entourage descended a steep hillside and found rocky shallows to cross the Otolum River between the Lak'in Temple and the partially built funerary monument. East of the river was a level meadow bordered by several spreading Ox-Ramon trees that provided welcome shade. Attendants quickly set up ground mats and canopies, and soon served tasty maize cakes, fruit and nuts, and strips of dried venison. Gourds were used to scoop cool river water for drinking. The porters waved large feather fans, attempting to create some airflow in the windless day.

The four young royals gathered on one mat, chatting casually about whatever came to mind. They were usually quite comfortable with each other, spending many hours together over the years studying, eating, exercising and playing. This day, however, Aj Ne felt awkward and remained quieter than normal. Hohmay, sitting opposite him, was more animated than usual, gesturing and tossing her hair repeatedly. Hix Chapat noticed nothing, being habitually self-absorbed and continuously refocusing conversation to his interests. Sak K'uk pursed her lips and took it all in, sensitive to the electric charge between her brother and Hohmay and irritated yet again by Hix Chapat.

As soon as they finished eating, she jumped up making excuses about needing to talk with her mother, and strode purposefully to the elders' mat. A little wheedling convinced Yohl Ik'nal to accompany her to the lowest rise to the east, so she could see what was beyond. Hand in hand they headed off, skirting the river along a narrow trail. When they were out of earshot, Yohl Ik'nal queried her daughter.

"You seem most eager to leave your companions."

"Aaah, they are boring me," Sak K'uk replied. "Aj Ne and Hohmay are particularly dull, all they can do is cast yearning glances at each other, while he pouts and she makes insipid remarks. Are they pledged to marry?"

"That is my intention, and I am certain that Chak B'olon Chaak gives his assent to this union."

"Thus is it when the urge to marry occurs? Normally intelligent people behave like fools . . . is this what it means to be love-sick? Yech!" Sak K'uk tossed her head disdainfully.

Yohl Ik'nal smiled and teased her daughter.

"Does not your affection stir for Hix Chapat?"

The girl's face clouded as if she entertained a terrible thought.

"It surely must not be your intention that I marry him! Unmarried rather would I remain than be bound to that strutting, puffed-up macaw who can think of nothing but his own deeds and desires. I do not need a man; I am perfectly fine by myself!"

Laughter burst from Yohl Ik'nal. Her daughter was nothing if not honest and direct.

"Rest assured that I have no such intention," she reassured. "Your assessment is quite accurate. He is far from deserving such a bright star as you. It is to your credit that you harbor no attraction to him. Soon he returns to his home city, and will annoy you no more."

Sak K'uk's relief was palpable. She smiled broadly and squeezed her mother's hand.

"Come, mother, let us hurry to look beyond the next ridge."

The girl trotted ahead but Yohl Ik'nal continued to climb slowly, catching her breath. She heard footsteps behind and turning saw Hun Pakal hurrying to catch up. She was very glad to have him take her arm and assist in the gentle climb.

Sak K'uk stood on the ridge top, looking east. The Otolum River ran almost straight across a long level meadow. Impressive, steep hills swept upward to the south, covered with trees. Another steep hillside veered west, crowned by the Nohol Temple. The far end of the meadow appeared to drop precipitously into a canyon as the river disappeared from view. A modest, rectangular structure bordered the left bank of the river not far from the ridge where she stood.

Her parents reached the ridge top and stood beside Sak K'uk. Tree branches rustled slightly as a breeze blew across the meadow. The sun behind them cast lengthening shadows on the waving grasses.

"What is that building?" Sak K'uk pointed to the lone building.

"In the time of my father, it was used for hunters to stay between forays into the forests," said Yohl Ik'nal.

"Occasionally the warriors use it to stage practices, since the meadow provides an open area for contests," added Hun Pakal.

"It seems empty now," observed Sak K'uk.

"Hmmm, I think it is," her father said.

Quiet descended upon the trio, as the breeze brought welcome coolness. Sak K'uk closed her eyes and appeared deep in contemplation. After some moments, she waved her arm to include the meadow.

"There, over that building I can see an immense palace," she whispered intently. "It is the most beautiful palace I have ever seen, with wide stairs ascending all sides, tall buildings and a most unusual square tower, many courtyards inside and . . . Oh, it has the most gorgeous panels and frescoes, with columns and windows and water flowing inside the rooms. . . Many people fill the palace and they wear strange clothes and come from distant places . . . Nothing like this palace has ever been before!"

Her parents exchanged glances, sharing the identical thought. Could this be a vision of the future? Or a young girl's daydream?

"How lovely," murmured Yohl Ik'nal.

"Yes, and I am there too." Sak K'uk spoke with startling certainty, eyes still closed.

3

The high-ranking ahauob of Lakam Ha maintained large home complexes, impressive structures with multiple courtyards, living quarters for family and servants, guest residences, separate cooking and dining areas, and even buildings resembling the royal court where the household head received his peers and supplicants. Here networks and alliances were shaped, loyalties and obligations established, and intrigue initiated. Most of these ahauob traced their family origins back to K'uk Bahlam I, the dynastic founder of the ruling B'aakal lineage. Their ancestors were the brothers and sisters of the rulers, family members who never acceded to rulership but who had legitimate claim through their sacred bloodlines.

Over generations, a large cadre of blooded ahauob were created. Some had diluted their bloodlines by marrying lesser nobility, and thus were farther removed from potential rulership. But others had bloodlines arguably as pure as the ruling Bahlam family. This created a scenario with many contenders for rulership at every change of ruler. Since determination of the next ruler was not strictly dictated by direct descent, or even by sex, an unstable situation existed in the large Maya cities. An excess of blooded ahauob eligible for rulership was inherently explosive.

Yaxun Zul was one of these blooded ahauob. He was a well-respected man of middle age who had acquired large farms and orchards; an astute manager of traders whose far-flung trade network brought exotic goods favored by the elite. While he inherited considerable assets, he expanded these holdings and was now among the wealthiest men in the city.

Yaxun Zul was also ambitious. When young, he had dreamed of becoming ruler himself. The wily manipulations by Kan Bahlam I, father of Yohl Ik'nal, had derailed this dream. Yaxun Zul still marveled at how smoothly the transfer of rulership to Yohl Ik'nal had been engineered. Indeed, he could learn much from studying the great ruler's tactics. Now Yaxun Zul dreamed again, this time for his 15-year-old son Kan Mo' Hix. Yohl Ik'nal was aging, and her heir not yet named. Few elites in Lakam Ha were unaware that her son, Aj Ne Ohl Mat lacked leadership qualities. Of course her daughter Sak K'uk possessed these qualities in

163

abundance, but her claim to rulership could be challenged more effectively than her brother's. Kan Mo' Hix was no less eligible than either of the ruler's children.

In the opulent household court of Yaxun Zul, a group of high-ranking ahauob gathered. These men came regularly to honor Yaxun Zul, and might be considered his courtiers. Most of them had reasons to desire the unseating of the Bahlam family; some held grudges, some were jealous, some had their own ambitions. Others were simply rebellious by nature or in search of exciting diversions.

Chief among this opposition group were Chak'ok, a fiery warrior who chaffed under the long period of peace and prosperity brought by the Bahlams, and Kab'ol, the brother of self-exiled Ek Chuuah. Ten men seated on floor-mats surrounded Yaxun Zul, who held forth from an elevated platform. Not as high as the ruler's throne platform, it none-the-less conveyed the message of dominance over the group. All present were dressed sparsely as the day was hot, wearing minimal adornments. They sipped cups of cool maize gruel mixed with cacao and ground chile, frequently replenished by servants. Other attendants stood waving huge reed fans to circulate air inside the chamber. Thick stone and plaster walls kept the interior reasonably cool as sunlight blazed on the white courtyard.

"Hix Chapat is departing with the dawn, returning to his ailing father in Popo' to prepare for rulership," Kab'ol remarked.

"His departure causes me no grief," growled Chak'ok. "The young macaw is much taken by his self-noted merits. Not that many others note them so well."

A ripple of laughter spread through the circle. The Popo' heir had never endeared himself among the ahauob of Lakam Ha because of his arrogance.

"Of more importance is the betrothal of his sister to Aj Ne Ohl Mat," observed Yaxun Zul. "Our ruler is securing a tight alliance with Popo' for reasons of her own. Better she should be courting Usihwitz and Yokib."

A few eyebrows rose at this remark and some men cast sideways glances toward Kab'ol, who remained impassive.

"It has not happened yet, that our ruler designates an heir. Might it be that this betrothal points toward her choice of Aj Ne Ohl Mat?" asked one of the youngest present, Uc Ayin, a talented artist quite popular among many circles in the city. He kept his connections fluid and was welcome in diverse groups. Yaxun Zul wanted to cultivate him as an informant, but the ever-diplomatic courtier deftly navigated through interrogations, not revealing anything of importance.

Murmurs of disagreement ensued. A couple of men emphasized Aj Ne Ohl Mat's lack of leadership qualities. Speculation about whether Sak K'uk might be named heir followed, with review of other possible candidates. A few present knew of Yaxun Zul's ambitions regarding his son, and the name of Kan Mo' Hix was mentioned more than once. Generally, the group agreed that neither of Yohl Ik'nal's offspring was a good choice for ruler. They thought another branch of the bloodline should be chosen.

"Chak'ok, what know you of happenings in other regions?" queried Yaxun Zul. The warrior had friends in several cities, forged through contests and exhibition battles over the years.

"It is said, of the Ka'an polity, that they are increasingly warlike since Uneh Chan became ruler," replied Chak'ok. "He is even more aggressive than his predecessor Yax Yopaat who advanced the spread of power over the southern regions instigated by Uitah Chan. Mutul still languishes following the destruction he brought to that city in the wake of the change of *may* seating more than a katun and a half ago. The Ka'an dynasty has been active spreading its influence, forming an alliance with distant Uxwitza. Closer to home, it is said by warriors of these cities, those who are friends of mine, that Ka'an holds strong influence upon the sahals of Pa'chan, Pakab, and Wa-Mut."

He paused, glancing around from Yaxun Zul to the other men present. All were attentive, although this was not news to most.

"Now comes something important," Chak'ok spoke slowly to add emphasis. "The sahals of Usihwitz and Yokib have received emissaries from Uneh Chan, Holy Lord of Ka'an. Exchanges of gifts and possibly promises of affiliation took place. What think you, Kab'ol?"

The sudden shift of focus to the brother of Ek Chuuah jolted the group. Yaxun Zul turned to Kab'ol, giving the hand sign to speak truly.

"We are among friends here," said Yaxun Zul. "You may speak freely."

Kab'ol seemed to consider this carefully. He had watched the opposition to the Bahlam rulership grow over several years among this group. Most were in support of Yaxun Zul's desire to make his son the next K'uhul Ahau of Lakam Ha. Only Uc Ayin was an unknown, not securely an ally but certainly not one to spread gossip. Perhaps the time had arrived to push his long-held agenda, fermenting inside him like heady balche, now ready to burst forth – revenge for the betrayal of his brother.

"That did occur," he began carefully. "Ahauob of Kan came to Usihwitz. After the death of Joy Bahlam, not long following the time his nephew Zac Amal did the First Tribute to our ruler, Yahau Chan Muwaan became the new sahal of Usihwitz. Uneh Chan of Kan sent emissaries to honor the new sahal with many rich gifts. There were long talks and much feasting. Ek Chuuah, my brother, attended most of these. He told me that these talks focused upon alliances between Usihwitz and Kan. Usihwitz sits among several cities bordering the K'umaxha River, cities long allied with Kan. For trade and protection, said these emissaries, Usihwitz would be better served by alliance with Kan than with Lakam Ha."

"And what did the new sahal of Usihwitz say in return?" asked Yaxun Zul.

"This did he say, that he would deeply consider these things, for perhaps there was much truth in their reasoning."

"What think you of the disposition of Yahau Chan Muwaan toward this alliance?" Chak'ok queried.

"Listen not to what I think. Hear the words of my brother, who is close by marriage and by interests to the rulers of Usihwitz. Ek Chuuah said that this alliance with Kan will happen. The alliance of Usihwitz with our city has cooled and will not last much longer."

Several men present nodded as others murmured in surprise. Yaxun Zul looked thoughtful, rubbed his chin and sipped more cacao drink.

"This also tell to us," he addressed Kab'ol. "What thinks your brother of the Yokib ruler's response to the Kan emissaries?"

"Of that he is less certain, but it is his assessment that the alliance of Yokib with Lakam Ha is weakening. He did know that the Kan emissaries were well-received there and stayed many days."

"This presents us with an opportunity," said Yaxun Zul. "The alliances of Lakam Ha with cities in its polity are weakening. They are shifting toward Ka'an polity, and that diminishes the position of our ruler. She is well liked and respected, but her children not so much. Aj Ne Ohl Mat is too timid and Sak K'uk is too outspoken. Yes, the opportunity is coming to make a change in ruling family."

Yaxun Zul paused to assess the group's responses, for he was now openly speaking what he had intimated before. He sensed all were with him, except perhaps Uc Ayin who remained thoroughly neutral in reaction. That did not matter, he decided. If the ruler's position could be undermined enough, the ahauob would take the question of heir to the Popol Nah for decision. He could wield tremendous influence in the council house, if events were properly manipulated.

"All here know that my family has as pure bloodlines to our founder Kuk Bahlam I as the family of Kan Bahlam," he continued. "My son Kan Mo' Hix is intelligent, brave and well-prepared for leading our city. Let us now seek the means to bring him to rulership. Let us find the way to attain heir designation for Kan Mo' Hix, that he will perform the deer-hoof binding ceremony instead of an offspring of Yohl Ik'nal."

Nods and murmurs of assent confirmed the group's support. A few ideas were advanced and briefly discussed, but none seemed effective. Yohl Ik'nal still had a wide network of support among the ahauob, and her ceremonies held great power. Many knew she was a seer and visionary, and were in awe of these powers. Something really significant was needed to discredit her as ruler. The discussion continued, wandering far afield as the nobles consumed more cacao drinks and trays of fruit.

Uc Ayin participated marginally, and then requested leave to return to his duties. He was painting several ceramic bowls for an upcoming ceremony. Yaxun Zul granted leave and thanked him graciously for being present.

Conversation drifted off after Uc Ayin left. Yaxun Zul gauged the time was right for serious commitment and planning. He dismissed the servants and signaled for the men to gather closely and speak softly.

"Now is the time for your pledge. If you cannot fully support action against the ruler, you must leave. What is needed is a change of regime. Remain here only if you are committed to this."

No one left. He looked each man in the eye and directly demanded their commitment, which they each gave.

"What we discuss now must not be spoken out of this room. Only those present must know of our plans," he continued. "What ideas have you for discrediting Yohl Ik'nal in a significant way?"

Kab'ol raised his head, meeting Yaxun Zul's eyes.

"Now I speak, for I have much considered this," he said softly. All leaned forward to hear better. "We will use the example of Kan to accomplish our ends. No small thing will bring down Yohl Ik'nal. We need something unprecedented, something devastating to our city. Here is what I am thinking. Launch a raid against Lakam Ha that brings destruction to the shrine of Kan Bahlam. This shrine is the work of Yohl Ik'nal, and to damage her father's monument will damage the daughter also."

"That would be significant," agreed Yaxun Zul.

"But we do not have the forces needed to accomplish such a raid," observed Chak'ok.

"That is so, but other forces will engage with our plan. My brother Ek Chuuah can gather men from Usihwitz who will gladly join a raid," said Kab'ol. "He knows warriors from Pakab who are ready to join forces. Of this I have no doubt. Ek Chuuah seeks rectification of the wrongs done to him by Kan Bahlam.

This thought, to stage a raid against his former city, already ferments in his mind. He has a large following of warriors and they will do his bidding."

"It can be accomplished with such forces," Chak'ok gauged, eyes narrowing.

Yaxun Zul was greatly pleased. The motives and source for the raid would lie outside Lakam Ha. He could remain an innocent bystander, a continuing loyal supporter of the ruler by all appearances. The foretaste of victory whetted his appetite.

"This is the plan we will pursue. You are to be commended for your strategy, Kab'ol. How soon can it be set in motion?"

"I will visit Ek Chuuah and discuss it further. Then he must prepare his warriors and arrange their travel and tactics. Several moons will be needed."

"To have the greatest effect, this raid should be a surprise," added Chak'ok. "We must make every effort to keep it secret."

"And for our own safety, the raid should appear planned and motivated by Ek Chuuah." Yaxun Xul relished this deception. "We can avoid joining in the attack if his forces are strong enough." The wealthy ahau intended to safeguard his position, should the raid fail.

"That will be arranged," said Kab'ol. "Ek Chuuah is only too happy to claim responsibility for a raid against the Bahlams of Lakam Ha."

4

Yohl Ik'nal tossed restlessly in her bed-chamber as images of destroyed buildings flashed before her, their carved frescoes and pillars shattered, their wood lintels and reed mats ablaze. Broken figurines, incense burners and offering cups littered the floors. Cries and shouts, clashing spears, pounding footsteps filled her ears as her breathing quickened and her heart raced. With a sudden gasp, she woke and sat upright, struggling for breath. Heart thumping against her ribs, she remembered the healer priestess' admonition, "Your heart is not as strong as before, you must rest more and walk less. Take care to guard your state of mind, keep inner calmness."

How could she remain calm with these recurring dreams of destruction?

Her movements awakened Hun Pakal. Sleepily he murmured: "What is it, my love?"

"The dream of destroyed buildings just returned again. It is so distressing, it frightens me. Then I have trouble breathing and must sit up."

He reached over to stroke her arm.

"Are you able to breathe now?"

"It is becoming better. This does not bode well." She might be alluding to her health as well as the dream. "I am not certain the city I see being destroyed is Lakam Ha. . . but I fear it must be. This is in keeping with my katun vision prophecy."

"That is so, but we have no evidence of actions being planned in the polity." Hun Pakal was now fully awake. "However, our sources in Usihwitz report difficulty getting information, and we have no direct agents in Kan. With Hix Chapat now acceded as ruler of Popo' this alliance is strong. The other cities have been calm."

He sat up and put his arms around his wife. Gratefully, she rested her head on his shoulders and sighed deeply, bringing more air into her lungs as her heartbeat slowed. They sat silently, listening to heavy rain pelting the roof and plaza in the darkness. Several rainy seasons had elapsed since the marriage of their son Aj Ne Ohl Mat and Hohmay, sister of Hix Chapat. As yet, the young couple had no children. The building program of Yohl Ik'nal was nearly completed, including most of her burial temple. She felt mixed emotions about it, for completing this goal seemed to foretell an ending.

"All these dreams, the prophecy . . . so must it be, something evil is coming to Lakam Ha. I will seek a vision to learn more, to get details. We need to be prepared," said Yohl Ik'nal.

Hun Pakal held her more tightly.

"Seeking a vision will tax your strength; it may harm your health. Did not your healer priestess admonish you to rest, to guard your heart?"

"My heart is devoted to the well-being of our city. It is my sacred duty to seek more information that may safeguard Lakam Ha. Surely my heart would be broken beyond repair if destruction comes to us."

He nodded in silent understanding of the K'uhul Ahau's responsibility, regardless of personal cost.

"When will you do it?"

"At the next Full Moon ritual done by the priestesses of Ix Chel. The Great Mother Goddess knows all, sees all the actions of her Middleworld children. When the moon is full, her sight is clearest and she sees into the hearts and minds of her people. Ix Chel can tell me what intentions are held against Lakam Ha."

The following morning Yohl Ik'nal set her plans in motion, arranging with the Ix Chel priestesses to include her vision quest in their Full Moon ceremonies. She deliberately included her daughter Sak K'uk, for she knew that the girl was instrumental in Lakam Ha's destiny. Sak K'uk needed experience developing her own visioning abilities. Her impatience and headstrong ways were impeding the subtle attributes of a seer.

Full Moon ceremonies during the rainy season were always a challenge, for clouds often occluded the moon. As Yohl Ik'nal and Sak K'uk prepared with a day of fasting and purification, dark clouds swirled overhead and rain pelted the palace intermittently. At dusk, they donned white huipils and cloaks, loosened their hair and proceeded barefoot to the small triangular temple of Ix Chel in the Nauyaka Group. The rain had ceased, but clouds still covered the darkening sky. In the plaza by the temple, the Ix Chel priestesses gathered, chanting and burning copal incense as they danced gracefully in a circle. The royals joined the circle, clad as simply as the priestesses, swirling to rhythmic drums with arms uplifted. Many voices trebled the moon chant.

"The very beautiful moon has risen over the forest.
It will light up the center of the sky, where it will be suspended.
It will illuminate the earth and all the forest and mountains.
Only sweetness comes as the air is fragrant.
There is happiness in all good people.

"Lady Rainbow, Mother of Waters, of fluids, of childbirth,
Lady Weaver of our lives' destinies, of fields and growing things,
She who sits upon the Moon with her Rabbit and sees all things,
Goddess who wears the Serpent Rainbow on her head,
Healer and herbalist, midwife and ender of life,
Wife of K'in Ahau-Lord Sun and lover of the stars.
We have brought the flower blossoms, the copal, the cane vines,
and we dance in your sacred light.

"With hair untied, wearing only your whiteness,
we scatter the flowers and the old times end. They end.
We welcome the new, the brightness that illuminates everything.
Lady Moon, very beautiful moon, you have risen over the forest
and illuminate the center of the sky."

As if by magic, dark clouds parted and became edged in silver. The women whirled and chanted, arms and faces lifted toward the sky. Slowly the brilliant white moon slid from behind clouds into the center of the sky, illuminating the plaza and glinting off eyes and teeth. Copal smoke curled like weightless snakes among the dancers, its heady incense altering perceptions of time and space. Again and again they repeated the chant, circling endlessly, floating effortlessly in their sinuous dance. Thus they would continue until exhaustion or trance overcame them.

Yohl Ik'nal gauged her state of consciousness and recognized readiness for her vision quest. Glancing at Sak K'uk, she knew the girl—actually now a young woman—was near trance. Arrangements were agreed upon before the ritual; the elder priestess had prepared a room inside the temple that opened on a small courtyard for the royal women to use. She also concocted a hallucinogenic brew made with secretions of the spotted toad, a common vehicle for visioning among rain forest Maya. Two attendants were ready to provide any support the royal women needed.

The Great Mother Goddess understood the bleeding of women, for She was in charge of these precious body fluids. Women's moon blood and childbirth blood were all the sacrifice She required of this life-giving itz. The Goddess approved methods of vision trance other than self-bloodletting, including toad secretions, plants and mushrooms. Sometimes simply fasting, dance and chants were sufficient to induce the visionary state.

Indeed, this was so for Yohl Ik'nal, in whom the patterns of visioning were well established. For her daughter's sake, however, she partook of the hallucinogenic brew, knowing the strong-willed Sak K'uk would have trouble releasing her mental control without it. They sat upon woven mats placed in the doorway facing the courtyard. From this vantage point, they could see the moon and bathe in her silvery rays.

Yohl Ik'nal lifted her face toward the moon, murmuring invocations. She saw the Rabbit in the full moon clearly, sitting with long ears perked. She knew that Ix Chel peered through the Rabbit's eyes onto the Middleworld below, and asked inwardly to be shown the danger that advanced toward Lakam Ha. Sinking deeper into trance, she was dimly aware of Sak K'uk beside her. Now the young woman must rely on the training she had received, for her mother could not intervene once the process was underway.

Gently Yohl Ik'nal's awareness slipped out of her body and floated up to the full moon. She sensed herself merging with the form of the Goddess, now taking shape as the full moon. Sliding into that brilliant orb, she expanded into roundness and light. Soon she settled into the Rabbit in the moon, blinking eyes several times to become accustomed to this perspective. The dark forests and mountain terrain of Lakam Ha stretched out below. Moonlight glinted off the rivers and white plazas. A few torches glowed in courtyards, but there was little movement. She marveled at the beauty of her city, seen from the sky far above.

She willed the Rabbit to look farther into the distance, following the K'umaxha River's winding course. Other cities emerged from the forests, those closest to Lakam Ha in the B'aakal polity. Her vision drifted over Popo', Yokib, Usihwitz and Sak Tz'i, as her expanded awareness entered into the collective thoughts emanating from each city. Only in Usihwitz did she sense animosity. Penetrating more deeply into these thought forms, she realized that an attack was being planned against Lakam Ha. Many warriors were involved and their hostile emotional energy was strong. There were energy strands connecting to warriors in other cities . . . she was unsure which cities, but not within the B'aakal polity. One strong strand linked directly to Lakam Ha itself.

The Rabbit suddenly shifted its eyes and gazed away from earth out into the vast cosmos. Millions of stars twinkled; space dust billowed in immense clouds of red and purple, constellations grouped in fantastic shapes. The Rabbit focused on one constellation, Scorpio, forming The Scorpion hanging over the earth's south horizon.

Ek Chuuah! She immediately knew who was leading this attack. His anger toward her father and family had never cooled. And the energy strand linked to Lakam Ha must be connected with his brother Kab'ol . . . and who else? Slowly familiar faces emerged to her sight; Chak'ok, a formidable warrior and several of his compadres. Uc Ayin seemed weakly involved, not clearly hostile. Her wealthy kinsman, Yaxun Zul . . . this pained her heart, even in her state of expanded consciousness. *And what of his son, Kan Mo' Hix?*

A startling image burst into her awareness. She saw her daughter Sak K'uk being married to Kan Mo' Hix. Struggling to avoid reacting, which could propel her out of the vision trance, she opened to accept this image . . . and saw once again the splendid future city Lakam Ha, numerous magnificent buildings glowing orange and white, many foreign visitors, and the prophesied Great Ruler of her lineage—the son of Sak K'uk and Kan Mo' Hix.

Yohl Ik'nal allowed her awareness to rest in this glorious imagery, simply accepting. The time for making judgments and developing strategies would come later.

In timelessness, there is no sense of time passage. Was it an instant, or a large portion of the night? Yohl Ik'nal began to sense the dissipation of the hallucinogen. Soon her trance would end, and she wanted more information. Re-focusing the

Rabbit's eyes, she peered far into the distance toward the northeast, into the Ka'an polity. Try as she may, her vision failed to penetrate into the city of the Kan dynasty, Dzibanche.

Thanking the Rabbit and the Goddess Ix Chel as the full moon, she allowed her awareness to slip away and descend gradually to earth. As she re-entered her own body, aching joints began protesting their period of immobilization. A wave of nausea reminded her of a long-empty stomach now aggravated by the drug. Her head felt fuzzy and heavy, as though simply being awake was too great an effort. With a flicker of concern, she realized her heart was beating rapidly.

The attendants were quick to note that the royal women were emerging from trance. They brought warm corn gruel and blankets, administering these comforts with compassion. Sak K'uk retched her first sips of gruel, but soon wanted more. After drinking she lay listlessly in the arms of an attendant. Her glazed expression indicated she had not fully eliminated the hallucinogen from her system. Yohl Ik'nal drank the gruel thankfully and drew blankets closely around her shivering body. When the royal women were able to walk, the attendants conducted them to a waiting palanquin for their return to the palace.

The following day the royal women met to discuss their visions with Hun Pakal, trusted court advisors, and the High Priest and Priestess; the successors to Lahun Uc and Wak Batz, who had entered the road, *Xibalba Be*, several years ago to be carried by the celestial canoe into the sky as ancestors. The group gathered in an antechamber of the royal residential complex, secluded from view. They settled onto mats with an expectant air. No attendants were present and one of Hun Pakal's warriors stood guard at the entryway.

Yohl Ik'nal's usual light brown complexion was noticeably sallow. Her eyes appeared deeply set with dark circles underneath. Sak K'uk, by contrast, had surprisingly bright eyes with a rosy hue coloring her tan cheeks. As the mother emanated fatigue and aging, the daughter radiated vibrant energy and blossoming womanhood. She had now reached her fourteenth solar year.

"All is secure," announced Hun Pakal. "You may begin."

Yohl Ik'nal looked closely into the eyes of each person present. The silence sizzled with intensity. She spoke deliberately but softly.

"Now it comes. Now comes the knowledge we sought, and it is heavy with sadness. It is fraught with turmoil and steeped in betrayal. But before I speak this, it is important that we hear the vision of my daughter, Sak K'uk. Of this, she has not yet spoken, even to me. Sak K'uk, tell fully all that you experienced in your visioning."

The young woman was taken by surprise and blushed more deeply. Regaining composure, she half-lowered her eyelids and recalled the vision.

"Lady Moon, Goddess Ix Chel took me into the night sky. She showed me the beauty of the stars and the vastness of the cosmos. She brought me to a future time in Lakam Ha, to a much larger city with structures and temples covering the eastern hills and plateaus. Such immense pyramids and huge complexes as I have never seen! They glow orange and white, their roofcombs reach high into the sky, and their plazas are enormous. Many more people gather before temples, fill the markets, and live in residences by the eastern river cascades. Lakam Ha has a great ruler; he builds the city and sits as a wise counselor for people from many distant places. I am overwhelmed."

She paused, breathing rapidly and fighting for composure. Opening her eyes, she looked quizzically at her mother. She tried to speak, but her voice faltered.

"Be at peace, my daughter," Yohl Ik'nal murmured. "You may speak here without fear, for none may judge what the Goddess revealed to you. This is your truth."

"I saw . . ." Sak K'uk began, but hesitated again. "I was shown the one who is to be my husband. He is . . . of our city. He is . . . Kan Mo' Hix."

Despite her intention to remain impassive, Yohl Ik'nal shivered at her daughter's revelation. Others present exchanged glances, a few murmured in surprise. Although the young man was of appropriate bloodlines, he had not been considered as a match for the ruler's daughter. His family was not closely aligned with the ruler, and his father was viewed as dissatisfied and critical.

Immediately Yohl Ik'nal made rapid calculations, weighing the profound import of this revelation given in both visions. That Sak K'uk received the same message from the Goddess confirmed its validity. The Divine Plan ordained the marriage of Sak K'uk and Kan Mo' Hix; and from their union would be born the greatest ruler Lakam Ha would ever see.

This meant that Yohl Ik'nal must not implicate his father, Yaxun Zul, as a traitor. She knew the ahauob and warriors supporting her family would be unable to accept the match with a family who betrayed and plotted against the ruler. How to handle the situation was not yet clear, but she trusted the way would unfold.

Sak K'uk looked stricken. She squeezed her eyelids tightly, teardrops trickling from the edges.

Yohl Ik'nal reached over and took her daughter's hand.

"Be comforted, Sak K'uk," she said tenderly. "For I too was given this same image during my vision. I saw that you are to marry Kan Mo' Hix. The intentions of the deities surpass our understanding. Know, my dear one, this is for the good of our beloved city, of our people. Ix Chel would not guide us wrongly."

The young woman's eyes popped open and she gasped. Taking a deep breath, she lifted her chin and straightened her shoulders. All present watched her intently.

"This am I glad to know," she said more evenly. "One more thing was I shown. The great ruler, the great architect of Lakam Ha's future, will be the child born of our marriage. Knowing this, I can accept the will of the deities."

The ahauob and priestly members present could not resist commenting to each other, exchanging reactions and thoughts. This was remarkable information, the more so that mother and daughter both had the same vision. Hun Pakal shook his head in astonishment; never had he considered that family for an alliance. After allowing time for venting the moment's intensity, Yohl Ik'nal continued.

"Turmoil and destruction are aimed at our city. This evil comes from Usihwitz, but it is augmented by a greater evil in our own city. Ek Chuuah has planned an attack, gathering many warriors from his city and others. His goal is to destroy something precious, something sacred to us. He is full of hatred, but those in our city who assist him are full of envy and ambition. Know that a cadre of warriors has planned this attack with Ek Chuuah. They are led by his brother Kab'ol and our own brave Chak'ok who have swayed their contingents to join in this evil. These have I seen in my vision."

She named those in the contingents of Kab'ol and Chak'ok, including the questionable Uc Ayin, but did not include Yaxun Zul. Heated discussion broke out amidst bursts of outrage, as the group pressed Yohl Ik'nal for details. Repeatedly she explained the nature of visions, that impressions given were often not complete or the visionary's memory not perfect. She reiterated that the timing of the attack was unclear, but soon. The precise target also eluded her grasp.

Tilkach and Itzam Ik, leaders among court advisors, pressed for immediate action to seize and imprison the plotters in Lakam Ha. The seasoned warrior Chakab, one of the few surviving from Kan Bahlam's time, was eager for quick execution of the suspects. But Hun Pakal's clear reasoning brought them up sharply.

"These actions are premature and unwise. We have no proof that our townsmen are planning to support this attack, and as yet no evidence that Ek Chuuah has plotted it. To seize them solely upon Yohl Ik'nal's vision is to leave ourselves open to criticism—not that I for one moment doubt what your vision has revealed," he added to his wife.

"Seizing them would inform Ek Chuuah that we are aware of his scheme, and permit him time to make adjustments in the plan of attack. Better to allow him to proceed, to catch his forces in the act, and also those traitors from our city. We will prepare, our warriors will be on alert. Let us post sentries at all routes into Lakam Ha, and send scouts to watch the passageways from Usihwitz both by the rivers and through the mountains. Runners will carry messages when movement of warriors is seen and we will mobilize our forces in readiness."

The High Priest and Priestess argued that Hun Pakal's plan was preferable. After more discussion, the courtiers agreed. Although the K'uhul Ahau had the power to order imprisonment or execution of enemies, it was not good for the social order to take such actions without clear justification.

Yohl Ik'nal thanked all for their contributions, especially Hun Pakal and charged him to organize the men needed for intelligence and battle. She requested runners outside her chambers, should she receive more insight about timing or target.

Later that day Hun Pakal and Yohl Ik'nal took afternoon refreshments of fruit and cacao drinks in the pale sunlight filtering into their private courtyard. Yohl Ik'nal reclined on a bench covered with soft mats, her face revealing the strain of recent events. Hun Pakal gently caressed her shoulder, trying to conceal his concern about her exhausted appearance.

"You must rest more, beloved," he murmured.

She nodded.

"Truly I am tired. There is so much to do . . . and I need your help."

"Always and in everything. Here I am beside you."

Several moments passed in silence as they sipped their cacao drinks. He urged her to take some fruit, so she nibbled on ripe papaya.

"There is something I must speak, for your ears only," she said softly.

Hun Pakal glanced around, waving the servants from the courtyard. He focused intently on his wife's tired face, nodding to continue.

"Involved in the attack plot was another of our city, whom I did not mention in the council. You will understand this when I whisper his name."

Hun Pakal bent his ear close to her mouth.

"It was Yaxun Zul."

He sat upright, startled. Quickly checking the courtyard to be sure no one was within hearing, he whispered back: "The father of Kan Mo' Hix! Both your and Sak K'uk's visions showed him as her husband. What make you of this?"

"In my vision I did not see Kan Mo' Hix among the plotters. This I do not understand, perhaps his father is protecting him. If the attack implicates this group from our city, they will all be executed as traitors. Perhaps Yaxun Zul wants to spare his son this possibility."

"I wonder how they plan to avoid implication," reflected Hun Pakal. "Any captured attacker from Usihwitz could be forced to reveal their names."

"Just so. And if Kan Mo' Hix knows nothing, has had no involvement, then they cannot identify him among the traitors."

"But he will be guilty by relationship. If his father is among the traitors, who will believe that he is not?"

"Ah, there you have my motive in not mentioning Yaxun Zul. Clearly the deities have ordained that Sak K'uk is to marry Kan Mo' Hix. For our people to accept this, neither of them must be found involved in the attack plot."

"Hmmm. That poses difficulties." Hun Pakal smiled appreciatively at his wife. "What plans have you? No doubt you have considered all these things."

"Indeed. First, you must go at once to Yaxun Zul and negotiate the marriage of his son to Sak K'uk. That will create a grand dilemma for him. If his goal is gaining more power in Lakam Ha, what better way than marrying into the ruling family? It is much more certain than a raid to elevate his status. He will quickly disengage himself from the plot. Ha! I should like to watch him scurry. This will create chaos within their group, much to our advantage."

"Think you not that the attack is meant to overthrow our dynasty? Or take over our city?"

"No. Ek Chuuah does not have enough forces to accomplish these objectives. He wishes to humiliate us and weaken our status among the ahauob and people. Then maybe internal competition will unseat our family. It is a risk, but by repelling this attack we will be stronger than ever."

Hun Pakal nodded. He thought a moment, and a dark shadow passed over his face.

"There is one more thing that must be done," he said grimly. "All our townsmen involved in the plot must be killed in the battle. If they survive to be questioned, they will reveal that Yaxun Zul was among them."

Wearily, Yohl Ik'nal agreed.

"Sadly, that must be so."

Another period of silence passed while the royal couple sipped cacao. Both appeared lost in thought, wrapped in the same concerns. Hun Pakal looked again at the lines of exhaustion on his wife's face. Reluctantly, he brought up the topic of royal accession.

"Beloved, I hesitate to speak of this, but it must be addressed. You have not designated an heir. With the troubles facing our city, this would add stability."

"Of this I am well aware," she replied. "It is a most difficult choice. Neither of our children is as yet ready for rulership. Sak K'uk has the character, but must refine and tame it. Aj Ne Ohl Mat does not possess such leadership qualities, but is more contained. Perhaps he would grow into a wise ruler."

"He lacks interest in affairs of state," observed Hun Pakal. "He is immersed in artistic pursuits, literature and poetry. Rarely does he attend the Popol Nah. Even today, informed of this most important meeting, he did not come."

"Our son causes me great concern. Rulership interests him not at all. This must I reflect upon, and seek divine guidance."

She took Hun Pakal's hand in hers, squeezing it warmly.

"Heart of my heart, you are ever my most worthy and trusted advisor. What you speak is truth; I will designate an heir with the hoof-binding ceremony soon."

Sak K'uk strode furiously through the main palace arcade, hands balled into tight fists. Two women servants scurried out of her path, gazes averted to escape her well-known wrath. Arriving at the chambers of her brother, Aj Ne Ohl Mat, she hovered in the doorway, taking in the scene. Aj Ne was reading his poetry aloud. The lilting tones of her brother's tenor voice hung like drops of honey in the expectant air. His circle of friends was listening in rapt concentration, while his wife Hohmay gazed adoringly, hands clasped to her breast. Sak K'uk curled her lip in disgust. That pompous, self-absorbed scrawny-necked crane! His arrogance and conceit were worthy of Wuqub Kaquix, the legendary bird who set himself up falsely as center of the cosmos. The whole scene made her want to throw up.

She hesitated, struggling to gain composure, waiting for a pause in Aj Ne's recitation. Mesmerized by his own creation, Aj Ne waxed eloquent with hardly time for a breath, his eyes lifted toward some phantom image, his right hand gesturing gracefully. Finally, she could bear it no more. Casting aside decorum, she strode into the room and stood defiantly in front of her brother.

"Aj Ne Ohl Mat! May I have your attention?!"

Startled, his voice sputtered and died out. He gazed quizzically at his sister, as though not recognizing her. Everyone present gasped. Shaking his head in perplexity, Aj Ne found enough voice to mumble: "Sak K'uk? Wh . . . what are you doing?"

"Clearly I am requesting to speak with you." Her voice rasped with irritation.

"But I am reciting," he complained in aggrieved tones. Waving his hand to include the courtiers, he continued. "We are in audience, and I am sharing my new poetry. Why do you interrupt us?"

"This is no time for poetry!" she said forcefully. "There are important things that I must discuss with you. Very important, but for your ears only. I must speak with you alone."

"Things that could not wait? Why so urgent? Disturbed I am by this uncalled-for interruption."

"Very urgent, Aj Ne. But for now, I can only speak with you about them. Please ask your courtiers to leave."

Brother and sister locked eyes. Often she had stared him down before, the very power of her will overcoming his timid nature. This was no exception. He broke the gaze first, sighed and requested his friends to leave. He entreated them to return after their noon meal, and the poetry readings would continue.

When all the courtiers were some distance from the open doorway, Sak K'uk made another demand of her brother.

"It is necessary that Hohmay leave also. What I have to say is a matter of state that I can only speak of with you. Please ask her to leave."

"What! Hohmay is my wife, we share everything."

"So you may share with her later as you see fit," snapped Sak K'uk. "But for now, I can only speak with you."

Aj Ne heaved another great sigh, his shoulders lifting and falling dramatically. His gesture clearly expressed "what can one do with such a sister?" Reluctantly he conceded.

"Dearest, do indulge my sister this strange request, and please overlook her rudeness."

To which Sak K'uk bit her tongue. Hohmay bowed obediently, smiled sweetly toward Sak K'uk and left.

Once they were alone, Aj Ne folded his arms over his chest, stretched his long thin neck to its limit and peered imperiously at his sister down his narrow arched nose. Again she noticed how his large head appeared to teeter on its thin stalk. That plus his prominent beaked nose made him look for all the world like a puffed-up crane.

"So? What is so urgent and important that you disband my poetry session and dismiss my wife like a servant?"

"Our city is in grave danger," she replied in a low voice. "An attack is being planned by a group of enemies, some from here but most from another city. I do not speak names now for security reasons."

"Where did you hear this? Perhaps it is just rumors." He waved a hand dismissively.

"Where were you this morning? Why were you not at the council our mother called?" she retorted.

"Oh, that. Mother's councils are so boring, always dealing with some problem or concern and taking much too long. And I had my poetry session already scheduled. That is much more to my liking than councils."

"This was a very important council; did not the messengers inform you? Mother and I made report of our vision quests, and these deal with our city's future welfare!" Sak K'uk was dumbfounded, unable to comprehend her brother's cavalier attitude.

"It is certain that Mother and Father can handle our city's welfare themselves— or perhaps even better with your sage advice," he noted sarcastically.

"Aj Ne! Some day you will need to take responsibility for Lakam Ha, when you become ruler. Does not this concern you? There is much to learn, you need experience . . . training . . . " Her voice trailed off as the thought arose that it might be she, not her brother, who became ruler.

"Perhaps so, but Mother has not yet ordered the hoof-binding ceremony to designate an heir." As if reading her thoughts, he said, "She might choose you. She has always favored you, and you certainly attend enough councils. Even if she designated me, we have a hoard of experienced ahauob and advisors to keep managing the city's affairs."

"You are hopeless. The Bahlam blood in your body is feeble." Sak K'uk could not conceal her contempt. "Just keep this in mind. Our city will be attacked sometime soon. There is internal treachery. You must not speak of this to others— not even your precious fool Hohmay. Mother and her advisors are developing a plan to protect us. If you want to know more, you must speak to her. Deities forbid that you would care to do anything."

Tossing her head, Sak K'uk spun on her toes and marched out of her brother's chambers.

Yaxun Zul waited nervously in his audience chamber for Hun Pakal to arrive. He was doubly worried about the visit; the request came suddenly from the K'uhul Ahau's consort and was characterized as both urgent and extremely important. What did the ruling family want of him? He was certain that this came not from Hun Pakal alone, but originated with the ruler. Might they have discovered his role in the attack plot? The very thought gave him chills, for he knew well how traitors were dealt with and it was not an easy death. Over and over he reviewed what the visit might mean; more tribute, sending his workers for building projects, confiscating his lands for food production, usurping his trade partners, or worse case, confronting him about the traitorous plot for a raid on Lakam Ha.

But if the latter were the case, why not simply send warriors to seize and imprison him? The worst was not knowing and having to wait. The wealthy ahau was not accustomed to such worry, and it discomforted him greatly.

A flood of relief washed through Yaxun Zul when his steward announced the arrival of Hun Pakal, but it was immediately followed by intense anxiety. His palms were sweaty as he clasped his shoulder and bowed to the ruler's consort, gesturing to the adjoining mat. Hun Pakal bowed appropriately, not too deeply or too shallowly, and nimbly settled onto his mat. Yaxun Zul made certain the two mats were at the same level on the floor of his audience chamber, declining to take his usual seat on the elevated platform. This was no time for holding court or elevating himself above the ruling family.

Immediately attendants served cups of atole mixed with cacao, and brought maize cakes made with nuts and dried fruits. After an exchange of pleasantries and inquiries into the wellbeing of each other's families, Hun Pakal asked how trade was going.

Keeping a bland expression, Yaxun Zul's mind spun wild fears that the ruler was planning to take over his trade routes and partners. His voice remained calm though he was quaking inside.

"Trade goes quite well. Recently my northern route traders brought some excellent obsidian from the central mountains, the finest I have seen of late. Might you be interested in new blades? There also is chert for spearheads, good quality and strong. And I received a small amount of exquisite jade of deep forest green color. Perhaps the K'uhul Ahau desires jade for jewelry? Of course to the royal family these would be an excellent value. . ."

His voice trailed off as he worried that he should have offered obsidian and jade as gifts. Now his mouth felt very dry, and he quickly sipped the atole-cacao drink.

Hun Pakal merely commented that they might be interested in seeing these objects, though not immediately. The conversation lapsed. Hun Pakal appeared deep in thought, while Yaxun Zul sweated more profusely. He waved for attendants to fan him with a large reed fan topped with feathers, and waited.

After what seemed an eternity to Yaxun Zul, his guest looked up and their eyes met.

"What it is, that I have come to speak about, is most important. It has great significance for the K'uhul Ahau and me, and for all people of our polity. Upon our decisions now will rest the future of Lakam Ha." Hun Pakal's face was serious and his voice carefully modulated to avoid emotions.

Yaxun Zul nodded, his hand gripping the cup tensely.

"I have come to speak with you about a union between your son, Kan Mo' Hix, and our daughter Sak K'uk."

Automatically Yaxun Zul lifted the cup to his lips and sipped, then almost choked on his drink. Suppressing a strong desire to cough, he sipped again more carefully.

"Kan Mo' Hix and Sak K'uk?" He was aggrieved that he could think of nothing better to say, but his mind was blank.

"Just so. Yohl Ik'nal and I have been thinking much of the correct match for our daughter. This is especially crucial as our son Aj Ne Ohl Mat has no children although married for over four tuns. It is possible the succession will be through children of Sak K'uk. We desire a broad basis of support for her children, and forming a union with your family will accomplish that. You are a greatly respected leader in Lakam Ha, have a wide circle of courtiers, many alliances within and outside our polity, and your lineage descends from our founder, Kuk Bahlam. Yours is a family of initiative and resources. Such a union would serve us both well, I believe."

Yaxun Zul's mind was racing, now in an entirely different direction. Marriage with the royal family! All his scheming to expand his power, to move his family closer to rulership, was co-opted by this amazing proposal. Hun Pakal was laying in his lap the very goal of his machinations, without his needing to risk his life or fortune, or even lift his hand! Except to signal agreement, which immediately he did.

"Immense is my honor, Lord Hun Pakal. Such a union offered by the royal family is more than I could have imagined. You will forgive me if I appear surprised, indeed I did not anticipate such an event. Of course, I completely agree with you, this will be most advantageous to both our families. My son Kan Mo' Hix will be honored, of this I am certain, with this great privilege and delighted to become husband of your most able and charming daughter."

He bowed while clasping both shoulders, the sign of ultimate respect and honor.

Hun Pakal smiled sardonically.

"Kan Mo' Hix is a young man of strong personality," he added, "and such a man is necessary for Sak K'uk. They will be a good match." He surprised himself with this spontaneous comment, realizing that he actually did mean it. Perhaps Yohl Ik'nal's idea was the ideal choice in any case.

"It is best that we proceed with this marriage without delay," he continued. "There has been some unrest within our polity, and the union of our families will do much to quell those ahauob who have become disgruntled with our dynasty. You are no doubt aware of these stirrings, for you are well-connected and have many information sources."

Yaxun Zul swallowed, his throat dry again. How much did Hun Pakal know? And if he knew, what motivated this move? New concerns rushed into his mind; he must disengage from the planned attack and keep himself removed from further plotting. Confusion filled him as he struggled to remain calm.

"That is so," he said, further confounded by which "that" he was referencing. "The marriage arrangements shall proceed at once. This day will I speak to Kan Mo' Hix and secure his agreement. Of which I am certain that he will be in accord."

"We will prepare the bride gifts with all due speed," replied Hun Pakal. "These will be most rich in keeping with the status of our royal daughter. Your family will see how great is the benefit of this royal alliance."

Even in his distracted state, Yaxun Zul did not miss the irony. Here was Hun Pakal offering him gifts, wealth and power while he had been worrying about losing both his fortune and his life. Was that a taunting glint in Hun Pakal's eye? If so, he was enjoying the game.

"So it is accomplished," Hun Pakal concluded. "We shall expect to receive you and your son tomorrow morning at the palace. Then the final agreements and plans for the marriage will be decided between our families. For our K'uhul Ahau, I express appreciation at your concordance with these proposals."

The ruler's consort rose to his feet, quickly followed by Yaxun Zul. Exchanging bows, the men's eyes met once again. Hun Pakal smiled briefly, then turned and was ushered out by the steward.

Yaxun Zul dropped heavily onto the nearest stone bench. Conflicting emotions and clashing thoughts raced through him. Could he abort the attack? No, the plans were already in motion, the time chosen, the strategies mapped. Should he tell his followers that he was withdrawing his support? They would surmise as much when the marriage was announced. How could he handle the consequences if anyone revealed his involvement? To this he had no answer. Even though the group had decided to keep out of direct action, some of the younger men were hotheaded and might join the battle, especially Kab'ol, the brother of Ek Chuuah. Any captives could expose the plot and implicate him as ringleader. By all the deities, what could he do?

He could deny everything. That is what he would do. Even as part of his mind doubted its effectiveness, simply having a plan comforted him. For now, he had many things to accomplish. Drawing a deep breath and straightening, he barked commands to the steward.

"Summon Kan Mo' Hix to me immediately," he demanded. "Prepare a list of updated assets. Bring the finest weaver and headdress maker here tomorrow afternoon; new clothing must be made. Speak not of this to the household until after the meeting with the royal family tomorrow, and so instruct all present. Many large changes are afoot."

5

The rains of the uinal Uo, month of the ground frog, were gradually decreasing. Uo ushered in spring, awoke the frogs from their winter sleep, nudged plants to send up new shoots. Low-lying land between mountain ridges was swampy. The rivers coursing through Lakam Ha flowed rapidly, swollen by rains and crashing loudly down cascades. Across the broad north plains, the K'umaxha River spread from its banks and deposited rich silt on farmlands. The river channel ran deep and swift, treacherous to navigate. Soon, however, the drier season would begin with its humid sunshine, blossoming flowers and easier travel.

In her reasoning mind, Yohl Ik'nal took these seasonal characteristics into consideration and surmised that the attack on Lakam Ha would occur after the rains of Uo. Try as she might, she received no further guidance from dreams or visions. Frustrated, she consulted her calendar priests, the Ah K'inob about calendar auguries in the next few months. Taking the most advanced priests into her confidence about the planned attack, she requested their interpretations. Each kin sign, uinal sign and their numeric coefficient produced different combinations fraught with meaning. To that was added the moon phase and lunation sequence, ruled by one of nine Lords of the Night. It was such a complex set of calendrics that the Ah K'inob had to study many tuns before attaining mastery that enabled them to make predictions.

The priests informed her that Uo, the Frog was characterized by magic and emergence, calling forth patience, serenity and understanding. It was most unlikely that aggressive or violent events would occur then. The next uinal, Zip, the Red Conjunction, honored the god of hunting and called forth bloodletting ceremonies. It augured ripeness, availability and completeness. This seemed to them a more likely time for the attack. Unless, of course, the enemy awaited the next uinal, Zodz, the Bat, associated with vision in darkness, intuition and clairvoyance. If they planned to attack at night, this would be a good uinal.

All of which Yohl Ik'nal found exceptionally unhelpful. With so many possibilities in each 20-day uinal, narrowing the time was impossible. One thing the priests said was significant, however; the day-sign Kimi held serious portent. Kimi meant "death" and was associated with the owl. The day of Kimi was a time for something to finish, change, remove or disappear. Its traits could be violent and vengeful, although also strong, tenacious and skillful.

She reflected much upon calendric meanings, her mind only partly focused on the numerous activities required for planning the marriage of Sak K'uk and Kan Mo' Hix. The date and time for this momentous ceremony was set by the Ah K'inob, who chose the month Mol, still five uinals away. Mol supported leadership and control, was a time for uniting and group activities. The chosen day sign, Lamat, had strong associations with success, good fortune, fertility, harmony and cultivation of the earth; things expected of a royal couple.

Amid the hubbub, a premonition arose on the fringes of Yohl Ik'nal's awareness that the attack would take place on the day of Kimi. There were twenty day signs that made up the Maya month, with 18 of these 20-day months in a 360-day tun. Since the solar year lasted 365 days, they added a short 19th month of five days at the end, called Uayeb. These five "days out of time" could be unpredictable and dangerous; usual activities were curtailed and no significant business conducted or decisions made then.

Another factor was the numeric coefficient of each day sign. Numbers also held important meanings and gave qualities to the day. The sacred Tzolk'in calendar used to plan ceremonies had 13 numbers; these flowed in continuous sequence through the solar and agricultural Haab calendar with its day and month signs. Therefore, the combination of number, day and month signs continued for 18,980 days (52 solar years) before returning to the original configuration. Within these 52 years, each configuration was unique.

As Yohl Ik'nal reflected on the day of Kimi, she calculated that it would occur three times in the near future, once in each month of Uo, Zip and Zodz. Some other clue was needed to help her determine which Kimi occurrence was the crucial one. Ever alert to messages from nature as well as the cosmos, she began to notice a recurring theme of four. When walking through an orchard, she saw four doves fly together from the underbrush. A *chik* (coatimundi) mother crossed her path with four babies trailing behind. Four ripe figs were placed before her as an afternoon snack. One evening a grouping of four stars hung above the horizon; the brightest she recognized as Noh Ek (Venus), often associated with warfare.

That is the date of the attack! The realization struck her. *It is 4 Kimi, the 19th day of Uo. And, it is only four days away.*

Baktun 9, Katun 8, Tun 5, Uinal 13, Kin 6 on the date 4 Kimi 19 Uo (April 19, 599 CE) matched the numerology and signs.

She sensed there would be something unusual about the attack, an unexpected twist. Calling Hun Pakal, close advisors and the warrior leaders together, she revealed these latest insights. Scouts had not seen any unusual activity in Usihwitz or strange travelers on the rivers. But, they respected her abilities as a seer and increased surveillance along routes leading into Lakam Ha. The Nakoms alerted their warriors to be prepared for action at any moment, but to conceal their preparations. Runners were stationed between the scouts in the field and the ruler's quarters. Observers hid near homes of the Lakam Ha plotters.

One final order was given to the warriors. They were to take no captives, and to kill all the plotters, their men and all Usihwitz attackers.

Sunrise on 4 Kimi 19 Uo spread fiery fingers across low-lying clouds on the eastern horizon. The city of Lakam Ha awoke to its usual morning activities, although intuitive residents might sense pervasive tension. The K'uhul Ahau and her contingent met in council, making final preparations. Yohl Ik'nal had slept little, and Hun Pakal even less during the ominous night. Warriors gathered along the two main entry roads into the city that followed the courses of the Tun Pitz and Ixha Rivers. Concealing themselves in the dense forests bordering these raised pathways, they settled quietly into readiness and waited. A small force of warriors occupied the ridges at the eastern edge of the city. From this vantage point, they looked over the undulating rises of heavily forested hills through which plunged two large rivers and several tributaries. The steepness of terrain, multiple cascades in rivers, and lack of substantial paths made this area unlikely for enemy invasion, but it must be watched. To the south and west, the mountain range lifted high toward the sky, rocky and virtually impassable.

As the sun progressed westward, breaking occasionally through billowing clouds, the ruler and her defenders waited. From time to time scouts came to the palace to report, but saw no unusual activity. Light food and drink were taken to sustain energy, but with little appetite. Hun Pakal had sequestered his son and daughter in one of the least accessible palace rooms, its only entrance heavily guarded. Assassination of heirs could be one objective of an attack aimed at the ruling family.

Shadows lengthened across the plazas of Lakam Ha. In courtyards of residential complexes, succulent aromas spread from cooking fires as the evening meal simmered. Some warriors slipped away from their stations, wearied of waiting and lured by smells of bubbling stew and roasting maize. When the setting sun peeped through clouds hanging just above the western mountains, a frustrated and worried group assembled at the palace.

Yohl Ik'nal sat in council with Hun Pakal, Tilkach, Itzam Ik and other trusted advisors, and several Nakoms including her father's friend Chakab. Questions were raised about the accuracy of her intuitions, phrased as politely as possible. The ruler was discouraged and puzzled; making inner inventory of all that the deities and natural forces had communicated to her, she could find no errors. The men discussed whether to recall the warriors and return to relying on scouts and observers. Night was about to fall, making attack most improbable. With only torches to navigate difficult terrain and unfamiliar city structures, invading forces would be ineffective against natives.

But, reasoned Yohl Ik'nal, 4 Kimi 19 Uo was not yet over. The day sign did not change until the next dawn. She listened to their reasoning against night attack, but did not defer, insisting the warriors remain in position. Food would be sent to them from the palace, which she ordered. As the Nakoms prepared to send their captains to keep warriors in place, Buluc Max the royal steward ushered in a breathless farmer.

He gasped out his message while bowing: "Warriors advance through the west orchards, bearing the standard of Usihwitz. There are many, I know not the count."

Chakab understood immediately, and his gaze swept the group.

"Their forces went west on the Chakamax River by night, crossed the hills and quickly traveled east on the Michol River, where we would never expect them," he said.

The Michol River flowed toward the west, the opposite direction from Usihwitz. Those maneuvers, combined with a late afternoon attack, were designed for maximum surprise.

The Nakoms leapt into action, shouting commands to their captains, bowing briefly to the ruler and rushing to the lines of defense. Hun Pakal had the foresight to send a runner to residential complexes to summon any warriors having dinner. He sent word to the guards of his children to intensify security measures.

Shaking his head in amazement, he turned to Yohl Ik'nal as the room emptied.

"Once again you are correct, my love," he commented. "Your vision never ceases to amaze me."

She appeared in deep reverie, not responding. Moments passed, he waited. Then her eyes flew open widely and she spoke with panic edging her voice.

"But that is not the twist! It is something else, a division of forces, something from the south and not the west!"

"What are you saying?" inquired Chakab, who had remained with them as the Nakoms left. He was far past the age of fighting.

"The south, the south!" she repeated frantically.

"Be calm, Yohl Ik'nal," said Hun Pakal, trying to sooth her. "Nothing can come from the south; it is too mountainous."

"Yes, a small force can ascend the footpaths over the mountains. They can be led by one who knows Lakam Ha intimately—Ek Chuuah!"

"You are again correct," said Chakab. "The path is narrow, steep and treacherous, but if led by one familiar with the terrain and taken slowly over a few days, it can be surmounted. That path leads to . . . let me think . . . the high plateau between the Bisik and Tun Pitz Rivers. Positioning forces well to invade the city center from the south. Summon runners! We must divert warriors to this area."

Hun Pakal immediately called more runners and Chakab gave them orders for the Nakoms. Yohl Ik'nal collapsed onto a mat, still in semi-trance. Hun Pakal kneeled and held her in his arms.

"Be comforted," he murmured. "We are as well-informed as possible; you have done our people an invaluable service."

Fighting broke out along the Tun Pitz road, the sounds of shouts, war cries and clashing weapons echoing up the hill into the city center. Word spread quickly that Lakam Ha was under attack. Boys and old men grabbed torches to help light the encroaching darkness, while women and children scrambled to find the safest rooms in their complexes. Warriors stationed on the eastern ridges ran rapidly toward the high plateau as instructed by runners. As they crossed the Tun Pitz heading in the direction of the palace and central plaza, screams from the area of Kan Bahlam's funerary pyramid diverted their course. Leaping steps to ascend the high platform, they encountered invading forces on the plaza, some already inside the temple throwing screaming priests aside. Crashing censers, pottery and statues resounded from within the temple atop Kan Bahlam's pyramid. Some attackers were setting blaze to the wooden lintels over entry doors. Others swung heavy stone axes against delicately carved panels on front walls, defacing the stone carver Uxul's exquisite work.

Lakam Ha warriors fiercely countered this attack, throwing chert-tipped spears and wielding obsidian daggers in hand-to-hand combat. Men grunted and howled, blood flowed freely and many fell motionless. As torches were dropped, priests grabbed them and held light onto the fray, hovering at the edges of combat and shouting encouragement to their forces. Invaders with stone axes turned these upon the defenders, but weight and clumsiness of the weapons gave little protection from spears and daggers. Soon no axes were in action, and the invading forces were driven down the steps away from the temple. The struggle continued on the plaza, but soon additional Lakam Ha warriors arrived and the forces of Usihwitz made a desperate retreat back toward the high plateau and mountain path by which they came. Although pursued intently, several escaped into the engulfing darkness of the steep forests. Mindful of orders, the warriors of Lakam Ha made certain all attackers were killed.

The battle along the Tun Pitz road continued longer, but eventually the enemy turned back and fled toward waiting canoes, carrying the Usihwitz standard with them. Many of their warriors had been killed, and those escaping did not wait for stragglers. Torches spreading light from prows of their canoes on the Michol River soon slipped into darkness. Again, the Lakam Ha forces put to death any Usihwitz warriors left behind.

During the fighting, a select contingent of Lakam Ha warriors led by Hun Pakal sought out the traitors named by the K'uhul Ahau. Some they found engaged in battle, ostensibly fighting with their city's forces, and managed to make their deaths look as if inflicted by the enemy. But on the plaza of Kan Bahlam's pyramid, Kab'ol was found fighting openly beside his brother of Ek

Chuuah. With intense fury, the select warriors overcame and killed Kab'ol, but when the bodies were tallied, it became evident that Ek Chuuah had escaped.

Darkness settled upon Lakam Ha, the night's quiet broken by wailing women who grieved the death of sons or husbands. Wounded warriors were taken quickly to the Ix Chel priestesses for treatment. The moon at mid-crescent cast pallid light upon plazas as it slipped between fast-moving clouds. At the pyramid temple of Kan Bahlam, priests accompanied Hun Pakal to inventory the damage. They were gratified that the front panels were minimally defaced, the interior friezes not touched, and the door lintels spared from fire due to the quick response by Lakam Ha warriors. Objects inside the temple such as vases and statues, many of which had been destroyed, could be replaced.

In the aftermath of the attack, Yohl Ik'nal met with the council to take measure of this extraordinary event. Inter-city warfare within a polity was not common among the Maya, but it appeared to be escalating. What made it more disturbing was that a few attacking warriors killed during the battle were from Pakab, a small town not within the Lakam Ha polity. Pakab was affiliated with Ka'an polity. While this did not prove that Kan was involved, it was suggestive. The belligerent, expansionary behavior of Kan was ominous. The council agreed that future aggressions were possible, and Lakam Ha must remain vigilant.

6

Sak K'uk and Kan Mo' Hix were married in regal splendor on the fortuitous date of 7 Lamat 6 Mol; seven was the number of energy and power, six the number of sprouting and hatching. The people rejoiced and enjoyed opulent feasting, their celebrations continuing through the night. Yaxun Zul, father of the new consort to the ruler's daughter, breathed more easily and counted his good fortune. More than five uinals had passed since the attack on Lakam Ha, and no murmurings had surfaced to implicate him. He was acutely aware that all the men involved in the plot had been killed, and no captives taken from the invaders. Again he reflected upon how much Hun Pakal and the K'uhul Ahau might actually know about the plot. Whatever their reason, they kept it to themselves, and for this Yaxun Zul was most grateful.

Life settled into its usual patterns in the city of many waters, perched upon verdant mountainsides above the broad plains crossed by great rivers. The royal court hosted courtiers, received tribute, entertained noble visitors. The Popol Na held regular council sessions, often presided over by Hun Pakal, because Yohl

Ik'nal needed to rest more. To those close to her, it was apparent that the K'uhul Ahau's health was declining, although she still made magnificent appearances at court. Sak K'uk frequently attended councils, though her brother Aj Ne Ohl Mat was frequently absent, pursuing the arts with his circle. Kan Mo' Hix engaged quickly with his new role, apprenticing to Hun Pakal and making an admirable impression both in court and at council.

Commoners worked the fields, prepared food and cooked, worked on city maintenance and building projects, and enjoyed their city's prosperity. Warriors trained and conducted field skirmishes, hunted and engaged in contests of strength and skill. Artisans, carvers, diviners, dancers, musicians and merchants plied their trades. The funerary monument of the ruler, a soaring pyramid on the east bank of the Otolum River, was near completion.

And none too soon, reflected Yohl Ik'nal. Her heart was growing weaker, limiting her ability to walk any distance and causing her to tire quickly. Whenever stressed, it beat rapidly and irregularly, making her gasp for breath. She realized that succession must soon be decided, but did not feel strong enough for a vision quest.

In the drowsy warmth of sun-drenched courtyards, in the quiet of moonless nights, Yohl Ik'nal began experiencing visitations as she drifted in the twilight of sleep. At first it was simply a presence, feminine and vast and powerful. It was enough to bask in this comforting presence, this profoundly mothering eminence. Perhaps the Great Mother was coming to welcome her home, to prepare the way of transition to the Underworld. After some time, the presence intensified, seemed to want something of her.

I am too tired, she thought. *Just allow me to rest peacefully.*

But the presence would not be denied. It meant to communicate something. Finally, Yohl Ik'nal acceded, made efforts to focus attention, to open her receptivity. The presence began sending her images and impressions as she dozed. The first one she received clearly was of herself performing the hoof binding ceremony to designate her son as heir. This startled her into waking, and she blinked rapidly in the hazy sunshine.

Aj Ne Ohl Mat as heir? Why was he the better choice? And who, she wondered, was this powerful presence.

That evening she set the intention to communicate with the presence and seek answers. As she drifted toward sleep and deliberately entered liminal space, she called to the presence to come forth, to reveal itself.

From the celestial vault, a thousand meteors plummeted toward her, bearing an immense star-strewn figure, a cosmic goddess with blazing eyes and shimmering tresses, wrapped in garments of cloud-nebula. Her soaring headdress of stardust streamers and sun-flare plumes bore an image of Muwaan Mat, the "duck hawk."

Muwaan Mat, the Primordial Goddess, primogenitor of the B'aakal Triad Deities, cosmic mother of creation, originator of the sacred ruling lineage of Lakam Ha. Her magnificence was beyond compare. Bowing deeply in the visionary field, Yohl Ik'nal acknowledged and saluted the Goddess.

Aj Ne Ohl Mat must be designated heir, the Goddess communicated into the liminal awareness of Yohl Ik'nal. *There are reasons for this, reasons to perpetuate the lineage. All is not yours to know. Aj Ne Ohl Mat will not rule long, will not leave successors. Succession will be through Sak K'uk, and she must be prepared to rule after him. It is her destiny to shepherd Lakam Ha through its darkest hours, and to propagate the great ruler to come, he who brings our sacred city to its apex. Time is short.*

Yohl Ik'nal's mind was spinning with questions, *What will happen to Aj Ne? The darkest hours of our city? What must Sak K'uk do to prepare? Time is short?*

The Goddess blasted her awareness with an explosion of shooting stars, burning away her questions.

All is not yours to know. Time IS short, so act now.

Shuddering and shrinking away, Yohl Ik'nal huddled at the Goddess' feet.

As you will, I shall do your will.

The Goddess softened her light and a sea of warmth engulfed the ruler.

Tell this to Sak K'uk. When the dark hours arrive, turn to me. I am the Way, I am the Answer, I am That which is sought in the depth of despair and the height of joy.

The immense glittering form began to withdraw, lifting skyward into the vast cosmic darkness, populating it with her constellations and nebula. A final communication drifted downward to Yohl Ik'nal on a sigh of celestial wind.

Soon you will join me in the sky of ancestors. The Goddess' voice sang more sweetly than the evening dove. *Your work is well done.*

On the steps of the palace, the deer hoof binding ceremony was performed as thousands filled the main plaza. In the ritual to designate the royal heir, Aj Ne Ohl Mat received from the K'uhul Ahau, his mother, the headdress featuring a deer hoof bound with a white cloth, bordered by B'aakal emblem symbols amid feathered finery. Within these intricate designs was the image of Unen K'awiil, the Triad deity of rulership and succession. Long trumpets blared and people cheered as Aj Ne ceremoniously placed the headdress upon his head, then walked slowly in procession around the main plaza, following his parents and flanked by priests and ahauob. After the ceremony ended, feasting, music and dancing began and continued well into the night.

Yohl Ik'nal, Hun Pakal and Sak K'uk participated for an appropriate length of time, and then retired to their quarters. It was not a joyful occasion for them. The ruler had explained to her husband and daughter the communications from Muwaan Mat and the coming course of events as best she understood them. Knowing that great tribulation was coming to their city, and that Aj Ne's time of ruling would be limited, by what catastrophe they knew not, saddened the royal family. They continued to prepare Sak K'uk for leadership, and Hun Pakal cultivated the abilities of Kan Mo' Hix. To their surprise, following his designation as heir, Aj Ne Ohl Mat began showing greater interest in governance and joined his father frequently in council and teaching sessions.

One great joy soon came to them, for Sak K'uk was pregnant. By Yohl Ik'nal's orders, conception was not delayed some years as was usual among royalty. Sak K'uk took her dynastic obligations seriously; she followed instructions of Ix Chel priestesses faithfully to ensure a successful pregnancy and healthy child. She ate recommended foods, took herbs as advised, exercised regularly, took cleansing baths, paid homage to Ix Chel as goddess of childbirth and healing. She blossomed as her belly enlarged, skin glowing and hair shining. Although her parents doubted that motherhood would come to her naturally, they appreciated her indomitable spirit. There would be ample wet-nurses and attendants to care for the child. Kan Mo' Hix was proud to have progeny so quickly, and Yaxun Zul simply beamed. But, it was difficult for Hohmay and her husband Aj Ne.

In the time of spring equinox, as K'in Ahau—Sun Lord found perfect balance between light and darkness, Sak K'uk completed the 260 days of pregnancy and went into labor. She was young, 19 solar years of age, robustly healthy, strong and determined. Her labor progressed rapidly and smoothly, much to the gratification of the Ix Chel priestesses. After less than one-half day of intense contractions, the midwife priestesses helped her stand on stone supports above the birthing bowl. She grasped birthing ropes tied to wall hooks, as one midwife encircled her waist with arms to help push the child downward. Another midwife held the birthing bowl as others chanted encouragement. Sak K'uk finished labor with a short time of vigorous pushing, and brought into the Middleworld a well-formed, healthy boy.

He touched the Earth on 8 Ahau 13 Pop, the child of Sak K'uk and Kan Mo' Hix, ahauob of Lakam Ha, of the sacred B'aakal lineage, the prophesied one.

Janaab Pakal, Lord of the Shield.

His birth was on Baktun 9, Katun 8, Tun 9, Uinal 13, Kin 0 (March 26, 603 CE).

Sounds of mournful drumbeats echoed through the palace complex. Slow and regular as heartbeats, the cadence invoked a meditative state. In the courtyard adjoining the ruler's private chambers, women and men sat cross-legged on mats, swaying to the rhythm. From time to time a woman's voice toned eerily, or a man's deeper rumblings evoked distant thunder. Copal smoke curled from multiple censers, filling the enclosed court with the sacred resin's entrancing scent.

These courtiers and warriors, women attendants and companions, were keeping a death vigil for their ruler. The entire city waited expectantly, cloaked in silence and sorrow. Yohl Ik'nal, their beloved K'uhul Ahau, their visionary and seer, their leader through adversity and abundance, lay dying.

Many days had passed since she last walked through the cool stone corridors of the palace, and many more since she passed among the people in the streets of Lakam Ha. For the last year and a half since her grandson's birth, she had not appeared in the Popol Nah or the throne room. Governance of Lakam Ha was in the capable hands of Hun Pakal, assisted by his two children. Now all was about to change, with the inherent uncertainty surrounding accession of a new ruler. The royal family had taken all the steps possible to assure smooth transition. The heir Aj Ne Ohl Mat was designated, a solid alliance formed through Sak K'uk's marriage, and loyalty assured among most ahauob and Nakoms.

The major unresolved issue was the city's relationship with Usihwitz. Since the attack nearly five solar years ago, interaction between two cities was suspended. No official visits occurred, and no tribute was offered by Usihwitz at the requisite occasions. Some ahauob grumbled about lack of initiative and show of weakness that Lakam Ha did not conduct a retaliatory strike. To diffuse this issue, Hun Pakal had called for a challenge ball game, to which Usihwitz responded by sending a team of players; Ek Chuuah was not among them. Safe passage was guaranteed to the Usihwitz contingent for the game.

The ballgame was played on 7 Chuen 4 Zodz, a few uinals after Pakal's birth; on Baktun 9, Katun 8, Tun 9, Uinal 15, Kin 11 (May 14, 603CE)

The game did not end well for Lakam Ha, whose players were defeated by one goal. In the small ball court at Lakam Ha, the stone rings on either wall were set lower than usual and the court was short and narrow, for it was seldom used. Usihwitz players were accustomed to larger and more challenging courts. Bouncing the hard rubber ball off well-padded hips and thighs, without using hands and arms, Usihwitz players sent more balls flying through the rings. The victors selected three Lakam Ha players to take back in servitude, cutting off their topknots. Symbolic blood was drawn from the losing captain's earlobes, a tribute to the Lords of the Underworld. When the Lakam Ha men's hair grew back full length, they could choose to return home or stay in Usihwitz.

This defeat of Lakam Ha was not taken well by ahauob and warriors. The issue of retaliation against Usihwitz was hotly debated in council. It was a source of discontent with which the new ruler would have to contend.

On this cool day as the sun moved close to its northern solstice, such concerns were far away from the dimming consciousness of Yohl Ik'nal. She reclined on her sleeping bench, propped up by cushions to ease her breathing. Each breath was a struggle, an effort to bring life-supporting air into her fluid-filled lungs, as her failing heart could no longer pump effectively. Nearby, her husband and children sat in silent concern. In the chamber were many other people, the Ix Chel priestesses administering care, the High Priest and Priestess, close courtiers including Tilkach, Itzam Ik, Chakab, Yaxun Zul, Kan Mo' Hix and Buluc Max, the Royal Steward. The ruler's long-time female friends, Sak Nicte, Na'kin and Tulix hovered as close as possible. The court dwarf Mas Batz stared mournfully into space at the foot of her bench. Her serving women clustered outside the door, tears streaming down their cheeks. She had always treated them kindly, and they loved their mistress deeply.

Yohl Ik'nal tried to open her eyes, but the lids were too heavy. Through a tiny slit she caught a glimpse of shadowy forms around her. She could sense Hun Pakal's strong presence and feel his warm hand upon her forearm. Their love had sustained her always, and still remained strong. As her vision dimmed, her hearing became acute. Through an open window to the courtyard came the lilting songs of birds, chirps and twitters as they gathered among courtyard trees. How lovely the music of the winged ones. Leaves rustled in a gentle breeze that sighed through stone lined alleys. The voice of Ik, the wind, was ever whispering secrets. In the kitchen courtyard, faint gobbles of ocellated turkeys and barks of spotted dogs drifted to her ears. The smell of stew cooking floated to her nose, but evoked no appetite. The sounds and smells of Kab—Earth, how beautiful, how precious, how impermanent.

Her breath rattled, she tensed in the effort to inhale then sank deeper into semi-consciousness. Awareness of otherworldly presences grew; many non-physical forms also surrounded her. Each form had its vibrational signature that impressed itself upon her consciousness, and she recognized the deities of the B'aakal Triad, those three who had formed and shaped and supported her lineage: Hun Ahau, One Lord of the Celestial Realm; Unen K'awill, Youthful Serpent-Footed Lord of Royal Lineages and the Earthly Realm; and Mah Kinah Ahau, Lord of the Underworld. The goddess of healing, weaving and birth-death transitions was present, the many-faceted Ix Chel, who had provided her with visions and much guidance.

Memory traces flitted across her awareness, faint and tantalizing. Someone from the distant past seemed to be calling her. A girl, a young woman, someone far away from a strange culture beckoned. Images formed of golden tresses wafting in moist breezes, of sky-blue eyes brimming with tears, and then dissipated into forest mists. She sensed the woman's confusion and pain, heard her cry of distress in a cruel and uncaring world. Men's voices, loud and angry, buffeted the woman's ears in a harsh unknown language. She was thrown to the floor and kicked viciously. Then she was stumbling through thick foliage, lianas entrapping her arms and thorns tearing at her clothes. The jungle was wet, the woman was soaked and her corn-colored hair hung in dripping tendrils.

The images faded as Yohl Ik'nal coughed and struggled for breath. Comforting hands supported her until she settled again into shallow breathing.

The woman with corn-colored hair and sky-blue eyes. Remember, remember . . . so long ago, so much has happened since . . . Elie! The girl from the windy hilltop in the land of the pale sun. Elie who said she would come to the lands of the Mayas, and appeared on an enormous boat traveling across an endless sea. She was in the jungle, running through dense bushes and tall trees, escaping from the thin-lipped man who intended to harm her. His rapacious eyes, small nose and hairy face were testimony to his merciless character. Elie was calling her, calling into the darkening jungle: *Yohl! Yohl! Help me!*

A stream of compassion flowed from Yohl Ik'nal's laboring heart to her distressed friend. She wanted desperately to help Elie, to guide her through the jungle to a safe haven, a village of her people. Even as these feelings formed, she glimpsed images of Elie inside a pole-and-thatch hut, sitting on a mat covering the dirt floor, taking a cup from the hands of an old Maya woman. A dark-skinned man hovered nearby, eyes filled with concern and something else . . . desire, passion, disbelieving hope.

Elie, Elie you have come . . . we will meet again.

She became aware of her surroundings once more, hearing the chants of priestesses and smelling the pungency of copal. Her fingers twitched and she felt the warmth of Hun Pakal's grasp, inhaling his beloved scent one final time. Him she would miss most of all when she departed the Middleworld. The blessing of his love was beyond anything she had dreamed might be her lot in a life dedicated to serving her dynasty. She felt his lips brush her forehead and knew it was complete.

Another powerful presence thrust itself into her awareness. It was the Great Mother Goddess, the primogenitor Muwaan Mat, who waited for her in the celestial realms and welcomed her with open arms. As dusk descended, Yohl Ik'nal yearned to surrender into the arms of the Great Mother. Her body wanted to drop away, to release her soul to its journey. Yet she had one more earthly task to complete, and Muwaan Mat urged her to action.

"Sak K'uk." Yohl Ik'nal's voice was barely audible.

"Mother, I am here," replied her daughter.

She felt the soft hand upon hers, recognized the scent of hibiscus flowers often worn by the young woman.

"When adversity comes, turn to Muwaan Mat," Yohl Ik'nal whispered between gasps. "Remember. Muwaan Mat."

She did not hear her daughter promise to remember. Already the soul, that White Flower Thing, was detaching from the body. In her last mortal thought, Yohl Ik'nal realized that dying was not so different than leaving the body for visioning journeys.

The celestial canoe appeared to carry her soul onto Xibalba Be, the road to the Underworld, the Great White Road of the Milky Way. The Jaguar Paddler god sat in the prow and the Stingray Paddler god in the stern of the long, narrow canoe. They invoked the Gods of power and sacrifice, symbols of divine rulership among the Maya. Riding in the canoe between the Paddler Gods from front to back were a spotted dog, a parrot, Hun Hunahpu—First Father the Maize God, a monkey, and an iguana. All held poses of grieving, hands to foreheads and mouths wide open and wailing. A space was open for Yohl Ik'nal between the parrot and Maize God, and there Ix Chel ushered her soul. As she settled, the canoe shot skyward and joined the Milky Way as it wrapped transverse across the night sky from east to west. It hovered for some time, then its prow tipped downward despite furious paddling, and it sank below the horizon as the Milky Way tipped just before dawn.

Yohl Ik'nal, K'uhul B'aakal Ahau, first woman ruler of Lakam Ha, had been transported into Xibalba, the Underworld.

Sak K'uk stood alone on the low rise near her mother's mortuary pyramid, gazing to the east across the large open meadow traversed by the Otolum River. The funerary rites and interment of the B'aakal K'uhul Ahau had been appropriately grand. The crypt was filled with luxurious ceramics and precious jewelry of jade and shells. Wails of professional mourners echoed off the pyramid for the requisite nine days, to inform the nine levels of the Underworld of this soul's importance. Codices inscribed with intricate glyphs provided instructions on navigating this dangerous place, giving secret word formulas that tricked the Death Lords and released the soul from their domain. Once she traversed the watery depths, Yohl Ik'nal would ascend into the sky and become a star ancestor.

But this was no comfort to Sak K'uk. All she could feel was grief over losing her mother, an untimely death. Yohl Ik'nal had only reached the age of an elder recently; many lived far beyond these 52 years. In her final year, she spoke to her daughter of mysterious things; great cycles of growth and decay, ominous events coming to their city, meetings with a strange woman in another dimension. It was so confusing to Sak K'uk, why had she not paid closer attention? Without her mother to guide her in visionary skills, she despaired ever mastering them.

Her despair deepened as she thought about her brother's accession. Aj Ne Ohl Mat would succeed to the throne of Lakam Ha after the traditional year of mourning. That he would provide inferior leadership she had no doubt. What this might portend, during a time of instability and dissension among the ahauob, she shuddered to think.

Although she stood at the place where she had once envisioned a magnificent city, today she saw only an empty field below, as empty as her heart.

The heart of one man rejoiced at the news of Yohl Ik'nal's death. In the aftermath of the failed raid against Lakam Ha, Ek Chuuah's prestige plummeted in his adopted city. His ambitions to become ruler were thwarted as his following dwindled. For years his simmering rage found no outlet except plotting more schemes to bring down the Bahlam dynasty. Now that his nemesis was dead, the major obstacle to success had been removed. He knew that her visions had foreseen the Usihwitz attack and allowed her city to prepare; this story was famous among the cities of B'aakal and beyond. He also knew that her daughter was not the accomplished seer the mother had been. Travelers along the rivers brought gossip to spice their trade, and tales about the B'aakal ruler's children captured people's interest. They spoke of the weak, irresolute son and the willful, undisciplined daughter who was deficient in visionary skills.

Ek Chuuah had evolved the perfect plan. It would require insider information, but he already had targeted his source. Perhaps more challenging was the need for powerful outside allies with seasoned warriors. For this he would play upon the expansionist politics of Kan.

Yes, this plan would work. Successfully carried out, it would position his son for rulership of Usihwitz. Without Yohl Ik'nal to obstruct his efforts, he knew the time had come to set this long-schemed revenge into motion.

Field Journal

ARCHEOLOGICAL CAMP

Francesca Nokom Gutierrez   Palenque, Chiapas, Mexico

May 16, 1994

Today is the most exciting day of my life! Our archeological team just discovered a royal tomb! Rumors are flying around camp that it's a woman—a Mayan queen. If it is, this will be the first queen's burial ever found in the Maya world.

"It's a woman, it's a woman." These words murmured by Fanny Lopez Jimenez after her first look into the sealed chamber hidden inside Temple XIII passed from mouth to mouth among workers, rippled across forests and rivers, soared over mountains, and soon will reach the ears of the world. But much work is necessary before we know what is inside the sarcophagus.

I must place this discovery in context, so it can be fully appreciated. Our team of young archeologists has been working in the ancient Maya site called Palenque since 1992, under the direction of Arnoldo Gonzalez Cruz. We are part of several Special Archeology Projects to explore and maintain Mexico's cultural heritage, created through INAH (Instituto Nacional de Antropología y Historia). During the 1993 field season, we concentrated efforts on the Great Plaza, especially the Palace and Temple of the Inscriptions. This season we are focusing on the string of smaller temples extending westward from the Temple of the Inscriptions; Temple XIII, Temple XII-A, and the Temple of the Skull. If the Temple of the Inscriptions, burial monument of Palenque's most famous ruler Janaab Pakal, were not so overwhelming these other three temples would be impressive in their own right.

Our field seasons are 6 months long, during the relatively dry period in the tropical forests of southern Chiapas. In winter months, the rains are so torrential that ground work is impossible, and scaling crumbling limestone stairs is dangerous. This is the last year of our project, so making this momentous discovery is all the more astonishing.

Let me reconstruct how the discovery happened. When the project began, each archeologist selected the temple, structure or pyramid they wanted to work. Fanny Lopez Jimenez, an archeology assistant; was assigned to Temple XIII because no one else was interested; everyone thought it was completely explored by Jorge Acosta in the 1970s and had no more information to offer. Fanny was happy with her assignment, working diligently to clear weeds from the base of the collapsed stairs and achieve structural stability.

On the morning of April 11, 1994, Fanny made a remarkable observation. While looking at the collapsed stairs of Temple XIII from a distance, she detected something more than the usual debris—a partially covered opening. At 2.8 meters above plaza level she saw a crack, its upper part still sealed by masonry but the lower portion was open about four centimeters where the debris had fallen away. It was a tiny crack, giving just enough space to create a fissure into the structure's interior. Fanny and her workers did not have lamps at hand, but one had a small mirror that they used to direct sunrays into the crack. Peering in, they saw a narrow passage about 6 meters long. It was completely clear and opened onto another passage at right angle, in which they saw a large sealed door.

It was a substructure inside Temple XIII. An unknown substructure buried inside the surface building that we see next to the Temple of the Inscriptions. In a temple that everyone had written off as fully explored. On this momentous day, a process began that will change our understanding of Palenque.

I've been working with the archeological team for two seasons. Our comradeship is very close and we share everything. Fanny immediately ran to let others know, and we gathered quickly in front of Temple XIII. Now with a flashlight, we took turns looking through the crack and marveling at the clear space within the passages. Often when substructures were covered with later construction, the Maya filled halls and chambers with rubble. Fanny got permission from Arnoldo, our project director who was then in Mexico City, to enter into the passage the following day.

To assist the archeologists with heavy excavation and restoration, the project hired local stoneworkers and laborers. Several of these men chipped away debris and removed part of the stone covering the opening. Fanny and her assistant climbed through the opening and felt as if they had entered "a tunnel of time" as she later told us. Their footsteps fell upon the silence of centuries and echoed off slumbering walls that had long heard no sound. Slowly they walked, taking videos and careful not to step on any object or offering. Archeologists learn to take extreme care when exploring sites, to avoid destroying any traces left by ancient people.

The narrow 6 meter passageway led to a long gallery 15 meters in length, built with large limestone blocks and oriented east-west. There were three chambers facing into the gallery; the first and last were empty while the central one was blocked by precisely fitted stonework covered with a coat of stucco that still had traces of black pigment. At either end of the gallery were two sealed doorways. The ceilings of the passageway, gallery and empty chambers were constructed using the Maya corbelled arch, a triangular shaped roof finished with capstones.

In front of the central closed chamber were remnants of charcoal on the floor. This is significant, because it indicates that rituals were performed for whatever this chamber contains. The limestone lintel above the chamber showed that it was once functional before it was sealed off.

When Fanny and her assistant emerged, we bombarded them with questions: "What is there? "What did you see? Can we go inside?"

In small groups we entered, treading into a forgotten world. The coolness of stone walls, the smooth stucco and damp air, the high corbelled arches drew us into mystery and wonder. This was no ordinary find, but one of the best-preserved galleries in all Palenque. It had never been entered before. Somehow it escaped the digs of prior explorers, archeologists or artifact thieves. What is even stranger is that Jorge Acosta barely missed it during his restoration of the northeast corner of the Temple of the Inscriptions. Alberto Ruz Lhuillier who discovered Pakal's tomb made test holes in Temple XIII that would have broken into the gallery if he had drilled one meter deeper.

The questions in everyone's mind were: "What lies inside the sealed chamber? Could the gallery and its passageways be connections between Temple XIII and the Temple of the Inscriptions?"

When Arnoldo returned and entered the passageway, he was astonished. Here was a temple, he declared, buried as a substructure and totally unknown. A week later, after intense work to consolidate and free the entrance, he decided to make a probe into the sealed chamber to see if it was empty or not. Although no one spoke it, we all suspected there was a tomb inside. He called for a minute of silence to ask "permission" of who or whatever was inside, that they would know we were only doing our work with the greatest respect for Mayan culture.

An experienced excavator made a 15 x 15 cm cut above the sealed door with his chisel. As it penetrated through the wall, he exclaimed as a burst of cold air hit his face.

"The space is hollow! Bring a lamp."

Arnoldo extended the long-neck lamp through the hole and gradually details of the interior were illuminated. Fanny was standing at his shoulder.

"What do you see? Tell me, what do you see?" Fanny could not contain her eagerness.

"I see . . . I see. ."

"Tell me, what do you see?"

"I see . . . better you should look, because we hit it! We hit it!" Arnoldo stepped aside, shouting "A tomb!"

When Fanny looked inside, she began crying: "It's a sarcophagus! A sarcophagus! Arnoldo, it's a sarcophagus!"

Shivers ran up my spine and all the team hovering around the opening stood in stunned silence. As the shouts continued from inside the structure, workers nearby dropped their picks and shovels and ran toward the opening. Arnoldo emerged and told them: "Enter and see what is also yours. Pass and see because it is yours!"

In small groups the archeologists and workers entered to marvel at the sight inside the sealed chamber: a sarcophagus carved in one single piece and painted red with cinnabar, a mercuric mineral used in burials. On top was a monolithic limestone slab. Standing in the center of the slab was a lidded censer, and at its foot lay a small bone spindle whorl. Ceramic vases and bones surrounded the sarcophagus. The chamber was perfectly vaulted and beyond the sarcophagus was the main entry door with five steps leading up to it.

A crowd gathered at the base of the temple. Curious tourists began applauding. Even though they did not know what was happening, they felt that something important had been discovered. Arnoldo looked at his watch and imprinted the time in his mind: 12:30 pm on the 16th of May, 1994.

He took out his radio phone and called for the presence of all members of the archeological team, including laborers and stoneworkers, at Temple XIII.

"Come because we have something to show you! Come immediately!"

Inside the gallery, I heard Fanny murmuring to herself: "It's a woman, it's a woman."

May 30—June 1, 1994

I'm thrilled to be part of the team working on Temple XIII. Due to the importance of the royal tomb, I was re-assigned to assist cataloging its contents, cleaning and restoring artifacts. I am fortunate, few doctoral students in restoration are considered skilled enough to work on such fragile treasures. All the hard work learning these exacting techniques was worth it!

It took over two weeks to carry out strategies for entering the funerary chamber in the Temple XIII substructure. The small perforation made on the north wall showed that the main entrance into the tomb was from the south. We thought that the sealed doorways at the ends of the gallery might lead to an access gallery, and possibly open onto connections with the Temple of the Inscriptions. After 15 days of exploration, the excavators found that the doorways led to inner, ascending stairways that originally gave access to a structure above, corresponding to the last stage of construction that we see now as Temple XIII. From the exterior they next made test pits 8 meters deep to see if these stairways gave access to the tomb, with negative results. Danger of collapse from working these areas led to the decision to enter the tomb through its north wall.

In royal burials, the head is pointed toward the north. Thus the north wall of a tomb might be decorated with murals, such as those found in Pakal's tomb. This discovery in 1952 by Alberto Ruz Lhuillier exploded onto the Maya scene: a royal tomb deep inside an impressive pyramid. Construction was initiated by Pakal and finished by his oldest son, with a huge sarcophagus decorated on all sides by carvings of his ancestors and a fantastic lid carved with the young Pakal ascending from the mouth of the Underworld Monster. Pakal is attired as the Young Maize God rising up the trunk of the World Tree—Wakah Chan Te; it is a depiction of his resurrection as the life-giving sustainer of his people and their world. The burial chamber walls were painted with exquisite murals and Pakal's body was adorned with jade and jewelry beyond imagining, including a jade mask. Ceramics, flints, shells, amber, and obsidian offerings in abundance as well as several sacrificial bodies were in place to accompany their ruler through his Underworld journey.

The riches in the tomb of Pakal have been compared with those of King Tutankhamen of Egypt. It is the richest, most luxurious burial yet found among the Mayas of Mesoamerica. Before Ruz made this discovery, archeologists doubted that Mayas buried their royalty in a sarcophagus within a dedicated temple, as did the Egyptians. Pakal's tomb proved that, at least on occasion, such extravagant burials did take place. Now we have the second sarcophagus found in the Maya world, and both at Palenque.

If Fanny's intuition holds true, this second royal burial might be a woman. Finding the spindle whorl on the lid adds strength to her belief, because these were used by noble women who excelled in the art of weaving.

After determining that there were no murals on the north wall of the chamber, the workers enlarged the small perforation to allow entrance. From the characteristics and location of the tomb, it was obvious that we were dealing with a person of highest rank in Maya society during the Classic Period. Located in the Great Plaza next to the Temple of the Inscriptions, the burial was without doubt a member of the ruling class. Perhaps the burial was of Yohl Ik'nal, grandmother of Pakal, Sak K'uk, mother of Pakal, or Tz'aakb'u Ahau, his wife—if it was a woman.

After entering the tomb, we began the work of describing, classifying, restoring and preparing the contents of the chamber for storage. The sarcophagus measured 3.8 by 2.5 meters; the lid was 10 cm thick and 2.8 meters wide by 1.18 meters long. In contrast to Pakal's sarcophagus, there were no carvings. Two sacrificial persons were present, their skeletons badly deteriorated. One was a female about 30-35 years old, the other an adolescent boy about 11 years old. His head showed the typical elite cranial deformation. Her teeth were encrusted with jade, indicating she was a noble. The chamber measured 3.8 by 2.5 meters, with smooth undecorated stucco walls.

From the ceramics, we dated the burial between 600—700 CE. But without glyphs, we still wondered who was inside the sarcophagus. In a niche in one of the chamber walls were three figurines in the form of whistles. One had a woman's shape; the others were fractured to show that they had no further utility in earthly life. Another clue?

Each artifact was located spatially within the chamber, catalogued, cleaned and placed in plastic bags to carry them to the laboratory installed in a nearby cabin. Initial analysis was done on site, and then the artifacts were sent to Mexico City for further study. The sarcophagus walls and lid were encrusted with dirt, snail fossils, mineralized stalactites, stone dust, and carbon deposits and needed careful cleaning. Using brushes and scalpels, we removed these testimonies of the past and bagged them for analysis. All this work was done inside a buried chamber whose temperature reached 40 C, causing our hearts to beat forcefully and rapidly. Everyone was drenched in sweat.

Arnoldo noticed something in the center of the lid, pointing with his scalpel. He found a small orifice that he thought could be a psychoduct. The ancient

Mayas created these small openings or tubes so the entombed person could communicate with the external world. In Pakal's tomb, a square tube psychoduct ascended from the sarcophagus like a snake up a long stairway to the floor atop the temple.

Putting on a mask, Arnoldo opened the orifice. Immediately cinnabar, the mercurial element giving red color to the sarcophagus, began to escape through the opening as mercury sulfide gas. Everyone quickly put on masks to protect against the toxic gasses. The eyes of some began tearing and others felt nauseated. Arnoldo ordered everyone to go outside immediately. Work for the day was finished.

Nobody talked of anything else in the camp at Palenque. Everyone was preparing for opening the sarcophagus. Many lingered after dinner near Temple XIII as the sun set, knowing their work would resume at nine the next morning. Leading functionaries in government and national culture would arrive the following day, flying from Mexico City and expecting that the archeologists would wait for them to raise the lid. But they did not take into account the charge of adrenalin coursing through our bodies.

Fanny advised us to stay close by.

"Don't think about moving away from here, surely Arnoldo is not going to wait and will open it as soon as he can."

The morning of May 31st Arnoldo visited the funerary chamber to re-visualize his strategy for raising the lid of the sarcophagus. He had decided to use the technique that Ruz Lhuillier applied successfully in Pakal's tomb. A workshop was set up in the plaza for carpentry and other tools necessary for operating the hydraulic lift that would raise the lid. He calculated how many people could work inside the chamber to provide enough assistance to prevent the lid from breaking.

The work inside the tomb began. Hours passed, the temperature rose but there was no movement of the lid. The carpentry workshop functioned at full throttle; metal tubes, wedges and cables entered and left the chamber according to Arnoldo's instructions. Finally, after 16 hours the frame connected to the hydraulic lift was raised four centimeters, at 3:00 in the morning. By 4:00 am, the intense silence and nerve-wracking anticipation was broken when joking began among the workers. This humor alleviated the fatigue from hours of work and waiting. The system was functioning. They knew the moment of revelation and danger had arrived; the enormous lid was moving and soon they would see what lay inside.

Outside, the night before June 1, 1994 was long and hot. Few could sleep, including the wildlife in jungles and mountains surrounding Palenque. Howler monkeys roared as never before, their eerie chorus echoing from crest to crest. Brilliant fireflies twinkled in dense darkness while millions of insects chirped and clacked. During the night the god Chaak celebrated with a brief but intense downpour of rain. All was in readiness for one of the most important discoveries in the history of Mexican archeology, the revelation of who had waited 1300 years in the tomb of Temple XIII.

As the lid slowly lifted, a strong odor of cinnabar emanated from the sarcophagus. Everyone put on masks. Cries of "Courage! Courage!" came from those in the passageways and lining the stairs of the temple. Most of the camp was present; our young team with average age 25 to 30 years was too eager to sleep. By 6:10 am, the lid had lifted about 20 centimeters and our photographers could insert cameras that sent pictures to a monitor so we could watch the discovery unfold. At 8:00 am the final cylinders were in position and the huge lid slipped off, little by little. Ten minutes later, as profound silence descended, Arnoldo said "Ready!" and the lid slid to the bottom, allowing all in the chamber to see into the sarcophagus.

In shades of red cinnabar and green jade, a skeleton lay on its back with head to the north. On the skull was a diadem of flat, round jade beads and hundreds of bright green fragments framed the cranium. More jade, pearls, shells and bone needles both covered and surrounded the skeleton. These probably formed necklaces, ear spools and wristlets that adorned the entombed body. On the chest were many flat jade beads and four obsidian blades. In the pelvis area were three small limestone axes which most likely were part of a belt.

The bones were completely permeated with cinnabar, and the interior sarcophagus walls coated with the red mercuric preservative. Red, color of the sun, of fire, of the east where all things begin. Green, color of jade, sacred symbol of life, water, immortality.

Arnoldo and Fanny stared in awed silence. As word spread that the sarcophagus contained a complete skeleton richly adorned with jewels and precious offerings, applause broke out. Our intense emotions were expressed in smiles and hugs, as we passed in and out of the chamber taking our turn to view. Fanny had tears in her eyes, and so did I.

June 10, 1994

"We have here 100 years of archeological study."

Arnoldo's words upon first viewing the contents of the sarcophagus continued to ring in my mind. We had made a momentous discovery, the intact tomb of Maya royalty inside an unknown substructure built during the 7th to 8th centuries CE. It was the second richest burial ever found, the second in a sarcophagus. But in fact we knew very little. The total lack of inscriptions left us without any epigraphic data. This is not so uncommon, however, for most burials at Palenque lacked glyphs to identify the occupants. Pakal's extensively inscribed tomb is the exception, not the rule.

Now we are waiting for further laboratory analysis. The ceramics found in the tomb gave us the dates, but this conflicts with the earlier time period in which the substructure was built. Possibly the substructure had another purpose originally, and was converted into a tomb following an unexpected royal death. The stairs giving access to the outer level indicate that the tomb was visited after it became enclosed by the newer structure. This layered building practice is common among the Maya. Many structures we now can see represent at least three levels of buildings, each layer constructed over the one below. They also used rubble from broken-up structures to fill the inside of later buildings.

Initial examination of the skeleton calculated its height about 1.54 meters and age at death around 40—45 years. Given the height and size of the skeleton, tall for ancient Mayas, our physical anthropologists think it is probably a male. The offerings in the tomb, however, are not typical for male burials. There were no stingray spines used for penile bloodletting, no obsidian axes or knives, no jaguar claws. In contrast, the objects found relate more to women: the spindle whorl, plates and vases for serving food.

The sex of the royal person entombed in Temple XIII is critical. I hope INAH will send an expert soon to further examine the skeleton for evidence of its sex. It would be interesting if they chose Arturo Romano Pacheco, arguably Mexico's greatest physical anthropologist, who examined the bones of Pakal forty years ago. Controversy surrounds his conclusions, because the age he attributed to Pakal was much younger than what was recorded in multiple glyphs in Palenque. Arturo declared that Pakal was no more than 40 years old when he died, while the glyphs record his death at 80 years old. We will see what comes of all this.

Meanwhile, our work goes on at the archeological camp in Palenque. Our camp has a long history, going back to the work of Alberto Ruz Lhuillier in 1949.

Initially camp was set up with tents pitched in overgrown plazas and hammocks hung inside musty chambers. INAH constructed some buildings on the flat area at the base of the 400-meter high escarpment, the northern edge of the Chiapas highlands. The ruins cluster on a narrow shelf a quarter of the way up. Many great scientists have stayed in this camp. In makeshift laboratories, they analyzed findings and wrote reports. Over the years, the camp was upgraded to provide better housing in cabins and more current laboratory equipment. It's quite pleasant here, our cabins tucked among tropical forests, not far from Palenque's numerous streams. Walking to the site through the cascade trail takes you past several beautiful waterfalls and through residential complexes clinging to the mountainside.

Living close to jungles brings frequent contact with its creatures. My roommate Sonia Cardenas found a baby boa constrictor in her footlocker last night, and I've brushed many spiders off my pillow. Everyone contends with stinging insects in the field, from ants to mosquitoes to the dreadful garrapatas, tiny ticks that burrow under your skin. They like areas where clothes are tight, such as your waist, panty line and wrists. Once embedded, they form red bumps that are terribly itchy and persist for weeks. We use lots of cortisone cream, though the locals prefer Xcoch (castor bean leaves crushed into a paste.)

Howler monkeys roar from the forest canopy day and night. It's hard to believe that these smallish creatures can produce such deafening sound. Their deep, throaty roars conjure images of primeval beasts stalking prey through Pleistocene jungles. Packs of howlers call back and forth, echoing over miles of terrain. Early explorers who set up campsites inside Maya ruins thought they were hearing roars of jaguars. Of course, jaguars do not roar. They are stealthy creatures that stalk silently, creeping up on prey and making soft grunts just before the attack. None of us walk the jungle pathways at night.

Sonia and I worked all day in the lab cleaning ceramic fragments from different structures, removing limestone deposits encrusted over the years and stabilizing with resins on all surfaces. A few pieces from Temple XIII have come to us, and we fantasize about the tomb's occupant. Even though team experts lean toward it being a man, we are siding with Fanny and betting it's a woman. Together we review what we know about Palenque's great "queens." We use the terms "king" and "queen" for convenience, even though these don't capture the true meaning of Maya rulership. Maya rulers were called *K'uhul Ahau*, best translated as "Holy Lord" or *K'uhul Ixik* for "Holy Lady." Female rulers were often addressed with the male title, however.

210

There were four "queens" named in Palenque glyphs and inscriptions who are candidates for the Temple XIII burial. We know quite a lot about the first two women rulers, the grandmother and mother of Pakal. About the others, Pakal's wife and daughter-in-law, we know much less.

Palenque is one of the few Maya sites with "queens" who ruled in their own right. The Palenque "queens" hold immense fascination for me. These women shaped dynastic succession and wielded influence for generations. Certainly they were among the most powerful women in the western hemisphere, yet almost no one has heard of them. Ruler succession was usually along the male line, but not always. We have epigraphic evidence of women rulers in Tikal, Dos Pilas and Yaxchilan but all these women acted as co-regents with husbands or sons.

The ancient city of *Lakam Ha*, "Place of Big Water," was by around 500 CE the dominant city in a region called *B'aakal,* the polity of B'aak or "bone" in Mayan. We call these regions "polities" because the geographic areas of a dominant city's influence contained several subsidiary cities. People lived in the western part of the site by 500 BCE, according to the ceramic record. By 400 CE the community had grown and become more complex, interacting with the Peten region to the east. The Bahlam or "Jaguar" dynasty was founded around this time by *K'uk Bahlam I*, the first ruler considered fully human. He acceded in 431 CE.

Before him, however, was a divine lineage going back to mythological time and the Primordial Mother Goddess, *Ix Muwaan Mat*. The dynasty hit its apex with the creative genius of Pakal in the mid-seventh century CE. It declined along with the other Peten and Chiapas sites in the late tenth century.

I should give Pakal's entire name and title: *K'inich Janaab Pakal I*, K'uhul B'aakal Ahau, called "Pakal the Great," the most renowned ruler of Palenque. His name translates to "Sun-Faced Lord Shield."

Around 150 years into the B'aakal dynasty, the first woman ruler acceded. Her name was *Yohl Ik'nal*, "Heart of the North Wind." She acceded in 583 CE and ruled in her own right for 22 years during times of both abundance and conflict. Most likely she was the daughter of Kan Bahlam I, the prior ruler. As more than one Mayanist said of her, "she must have been a remarkable woman." She guided her polity through attacks from Bonampak and Dos Pilas, plotted by archrival Kalakmul (Kan in Classic times), and kept succession in her family against opposition. She was Pakal's grandmother.

The second "queen" was *Sak K'uk*, "White Resplendent Quetzal." Daughter of Yohl Ik'nal and mother of Pakal, she acceded in 612 CE and ruled for three years until Pakal acceded at the age of 12 in 615 CE. Probably she was co-regent for some years and continued to advise him. However, there is controversy about exactly who ruled from 612-615 CE. Glyphs name Muwaan Mat as ruler, though some contend this was another name for Sak K'uk. Most intriguing is the link back to the Primordial Mother Goddess Ix Muwaan Mat. Maybe Sak K'uk joined forces with the Goddess to cope with the chaos that befell the city after Kalakmul's devastating attack in 611 CE.

The third "queen" was *Tz'aakb'u Ahau*, "Accumulator of Lords." Wife of Pakal, they married in 626 CE. She was from Tortuguero (B'aak), a site that had close ties to Palenque. The inscriptions refer to her as "from Toktan" the legendary city where the dynasty originated. Also called "Lady of the Succession," she bore three or four sons, two becoming rulers after Pakal. The Mayan word *tz'aakb'u* was important in ancient Maya politics, and refers to the ordering of royal succession. This honorific name was undoubtedly given to her when she married Pakal. Her actual name is not known.

The fourth "queen" was *K'inuuw Mat*, "Sun-Possessed Cormorant." Also from another city, she was the wife of Pakal's youngest son. Although this son did not accede (he died earlier than his older brothers), he was the only one to produce heirs. Their son K'inich Ahkal Mo' Nab III acceded in 722 CE, and the Bahlam lineage of B'aakal continued through this union. As mother of the royal succession, she wielded influence during a time when nobles were gaining power and there was foreboding of dynastic and cultural decline. Her role in preserving Maya cultural heritage bears examining.

June 17, 1994

The hot, humid climate of Palenque accelerates both growth and decay. After the ancient city was abandoned around 1000 CE, voracious jungle vines quickly climbed stairways while trees sprouted in plazas and brush grew between stones of walls and terraces. Within 100 years the city was hidden beneath waves of greenery forming forested hills where once pyramids stood. Another few centuries and the stone walls crumbled while torrents of rain dissolved the bright paint covering Palenque's structures and eroded exquisitely carved panels and glyphs. By the time the Spaniards arrived, only a few roofcombs peeped through forest panoply and the great city was but a faint memory among local Maya descendants.

I've become accustomed to the cool, dry climate of Mexico City where my school (Escuela Nacional de Conservacion, Restauracion y Museografia) is located. Today the heat in here Chiapas is oppressive. Sweat drips as I write, moistening my notebook. But I will soon adjust, for this area is my home. I was born in the village of Palenque, a few miles from the ancient Maya site. Maya people have always lived here; early Spanish explorers gave the name to my village in the 1500s. Perhaps my family is descended from the Mayas that mysteriously abandoned their great city during the Classic Maya "collapse."

Palenque—the most magical and exquisite ancient Maya city. This place has been dear to me all my life. Spread across a plateau of the Sierra de Chiapas Mountains, the city looks north and west over the Tabasco plains. It has abundant water; seven streams cross its terrain and cascade through ravines. Lush tropical forests rich in edible fruits, plants and wildlife surround it. Mountains rise tall to the south, their peaks often draped in mist.

The mists of Palenque. How often I've watched swirling mists furrow through mountain crevices, hover like silvery drapes, seep across plazas to lap at broad stone stairways. Mists that hide more than palaces and pyramids and temples. They obscure from our sight the lives of those ancient Maya people who once lived in this magnificent city. I yearn to see Palenque, ancient Lakam Ha, through their eyes. What did the delicate roofcombs and graceful temples look like in their original colors, walls painted red-orange, friezes etched in vivid blue, yellow, black and green? The city perched on a narrow ridge partway up the mountain's northern edge. Buildings draped over steep hillsides, their stepped platforms and multilevel plazas ordered by natural contours. In its heyday up to 8,000 people lived there, gathering below temples and filling plazas for ceremonies and feasting.

I can almost smell copal incense drifting from incensarios lining pyramid steps, and hear the rhythmic beat of wooden drums and plaintive flute melodies.

Palenque is disconcerting to archeologists, while holding us in its mesmerizing grip. Buildings were constructed differently than at other sites near the Usumacinta River, called K'umaxha by ancient Mayas. Palenque has a striking style of simple stepped pyramids supporting a temple on top with sloped roofs crowned by airy roofcombs. Many buildings were decorated with exquisite friezes on pillars, side panels and interior tablets. In contrast with other sites that had many freestanding monuments such as stela, Palenque had only one. Lakam Ha glyphs expressed religious and lineage themes, while its neighbors' glyphs were of a more bellicose nature, recounting victories of rulers.

There was only one quite small ball court in the city. Most important Maya sites had several large ball courts, because the ball game re-enacted Maya creation mythology as told in the *Popol Vuh*. This was central to Maya religious practices, but at Palenque greater focus was placed on the Triad Deities. The great Mayanist Heinrich Berlin first deduced their existence in 1963, designating them as God I (GI), God II (GII), and God III (GIII) because he could not read their name glyphs. Progress in epigraphy deciphered their Classic Mayan names and how they fit into Palenque's creation mythology:

God I is *Hun Ahau* (One Lord), first born in the mythical realm of Matawiil. Around the time of Maya creation, he occupied "Six Sky Ahau Place," a position on the Maya zodiac. His domain is the celestial realm, the Upperworld. His rebirth as a Triad member signaled his resurrection into a new, local religious order at Palenque.

God II is *Unen K'awiil* (Infant Powerful One), third born though Berlin identified him as the second god. The youngest, he assumes a baby jaguar form with a snake leg. As dynastic patron, he symbolizes royal power. His domain is the earthly realm and agriculture, the Middleworld. His title "Young Lord of the Five Heavenly Houses" refers to the Maya zodiac.

God III is *K'in Ahau* (Sun Lord), second born on 13 Kimi, day of death that ends the 13-day cycle. His domain is the Underworld. He is depicted as K'in Bahlam the Underworld Sun Jaguar represented by the full moon, or Waterlily Jaguar swimming in the watery Underworld.

The Palenque Triad Deities had an interesting birth sequence. All were born the same year (2360 BCE). GI and GIII were born four days apart, and then GII came 14 days later. They all had the same mother, the Primordial Mother Goddess Ix Muwaan Mat. It's not clear who fathered them, maybe the very ancient God

I "The Father" who seemed to reincarnate himself as his firstborn "The Son." The Triad Deities created the liminal quasi-human *U K'ix Kan*, who "came to be" in ancient times and lived hundreds of years. He brought forth the first truly human ruler, K'uk Bahlam I, who lived a normal mortal life in historic times, and founded the B'aakal lineage that built Lakam Ha.

The Maya of Lakam Ha were unique in their emphasis of these three deities. They were patrons of the ruling dynasty, the Holy Lords of B'aakal. Although the Gods are found in many other Maya sites, only in Lakam Ha did they have such special roles with the rulers. The rulers embodied—actually became—Triad Deities and brought their beneficence to the people. Religion, history and politics were one and the same. Society was organized according to religious beliefs and cities constructed to mirror cosmology. While all Maya cities integrated religion and sociopolitical structures, Palenque was obsessed with weaving them together to demonstrate the ruling dynasty's oneness with the deities.

The Maya title for ruler, K'uhul Ahau or Holy Lord conveys their role as divine emissaries, mediating between Gods and people, maintaining the cosmic order of their universe. Rulers were not kings or queens in the European sense. We must be careful of super-imposing a Eurocentric view upon Maya culture, which was radically different from the kingdoms and warfare of medieval and renaissance Europe.

June 28, 1994

Today is Sunday, and the team takes every Sunday off to rest. I'm impatient to continue the work, but everyone else seems to enjoy lounging around camp, visiting nearby towns or going to Villahermosa to the movies. Last evening I went to Palenque town for dinner with my family. They are thrilled at the opportunity to have me close by; most of my last six years have been spent in Mexico City. While they're proud of me, the first in our family to get advanced degrees, they seem uncomfortable about the results. I'm still unmarried at age 26, too educated for men of our town, and probably destined for a university position far away from home.

It's the perennial dilemma of villagers around the world. Parents want a better life for their children, send them away to get educated, hope they will return to the village and help local people, but inevitably we're lured into city life with its work and cultural advantages. In addition, the educational and cultural gap separates us from village society. Our poor parents are left alone in their old age, or uprooted to live in alien urban settings. Tanto trieste! How sad, but probably my fate, too.

My family was interested in happenings at the archeological camp, because locals take much pride in their famous Maya ruin. It supports a large part of local economy with an unending stream of tourists, filmmaking, spiritual conferences and scientific research expeditions. They listened to my stories and took part in a vivacious discussion, my father never lacking in opinions about the import of our discoveries. He's somewhat of a self-styled Palenque expert and frequently takes friends on tours of the archeological site. My mother liked best the descriptions of our cook's talents, though she couldn't believe their cooking might taste as good as hers.

I described last evening's dinner at the archeological camp kitchen; it was especially delicious. How the cooks can prepare such tasty food with limited facilities amazes me. They brought typical south Mexican cuisine to a fine art; stews of pork and chicken, black bean sauce, tamales of chili and cheese, and tortillas as only village women can make—small, thick and cooked on a griddle stone placed over an open hearth. Add local fresh papayas, mangos, bananas and melons for the finishing touch and you have a meal for a Maya king; a K'uhul Ahau, that is.

My abuelita, "little grandmother," watched all this with a twinkle in her eyes. She is a great one for telling stories, my abuelita. I learned all I know about storytelling arts from her. She told me many tales about growing up in Tumbala, a tiny Mayan village far into the forests east of Palenque. To help support her family, she walked three hours through trails to Palenque town to work as a housekeeper. After a long day scrubbing floors and washing clothes by hand, cooking meals and tending children, she returned home in gathering darkness. According to her, she could walk that trail if the night was pitch black or she was blindfolded.

She met my grandfather in Palenque. He worked in the grocery store owned by his uncle. One day their eyes met across a table of squashes, and they fell in love. He bargained with her father, who was loath to lose the family's best source of income. Legend has it that grandfather paid a royal bride price for her; at least it seemed so to villagers of that time. They lived in Palenque and built the house my father inherited, where my parents are today. Abuelita's squash dishes are still a family favorite.

She promises to tell me the story of how I got my blue eyes—the same color as hers—later, always later, when I am old enough. Well, I should be old enough now! When I asked tonight, she demurred, saying: "Maybe on your 30th birthday, or when you marry."

"Why when I marry? What if I don't marry?" I chided her.

"Not marry? Do not say such a thing, querida," she scolded. "Of course you will marry, and have children, and continue the family. That is what women must do."

She is still very much a Maya villager, my abuelita Juanita. A tiny, slender woman, she has the narrow face, prominent cheekbones and large nose of the highland Maya. Her skin is dark chocolate color and makes a startling contrast with her blue eyes. Papa, her son, looks more Spanish with lighter skin and smaller nose. He more resembles my grandfather, now passed on. Mama also looks less typically Mayan. They are all mestizos, my family. From earliest times the Spanish interbred with natives, initially by keeping mistresses but eventually by marrying.

Mama seems unimpressed by Abuelita Juanita's secrets.

"Every Maya today has some blue-eyed Spaniard ancestor. What's to be so special about your eyes? Mexico is populated by mestizos; we are all a mixed breed. Juanita makes much of nothing."

But I'm interested in our heritage and her village memories.

"Maybe if you tell me the story about our blue eyes, then I will want to get married," I tease.

"We will see, we will see," is all she would say.

I am nearly moved to tears, some of joy and some of sorrow, when I think about Palenque's legacy of exploration going back to the early Spaniards. Some came for official documentation, some as explorers and opportunists, a few as lovers of antiquities and exotica. Among them were serious archeologists and anthropologists seeking to penetrate the mysteries of the fabulous ancient civilization lost in dense jungles.

What did the site look like to early explorers? They had to endure daunting hardships getting here. With Papa's help, I'm summarizing the history of Palenque's exploration.

In the 1780s, a couple of Spanish expeditions came to Palenque and made crude drawings of structures and art. The King of Spain was interested in the geography and history of his overseas colonies, and dispatched Artillery Captain Antonio del Rio from Guatemala to bring away samples. Del Rio removed stucco hieroglyphs, parts of figures and small panels that now reside in Madrid's Museo de America. Numerous drawings by artist Ignacio Armendariz from this expedition were the first reasonably accurate reproductions of Palenque's huge array of art.

Another Spanish expedition in the early 1800s produced 27 drawings of panels and tablets, floor plans, and sketches of buildings, a bridge and aqueduct. Guillermo Dupaix, Dragoon Captain stationed in Mexico, and artist Jose Luciano Castaneda took a 50-mile trek from Ciudad Real (now San Cristobal de las Casas) to Palenque that required eight days on a trail winding through mountains that were "scarcely passable by any other animal than a bird." Unfortunately, the work of these two Spanish artists got confounded and appeared in a book by Alexander von Humboldt in 1810 labeled as "Mexican reliefs found in Oaxaca," a city nowhere near Palenque.

The flamboyant artist, traveler and antiquarian, self-styled "count" Jean-Frederic Maximilien de Waldeck adapted Armendariz-Castaneda's art with his own embellishments of musculature and costumes that gave a distinctly Roman look. Waldeck, like some other early explorers, believed the people who built these cities came from the "old world," perhaps Rome, India or Egypt. This art appeared in an 1822 publication of the del Rio report, with many images copied into Lord Kingsborough's sumptuous volume the *Antiquities of Mexico* in 1829. Waldeck resided at Palenque in 1832, building a pole-and-thatch house near the Temple of the Cross and recruiting a local Maya girl as his housekeeper. The structure called Temple of the Count is named for him. He made numerous drawings of reliefs and glyphs, some were careful reproductions but many were fanciful with evocative views of buildings and romantic landscapes used later for paintings and lithographs.

I can forgive Waldeck for many of his absurdities, such as including elephant heads and Hindu designs in renditions of Maya art. But I cannot forgive him for partially destroying one of Palenque's loveliest stucco sculptures, the "Beau-relief" that once adorned the Temple of the Jaguar. It depicts a graceful figure with flowing headdress and geometric-patterned skirt, seated on layered cushions upon a double-headed jaguar throne. The figure's arms and legs hold elegant, ballet-like poses. Waldeck did draw the figure first, as did Armendariz half-a-century earlier. Why he destroyed it is a mystery.

These drawings were reproduced in a number of books and magazines, and caught the attention of two men in the United States who really "put Palenque on the map;" John Lloyd Stephens, American popular travel writer and Frederick Catherwood, English architect and illustrator. Intrigued by the fantastic images and cities depicted, they determined to travel in search of Maya ruins and publish a book with illustrations about these wondrous things. They went first to Belize to visit Copan (now in Honduras), and then planned visits to Uxmal, Palenque and other sites.

Belize was under British control then, and some international competition got sparked. Patrick Walker, aide to the superintendent of British Honduras, and Lt. John Caddy of the Royal Artillery heard about Stephens and Catherwood's plans to visit Palenque. Irked that the American expedition might reach Palenque before the British, Walker and Caddy quickly put together their own expedition. The Britons planned to reach Palenque first by going due west along the Belize River and across the Peten in Guatemala. They endured a grueling journey through swamps and jungles, arriving two months ahead of the American team.

Walker and Caddy made some quite accurate drawings of figures, panels and buildings and produced a report that remained unpublished for over 125 years. Their primary goal seemed to be winning the race with the American team, and Walker's greatest interest was hunting game along the way. Caddy's report did make prophetic observations; saying that the massive buildings, elegant bas-reliefs, and beautiful ornaments prove that in ancient times the city was inhabited by "a race both populous and civilized." He also concluded that many more buildings once stood at the site that extended for several leagues. One entry remarked on a Spanish manuscript from around 1796, in which the local priest claimed that he "discovered the true origin" of these ancient people because of their "perfect knowledge of the Mythology of the Chaldeans."

More of Stephens and Catherwood's work later. Mama just called for dinner and I'm hungry.

July 2, 1994

On this rainy afternoon, my work for the day finished, I'm continuing my notes about early explorers. At camp we really enjoy occasional rains during the dry season; it cools the air a little. The humidity increases; it must be close to 100% now judging from my totally damp clothes. The ceiling fan helps by moving the air. I marvel at the stamina of those early explorers who visited Palenque in the 19th century, without cabins and electricity. Thanks to the remarkable four-volume books *Incidents of Travel*, by Stephens and Catherwood, we are given much insight into the hardships of travel and the impact of this splendid and high civilization on these explorers.

John Stephens is a masterful storyteller and Frederick Catherwood a fine artist. Their first two-volume book, featuring Central America, Chiapas and Yucatan, was published in 1841. It became an instant success, with publisher Harper and Brothers in New York making 11 printings of 20,000 copies each in only three months. I keep a copy with me to enjoy comparing their impressions with present-day Palenque. Although his prose is typical for that period, it's richly descriptive and amusing. Stephens weaves details of their harrowing adventures, gives astute character profiles, evocative descriptions and levelheaded reasoning, spiced with wry humor. Catherwood provides distinctive drawings and quality architectural designs with floor plans, elevations and outside views of Palenque's major structures. Thirty-one of his Palenque drawings were converted to engravings and published in the two Central American volumes.

You get a real sense of travel in the mid-1800s in the backcountry of Mexico and Central America. Stephens and Catherwood came from Guatemala to Ocosingo and followed the same route Dupaix took thirty years earlier, an ancient Indian path over mountains giving "one of the grandest, wildest, and most sublime scenes I ever beheld." They made the trip in five days to reduce nights in the wild during the rainy season. Clambering along steep paths hovering over thousand-foot precipices, they mostly walked leading mules and occasionally risked being carried in a chair by an Indian using a tumpline across his forehead. The chair-bearer's heavy breathing, dripping sweat and trembling limbs failed to inspire confidence and made them feel guilty, so they used the chair very little. The descent was even more terrible than the ascent, and the sun was sinking. Dark clouds and thunder gave way to a violent rainstorm, men and mules slipping and sliding. Stephens admits ". . . it was the worst mountain I ever encountered in that or any other country, and, under our apprehension of the storm, I will venture to say that no travelers ever descended in less time."

Once on the plains below and camped for the night, they suffered an onslaught of "moschetoes as we had not before experienced." Even fire and cigars could not keep the vicious insects at bay. After a sleepless and much-bitten night, Stephens went before daylight to the nearby shallow river "and stretched myself out on the gravelly bottom, where the water was barely deep enough to run over my body. It was the first comfortable moment I had had."

"Moschetoes" and rainstorms continued to plague the explorers after they arrived at the ruins of Palenque. They no sooner got their wood frame beds and stone slab dining table set up, with a meal of chicken, beans, rice and cold tortillas prepared proudly by their mozo Juan, than a loud thunderclap heralded the afternoon storm. Though located on the upper terrace of the palace and covered by a roof, the fierce wind blasted through open doors followed instantly by a deluge that soaked everything. They moved to an inside corridor but still could not escape the rain, and slept with clothes and bedding thoroughly wet.

Rather, they tried to sleep but "suffered terribly from moschetoes, the noise and stings of which drove away sleep. In the middle of the night I took up my mat to escape from these murderers of rest." Finding a low damp passage near the foot of the palace tower, Stephens crawled inside and spread his mat as bats whizzed through the passage. However, the bats drove away the mosquitoes, the damp passage was cooling and refreshing, and "with some twinging apprehensions of the snakes and reptiles, lizards and scorpions, which infest the ruins, I fell asleep."

They solved the mosquito problem by bending sticks over their wood beds and sewing their sheets together, draping them over the sticks to form a mosquito net. Not all insects were odious. At night the darkness of the palace was lighted by huge fireflies of "extraordinary size and brilliance" that flew through corridors or clung to walls. Called locuyos, they were half an inch long and had luminescent spots by their eyes and under their wings. "Four of them together threw a brilliant light for several yards around" and one alone gave enough light to read a newspaper.

To explore the heavily forested ruins they hired a guide, the same man employed by Waldeck, Walker and Caddy. It's hard now to imagine how dense the jungle was then, trees growing on top of every structure and filling plazas. Without the guide, they had no idea where other structures lay and "might have gone within a hundred feet of all the buildings without discovering one of them." The palace was most visible and could be seen from the northeast path leading to the ruins. Stephens described its many rooms, stuccos, tablets and ornaments while Catherwood rendered detailed floor plans and copied images. Stephens hoped their work would give an idea of the "profusion of its ornaments, of their unique and striking character, and of their mournful effect, shrouded by trees." Perhaps readers could imagine the palace as it once was "perfect in its amplitude and rich decorations, and occupied by the strange people whose portraits and figures now adorn its walls."

According to the guide, there were five other buildings that Stephens numbered, but none could be seen from the palace. The closest was Casa 1, a ruined pyramid that apparently had steps on all sides, now thrown down by trees that required them to "clamber over stones, aiding the feet by clinging to the branches." From descriptions and drawings, this structure is the Pyramid of the Inscriptions. Bas-relief stuccos on the four piers of the upper temple were reasonably well preserved, depicting four standing figures holding infants. The famous hieroglyphic tablets covering the interior wall were also in good condition.

Casas 2, 3 and 5 are part of the Cross Group. Stephens and Catherwood were deeply impressed by the stuccos and tablets that we now know belong to the Temple of the Cross and Temple of the Foliated Cross. The fantastic tablets from the first temple were incomplete and only the left tablet containing glyphs was in place. The middle tablet with two figures facing a cross had been removed and carried down the side of the pyramid, but deposited near the stream bank below. A villager intended to take it home, but was stopped by government orders forbidding further removal from the ruins. The right tablet was broken and fragmented, but from remnants they saw it contained more glyphs.

The second temple contained another tablet in near-perfect condition. It had a central panel with two figures facing a large mask over two crossed batons, flanked on each side by panels of glyphs. The four piers of the temple's entrance once contained sculptures; the outer two adorned with large medallions were still in place. The other two panels had been removed by villagers and set into the wall of a house. Copied earlier by Catherwood, these panels depicted two men facing each other. One was richly dressed and regal, the other an old man in jaguar pelt smoking a pipe. Later these famous sculptures were moved to the village church, and again later to the Palenque museum.

Casa 4 was farthest away, southwest of the palace. It sat on a pyramid 100 feet above the bank of the river with the front wall entirely collapsed. The large stucco tablet inside showed the bottom half of a figure sitting on a double-headed jaguar throne, the lovely beau relief partially destroyed by Waldeck. Stephens regretted this loss greatly (as do I) because it appeared to be "superior in execution to any other stucco relief in Palenque." This small structure is now called Temple of the Jaguar.

Stephens complains that artists of former expeditions failed to reproduce the detailed glyphs in Casas 1 and 3, and omitted drawings of Casa 2 altogether. He believes these artists were "incapable of the labour, and the steady, determined perseverance required for drawing such complicated, unintelligible, and anomalous characters." Catherwood used a camera lucida to project a light image of the glyphs and sculptures onto paper, and then drew the images to accurate scale and detail. He divided his paper into squares for copying glyphs to give accurate placement, reducing these large images and hand correcting the later engravings himself.

One must admire these two men, working under terrible conditions with limited equipment, yet providing such a thorough account of the Palenque structures they saw. They needed to scrape off green moss, dig out roots, clean away layers of dissolved limestone, use candles to light dark inner chambers, build scaffolds to access high places, and endure a plethora of climate and insect assaults. They paid the price of multiple mosquito bites, for both men contracted malaria and suffered repeated episodes of illness.

They left us a few astute conclusions. Stephens proved more insightful than later Mayanists by writing, "The hieroglyphics doubtless tell its history" and "The hieroglyphics are the same as were found at Copan and Quirigua . . . there is room for belief that the whole of this country was once occupied by the same race, speaking the same language . . ."

"Here were the remains of a cultivated, polished, and peculiar people, who had passed through all the stages incident to the rise and fall of nations; reached their golden age, and perished, entirely unknown . . . wherever we moved we saw the evidences of their taste, their skill in arts, their wealth and power."

July 10, 1994

Over a month after opening the sarcophagus lid, we still have more questions than answers about the tomb in Temple XIII. On July 5th, Arnoldo and Fanny decided to continue searching for the passage leading to the south door, the original main entrance to the burial chamber. Two observations spurred them on; the five steps ascending from the chamber floor to the south door, and a fresh breeze that came from around the door. They speculated that the steps might lead to another substructure contained in the six meters between the tomb and the top of Temple XIII.

When workers removed the stones that closed the south door, they ran into huge rocks weighing 30-40 kilos filling the stairway. Little by little they broke up and removed rocks. After proceeding upward one meter and 13 more steps, Arnoldo had to call off the operation. They encountered only more large rocks, and risked danger of collapsing the structure with more excavation.

The question of what else remains inside Temple XIII could not be answered yet. Everyone took a break that afternoon and most went to a hotel in Palenque town to watch the Mexican soccer team play against Bulgaria in New York. It was the Soccer World Cup of 1994. Sonia and I were not interested in watching the game, unlike most of our compadres and they accused us of being unpatriotic.

We decided to take a walk to the older section of the site, rarely visited because of poorly marked trails through heavy forests. The old section west of the Great Plaza where we are working is very large and little excavated. Archeologists believe there are many structures buried under trees and brush, and tantalizing glimpses of rocky piles peering through foliage convinced us that an unknown treasure resides here. The trail was narrow with fallen branches and tangled roots. We had obtained a rough map from a local Maya who claimed he knew how to reach Templo Olvidado. It's called "Olvidado" or Lost for good reason; it's far from the main area, poorly restored, visited by few.

After crossing three streams and climbing over several hills, we reached the flat, east-west running plateau on which most of the western settlement was built. This area probably was downtown Lakam Ha in its early years. There is not much to see except tree-covered mounds with stones peeping out between roots. Some speculate that this older western portion of the site might be the legendary "Toktan," origin place of the Palenque dynasty.

Our destination, Templo Olvidado, is halfway across the older section. Current thinking holds that Pakal built this temple around 640 CE, possibly as a funerary structure for his parents. It's been partially cleared and the top structure restored, though the sides are still rubble and brush. Knowing the Maya propensity to build on top of existing structures, there may be substructures from even earlier times.

After a few wrong turns and thorny bush scratches, we followed our map past an aqueduct and up a steep hill. Breathless after climbing the steep path to the temple, we sat on the upper steps, peering between tall trees toward the Tabasco plains far below. The temple has only two rooms with several doorways, the roof still mostly intact but no decorations remain. Once it surely had sculptures on piers and panels on inside walls, with a decorated roof and tall roofcomb. Surrounded by smaller mounds and rising visibly above them, this area was not residential and must have been ceremonial.

The breeze wafting upward was refreshing and the trees shaded us from the warm afternoon sun. We talked about our attraction to archeology. Though we're in the same school, Sonia is in the class ahead of me and we did not know each other before.

"Franci, why did you choose restoration?" she asked me.

"I always knew, since childhood, that I wanted to work in archeology. Growing up next to the Palenque ruins, visiting often with my father who loves them, I felt deeply connected. But I also love art and ceramics; I've been a potter for years. So I combined these two for a career restoring ancient Maya artifacts."

"Similar to me, growing up in Oaxaca," she said. "Different people, the Zapotecs, but also surrounded by ruins. Painting and calligraphy are my passions, and preserving ancient glyphic works seems so important."

Though our ambitions are close, our family backgrounds are far apart. Most of her family was well educated and some were professors. When I described my village family, she was surprised that I'd gone so far in school. Not the least of it, women having a professional career was expected for her. My situation is anything but that and it takes some determination to overcome pressure from my mother and grandmother to get married. But I will finish my degree and work in the field, this I've promised myself.

Warmed by the sun into drowsiness, my mind drifts to the ancient Maya as we sit in silence after a long talk about our lives. When did residents of Lakam Ha last stand upon the platform where we sit, last conduct ceremonies in this temple? Fleeting images cross my inner vision of priests and nobles with elaborate costumes ascending the stairs, a plaza below filled with commoners in loincloths and huipiles, processions carrying standards and playing exotic instruments. My ears almost hear the sonorous blasts of long trumpets, the reedy melodies of flutes and steady drumbeats.

If only I could transport myself back to those times, if I could experience the world of Lakam Ha during its heyday. Then I would see the queens in their full glory and magnificence, these powerful women who fascinate me so much, who changed the destiny of their city. Then I would know which one of them lies in the sarcophagus in Temple XIII—if it is a woman's skeleton.

A Sneak Peek into Book 2 of the Mists of Palenque Series

THE CONTROVERSIAL MAYAN QUEEN: SAK K'UK OF PALENQUE

THE MAYAN QUEENS' series continues with Sak K'uk, daughter of Yohl Ik'nal. A strong-willed young woman, Sak K'uk struggles to preserve her family dynasty. She is more fit to accede than her indecisive, artistic brother and she chafes at his lack-luster leadership. In visions she sees that her son K'inich Janaab Pakal is destined to become the greatest ruler of Lakam Ha, but how it will happen is uncertain. A sudden attack by archenemy Kan, plotted by vengeful Ek Chuuah who was exiled from their city by Sak K'uk's grandfather, changes everything. Lakam Ha is thrown into chaos by the desecration of their most sacred shrine, destroying the portal to Gods and Ancestors. The royal family is humiliated, and the capture and death of her brother and father leaves the city without leaders. Since the sacred portal is in collapse, the help of the Triad Gods cannot be attained. In desperation, Sak K'uk undertakes perilous journeys into the Underworld for guidance. She meets the Primordial Goddess Muwaan Mat who promises to co-rule with her until her son Pakal is old enough to accede. Can Sak K'uk convince dissident nobles to accept this joint rulership, when they are disillusioned with her family over the Kan defeat? All her willpower and skills are needed to navigate through this spiritual crisis and hold the throne so her son can fulfill his destiny to restore the collapsed portal. Through these intense trials, a special bond is forged between them that proves both a blessing and a curse.

SAK K'UK—I

BAKTUN 9 KATUN 8 TUN 12
606 CE—607 CE

1

PAKAL'S NURSEMAID WAS worried. Creases marred her smooth forehead, her lips drawn tight as a purse-string. She scurried through long corridors, eyes darting to every door and scanning the small chambers within. Crossing the inside patio, she quickly assessed each corner and glanced behind benches and plants.

Not yet two solar years old and the child was a master of escape. How far could his toddler's legs carry him? Her mistress would be most annoyed that he once again eluded supervision. Or much worse if any harm came to him.

Her search of Sak K'uk's quarters in the palace was fruitless. She enlisted help from other attendants, but none could locate the child. The sun was near zenith, its intense brightness almost blinding when reflected off white stucco walls and plazas. There was nothing to do but report Pakal's absence and muster a larger search.

Trembling and bowing low to the ground, Tunsel approached Sak K'uk, whose temper was well known among her attendants.

"My Lady, much is it my sorrow to report we cannot find your son, the sun-blessed Pakal."

Sak K'uk's face was stony, her voice hard.

"So it is, yet another time, you have failed in your duties. What is so difficult in knowing the whereabouts of a child? Find him at once, or I shall dismiss you this day." She signaled to the palace guard standing nearby. "Summon several men and search the entire palace complex. Bring Pakal to me as soon as you find him."

Tunsel and the guard rushed away and Sak K'uk dropped onto a stone bench. Tears smarted her eyes and she blinked them away, loath to reveal any weakness. But she was concerned, not just about her son's safety but her own abilities as a mother. Though the depth of her love for Pakal surprised her, mothering did not come naturally. She was not mesmerized by babies as were other women, she did not enjoy their nonsense babbles and disliked the drooling and feeding and toileting that seemed to go on endlessly. Those functions she gladly relinquished to nursemaids.

Any good mother should know where her children were, however. Simply because supervision was delegated to nursemaids did not absolve her of responsibility.

She would rather be in the Popol Nah, Council House, discussing Lakam Ha governance with leaders and interrogating messengers about happenings in the B'aakal polity. Especially so, since her brother was proving an ineffective ruler. She never respected Aj Ne Ohl Mat despite his attempts at leadership; his mind did not grasp political subtleties and he had little skill in the art of influence and intimidation. Only the abilities of her father and husband kept the ahauob in line and the city functioning. She kept away from the Council House because she might lose control of her tongue and berate her brother in front of his courtiers.

The sun began its afternoon descent as Tunsel conferred impatiently with guards and palace attendants. None had seen the child despite repeated searching within the palace complex. They agreed to widen the search to nearby complexes and walkways. The nursemaid was frantic, gripped by fear for her charge and also herself. Dismissal from service to the ruler's sister would bring shame upon her family. Their standing would fall in status-conscious Maya culture, reducing opportunity for lucrative positions and advantageous marriages. Tunsel came from minor nobility, and her palace affiliations were much prized by her parents.

"Where can the boy be?" she moaned to herself, reviewing where she last saw him and what he was doing. It was at the edge of the patio adjoining his quarters, and he was throwing handfuls of dust into a beam of sunlight breaking through slots in the roofcomb. She left briefly to fetch a cloth for cleaning his hands, and upon returning he was gone.

The sun! Suddenly her mind was sharply focused. Pakal loved the sun; he sought it and often danced in sunbeams. In fact, his first word was "*k'in*" as the Maya called the sun. He must be in search of the sun, trying to get closer. That meant climbing a hill or temple pyramid. Someone would see him climbing a pyramid, but brush on a hill would easily conceal his small form.

Her legs pummeled as she raced toward the nearest hill, rising just west of the palace complex, the beginning of foothills that soon soared to cresting heights. Racing through the west plaza and crossing the footbridge spanning the Bisik River, Tunsel marveled that no one sighted the child on his excursion. Though his legs were long for his age, it was surprising that he could cover this distance. How she knew with such certainty that he took this path she did not question.

She sighted the trail wending across the hill, but saw no small form along its path. Sandals crunching on pebbles, Tunsel bounded up the trail with pounding heart. She gasped for breath, cursing her laziness from soft palace life. That life she would soon lose or perhaps all life if she did not find Pakal soon. The hill summit was just ahead and she called inwardly for the goddess Ix Chel's largesse.

Please let the boy be there!

Salty sweat mingled with tears as she ascended the final rise and spotted the boy. He was standing on a small boulder, arms lifted to the sun, singing in a high sweet voice. She rushed up and grabbed him into her arms. The surprised boy thrashed momentarily then relaxed into her embrace as she dropped to the ground. He reached to wipe away her tears and smeared her dusty face.

"Tunsel cry?"

"Tunsel happy Pakal is safe. Can we go home now?"

He studied her face solemnly and nodded. Then he turned his face toward the sun and burst into a huge smile. His almond eyes shone and he pointed at the sun.

"K'in Ahau. K'in Ahau loves Pakal."

"Yes, and Pakal loves his Father Sun." Tunsel in turn studied Pakal's face. "You are k'inich, sun-faced. We must call you K'inich Janaab Pakal. That is perfect, let us tell your mother and perhaps she will forgive us."

"Mother wants Pakal now?"

"Yes, let us go home now. Your mother waits. I will carry you; your legs must be tired from such a long climb." Rising with renewed vigor, Tunsel held the child tightly as she descended, silently thanking Ix Chel and resolving to never let Pakal escape her sight again.

Torchlight flickered from walls of the dining chamber in Sak K'uk's quarters. Dusk settled over the plateau of many waters as attendants served bowls of bean and squash stew seasoned with peppers and green herbs. Only two dined this evening with Sak K'uk, her father and husband. She regaled them with Pakal's latest adventure, his quest to reach K'in Ahau—Sun Lord on the hilltop.

"Tunsel conferred a new title on him, calling him k'inich, sun-faced. The cadence of this pleases me—K'inich Janaab Pakal."

"It is most fitting for the royal ahau of Lakam Ha," Hun Pakal said.

"So it is. We are descended from Hun Ahau, the son of the Sun Lord who we also call K'in Bahlam, the Sun Jaguar. The Bahlam family and the Sun are inseparable." She smiled at her father, while noticing how he had aged since her mother's death. Strange that only two years could reap such havoc; but he and Yohl Ik'nal had been exceptionally close and he missed her terribly.

"You should dismiss that girl," Kan Mo' Hix opined. "Tunsel does not watch Pakal closely enough; the boy is always running off. It makes me concerned."

"Hmmm," murmured Sak K'uk. She dipped maize cake into her bowl of stew and chewed thoughtfully. She disliked contradicting her husband, they had enough issues already ripe for conflict, but she had decided to retain Pakal's nursemaid.

"That I have considered," she replied. "Pakal is very fond of her. Think on it, I must." Quickly changing the subject, she asked her husband: "What transpired in Council today?"

"More debate over extracting tribute from Usihwitz. That testy contingent of our ahauob cannot let go of our defeat in the ballgame. This sully on the reputation of Lakam Ha seems more important than our prosperity and peaceful life. And Aj Ne Ohl Mat does little to deflect their criticisms; I doubt he has one creative political thought, devoting all his talents to poetry and music." Disdain fairly dripped from Kan Mo' Hix' voice and his hand sign conveyed dismissal.

"Peace and prosperity indeed are the problem," observed Hun Pakal. "They are bored; they have not enough to occupy their small minds. Warriors want to ply their skills in more than flower wars or ballgames. Some ahauob thrive on conflict, their lives lack spice without it."

"Aj Ne cannot manage this situation," Sak K'uk said flatly. In her heart she believed she could, but her brother was ruler.

"We must find ways to divert this wave of discontent," said Hun Pakal.

"Is not the artist Uc Ayin among the circle of opposition? And also frequent courtier in Aj Ne's artistic gatherings?"

Sak K'uk's eyes caught her fathers' in unspoken caution. They knew the questionable role Uc Ayin had played in Usihwitz' unsuccessful raid several years earlier. Only by leaving the city had he escaped death.

"Uc Ayin could be a source, yes, if we can obtain his cooperation, for he does move among camps," said Kan Mo' Hix.

"If he can be trusted," Hun Pakal noted.

"He rides the winds of advantage. I will cultivate him; that will be flattering. He did spend much time in my father's house but comes less often now that the ruler includes him as a fellow artist. What need have we of artists as leaders? Warriors, men trained in skills of strategic attack and managing resources make the best rulers." Kan Mo' Hix gestured toward Hun Pakal. "You or I would be a better ruler for Lakam Ha. This designation of Aj Ne Ohl Mat as heir, his selection for succession was a mistake. Not to imply disrespect for our late ruler, your honored mother." He nodded toward Sak K'uk.

It took great determination for Sak K'uk to withhold her caustic remarks. She chewed a piece of maize cake furiously. Kan Mo' Hix was oblivious to both the embedded insult and exposure of ambition in his remarks. It was becoming apparent that her husband aspired to rulership. "Fine ruler he would make," she thought, "with such lack of diplomacy."

Hun Pakal's face was clouded, but he said nothing.

Their meal finished with cups of cocoa laced with chile. They agreed to meet again once Kan Mo' Hix obtained information about the opposition's objectives. He left first, bowing and touching fingertips with Sak K'uk in a gesture of affection. She responded as expected, reaching toward his fingers with hers and smiling, though her true feelings dictated a slap.

When her husband disappeared through the door drape, she sank down with a sigh.

"Often it is, he is insufferable," she whispered to her father.

"Insufferably ambitious. That he would make an admirable ruler, I doubt. This situation we have is not good. Aj Ne is weak and distracted, discontent is mounting, and Pakal is years away from being capable of acceding. Were it not so disruptive, I might even support the idea of Kan Mo' Hix as ruler."

"Father, this is not wise. He would bring difficulties to us, for he is rash and lacks judgment. He is too reactive about the Usihwitz situation. Can you imagine him spreading the cloak of reason and calmness over our nobles?"

"Ah, no . . . he would create quite the opposite effect. There is trouble gathering in our recalcitrant subordinate city, however. Never believe that Ek Chuuah is finished with his lust for revenge. It is certain he has used these years to perfect his plans, even if the defeat he suffered in the first raid diminished his status in Usihwitz. Would that our intelligence was better."

"Lack of information about neighboring cities is a major detriment," agreed Sak K'uk. "We cannot be prepared without some knowledge of hostile intentions. It appears we must work with the leadership situation we now have, faulty as it may be. Can we not give more support to Aj Ne?"

"Perhaps we can. I will again try to interest him in court rituals and council strategy, though he shows little aptitude. Your mother was a master at courtly arts; it is regretful that he inherited so little of it from her."

Hun Pakal cast his eyes down, but not before his daughter caught the shadows of sadness in their depths. After a few moments, he said wistfully: "The poetry of Aj Ne is quite good, think you not?"

Sak K'uk placed a hand on her father's shoulder.

"Mother was a great ruler. I also miss her presence, her strength and vision, so much. Yes, Aj Ne does write poetry well."

They sat in silence, sipping cacao. Sak K'uk cared little for her brother's poetry, but she yearned to give comfort to her father, some acknowledgement of his son's value.

"You are intelligent and determined." Hun Pakal simply stated facts with no hint of flattery. "Perhaps you can improve your husband's judgment and hone his leadership abilities."

Caught by surprise, Sak K'uk laughed aloud. Seeing that her father was serious, she conceded: "So it might be possible. Yes, I will try applying my intelligence to this daunting task."

They embraced warmly and Hun Pakal left. Sak K'uk reflected on how different her parents' marriage was than her own. By custom, Maya nobles each had private sleeping chambers and different sets of attendants. Her parents, however, slept together more often than not. Their closeness was remarkable, something she admired but did not understand. In her own marriage, Kan Mo' Hix visited her sleeping pallet often enough, but never stayed with her through the night. She enjoyed the physical contact, but could easily remain alone for long periods. It was not correct timing for them to conceive another child, and she was taking herbs to prevent pregnancy, so frequent intercourse was not necessary.

The Maya were sexually continent people. They viewed male and female sexual union as a sacred act, one that combined powerful creative energies and augmented inner spiritual processes. It was undertaken consciously and deliberately, treated with honor and respect. To overindulge sexually was to squander one's life force, the *itz* that permeated all existence with sacred essence.

Sak K'uk was not troubled that her husband might lie with other women. This was not common practice among Maya ahauob, especially those in the highest positions. He was too focused on building personal power to waste any on such frivolities. She was troubled about his ambitions, his self-focused perspectives that fell short of true dedication to the welfare of the B'aakal polity and Bahlam dynasty.

Her thoughts returned to her wandering son. He was already precocious, walking and speaking early, exuding a magical presence that entranced those around him. Everyone basked in the radiance of his loving nature, kind and comforting. He certainly exhibited qualities of Yohl Ik'nal, his visionary grandmother, including the ability to elude attendants and explore other dimensions. Tunsel said he was communing with the sun on the hilltop; often he related to this deity as though he were actually the son of K'in Ahau.

As indeed he is, she mused.

Sak K'uk often brought Pakal with her on visits to the underground chamber, the most sacred shrine of Lakam Ha, the Sak Nuk Nah or "White Skin House." When he had just passed his third solar year, she visited the shrine to honor her grandfather Kan Bahlam's voyage to the celestial realms. Seated on the altar-throne in the hidden sanctum, she meditated with closed eyes while Pakal sat on a mat at her feet. After a short time of silence, the boy's gleeful giggles interrupted her reverie. Too curious to concentrate, Sak K'uk peeked under lowered eyelids at her son.

Pakal was dancing in small circles, waving his hands furiously in the air. He lunged and swatted with one hand, then the other, and burst into a ripple of laughter. Next he jumped backward, danced in more circles, and repeated the gestures.

Sak K'uk could not contain her curiosity.

"What are you doing, Pakal?"

He glanced at her, but continued his movements.

"See, mother, see!" he exclaimed, pointing into the air at his chest level.

She focused where he pointed but saw nothing except wavering torchlight.

"Dearest, I do not see anything. What do you see?"

"The Baby Jaguar, see he plays with me."

"The Baby Jaguar? Unan K'awiil in his baby jaguar form?"

"Yes, yes, do you see him? His paws, he paws at me, I jump away." Pakal swatted again in the air and laughed. "He will not get me, I am fast!"

Sak K'uk frowned, squinting to bring ephemeral forms into sharper contrast, but was unable to see her son's playmate.

"Much to my regret, I cannot see the Baby Jaguar."

Pakal stopped his movements and stared at his mother, his surprised eyes conveying confusion.

"You cannot see him? He is here . . . Oh, he has gone! Mother, you made Baby Jaguar go away!"

"Truly I am sorry, dearest," she enjoined. "What did he look like?"

"Like Baby Jaguar!" Pakal said with annoyance, then softened and hugged his mother. "He has black spots, many spots, he lies on his back and waves his paws and wiggles his tail. He smiled at me, I saw his little fangs, but he was careful not to bite. He wants to play. He is very cute. I am sorry you cannot see him."

"Perhaps I will see him the next time he comes to play with you. Does he come often?"

"Yes, often when we are in the White Skin House. First he watched me; today he played the most ever. Can we come here tomorrow? I want to play with Baby Jaguar."

"Of course, my love. We can come very often."

Sak K'uk was eager to discuss Pakal's experience with the High Priest. To her knowledge, never before had such a young child with no training been visited by a Triad God, much less been able to clearly see and interact with the deity.

2

Pasah Chan, High Priest of Lakam Ha, contemplated the significance of what Sak K'uk told him about her son. Although holding the exalted office as head of his city's priesthood for less than five solar years, his lengthy preparation in calendric and occult arts and the rigorous selection process leading up to his nomination gave him confidence in his spiritual leadership. He searched his memory for similar scenarios in which very young children demonstrated unusual psychic and inter-dimensional abilities, but could not recall anything similar. Of course, Pakal's grandmother Yohl Ik'nal was known for her skills at journeying since her middle youth and for her prowess as a seer later in life. As ruler she clearly embodied the Triad Gods in rituals and communicated with various deities. But at such an early age, to become playmate to Unen K'awiil? Of this he had never heard.

Tall for a Maya with sinewy limbs and slender frame, Pasah Chan came from a minor noble family fortunate enough to cultivate favor with the former High Priest Wak Batz. Through gifts and tribute that stretched the family's resources, the eldest son gained admittance into priestly training. There he excelled, using his keen memory and natural intelligence to advance in studies. His aptitude for ruthless competition played no small role in his progress, and he became the old High Priest's favorite acolyte. Partly through admiration for his command of esoteric knowledge, and partly due to his intimidating personality, the Council of Priests nominated Pasah Chan upon the passing of Wak Batz. He underwent the series of trials required of High Priest candidates to demonstrate his mastery over emotions, body functions, elements of nature, and spirit world assistants. In all tests he exceeded expectations.

The face of Pasah Chan resembled a bird of prey. Beaked nose overshadowed thin lips drawn tight against jutting cheekbones, half-lidded eyes held the penetrating glare of a hawk. Over his small-domed crown, dark hair crested from his narrow forehead, pushed upward by a feathered band with a long braid falling down his back. Although the crest was intended to mimic the elongated skulls of high-ranked elites, it did not conceal his defect. His parents had failed to apply the headboards used to elongate the skull properly during his infancy. Of this defect he was quite self-conscious.

His eyes narrowed into slits as he concentrated. Again he reviewed his conversation with Sak K'uk and her father, Hun Pakal.

"Surely this means Pakal is favored by Unen K'awiil, perhaps destined for rulership?" Sak K'uk tried to keep her voice tentative, but Pasah Chan could sense her conviction.

"The Baby Jaguar, designator of royal lineage, would not appear to such a young child were it not significant," added Hun Pakal.

"Perhaps, perhaps," Pasah Chan murmured, rubbing his chin. "Yes, it is most unusual, and the child is advanced for his age. Yes, this bears contemplation, to discern the hidden meanings and the intentions of the deity. I must reflect, seek precedence and spiritual guidance."

Sak K'uk persisted.

"Would it not seem an indication to begin Pakal's training early? His abilities are unfolding naturally; these must be shaped by adepts in the priesthood so the proper skills are developed."

"And to keep him safe," said Hun Pakal, thinking of Yohl Ik'nal's untutored travels and the risks involved.

"Indeed, indeed, these are important considerations," the High Priest replied. "It is highly irregular for a child not yet attained of four tuns to enter shamanic training, when the normal age for elite boys is seven tuns. His abilities are advanced for his age, of course, and this brings other elements into the situation. As you both note, his safety is a concern. And he is of ruling lineage with no heir yet born to the ruler, although that might change soon."

Sak K'uk and Hun Pakal exchanged surprised glances. Pasah Chan gloated that he possessed information the two royals did not have. Just two days ago the Chief Priestess of Ix Chel informed him that Aj Ne Ohl Mat's wife Hohmay was pregnant. After years of barrenness, the arts of the healing priestesses had finally succeeded in bringing about a conception. It was a precarious pregnancy founded on extreme measures, secrets the healers would not reveal. They had great concern over the outcome and planned ceaseless surveillance of Hohmay and a rigid protocol of diet, herbs, spiritual ritual and careful activity.

"The Ix Chel priestesses have assisted Homay to conceive." Pasah Chan allowed the words to roll from his tongue deliciously, savoring their impact.

Sak K'uk could not conceal her shock. Hun Pakal looked crestfallen.

"Only two days ago was I informed of this momentous event," continued the High Priest. "As you can imagine, the Ix Chel priestesses will be at her side every moment, and continue to apply their skills to support the pregnancy."

"Ix Chel be praised," Sak K'uk managed to mutter. "Truly her priestesses are exceptionally skilled, may all go well."

"When is the child to be born?" asked Hun Pakal.

"In seven moons."

"Should all go well. Truly remarkable. Yet the child may be a girl, leaving Pakal the more logical choice," Hun Pakal observed.

"Given the great difficulty Hohmay had conceiving, perhaps it was impossible to follow all procedures to assure the child's gender," Pasah Chan admitted. "Although the Ix Chel priestesses do believe the child conceived is male."

"But they are not certain," suggested Sak K'uk.

"That is true. We will see, there is much that must pass until the pregnancy is culminated. Concerning Pakal, I will reflect upon his early entry into training."

"This we deeply appreciate," said Sak K'uk. Eyes bright with intense passion, she directed a piercing look at the High Priest.

"Pakal is destined for greatness. I have been given many signs of this, and have no doubt of its truth. My mother Yohl Ik'nal also envisioned Pakal bringing Lakam Ha to its zenith. He must be trained soon."

Pasah Chan blinked, bringing himself into the present. That look in Sak K'uk's eyes had shaken him, and her mother's visions were always to be taken seriously. Was Pakal destined to rule Lakam Ha, to bring forth its apogee?

The High Priest intended to become even more important than his position demanded. He wanted to be the most powerful man in Lakam Ha, the shaper of its course, the master of rulers. Watching the current ruler Aj Ne Ohl Mat, observing the weakness of his leadership and his passive personality, gave Pasah Chan reassurance. He could easily influence and control this ruler, and most likely his progeny. The Council was divided and contentious, they could be manipulated and one contingent played against the other. Should rulership remain in this line, his goals were as good as accomplished.

But rulership in Sak K'uk's lineage was another issue. Already Hun Pakal and Kan Mo' Hix aggregated a strong group of supporters, ready to follow their leadership. Rumors circulated that Kan Mo' Hix should be made ruler. He would certainly bring a stronger hand to leadership, but his impulsiveness might spark serious disruptions. Just how far the opposition group would go was an unknown. Civil strife and possible internal battle were unappealing possibilities.

If it was true that Pakal was destined for greatness, for rulership, then Pasah Chan was cultivating the wrong branch of the family. Maybe Hohmay would bear a son to keep succession in their line, but that was far from certain. He doubted the pregnancy would end successfully. If Pakal did become heir, and if he trained the boy from an early age, his opportunity for influence would be immense.

His brows knitted, Pasah Chan struggled to remember ephemeral images from ancient codices written in early forms of the Mayan language. Was there some distant prophecy about a great ruler, one whose mission was to guide his people to remember their celestial mandate, to inspire art and architecture that reflected cosmic harmony, to spark a creative vortex that would draw admiration from all parts of the world? Just beyond the fringes of memory some tantalizing fragments danced, but remained elusive. He must consult with the elderly priest who was the most revered codex expert.

The High Priest ascended the temple plaza as the sun caressed verdant peaks of the western mountains, sliding toward the distant great waters. Although the afternoon was warm, the old priest sat bundled in his blanket, cross-legged upon a low wall bench flanking the plaza. From this uppermost plaza of the High Priest's Temple, a spectacular view spread below. Hazy plains rolled toward the horizon, patches of green mingling with golden fields of maize and olive leafed orchards. Like a traveling serpent, the Michol River curled across the plains, as towering trees that lined the river trailed lianas in its turbid waters. A few canoes plied the swift currents, hugging the banks as pilots propelled them with long poles.

The old man seemed oblivious of his visitor, eyes closed and head nodding in the sunlight. Pasah Chan noted the deeply wrinkled face, each crease representing cycles of time. Surely the old man had passed 104 tuns, twice the 52-tun age of elders. It was said that when 104 tuns were attained, the person had completed all the cycles of life and became living repositories of history and wisdom. Young people would sit in their hallowed presence to reflect upon time's passages and the phases of earthly and celestial life. Simply to touch their wrinkled faces and hands was to receive blessings and attain deeper understandings.

Pasah Chan cleared his throat noisily. Slowly the old man turned toward him, watery eyes blinking and toothless mouth opening. His corneas were clouded and whitened. He tilted his head to obtain better view of this visitor, wrinkled lips pursing and popping like a gasping fish. His thin, clawed hands picked tremulously at the blanket.

"Greetings of the afternoon, Ah K'uch, Honored Ancient One," said Pasah Chan. "It is good to enjoy Father Sun's warmth, is it not?"

"K'in Ahau is good, he warms my old bones," replied Ah K'uch in a high reedy voice. "Greetings to you, Pasah Chan, High Priest. How passes your day?"

"It is well, and I am happy to be with you again. May I join you?"

Ah K'uch nodded and gestured to the bench beside him. Moving his clouded gaze to the view below he gave a gummy smile.

"Such beauty does Hun Ahb K'u, the Infinite Creator of All give to this world. So shall I miss it, when I traverse the sky in the Celestial Canoe."

"Let us hope that is yet far in the future."

"Ah, hah," the old man chuckled. "Not so far, not so far."

Both men fell silent, each contemplating their destinies and life's temporality.

"There is a task you might yet do, something of great importance to our city's future." The High Priest spoke softly but with crisp enunciation. "It is something that means much to me. A personal favor."

Ah K'uch tilted his head back, looking upward into the young priest's face.

"What would you have me do?"

"Search among ancient codices for a prophecy for Lakam Ha. A prophecy for these current times, about a great leader who is destined to bring Lakam Ha to its highest point. It is likely that the leader would also be the ruler, one yet to come, but soon."

"Why do you ask me? You are a codex expert yourself, you could do that search." Ah K'uch shrugged and wagged his head. "Here am I, a very old man. My wits are not as sharp as yours. My eyes are failing me. My limbs are frail and weak."

"Your knowledge of codices far surpasses that of any priest, myself included," Pasah Chan replied. "You say your wits are not so sharp, but your memory is boundless. It is such that should you command it, focus your mind, set your intention, that you can remember which among the thousands of codices speaks of this prophecy. I vaguely recall some prophecy concerning Lakam Ha's destiny, but would spend countless days in fruitless searching. You can summon it to mind, scanning your memory."

"Ah, perhaps that is so. Might not it take me countless days also? I have fewer days to count than you." Enjoying his own humor, Ah K'uch chuckled.

Pasah Chan smiled, giving the hand sign for losing a point.

Time passed as the men sat in silence. The sun hovered at the mountain's edge, sending golden beams across the plaza. Birds called in the forests, jostling for position among branches. Pasah Chan sighed, resigning himself to doing the search. It would take a long time, and Sak K'uk would keep pressing him to train Pakal. He had hoped to get the information quickly upon which to base his decision.

"I will do it." The old priest's reedy treble startled Pasah Chan.

"Something to amuse my old mind before I join the ancestors. Yes, I know where to begin. It is a good thing, High Priest, that you reminded me of my memory." He coughed and chuckled simultaneously while the younger man bowed and smiled.

A special chamber in the Temple of the High Priest was devoted to housing the codices. It was the uppermost chamber of the temple school, chosen to receive maximum light and air. The school was a two-tiered square building opening into a secluded courtyard. On the lower level were numerous classrooms; the upper held small chambers for meditation. The entire western-facing side of the upper level was a series of interconnected rooms with stone shelves lining the walls. These shelves held thousands of codices, the heritage of untold years of scribal work reaching far into Lakam Ha's mythohistoric past. The codices held the arcane knowledge of the Maya; astronomy, astrology, divination, sacred geometry, numerology, healing arts and herbalism, calendars, alchemical recipes, history of dynasties and rulers, tales of Gods and ancestors, philosophy, language, arts and music. It was an unparalleled library, a hidden font of wisdom from ancient times.

Each codex was made of bark paper in long strips, folded like an accordion that fanned out when extended. The Maya harvested inner layers of bark from the wild fig tree, soaked and boiled it in maize water treated with lime or ash. Then the bark was rinsed and pliable strips were laid out on a wooden board. The first layer was lengthwise and the next was crosswise. The damp bark was pounded with a hafted stone beater into a continuous sheet of paper, some as long as three arm's length. After drying in the sun, the paper was peeled off the wooden board and smoothed with a stone. Since the bark was never made into a pulp, it retained a fibrous texture that was not smooth enough for Maya scribes to write easily. They covered the paper with a thin layer of plaster before writing on it.

Natural dyes were prepared in many colors; black, red and yellow were much favored though blue and green also were used. The particularly lovely shade of Maya blue was made from indigo fused with palygorskite by the heat of burning copal incense in ceremonial bowls. Scribes used quills from turkey or wild bird feathers, dipping them in dyes held in seashells or conches. The monkey scribe or rabbit scribe were the animal uay—companions who represented the sacred art of glyphic writing, recording numbers and drawing pictures that filled the codices.

Ah K'uch sat on a raised platform covered with a woven mat. A rectangular wooden box served to elevate and display unfolded codices as he examined them. Positioned next to a window opening toward the west, he took full advantage of sunlight to improve his ability to see. Beside him sat three assistants, acolytes assigned to fetch and shelve codices and explain images he had difficulty making out. They also plied the old priest with warm cacao drinks and maize cakes to keep up his energy.

It was his third day of work, and he was beginning to wonder if his memory had failed him. After examining over 30 ancient codices, he had not found the one containing the Lakam Ha prophecy. He was certain there was such a prophecy, he clearly recalled having read it in his youth, but could not remember all the details.

This called for different tactics.

"I will sleep now," he announced to his assistants.

They were perplexed, for they knew he was on a time-sensitive assignment.

"Master, is not your intent to find the codex today? Very soon, is that not important?" asked one young acolyte.

"You are correct, that is my intent," replied Ah K'uch. "My methods may seem strange to you. Now I am called to sleep, to dream and to remember in the dreamtime. In this way shall the codex come to me."

Obediently, the acolytes prepared a pallet for the old priest in a darker corner of the chamber. Sighing, he reclined his achy body and soon was snoring loudly.

Patiently the assistants sat in vigil as the old man slept. The sun crossed overhead and began its afternoon descent, bright squares of light forming through windows and moving slowing across the floor. After a series of snorts that interrupted throaty snores, the old priest woke, blinked furiously, wiped his watering eyes and sat up.

His voice gurgled, requiring some coughing to clear his throat.

"Bring me the codex on the farthest shelf to the west; it is low and close to the floor. It is called the Noh Ek Almanac of Baktun 8 Katun 18. Be careful! Handle it gently, it is very ancient. From the times of our venerated lineage founder, Holy Ancestor K'uk Bahlam."

As the assistants scrambled to retrieve the codex, Ah K'uch groaned and lurched to his feet, limping slowly to his scribe platform. Stretching and sighing, he sat cross-legged and reached to receive the dusty codex from his assistant. Spreading it and gently turning the flaps, he scanned through pages of Noh Ek (Venus) almanacs with neat rows of day and month signs, dot-and-bar numbers, and pictures of deities. Columns of glyphs along page edges or across the top added further information.

"Ah!" he exclaimed, bony finger tracing a glyph column that accompanied numbers and images. The three assistants crowded around, straining to see. They could not decipher the antiquated glyphic forms, though the numbers and deity images were familiar.

"What does it say, master?" asked one assistant.

"Bring writing materials, copy this down as I read," ordered Ah K'uch.

As soon as the assistant scribe was set up with new bark paper, quill pen and dye, the old priest read slowly.

"Dawn counts the drumbeats,
counts the Katuns, the bundles of stones.
Dawn counts the guardian spirit of the sun-eyed torch
at the center of the sun, the Sun Eyed Lord of the Shield.
The sun-eyed torch at 12th Sky Place, B'aak (skeleton).

"When T'zek (scorpion) falls in the Waters of the Night.
Baktuns make 1, Katuns make 10, Tuns make 9 at Toktan,
Place of Clouds and Many Waters.
The Celestial Twins sit upon the Earth-Sky Band.
Noh Ek the "Great Star" shines, the False Sun,
begins the Count of Days of the Sun Passer, Noh Ek.

"Lady Moon-Ix Uc ascends in Uo (frog), 8th Sky Place.
She dangles below her K'awiil Ek and Chak Ek,
above the Waters of the Night.
And the Katun Lord, he of the mirror scepter, K'awiil Ek,
turns around at the heart of 8th Sky Place.
It happens, it is done.
The Sun Eyed Lord of the Shield,
he touches the earth, the 8 Ahau Lord,
And the white paper headband is handed over to him.
And great things come to the Place of Clouds and Many Waters.
So is it written upon the sky, so is it written upon the earth."

As soon as the dyes dried upon the new codex, Ah K'uch had his assistants bundle it together with the ancient codex in soft white blankets. To their disappointment, the old priest gathered up the bundle himself and carried it to the chambers of the High Priest. Although he had translated the archaic glyphs into current language, and this they had carefully written in modern glyphs, they did not understand the arcane imagery. Nor were they likely to be told the meanings, for this appeared to be meant for the High Priest alone. Only so much were acolytes given to understand.

Pasah Chan sat alert and eager as the old priest displayed the two screen-fold codices, one still smelling of new dyes and the other musty and discolored with age. First Ah K'uch read the translation, and then the High Priest re-read the glyphs himself. He looked over the ancient codex, understanding most of the glyphs, checking the translation. All appeared accurate, as best he could ascertain.

"Much here relates to the stars and zodiac," he said. "When was the original codex written?"

"In Baktun 8 Katun 18 (397 CE), in the time of Holy Ancestor K'uk Bahlam. Our revered lineage founder was born in that Katun, and acceded when he had attained 20 solar years in the next Katun. He must have been a child when it was written," Ah K'uch remarked.

"Let us examine these verses together. They begin with dawn and a count of Katuns that relate to the sun and some being 'at the center of the sun' called Sun Eyed Lord of the Shield. K'in Ahau, Sun Lord, is not called this way," observed Pasah Chan.

"See the use of 'Lord of the Shield' that calls to mind young Pakal's name, which is shield. But 'sun-faced'? What make you of that?"

The High Priest pondered for a few moments, and then his eyes lit up.

"Know you that the household of Pakal often calls him 'k'inich' or sun-faced?" he exclaimed. "This I learned only recently. It appears his nursemaid gave him that appellation because he loves to lift his face to the sun. The boy seeks the sun; there was an incident where he wandered away from home all alone, and she found him sitting on a high rocky outcropping gazing at the sun."

"K'inich Ahau Pakal, Sun-faced Lord of the Shield," repeated the old priest. "But the boy's other name is Janaab."

"Is that not an old-fashioned way of saying Lord, Ahau?"

"Why, so it is!" chimed Ah K'uch, chuckling. "K'inich Janaab Pakal. Your memory is better than mine."

"That I doubt," Pasah Chan smiled. "You found the codex from memory. Let me see. This Sun Eyed Lord of the Shield is guardian spirit of the sun when it rises at dawn at 12 Sky Place of B'aak. That is the twelfth zodiac sign, the skeleton."

"That is so. It is occurring when the zodiac sign T'zek, the scorpion, falls below the horizon. Then we have a distance number placing this event in the future, 1 Baktun, 10 Katuns and 9 Tuns from when the codex was written. At Toktan, the earlier name given Lakam Ha. Can you calculate this future date quickly? My mind is too weak for such calculations without figuring the numbers on paper." The old priest chuckled.

Pasah Chan closed his eyes and ran the numbers internally. He had trained many hours to perfect this skill that required manipulating 5 sets of numbers in base 20. Since the Maya used zero, their count was from 0 to 19, except in the second lowest position when the highest number was 18. When the k'in (day) count reached 19, then the uinal (month) advanced by one. When the uinal reached 18, then the tun (year) advanced by one. When the tun reached 19, then the katun (20-tun period) advanced by one, and when the katun reached 19, then the baktun (400-tun period) advanced by one.

Now he was required to subtract, and the mental gyrations were demanding. Soon he worked it out, and again his eyes lit with excitement.

"Although we do not have the exact day and month, the other future time positions arrive at Baktun 9 Katun 8 Tun 9, which matches when Pakal was born. I can check the exact day and month using the other astronomic clues. They are quite precise. The Celestial Twins, Noh Ek (Venus) and Xux Ek (Mercury) are close to the horizon when Noh Ek appears as Eveningstar. This begins a new Noh Ek cycle that initiates the count of days until he becomes Sun Passer as Morningstar. The Moon rises in the eighth zodiac sign of Uo (frog), and below her in a line are K'awiil Ek (Jupiter) and Chak Ek (Mars). They are just above the western horizon at dusk. K'awiil Ek is resuming his forward motion after being still."

"Ah, there we have it. The Sun Eyed Lord of the Shield, young K'inich Janaab Pakal, is born, he touches the earth. Was he not born on the day 8 Ahau?"

"It is so. And he will receive the white paper headband of rulership. The verses finish by saying this brings great things to Toktan, our city Lakam Ha."

Both priests settled into silent contemplation, each pursuing his thoughts. Ah K'uch was pleased that his service to the High Priest was so successful; gratified that in his waning years he could still accomplish something significant. Pasah Chan was astonished at the clarity of the ancient prophecy, and its congruence with everything Sak K'uk and her mother Yohl Ik'nal had envisioned. He felt certain that when he checked the records of the sky's configuration on the date of Pakal's birth, he would find exactly the astronomical pattern the codex described.

"May I ask, honored High Priest, what you will do with this information?" Ah K'uch was curious. "Needless to say, this information shall I keep solely to myself."

Pasah Chan smiled warmly at the aged man, sincerely appreciative of his help.

"It is you who are the honored one, Elder Priest, for your exceptional work. This shall I do: I will take the boy Pakal into training early to become a shaman-ruler."

The old priest nodded and chuckled.

"It is fitting. Now have I one request for you. Allow me to also teach the boy, while I have yet the mind and strength. For he should know the antiquated language of our forebears and study their prophetic codices."

"It is done."

Dynasty of Lakam Ha (Palenque)

Codes: B. Born A. Acceded
D. Died R. Ruled
All dates are CE

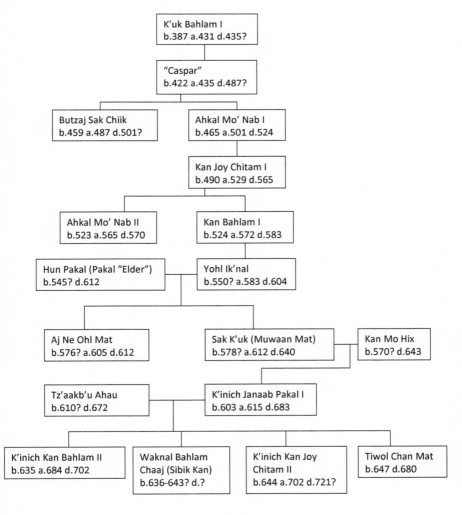

K'uk Bahlam I
b.387 a.431 d.435?

"Caspar"
b.422 a.435 d.487?

Butzaj Sak Chiik
b.459 a.487 d.501?

Ahkal Mo' Nab I
b.465 a.501 d.524

Kan Joy Chitam I
b.490 a.529 d.565

Ahkal Mo' Nab II
b.523 a.565 d.570

Kan Bahlam I
b.524 a.572 d.583

Hun Pakal (Pakal "Elder")
b.545? d.612

Yohl Ik'nal
b.550? a.583 d.604

Aj Ne Ohl Mat
b.576? a.605 d.612

Sak K'uk (Muwaan Mat)
b.578? a.612 d.640

Kan Mo Hix
b.570? d.643

Tz'aakb'u Ahau
b.610? d.672

K'inich Janaab Pakal I
b.603 a.615 d.683

K'inich Kan Bahlam II
b.635 a.684 d.702

Waknal Bahlam Chaaj (Sibik Kan)
b.636-643? d.?

K'inich Kan Joy Chitam II
b.644 a.702 d.721?

Tiwol Chan Mat
b.647 d.680

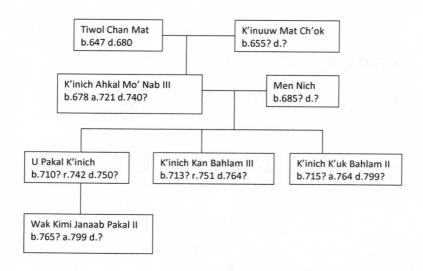

Long Count Maya Calendar

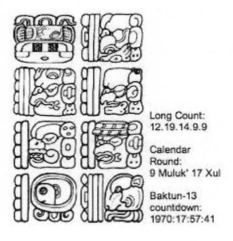

Long Count:
12.19.14.9.9

Calendar
Round:
9 Muluk' 17 Xul

Baktun-13
countdown:
1970:17:57:41

ALTHOUGH CONSIDERED A vigesimal (20 base) system, the Maya used modifications in 2 places for calendric and numerological reasons. In Classic times the counts went from 0 to 19 in all but the 2nd position, in which they went from 0 to 17. Postclassic adaptations changed the counts to begin with 1, making them 1 to 20 and 1 to 18.

Mayan Name	Count		Solar Years	Tun
Baktun	0-19	144000 kin = 20 Katun = 1 Baktun	394.25	400
Katun	0-19	7200 kin = 20 Tun = 1 Katun	19.71	20
Tun	0-19	360 kin = 18 Uinal = 1 Tun	0.985	1
Uinal	0-17	20 kin = 20 Kin = 1 Uinal		
Kin	0-19	1 kin = 1 Kin		

After 19 Kin occur, the Uinal count goes up by 1 on the next day; after 17 Uinal the Tun count goes up by 1 on the next day, after 19 Tun the Katun count goes up by 1 the next day, and after 19 Katun the Baktun count goes up by 1 the next day.

Thus, we see this progression in the Long Count: 11.19.19.17.19 + 1 kin (day) = 12.0.0.0.0

Increasingly larger units of time beyond the Baktun are Piktun, Kalabtun, Kinchiltun, and Alautun. These were usually noted by placing 13 in the counts larger than Baktun, indicating 13 to a multiple of the 20th power: 13.13.13.13.13.0.0.0.0

When a 13 Baktun is reached, this signifies the end of a Great Cycle of 1,872,000 kins (days) or 5200 tuns (5125.2567 solar years). But this does not signify the end of the Maya calendar. Larger baktun units occur on stela with numbers above 13, indicating that this count went up to 19 before converting into the next higher unit in the 6th position. When the 5th position (Baktun) reaches 19, on the following day the 6th position (Pictun) becomes 1 and the 5th position becomes 0. This results in a Long Count such as that projected by glyphs at Palenque to a Gregorian date of 4772 AD (GMT correlation), written as 1.0.0.0.0.0.

The Tzolk'in and Haab Calendars

The Tzolk'in (Sacred Calendar)

T HE TZOLK'IN IS a ceremonial calendar that orders the times for performing rituals honoring the Maya Deities. It is the oldest known Mesoamerican calendar cycle, dating back to around 600 BCE. The Tzolk'in has a 260-day count, believed to be based on the nine months of human gestation which averages 260 days. The mathematics of the Tzolk'in combines 13 numbers with 20 day names: 13 x 20 = 260. Mayan culture assigns the value 13 to the circle, a sacred number representing spirit and movement. This number also represents the 13 great articulations of the human skeleton, the 13 yearly cycles of the moon, the 13 planets known to the ancient Mayas, and the 13 constellations of the Maya zodiac. Additionally, they subdivided the day into 13 segments each divisible by 13, similar to modern hours, minutes and seconds.

The Maya "month" has 20 days, each with a name. To create the Tzolk'in, each day is combined with a number between 1—13. Since 20 is not evenly divisible by 13, the two sequences do not pair exactly. When the 13th number is reached, the count starts again at 1 while the day names continue from day 14 through day 20. This forms unique combinations until the numbers and names run through a complete 260-day cycle. Then, the Tzolk'in count starts again at day 1 and number 1.

The Haab (Solar Calendar)

The Haab is considered a secular or agricultural calendar, was in use by at least 100 BCE, and has deeply significant numerology. It is composed of 18 "months" of 20 days, creating a mathematical system that resonates through vast cycles and synchronizes with many other calendars through its multiples: 18 x 20 = 360. Each month has a name, combined with a number between 1—20 which is assigned to each day. In ancient Maya counting, the month begins with a "seating" that is recorded as zero, and then the patron deity of the month assumes the throne on day 1 and reigns for the next 19 days. The Haab is used to track solstices, equinoxes and eclipses of moon and sun. Since the Haab count is 360 days, it does not match the solar year of 365.25 days, and the Mayas add a short 5-day "month" to coordinate with the sun's annual cycle. They account for the fractional day by adding one day to the count every four years.

In ancient hieroglyphic texts, the Haab date is recorded next to a Tzolk'in date. This appears as a month name-number combination next to a day name-number combination: 4 Kan 12 Pax, for example. In operation together, the Tzolk'in and Haab create a larger, 52-year cycle called the Tunben K'ak or New Fire Cycle. It is known as the Calendar Round, and is used widely throughout Mesoamerica. The Haab also synchronizes with the Tzek'eb or Great Calendar of the Suns, which tracks cycles of the Pleiades over 26,000 years.

Most Mayan texts that track time combine a Long Count date with a Tzolk'in-Haab date. Using these two separate systems for counting time, the Mayas present amazingly accurate dates.

About the Author

L EONIDE (LENNIE) MARTIN: Retired California State University professor, former Family Nurse Practitioner. Author and Maya researcher, Research Member Maya Exploration Center.

My books bring ancient Maya culture and civilization to life in stories about both real historical Mayans and fictional characters. I've studied Maya archeology, anthropology, and history from the scientific and indigenous viewpoints. While living for five years in Mérida, Yucatán, Mexico, I apprenticed with Maya Elder Hunbatz Men, becoming a Solar Initiate and Maya Fire Woman in the Itzá Maya tradition. I've studied with other indigenous teachers in Guatemala, including Maya Priestess-Daykeeper Aum Rak Sapper. The ancient Mayas created the most highly advanced civilization in the Western hemisphere, and my work is dedicated to their wisdom, spirituality, scientific and cultural accomplishments through compelling historical novels.

My interest in ancient Mayan women led to writing the Mayan Queens' series called "Mists of Palenque." Three books of the 4-book series are published, telling the stories of powerful women who shaped the destinies of their people as rulers themselves, or wives of rulers. These remarkable Mayan women are unknown to most people. Using extensive research and field study, I aspire to depict ancient Palenque authentically, and make these amazing Mayan queens accessible to a wide readership.

My writing has won awards from Writer's Digest for short fiction, and *The Visionary Mayan Queen* received a Writer's Digest 2nd Annual Self-Published eBook award in 2015. *The Mayan Red Queen* was nominated for Dan Poynter's Global Ebook Awards for 2016.

My hobbies include gardening, walks in nature, wine tasting, cooking, and of course reading good books. I live in Oregon with a wonderful husband and two gorgeous white Angora cats, and keep up with grandkids through Facebook.

For more information about my writing and the Mayas, visit:
Website: www.mistsofpalenque.com
Blog: http://leonidemartinblog.wordpress.com/
Facebook: https://www.facebook.com/leonide.martin

Author Notes

WISE PEOPLE SAY "all history is interpretation." When writing historical fiction, this becomes even truer. There are contending views of nearly every historical event, and authors must select one viewpoint and forge ahead. Ancient Mayan history is fragmented, because the early Spaniards destroyed innumerable texts. With recent progress in epigraphy experts are able to read most of the complex hieroglyphs left on walls and monuments in many Maya cities. However, new subtleties are emerging in the interpretation of inscriptions and experts' ability to understand the complex symbolism of this sophisticated language.

Readers familiar with Maya research will see that I have taken a particular interpretation of dynastic succession at Palenque, based on work of Peter Mathews and Gerardo Aldana. Different successions were proposed by David Stuart, Linda Schele and David Friedel, Simon Martin and Nicolai Grube. For my focus on the women rulers, succession makes more sense by placing Yohl Ik'nal as the daughter of Kan Bahlam I, Hun Pakal as her husband and not her son, Aj Ne Ohl Mat as her brother and not her son, and Sak K'uk as her daughter who becomes the mother of K'inich Janaab Pakal the Great.

In the ruler list of the Palenque dynasty, experts seem to agree that Yohl Ik'nal ruled in her own right for 22 years, the first woman ruler of Lakam Ha. Some contend that Hun Pakal was also a ruler, and designate him Pakal I. In my view he was a royal consort, not ruler, and did not have the name Janaab. I gave him the name "Hun" which means "one" in Mayan, to distinguish him from K'inich Janaab Pakal (designated by some as Pakal II, but by others Pakal I). The next three rulers are controversial. Aj Ne Ohl Mat is left out of some ruler lists. In older lists, Sak K'uk follows Aj Ne Ohl Mat, but newer interpretations contend she was not a ruler. The successor is given the name glyph Muwaan Mat. Some think Sak K'uk and Muwaan Mat referred to the same individual, others that Muwaan Mat was actually a man. From this maelstrom of disagreement, I selected one stream to follow, the story told in this novel of their extraordinary co-regency.

The "axing" events in which Lakam Ha was "chopped down" in 599 CE, 603 CE and 611 CE also required making interpretations of history. Yohl Ik'nal was ruler during the first and second attacks, Aj Ne Ohl Mat during the third. My interpretation portrays her as a visionary who rebuked the first attack from Usihwitz (fueled by Kan) so her city suffered minor damage. The second attack is obscure but probably involved the same enemies. Many years later, Janaab Pakal inscribed these events on the steps of House C in the Palace, providing rationale for his subsequent aggressions against Kan. I chose to treat the 603 CE event as a ritual ballgame conflict in which Lakam Ha was the loser. The 611 CE attack was devastating, for "god was lost; ahau (Lord) was lost."

Names of ancient Maya cities posed challenges. Spanish explorers or international archeologists assigned most of the commonly used names. Many original city names have been deciphered, however, and I use these whenever they exist. Some cities have conflicting names, so I chose the one that made sense to me. The rivers were even more problematic. Many river names are my own creation, using Mayan words that best describe their characteristics. In the front material, I provide a list of contemporary names for cities and rivers along with the Mayan names used in the story.

Notes on Orthography (Pronunciation)

ORTHOGRAPHY INVOLVES HOW to spell and pronounce Mayan words in another language such as English or Spanish. The initial approach used English-based alphabets with a romance language sound for vowels.

Hun – Hoon	Ne – Nay	Xoc – Shoke	Ix – Eesh
Ik – Eek	Yohl – Yole	Mat – Maat	May – Maie
Sak – Sahk	Ahau – Ah-how	Yum – Yoom	Ek – Ehk

Consonant sounds as originally pronounced.

H – Him	J – Jar	X – "sh"
T – Tz or Dz	Ch – Child	

Mayan glottalized sounds are indicated by an apostrophe, and pronounced with a break in sound made in the back of the throat:

B'aakal	K'uk	Ik'nal	Ka'an	Tz'ak

Later the Spanish pronunciations took precedence. The orthography standardized by the Academia de Lenguas Mayas de Guatemala is used by most current Mayanists. The major difference is how H and J sound.

H – practically silent, only a soft aspiration as in hombre (ombray)

J – soft "h" as in house or Jose (Hosay)

There is some thought among linguists that the ancient Maya had different sounds for "h" and "j" leading to more dilemma. Many places, roads, people's names and other vocabulary have been pronounced for years in the old system. The Guatemala approach is less used in Mexico, and many words in my book are taken from Yucatek Mayan. So, I've decided to keep the Hun spelling rather than Jun for the soft "h." But for Pakal, I've resorted to Janaab rather than Hanab, the older spelling. I have an intuition that his name was meant by the ancient Mayas to have the harder "j" of English; this gives a more powerful sound.

For the Mayan word Lord (Ahau) I use the older spelling. You will see it written Ahaw and Ajaw in different publications. For English speakers, Ahau leads to natural pronunciation of the soft "h" and encourages a longer ending sound with the "u" rather than "w."

Scholarly tradition uses the word Maya to modify most nouns, such as Maya people and Maya sites, except when referring to language and writing, when Mayan is used instead. Ordinary usage is flexible, however, with Mayan used more broadly as in Mayan civilization or Mayan astronomy. I follow this latter approach in my writing.

Acknowledgements

THE CONTRIBUTIONS OF many people provide a supportive framework for this book. My greatest respect goes to the archeologists who devoted years to uncovering hidden ruins and analyzing the messages communicated through stones, structures, artifacts and hieroglyphs. Seminal work uncovering Maya civilization was done by Teobert Mahler, Alfred Maudslay, Sylvanus Morley and J. Eric Thompson. Early decipherment made progress through Ernst Forstemann, Eduard Seler, Joseph T. Goodman and Juan Martinez. Franz Blom made early maps of Palenque structures and Heinrich Berlin advanced epigraphy by identifying emblem glyphs for cities.

Alberto Ruz Lhuillier made the famous discovery of Janaab Pakal's tomb deep inside the Temple of the Inscriptions. Merle Green Robertson, whose drawings of Palenque structures still captivate researchers, gathered an inter-disciplinary team in the Mesa Redondas held near the archeological site. The Palenque Dynasty was identified by the Mesa Redonda teams including Linda Schele, Floyd Lounsbury, Simon Martin, David Stuart, Peter Mathews, Nicolai Grube and Karl Taube. David Stuart and his father George Stuart continued to advance knowledge of Palenque rulers, while Michael Coe captured the public's interest in books about Maya culture and deciphering the Maya hieroglyphic code.

Two Russian scholars figured large in Maya research. Tatiana Proskouriakoff rendered beautiful reconstructions of cities and uncovered patterns of dates that recorded historical events on monuments. Epigraphy leapt forward with the work of linguist Yuri Knorosov showing that Maya symbols were both syllabic and phonetic. Later scholars added the concept polyvalence, when a single sign has multiple values and a sound can be symbolized by more than one sign.

Dennis Tedlock translated the *Popol Vuh*, giving us a poetic rendition of Maya creation mythology. Edwin Barnhart oversaw the masterful Palenque Mapping Project, uncovering numerous hidden structures west of the Great Plaza and demonstrating that Palenque was a very large city. Prudence Rice provided fresh and instructive interpretations of Maya social and political organization, including the *may cycle* in which ceremonial and political leadership passed cooperatively among cities.

Gerardo Aldana explored different interpretations of Palenque dynasties, power structures and astronomy. The amazing intellectual feats of Maya royal courts were exemplified in the 819-day count, a calendric construct used to maintain elite prestige. Aldana's acumen in reading glyphic texts was pure inspiration for me, leading to major ideas for the succession surrounding Sak K'uk and Muwaan Mat, and Pakal's reconstruction of the destroyed portal to the Gods.

Arnoldo Gonzalez Cruz directed the excavations at Palenque that revealed the tomb of the "Red Queen," first uncovered by Fanny Lopez Jimenez. The story of discovering the first Mayan queen's sarcophagus was told in lively fashion by journalist Adriana Malvido in *La Reina Roja*. Arturo Romano Pacheco determined that the bones were those of a woman, one of the queens in my novel.

The richness of my experiences with indigenous Mayas goes beyond description. I could not write about the ancient Maya without the insights and revelations gained in ceremony and study with mentors Hunbatz Men and Aum Rak Sapper, who initiated me into Maya spirituality, and the examples of ancient rituals provided by Tata Pedro Cruz, Don Alejandro Cirilio Oxlaj, Don Pedro Pablo, Miguel Angel Vergara, and members of the Grand Maya Itza Council of Priests and Elders.

Every author needs a cadre of readers willing to suffer through first drafts and catch errors. Thanks to my kind but incisive readers Lisa Jorgensen, Cate Tennyson, Becky Rowe, Karen Van Tassell, and Ginger Bensman. Endless accolades and many hugs to my husband David Gortner, inveterate web researcher who ferreted out esoteric facts and elusive images, tirelessly re-read chapters, dissected grammar, and always challenged me to get things straight and make them clear.

Other Works By Leonide Martin

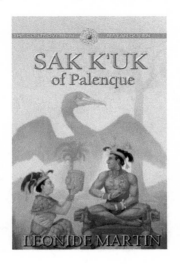

The Controversial Mayan Queen: Sak K'uk of Palenque

Mists of Palenque Series Book 2

Strong-willed Sak K'uk, daughter of Yohl Ik'nal, assumes rulership of Lakam Ha after her brother is killed in the devastating attack by arch-enemy Kan, which leaves her people in chaos. She faces dissident nobles and spiritual crisis caused by destruction of the sacred portal to the Gods. Undertaking a perilous Underworld journey, she invokes the powers of Primordial Goddess Muwaan Mat to help her accede to the throne and hold it for her son, Janaab Pakal, until he is old enough to become ruler. His destiny is to restore the portal and bring Lakam Ha to greatness. Their intense trials together forge a special bond that proves both a blessing and a curse.

In modern times archeologist Francesca continues her quest to uncover the identity of the crimson skeleton found by her team at Palenque. Further examination of the bones confirms that the skeleton was a royal and important woman, dubbed The Red Queen. Francesca is also perplexed by her grandmother's cryptic message to discover her true self by listening to the lightning in her blood.

The Mayan Red Queen: Tz'aakb'u Ahau of Palenque

Mists of Palenque Series Book 3

The ancient Mayan city of Palenque has a new young ruler, Janaab Pakal. His mother and prior ruler, Sak K'uk, selects his wife, later called The Red Queen. From a small city, Lalak is shy and homely, relates better to animals than to people, chosen for her pristine bloodlines and lack of beauty. She is overwhelmed by the complex royal court, intimidated by her mother-in-law's hostility, and puzzled by her husband's aloofness. She struggles to find her place and win Pakal's love, for she discovers he is smitten by a now-banished beauty. Facing shattering loss and heartbreak, she must discover her inner strength and unleash hidden powers. Lalak sees she can play a pivotal role in Pakal's destiny by bringing the immense forces of sexual alchemy to help him restore the collapsed spiritual portal, destroyed by enemy attack. But first, he must come to view his wife in a new light.

Modern archeologist Francesca, ten years after discovery of the Red Queen's tomb, continues her research on the mysterious crimson skeleton. She teams up with British linguist Charlie to decipher an ancient manuscript left by her grandmother. It gives clues about family secrets that propel them to explore what a remote Mayan village can reveal.

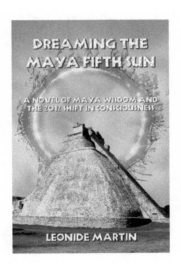

Dreaming the Maya Fifth Sun: A Novel of Maya Wisdom and the 2012 Shift of Consciousness

Suppose your dreams were portals to a different reality? ER nurse Jana's recurring dream compels her journey to jungle-shrouded Mayan ruins where she discovers links with ancient Maya priestess Yalucha, mandated to hide her people's esoteric wisdom from the Conquistadors. Jana's reluctant husband has strange experiences when they visit Tikal, and warns against further involvement. Risking everything, Jana follows her inner guidance and returns to Mexico to unravel her dream. In the Maya lands, dark shamanic forces attempt to deter her and threaten her life.

Ten centuries earlier, Yalucha's life unfolds as a healer at Tikal where she faces heartbreak when her beloved, from an enemy city, is captured. In another incarnation at Uxmal, she is his spiritual teacher but circumstances thwart their relationship. She journeys to Chichen Itza to join the priesthood in a ritual critical to future times. This ritual to balance Earth energies must be performed again at the end of the Mayan calendar Great Cycle, Baktun 13, when the calendar resets.

As December 21, 2012 approaches, Jana answers the call across centuries to re-enact this mystical ritual for successful transit into the new era. She contends with shamanic forces bent on preventing her mission, and faces her husband's devastating ultimatum – their marriage or her mission. Her choices activate forces that could heal or destroy their relationship and the planet.

CPSIA information can be obtained
at www.ICGtesting.com
Printed in the USA
BVHW072355300519
549745BV00001B/5/P